TO SPARK A FAE WAR

THE FAIR ISLE TRILOGY BOOK THREE

TESSONJA ODETTE

1

No one dreams of starting a war.

A revolution, maybe, but never a war. Personally, I've never been one for revolutions or warfare, preferring to fight death and illness in the surgery room. Instead of a sword, I once favored the scalpel. Laudanum. Chloroform. All essential weapons against threats to mortal lives.

But that was back when I thought I *was* mortal. Human.

Before my mentor betrayed me and I used a scalpel not to save a life but to end one.

Before a human shot my mother with an iron bullet and tried to turn the gun on me.

Before I tore out the throat of a fire lizard to take his throne as my own.

After all that, I think I understand warfare. The pursuit of justice.

With the blood of fire fae and ruthless kings flowing

through my veins, I admit I was born to inherit a legacy of violence.

I carry that legacy now, feeling it rushing through my blood and veins as I walk down the darkened street—a human street, in the same city my mother was killed. The night is blanketed with smoke and shadows and sounds of evening merriment. I'm in the pleasure district of Grenneith, where brothels, taverns, and gambling halls cluster side by side.

I keep my head held high, trying my best to exude confidence as I walk by a particularly rowdy-seeming pub where several men loiter outside the door. They leer at me, whistling. I pat the obsidian dagger—a gift from Queen Nyxia—strapped around my waist beneath my coat. The blade isn't iron, like I once carried in the past. But it isn't iron I need for what I'm about to do. Still, blade or no, I'd rather not deal with any interruptions to my night's plans.

One of the men breaks off from the group and comes toward me, sending my heart racing. The swagger in his steps tells me he's clearly had more than his share of drink tonight. I allow my fire to flood my palms, but only enough to keep my mind clear without burning my kid gloves.

The man smirks as he looks me up and down, eyes trailing the modestly high lace neck of my gown to the black and white striped satin hem that brushes the cobblestones at my feet. "What's an elegant lady like you doing walking the streets unaccompanied this late at night?"

For the love of iron, perhaps I should have come dressed as a man tonight. I wasn't sure I could pull it off once I reached my destination, but I hadn't accounted for the perils on my journey there. Now what to do about it? I could brush past him, ignore him, hurry my pace, but that would show fear. Instead, I look him straight in the eyes. "Same as you."

"Oh, I doubt that, miss."

I put a hand on my hip, an innocent gesture, if not for the blade sheathed and hidden within reach. "Am I close to the Briar House?"

The man draws back in surprise before a crimson flush rises to his already ruddy cheeks. "The Briar House? You?"

I keep my eyes pinned on his and flash him a dangerous smile. "I have exotic tastes."

He seems encouraged by this, taking a bold step closer, hand resting on the waistband of his trousers. "I have something exotic you could taste."

"I doubt that." A surge of fear leaps in the back of my awareness, but I burn it away. I focus on his eyes on mine, drawing his attention deeper until the imagery of a bird in a cage floods my mind. His face goes slack, and I know that I have him. This is only the third time I've glamoured someone, and only the second time I've attempted it consciously. The first was an accident with Mayor Coleman, and the second was earlier this morning when I— well, let's just say *borrowed*—this dress.

I keep my voice low and even as I speak to him. "You will tell me where the Briar House is."

He doesn't hesitate to answer, his tone flat. "Next block over. Right side of the street. Second building from the corner."

"Thank you. Now, you are going to return to your

friends and pay me no heed as I continue on with my business. You will allow none of your companions to harass me either."

He nods, pointing a thumb at the group of men eyeing us from near the pub door. "I'm going back to my friends."

"Wonderful." Now the true test begins. He takes a step back, then another, and turns. Our eye contact is severed. My breath hitches as I watch him walk in the opposite direction. Any moment he could turn back around. As far as I know, most glamours end when eye contact is lost. However, I gave him an active order. Will the glamour last long enough for him to do as he was told? I didn't stick around the dressmaker's shop long enough this morning to find out what happened once I left with my borrowed goods.

I remain in place as I watch his unsteady progress back to the group. Only when he rejoins them and lets out a casual laugh do I feel I can breathe again. With a turn on my heel, I continue on my way.

To the Briar House.

I've never been inside a brothel—nor outside one, come to think of it—and I've never wanted to be. Not until I learned Henry Duveau, the councilman who shot and killed my mother, brings unfortunate fae females to this particular pleasure house after illegal capture. Over the last week since Mother's death, I've thought mostly of two things: killing Mr. Duveau and taking down the Briar House.

If I'm lucky, I'll do both tonight.

The brothel's foyer is a mass of scarlet silk, maroon velvet, and gold lace as far as I can see. The lights are dim; no electricity, only several lanterns with red or gold glass covers. Plush couches line the walls, strewn with pillows bearing an ungodly number of tassels. Partitions that look like dressing screens separate certain corners and alcoves, and I can hear tittering laughter behind at least two.

I try not to allow discomfort to show on my face as a stately woman in a dark pink gown steps into the foyer from one of the halls. The cut of her dress is modest like mine, her gray-streaked brown hair arranged in a neat pile on the top of her head. My auburn tresses, on the other hand, are hidden beneath a wide white hat decorated with black peonies. Anything to keep me from being immediately recognized should I come into contact with Mr. Duveau. Hence my human state of dress.

"I am Madame Rose," the woman says. A false name, obviously, considering it fits a little too neatly in with *Briar House*. Nonetheless, she's whom I came here to see. Her posture is confident, her eyes are keen, and her smile is welcoming. "What can I do for you? Have you come seeking companionship tonight?"

"I have, Madame." I take a step closer to her, lowering my voice. I repeat the same thing I said to the drunk man outside, use the same term I once overheard Henry Duveau use when mentioning the Briar House. "I have... exotic tastes."

She nods, a knowing twinkle in her eye. "And might I ask how you came to know of my wares? I do not recognize you as a regular patron."

I know she's testing me, but I have my lie prepared. "I was referred to your establishment by a colleague of my father's. We are visiting from out of town, and I needed to sate my unusual appetites, if you know what I mean."

She eyes me with scrutiny, although her smile remains on her lips. "How did you sate these...*unusual* appetites before? The Briar House is the only of its kind in all of Eisleigh."

It takes no small effort to hide my giddy relief. If this is the only brothel peddling fae females as merchandise, then what I'm about to do will be far more satisfying than if I'd learned there were several more establishments like this. I hide my relief behind a conspiratorial grin and lower my voice further. "I have my ways."

She gives me an approving nod and extends her hand toward a velvet divan strewn with gold satin pillows. "Then tell me more about your tastes and I will see if I can find something to satisfy you."

We take a seat on the divan and I pretend to ponder. "I like them to have a tendency to put up a fight." My voice remains steady as I say it, but my words make acid churn in my stomach. I can't help but recall how similar they are to what Lorelei had said about Mr. Osterman. *I think he liked his prey to put up a fight.* Mr. Osterman was one of the two men who'd captured me and Lorelei and tried to do unspeakable things. The other man was my mentor, who I apprenticed under during my training to become a surgeon. Both men are now dead.

Good riddance.

"You like a fight, do you?" Madame Rose's lips quirk at the corners.

"A little," I say. "I prefer if you have someone who has remained a bit...untamed, shall we say? Feisty."

She assesses me from head to toe. "Now, you are a surprise, aren't you? Who did you say referred you to me?"

I lean in, my voice a whisper. "I dare not say his name, but he is a well-respected councilman. You do know who I speak of, do you not?"

"Ah," she says. "Yes, I know exactly who you mean. He is my establishment's prime patron. One would even call him a partner in my business. Although, I'm hurt he's never mentioned you to me before."

Is that suspicion I'm sensing? I hardly falter, continuing my feigned conspiratorial air. "Like I said, my father and I are on business from out of town. Father's acquaintance with the councilman is new, but I must say it has grown quite intimate. This won't be the last you see of me here." I end that with a wink.

"I should think that's the case, for I'm confident once you sate your appetite, you will hardly be able to keep away."

"That's what I'm hoping for."

Madame Rose rises to her feet. "I think I have the perfect specimen in mind. Give me just a moment and I will prepare her for you."

"One more thing," I say, standing before she can turn away. "Father was under the impression his colleague would be here tonight. He has an urgent message he'd like me to pass on to him. Could you arrange a meeting for us?" I have no grounds to assume anything I've just said. No intel that Mr. Duveau is here, only the barest hope.

She cocks her head slightly to the side. "The man you speak of is not here tonight, so I apologize that I will not be able to satisfy that request."

Damn. Still, there's one more chance. I lock my eyes on hers, pulling her attention to me, drawing that imaginary bird into the cage of my hands—

Nothing. There's no give in her attention, no sway in pulling her gaze. I adjust my hat as an excuse to break eye contact and glance at her wrist. There I see what I should have sought before: a hint of red beads around her wrist, barely visible beneath the lace cuff of her gown. Of course she wears rowan. In a brothel full of enslaved fae, it would be idiotic not to. Still, I had to try.

Try and fail.

Even though I went into this knowing the chance of finding Mr. Duveau was slim, I can't stop the crushing disappointment. However, my mission is far from over.

I plaster a false smile over my lips. "Never mind that. I'll seek him out myself."

That's a promise.

2

Madame Rose leaves me in the foyer for several minutes. When she returns, she guides me into one of the halls that branch off from there. The carpets are plush and red, the walls papered with red and gold designs of roses and vines. Before I went to Faerwyvae, I might have considered the decor luxurious. Compared to fae luxury, however, this place is hideous.

We walk past several doors as we make our way down the hall, and I try not to blush at the sounds of pleasure that emanate from behind them. I constantly summon my inner fire to keep my nerves at bay until Madame Rose pauses outside a door at the end of the hall. "Your merchandise awaits."

I give her my thanks and enter the room. Inside is a modest accommodation with more gaudy crimson satin and papered walls. A vanity and wash basin peek from behind a dressing screen next to a narrow wardrobe. The only other furnishings in the room are a high-backed chair and a small bed. Upon the latter rests a petite female with lavender hair and pale green skin.

"Enjoy," whispers Madame Rose before she closes the door.

"Welcome," the fae female says without warmth. She lies on her side wearing a sheer nightgown, head propped up by one arm while the other hand is draped over her hip. Her pose would be seductive if it weren't for the scowl etched over her face that no false smile could hide.

With slow steps, I approach the bed. She tenses as I near her, violet eyes trained on me, burning me with their hate. "Finally, I can take this off," I say, pulling the enormous hat from my head and tossing it on the ground. With a sigh, I lower myself into the chair and adjust my bone-crushing corset to no avail. I can no longer stand restrictive human clothing, and corsets are the worst offenders. Another reason I should have come dressed as a man today.

But would Madame Rose have bought my disguise? I've barely begun to test my fae powers over fire, and glamouring others is a gamble. There's no way I would have been able to conjure a physical glamour over myself.

Still, what's done is done, and there is more yet to do.

The fae courtesan looks visibly alarmed by my behavior as she watches me from the bed. "Do you...want me to come to you?"

"No need." I wave my hand dismissively. "We can talk as we are."

She furrows her brow. "Talk?"

"Yes. Go ahead and make yourself comfortable. There's no need to sprawl out for my sake."

Her eyes widen, and she makes no move to change positions. Meanwhile, I fiddle with the pins in my hair until half of it comes down from its achingly tight updo. For some reason, this seems to set the fae at ease. Slowly, she folds in on herself and moves into a seated position, shoulders hunched. "May I put on a robe?"

"Do what you will," I say without looking at her. However, as soon as she stands and turns her back to me, I take the opportunity to study her. She's smaller in stature than Lorelei, with narrow hips and dainty limbs. Thin iron cuffs circle her wrists and ankles, the skin beneath them visibly red. She approaches her wardrobe and retrieves a colorful robe. I'm about to look away as she drapes it over her shoulders, but my attention is snagged on something I can barely make out beneath the sheer back of her gown—two jagged marks over her shoulder blades. Scars.

Bile rises in my throat as I recall the sets of wings I saw in Mr. Meeks' underground laboratory. Did any of them belong to her?

The fae returns to the bed, sitting at the edge. She leans back halfway, chest arched slightly forward, before she seems to reconsider. Straightening upright, she crosses her arms over her torso and fixes me with a glare. "I don't understand what you want me to do."

"Let's start with your name."

"Mikaela," she mutters.

"Pleasure to meet you, Mikaela. I am Evelyn, Queen of the Fire Court."

She rolls her eyes with a grunt of irritated laughter. "Right. So that's the fantasy you came here for."

I ignore her. "Are you a pixie?"

Her expression hardens. "I'm whatever you want me to be," she says through her teeth.

"But what are you really?"

Another eye roll. "Yes, I'm a pixie."

"What court are you from?"

"Summer."

"I see. How many of your kind are there in the Briar House? Not pixies, exactly, but fae."

She shrugs. "Seven, unless you count the children."

The blood leaves my face. "Children?"

"There are two who haven't been taken from their mothers yet."

"Are these half-fae offspring born from relations had here?"

She scoffs at the word *relations* but nods.

"What is done with the children who are taken from their mothers?"

"Madame Rose sells them," she says, and her fury is written on her face. I'm sure it's reflected on mine as well, because my gloves are growing dangerously hot. "Rumors mention experiments."

A chasm of grief threatens to open up beneath me, pulling me under as the slice of a scalpel flashes through my mind. I channel my pain into rage, let my fire burn it away until I can breathe again. I curl my fingers into fists. "So, Madame Rose is complicit in everything that happens here?"

"Yes."

There goes my final doubt that Mr. Duveau could be the sole offender in this operation. Madame Rose must not be spared from my wrath. I lean forward. "If there were to be an emergency here, what would happen?"

She lifts a brow. "An emergency?"

My lips curl into a smile. "A fire, let's say."

"Chaos, I suppose. Everyone would fight to flee out the front door, and hardly a man would be wearing pants."

"Is there a back door?"

"Yes, outside the kitchens, but it opens into an alley. Not the best escape in the event of a fire."

"I see." I ponder this for a moment. "When would be the worst time for such a tragic emergency to occur here? Meaning, when might it be the most difficult to escape?"

Mikaela's green skin goes a shade paler. "Is this really what gets you going?"

"Just answer the question honestly."

She pulls her arms tighter around her. "I would have to say around three in the morning. The last patron has left by then and everyone is asleep."

"Does Madame Rose retire by then as well?"

She nods.

"How much time would you need to ensure your fellow courtesans knew to escape through the back door during a fire?"

Her body goes still as stone. "Why are you asking me this?"

I rise to my feet and take a step closer to her, summoning every ounce of regal air I can find. To be honest, it isn't much. I haven't been Queen of Fire for more than a week. At least I know how to fake it. I repeat my question, slower, firmer. "How much time would you need?"

Her answer comes out in a whisper. "A few hours, I

suppose. I would circulate word during our nightly bathing hour."

"Good. See that it's done. Discreetly." I retrieve my hat from the floor and begin pinning my hair back up under it. I can feel her eyes on me, her expression dumbstruck. "I must confess I cannot pay you. When are you required to pay your mistress her dues?"

"You mean give her everything?" Her voice is heavy with venom. "At the end of each Sunday."

"Good. Since that's the case, may I borrow some coin from you? If I must remain in town until three in the morning, I should probably have dinner."

She eyes my gown. "*You* need money? From *me*?"

"I don't have any of my own."

"You don't understand. Madame Rose requires I give her every last coin—"

I round on her, leaning in close. "No, *you* don't understand. You won't be here by Sunday to pay her. Nor will this building be left standing by morning."

Her mouth falls open. "Who are you really?"

"I told you who I am," I say flatly. "Now do what I've asked of you. Speak to your fellow courtesans. A fire will occur at three in the morning. Anyone who wishes to escape must flee to the alley in secret by then and meet me there. Must I make it clear Madame Rose is not to be privy to this information?"

She shakes her head.

"Good. Will you do it?"

Her lower lip quivers. "If this is part of your game for pleasure, it is cruel and I beg you not to play it with me."

My first instinct is to lay a comforting hand on her shoulder, the way Lorelei often does with me. However,

knowing the unwanted touch the pixie is forced to toler-
ate, the gesture seems inappropriate. Instead, I turn to my
fire.

I pull the glove off my right hand, let my rage burn to
my fingertips until a ball of fire ignites there, swirling
purple, pink, and aqua. "This is no game, Mikaela. I am
burning down the Briar House. Now I will ask you one
more time. Will you do as I've requested?"

She swallows hard, hopeful tears swimming in her
eyes. "I will."

3

The city clock chimes three times, its bells echoing through the otherwise silent, sleeping city. With bated breath, I fix my eyes on the back door of the Briar House, the view clear from where I lurk in the shadows farther down the alley. Unwelcome thoughts threaten to shake my resolve; the chimes recall memories of the first time I heard them in the city and the fate that visit led me to. The alley, on the other hand, reminds me of Aspen's lips on mine, the weight of him pressing me into the wall behind my back. One memory fills me with terror while the other teases me with joy. Both are distractions I can't afford right now.

I refocus on my anger, my mission at hand. As the echo of the third chime fades, panic rises within me. What if something went wrong? What if Mikaela got caught or needed more time to spread the word? What if she didn't take me seriously? There's no way I can stay in this city any longer than I already have. It's taken nearly everything I have not to succumb to the grief Grenneith stirs within me, and I know from experience I can only ride the wave of my rage so far before I suffer for it.

Just as I'm tempted to storm inside and drag each courtesan out of the building by force, the door swings open. My hand moves to my obsidian blade, ready to strike should danger be revealed behind the door. I release a heavy sigh as the figure emerges and moonlight illuminates a hint of lavender hair and green skin. I'm even more relieved when I see several other figures file into the alley behind her.

I move from my hiding place and approach the growing crowd. There are far more than seven, but not all of them appear to be fae, and more than a few look like servants. The pixie must have warned all the courtesans and staff, not just her own kind. I'm relieved to find this to be the case, for I don't want to consider what I would have done if I knew anyone but Madame Rose was left inside to handle their own fate.

Mikaela's eyes widen upon seeing me, as if she never truly expected I would follow through with my plan.

"Is this everyone?" I whisper, scanning the crowd. Mikaela nods, the fae huddled close to her, eyeing me with suspicion. Two of the females hold wrapped bundles in their arms, which I can only assume are their sleeping babies, and I'm surprised to see one of the fae courtesans appears to be male. Their human comrades hesitate only a moment longer before taking off into the night.

"What do we do now?" Mikaela asks.

"Now you run," I say. "Get at least three blocks from here and wait for me to find you."

One of the fae mothers—one with enormous black

eyes and a squirrel-like face—squints at me through slitted lids. "Why should we even trust you? Why shouldn't we run off on our own like the humans did?"

My gaze slides to the iron cuff around her wrist and the puckered red skin around it. "Do you have means to get that cuff off?"

She purses her tiny lips. "No."

"Then you'll need someone who can touch iron. Someone like me. Now go. I'll find you."

Mikaela turns toward the group and ushers them toward the mouth of the alley. I, on the other hand, turn away from it toward the Briar House.

With slow, silent steps, I creep into the open door and find myself in a dark kitchen. Aromas of rotting food and pungent perfume assault my senses the farther I step into the room. I remove my gloves and toss them to the ground. Raising a palm out before me, I shape my intent into a need for light. With that, a pale blue flame hovers over my hand, lighting my way as I leave the kitchen to enter a hall. I follow that hall until I find my destination: the foyer I was in mere hours ago.

My blue flame throws the crimson room under an eerie glow. I glare at the pillows, the privacy screens, the papered walls, recalling Mikaela's scarred back, her mention of half-fae children being sold for experimentation. Such a thought can't occur without memory of Mr. Meeks' laboratory, the severed wings, Mr. Osterman's dark room, the iron chains he had Lorelei strapped into. Lastly, for no more than a second, I allow myself to remember an iron bullet lodged between Mother's eyes.

Just like that my blue flame turns a pink so dark it's almost red.

I stalk the perimeter of the room, hand outstretched as my fire-laced fingertips brush the seat of the divan, the tassels of the pillows, the paper of the privacy screens. In a matter of seconds, the room has fallen beneath a beautiful, rosy inferno. Turning my back on my work, I exit the same way I came and return to the alley. Keeping my anger burning hot inside me, I close my eyes and take it to the Twelfth Court.

I wish the effect were immediate, the way it seems to be for fae like Aspen, Franco, and Nyxia. But quarter-fae that I am, and new to the ability to shift forms, I'm stuck seeking for a frustrating stretch of time. Violet fills my inner vision, turning the alley into swirling particles of light. I continue to turn ever inward, seeking my inner firefox, my instinct, my wild birthright.

Finally, calm settles over me. My body shrinks in on itself, while my senses grow sharper. Slim legs replace my four human limbs, each ending in dainty white paws. Sound becomes louder, the night more alive now that I can hear the bats fluttering in the sky, the distant hoot of an owl. Smoke tickles my nose, even though it has yet to enter the alley.

Fully in my firefox form, I sprint away from the Briar House and into the streets beyond.

As a fox, I find the fae with ease and guide them to the outskirts of the city just as the first siren begins to wail. Ignoring the sounds of alarm, I focus on the distant smell of dew-soaked grass, of towering trees. The woods. I traveled through them with Aspen, Foxglove, and

Franco the first time I came to Grenneith, but even if I hadn't, I'd be able to find them now. They call to me, with their sounds and aromas, with the sense of peace left in the absence of human houses and bustling cities.

Only once we are safely beneath the blanket of trees do we rest. That's when I return briefly to my human form to melt the cuffs from each fae's wrists and ankles. Without the iron bonds suppressing their powers, a few of the stronger fae are able to shift into their unseelie forms and head north to find the faewall on their own. The remaining four, plus the two babies, stay with me. This includes Mikaela and the fae male, who I think must have had his wings shorn as well, considering the way he absently rubs his shoulders.

I know I should let them rest. I should let them sleep. They cannot keep up with a fox, and being this far from the faewall cannot offer them the ability to heal from blistered feet and torn heels. The two mothers need to nurse their babies and rest their weary arms from carrying their charges so long already.

But we must keep moving.

Shifting back into my fox form, I prod them onward.

PROGRESS IS SLOW AS MORE THAN A FULL DAY OF TRAVEL passes. In my fox form, I fight the urge to race on without my companions. Although my instincts tell me I'd reach my destination much faster on my own, a part of me remembers that this journey means nothing without those I lead.

By the time we make it past the faewall, the sun is

lowering in the sky and creeping toward evening. Just as planned, I've brought us to the Lunar axis, where I know we'll all be safe. The dusky light is a welcome respite from the glaring sun combined with the unforgiving late-October cold of the Eisleigh side of the wall.

I return to my human form, although my ribs protest at being back inside my corset. I should have had the foresight to keep the fae clothing I'd discarded when I borrowed this stupid dress. Although, when I first set out to do this, I didn't exactly have a plan. Just a need. A need to run, to flee, to seek vengeance on *something* before the empty void inside my heart swallowed me whole.

The four fae fall to their knees. Mikaela sobs into her hands while the male stares blankly ahead, shoulders slumped. The squirrel-like mother rocks her child with tears streaming over her round cheeks, and the other, a petite fae with gnarled brown skin, begins to wail a mournful song in a language I don't understand.

I remember feeling this way when Lorelei and I made it past the wall after the incident at the laboratory. It was the most agonizing grief mixed with solace I'd ever felt. The main difference between myself and the fae before me is that none of them were forced to become murderers tonight.

That burden lies on my shoulders alone.

With a sigh, I sink into the grass, letting my satin skirt pool around me. What remains of my inner connection to my fox form slips away, leaving nothing but aching limbs and a pounding headache. I breathe the pain away, too tired to even summon my flames for relief. There's nothing left to do but let the magic of Faerwyvae do its work.

"Do you have homes to return to?" My voice comes out small, revealing the truth behind my feigned confidence. The broken girl is showing beneath the mask of the unseelie queen, and I've exerted too much energy to keep her hidden a moment more.

Only the male nods, but his expression isn't hopeful.

"You are all free to stay in Lunar," I say. "Queen Nyxia will welcome you. And when I claim my palace in Fire, you will be welcome there as well."

Mikaela's gaze whips toward me. "Are you truly Queen of Fire?"

I nod.

"How is this possible?" the squirrel fae asks. "King Ustrin has ruled Fire as long as I've been alive."

"And you—you can touch iron." The male rubs his wrists, the red welts left by the cuffs only now beginning to fade.

I open my mouth, but again exhaustion drags me under. "It's a long story, but King Ustrin is dead and I have taken his place."

With that comes an image of orange scales covered in tricolor flame, of my teeth sinking into a scaly neck. Blood in my mouth. Smeared on my fur. I can almost taste it all over again, as well as the bile that rose in my throat afterward. My eyes unfocus as the moment I ended his life replays over and over in my mind.

I'm so lost in the memory that when I return my gaze to the fae, they're gone. I barely recall them leaving, but now that I think about it, I remember each one offering at least a parting glance, if not a distinct farewell. Whether they continued on through Lunar or went to their home courts, I do not know. I can only hope they're safe. And that the ghosts of what has been done to them will cease haunting them one day.

I wish the same for me.

As I rise to my feet, I expect to feel a surge of triumphant pride over doing exactly what I set out to do. I took down the Briar House and put an end to one of Henry Duveau's disgusting operations. I set seven fae free and just as many human courtesans who were probably also kept there against their will.

I may not have claimed my vengeance against the councilman who killed my mother, but I did something. Something good.

Good? The word strikes a painful chord inside me. *Is ending yet another life* good?

My stomach lurches as Madame Rose's face flashes through my mind. As much as her actions disgust me, the weight of what I've done to her hits me for the first time. Without the fire of rage burning away my fears and pain, I am defenseless against my own cruelty. My own violence.

Was it really me who set that fire, condemned a woman to die?

Or was it the fox inside me?

Is there even a difference?

Something builds in my throat, something enormous and painful. It's a sob, and with it comes stinging tears and an agonizing guilt so vast, I think my vision will go black from it.

I sink to my knees with a wail, and suddenly all I can think about is Mother. Mother at the trial. Mother in chains. Mother in a tub of freezing water. Mother shouting to defend my honor. Mother fighting the guards. Mother with a bullet between her eyes.

And between all that lies every cruel thing I've ever said to her. Every right thing I've ever dismissed. Every eyeroll. Every instance where I denied her magic and spouted off about how superior Mr. Meeks was.

Burning down the Briar House was supposed to make me feel better. It was supposed to alleviate this pain that continues to plague me. I thought I'd faced the full depth of my grief when I cried in Aspen's arms the night I defeated Ustrin. I thought I'd at least begun to recover from my mother's loss.

But I haven't.

My cheeks grow hot, breaths too shallow. My lungs feel like they're shrinking into nothing. All around me spin images I cannot bear to face. For if I do, I'll be buried beneath them forever. Instead, I seek my fire, let it burn my pain, my regrets. I let it build within me, let it light my way from the bottomless sorrow I've fallen into.

With a deep breath, I turn it into rage. Then I take it to the Twelfth Court.

4

The fox's feet are almost silent.

She stalks over the forest floor, padding over grass and brambles on quiet paws, ears attuned to the sounds around her. Right now, all her senses are focused on what awaits on the other side of the brambles.

The fox crawls closer, peering through a gap in the tangled thorns to her unwitting prey.

A blackbird, some strange part of her notes.

Meal, says another part.

The plump bird pecks the damp earth, seeking its own sustenance. The fox watches as it moves closer and closer to her hiding place, salivating in anticipation of the kill. She hasn't eaten anything but berries since she can remember; it's as if she woke up this morning with the sudden realization there were other things in the forest to eat. Why hasn't she noticed before?

The fox's prey inches closer.

Her body quivers as she prepares to pounce.

"A bird, Evelyn?" The voice startles both the fox and her prey, resulting in a flutter of wings as several black-birds take off into the sky, chirping with alarm. "I resent that, you know."

Familiar, the fox assesses about the voice. She whirls toward the source and finds a slim male on two legs leaning against a tree. He watches her without fear.

He's too large to be prey, but his presence is a threat, considering how easily he drove away her meal. Her fur bristles along her back, and she emits a warning growl.

To the fox's surprise, the male doesn't seem even remotely alarmed. Instead of backing away, he crouches down before her. "Aspen sent me to find you."

Something about the name makes her mind go still. *Aspen. Aspen. Aspen.* What does it mean?

"He's worried about you."

The fox is still trying to place the name, while another part of her argues that names don't matter to her. In fact, she should bite his hand. His pale fingertips are only several inches away—

"Hey, Evelyn."

The fox's eyes dart toward the male's face just as he pulls his lips from his pointed teeth. His face contorts with a terrifying snarl, eyes going black, skin nearly translucent as purple veins bulge beneath the surface. The monster lets out a shrieking hiss.

The fox's shock is so strong, she's left blinking several minutes. No, *I'm* left blinking. *I'm* the fox. Wait, not a fox. A...person. Oh, for the love of iron, what just happened?

I'm sprawled on my back, suddenly aware of rocks and twigs digging into my palms. I glare up at Prince Franco—the familiar Prince Franco, not the nightmarish glamour he donned to frighten me—smiling over me with his hand extended.

"I thought that might do the trick," he says.

At a loss for words, all I can do is take his hand and allow him to pull me to my feet. Vertigo seizes me as I adjust to the feeling of standing on two legs. As my vision returns to normal, I glance around. I'm in the forest. Based on the muted quality of light, I'm in Lunar. Have I been here since I crossed the faewall? Finally, I manage to shape my burning questions into words. "How long have I been away from Selene Palace?"

Franco shrugs. "Five days, I think."

My eyes bulge. "Five?" It shouldn't be possible. I was only in Grenneith for a single day, then another day or two of travel back to the faewall. After that—

I shake my head, finding my mind oddly blank aside from flashes of images. Trees. Underground burrows. Berries. The bird.

"I don't understand. I shifted into my unseelie form, and..."

"You got stuck," Franco finishes for me.

"But why? I was starting to shift faster and faster between forms."

"You must have lost touch with your seelie side."

I suppress a shudder. Aspen warned me about the possibility of forgetting who I am in fox form, but I never thought it would be so easy to do. What would have happened if Franco hadn't found me? Would I have stayed a fox forever? Surely, I would have remembered who I really am.

I recall one of my last coherent thoughts before I shifted forms.

Was it really me who set that fire?
Or was it the fox inside me?
Is there even a difference?

Anxiety rushes through me, but my fire is ready to burn it away. I don't let it burn too hot; just enough to keep my mind clear. Then I recall what Franco had said before he scared me out of my fox form—something that makes my heart flip. "Aspen sent you?"

"Yes, and it's a good thing I found you. Do you have any idea how hard it is to find a fox in the woods? Luckily, you glow."

"I...glow?" I furrow my brow, and Franco nods. I haven't given much thought to what I look like in my firefox form. When I first glimpsed my reflection in the Twelfth Court, I noted white fur rippling with pink, purple, and aqua flame. After I killed Ustrin, I remember looking at myself in a stream and saw my flames had died down to a harmless glowing light. If that's always the case with my fox appearance, it's a wonder I managed to sneak up on that bird at all.

"Why didn't Aspen come himself?" I ask, keeping my voice casual despite the way my heart tightens at the question.

"He said he made you a promise that he wouldn't use the Bond to look for you, whatever that means."

I snort a laugh, his answer relieving me of my momentary tension. "So he sent you to find me. A clever way to work around a promise."

He lifts his chin with a smug grin. "I'm sure it also had to do with the fact that my power of flight has an advantage over his unwieldy hooves."

I roll my eyes, but a more serious question drains my mirth. I bite my lip. "Did you tell him where I went?"

"How could I? It's not like I knew myself."

I avert my gaze to stare guiltily at the ground between us. "I'm sure it isn't difficult to guess. You're the one who flew to the Briar House to gather intel on the brothel at my request. Surely, you must have guessed what I was planning on doing with the information once you gave it to me."

"When I saw for myself what went on inside that brothel, I thought you might set off on some heroic mission to rescue the enslaved fae there," he says. "However, I never would have guessed you'd go alone or that you'd burn the entire building down once you did."

My eyes flash to his, a spark of alarm running through me. "You know about that?"

"Where do you think I first flew to look for you?"

I turn my gaze to my skirt—the stolen human gown that serves as further evidence of my guilt. Surprisingly, the dress has held up during my travels as a fox, although the hem is coated in black. My obsidian dagger remains at my side as well.

"Thank you, by the way," I say. "I honestly can't remember if I said that when you gave me the information about the brothel."

He lifts his chin. "I don't believe you did thank me. Turned a fiery shade of scarlet, I think was your response. Not an hour later, you were gone from Selene Palace. On that note, it seems I've done quite a bit more for you than you've done for me, and I've yet to be repaid for that *errand*, as you called it."

I put my hands on my hips and give him a pointed

look. "I think saving your life after an iron injury should count as payment for several favors, don't you think? Besides, I don't recall promising you anything in return."

"A fae never does anything for free," he says with a teasing smirk.

"Well, a *smart* fae shouldn't perform a favor without requesting a bargain beforehand."

"And only the most ruthless fae would deny fair compensation." He takes a step closer. "Better late than never, though. Worry not, I can think of several things you could do to pay me and none of them would take too long." He looks at me from under his lashes.

I bark a laugh. "Wouldn't take too long? Now that's a ringing endorsement."

"You'll find I'm long in the ways that matter the most."

"If you haven't noticed, Franco, King Aspen is my mate."

At that, the laughter is leeched from his expression. His voice comes out quiet, hesitant. "I have noticed, actually."

Guilt drags my stomach as the air grows heavy between us. I could ignore it, I could laugh it off and change the subject. But Franco is right about one thing: he's done far more for me than I've ever done for him. He deserves candor from me. Even so, I can't stop the blush that warms my cheeks before I even say a word. "Franco, I know we had a moment before Aspen came to Selene Palace. Unless I imagined it, there was something between us. But...Aspen is..."

Words dry in my throat as I struggle to express my love for my mate without hurting Franco.

To my relief, his lips pull back into a smile, although

it doesn't quite reach his eyes. "You don't need to explain, Evelyn. You did not imagine what was, for a time at least, between us. Even now, I confess you give me a thrill. Much of what I say to create a rise out of you is said in jest, but only partially so. No part of me would deny you if you wanted me. But in matters of the heart, I knew you belonged to another long before I kissed you. I could taste it in the air around you. I still can."

Tears prick my eyes. "I love him," I whisper.

Somehow, his smile grows both wider and sadder at the same time. "I know you do. I hope to find a love like that myself someday."

"Have you never loved anyone?" My breath hitches in my throat as I imagine with terror what would happen if he says he feels that way about me. *Please, don't say it...*

His eyes grow distant as he averts his gaze. Finally, he says, "I've felt it. Tasted it from others. But experienced love myself? No, I don't think so. When you can taste the emotions of others, it leaves a lot to be desired when your own feelings are lacking."

My heart sinks at that. I never imagined such an unfortunate downside to being a psy vampire. "Well, I do hope you find that person who makes you feel that way. Better than that, in fact."

"So do I. In the meantime, if you and the Stag King find yourselves on the outs, come to me for a revenge tryst." He winks.

I shake my head with a chuckle. "Are we friends, then?"

"Yes, Evelyn. We're friends. I didn't risk my wings for you at your mother's trial because I thought I stood a chance at winning you from Aspen. Same reason why I flew to the Briar House for you without question. I did it because we're friends. I like you and I always will."

I tilt my head. "Are you sure you don't just like the violence that seems to trail in my wake?"

"Well, there's that too," he says. "And don't think for a minute that this means I'll stop baiting your mate. I can't help it, nor will I give it up. He emits the most delicious emotion when it comes to you." His expression turns wistful, as if savoring the memory of the last time he got under Aspen's skin. "Speaking of violence, did you get what you were looking for? At the Briar House?"

I cross my arms over my chest to keep my mind from spinning down the wrong path. "Not exactly," I say. "I thought my mission would make me feel better, but it didn't. Perhaps if I'd been able to find and kill Mr. Duveau as well, it would have felt more meaningful."

"Are you sure even that will make you feel better about losing your mother?"

I swallow the lump in my throat and replace it with fire. "It has to. We're at war. I can't have my grief distracting me."

"Why is that?"

"Grief makes me weak."

He furrows his brow. "I don't think anything could make you weak. If you let it, I have a feeling it could make you stronger."

His words tug at my heart, but I don't let them pull me far. I can't afford where they might take me if I do. Instead, I give a casual laugh and bat him playfully on the shoulder. "Since when are you one to get serious? Are you aiming to become some great fae philosopher next?"

He winces. "I don't like the taste of your teasing at my expense. Remind me never to be serious with you again."

"Agreed."

Another wince. "Well, actually, I have one more thing to be serious about. It's why I was sent to find you in the first place."

"I thought Aspen was worried about me."

"Oh, he was. Stalking around the palace like a caged bull for days. However, I think he would have let you frolic around the woods a while longer if it weren't imperative that you return at once."

Despite his casual demeanor, I can't help but shiver with dread. "Why? What's happened?"

"The rebels have called an emergency meeting. It's about you."

5

By the time Franco flies us to Selene Palace and sets me on my feet outside the palace doors, my stomach is a roiling mess. And it isn't just from soaring terrifying heights in the sky; my panic stems more from anxious anticipation. Anything could have happened in my absence. Anything could have prompted this mysterious meeting, and none of my imagined causes are good.

As soon as the doors open, Nyxia is standing before us, arms crossed over her chest. Like always, she's dressed in a way that is stunning, eccentric, and elegant all at once. Her top is like a waistcoat, but it's composed entirely of small, black beads, and she wears nothing underneath. Her trousers are skintight silk that show off every curve and muscle of her long, slim legs. As she stands there staring daggers at me, I can't help but wonder if one of her owl messengers announced our arrival or if she's been waiting here endlessly for dramatic effect. I wouldn't put the latter past her.

"And hello to you too, sister." Franco greets the queen with a crooked smile, but she ignores him, her eyes fixed on me.

"Look who decided to show up," the Lunar Queen says, running a hand through her hair. That's when I realize her short silver strands are wet, as if she's recently stepped out of the bath. "Where in the name of iron have you been?"

I open my mouth, but all air is stripped from my lungs as I glimpse the figure strolling down the hall toward us.

My heart lurches, first from the joy at seeing Aspen. Even though I was unconscious of the passage of time when I was stuck in my fox form, my absence from him suddenly comes crashing down on me, the space between us a painful and tangible thing I want to destroy at once. I dart toward him, but my steps falter, my heart lurching a second time as I take in his appearance.

Aspen's face is splattered with what looks like dried blood, smears of dirt crisscrossing his forehead. His russet shirt is filthy and torn, the sleeves rolled up to his elbows to reveal bloodstained forearms. Only his hands appear clean. I finish closing the distance between us, my throat tight as my fingers reach his face, seeking signs of injury.

Before I can prod him further, he stills my fluttering hands with his. "I'm fine." His tone is gentle as his eyes drink in mine. I can feel his relief at seeing me surging through the Bond between us.

I lower my hands and rest them on his chest, over the caked dirt and blood. "What in the name of iron happened?"

"There was a skirmish at the border between Solar and Lunar," he says. "It was nothing."

From his state of dress, I highly doubt that's true.

"It really was nothing," comes Nyxia's airy voice. "Just like every other minor skirmish they've attempted this past week. Do they honestly think they're intimidating us, sending their pathetic soldiers to feign an attack only to flee at the first draw of blood? The royals don't even have the decency to show their faces and fight us themselves."

Aspen ignores Nyxia, eyes still locked on me. "Are you all right?"

"I'm fine—"

"What in the name of night are you wearing?" Nyxia has come up beside me and my mate, gaze burning into the length of my gown. Franco trails behind her, lips pulled into a grimace. "Is that…"

Aspen pulls away slightly, just far enough to study my dress. Guilt burns a hole in my heart as Aspen's eyes turn steely. "Human clothing," he mutters, and the scorn laced into those two words can only be met with my fire.

"So what if it is?" I say, lifting my chin in defiance.

"That's my cue to leave," Franco says under his breath as he inches away from us. After an exaggerated bow, he shifts into his raven form and takes flight down the hall.

Nyxia beams at me and Aspen. One would think she was oblivious to the tension rippling between us, but I know she's probably relishing the energy we're emitting. She almost sounds disappointed when she says, "I suppose I should make sure everyone is ready for the meeting. Don't take too long."

Aspen's eyes don't leave mine as Nyxia exits the corridor. I force myself not to waver beneath his glare, knowing if I do, he'll see all the guilt I'm hiding inside.

"You promised me you'd stay safe," Aspen finally says. "In turn, you made me promise not to seek you through the Bond. You said you needed time to be alone. Time to heal. You lied."

I lift my chin. "I didn't lie."

"Since when is setting foot on human soil while we're at war considered *staying safe*?"

I feel a ripple of hurt through the Bond, and it isn't mine. It's enough to extinguish some of the fire in my veins. My shoulders slump, and I break his gaze, eyes resting on his chest. "I'm sorry."

He runs a hand over his face, smearing the dirt and dried blood. His expression softens. "We'll talk later." There's only a hint of resignation mixing with the frustration in his tone, telling me this conversation is far from over. He turns away and motions for me to follow. "Let's join the meeting."

"What's this about?" I ask as I hurry to his side.

"We'll find out," is all he says.

Icy silence falls between us, but I walk with my head held high.

We enter the throne room, and my attention is immediately drawn to the large table at its center. Around it stands Nyxia and three other fae rulers I've grown somewhat accustomed to seeing at Selene Palace: King Aelfon of Earthen, King Flauvis of Winter, and Queen Minuette of Wind. The first two are in equal states of disarray as Aspen, smeared with grime from the battle they too must have joined. But there are two additional fae I only vaguely recall seeing before. One is a tiny pixie who resembles a brown stick with a pair of pink, fluttering wings and a cherry blossom for a head. The other is a tall female figure—which I only know because she's without clothing—composed of particles of shimmering white light from her toes to her hairless, humanoid head.

All eyes fall on Aspen and me as we join the fae around the table. I realize this is the first time I've been present at a meeting of the rebels, the first time I've confronted these rulers as a queen myself. Without meaning to, I've inched closer to Aspen's side for comfort. I go still as I feel his pinky wind around mine, our linked fingers hidden behind the folds of my dress. The touch of his flesh, despite the current grudge we hold between us, helps steady my nerves.

"Queen Estel." Nyxia nods at the shimmering fae, then faces the winged one. "Queen Tris. I present to you Queen Evelyn of Fire."

I freeze, unsure if I'm supposed to curtsy. I'm still so uncertain what customs are universal to faekind and which are adopted only by some as preference. Besides, I'm a queen now. Am I ever expected to curtsy? When both offer me only nods of acknowledgment, I do the same for them. "Have you joined the rebellion?" I ask.

Flauvis, the wolf king, lets out a growl that sounds more like a laugh. "I'd like to know that answer too," he says, gaze locked on Queen Estel.

"I gave you my answer days ago," Queen Tris says in a minuscule voice. She shudders, and suddenly the pixie stands as tall as Queen Nyxia. Her skin remains brown and bark-like, decorated in elegant whorls. Her hair is composed of brambles and bright pink cherry blossoms, her dress like woven branches laced with pink petals.

Translucent pink wings fold down her back. I suppress a rush of nausea as I'm reminded of Mikaela's scars where wings should have been. Queen Tris gives an audible huff and crosses her arms over her chest. In this form, she looks much more familiar as one of the rulers I recall seeing at the council meeting where Aspen fought Cobalt for his throne. She must be Queen of Spring.

"And my presence here today is my answer," Estel says. Her voice is light and musical, like the tinkling of distant bells or wind chimes. The particles shift and sway over her face, rearranging until they form the semblance of a smile. I can only imagine she's Queen of Star.

"It took you long enough." If a wolf can scoff, Flauvis certainly does now, an expression I can't even imagine on a common canine.

Estel remains composed, giving no reply.

I glance from Estel to Flauvis when I'm suddenly aware of a pair of eyes burning into me. I look across the table at Queen Tris, who stares as if seeing me for the first time. However, if I recognize her, she should damn well recognize me. I was certainly hard to miss when I was presented as Aspen's champion before the entire fae council. Regardless, her scrutiny feels invasive as her eyes bore into me, lingering on my dress. I wonder if that's the primary reason she shifted from her smaller form into this one—to unsettle me with her glare. Her upper lip lifts in clear distaste. "*You* defeated King Ustrin?"

I meet her eyes without falter, lips pursed. Indignation dances down my arms to my fingertips. I lift a hand, let flames flicker over my palm. "I tore out his throat with my teeth. Would you like to scrutinize them too? You might still find one of his scales if it's proof you're after."

Tris pales to a lighter shade of brown, pink eyes locked on my menacingly pleasant smile.

Aspen chuckles next to me.

"We aren't here to discuss the virtues of oral hygiene," Nyxia says in a bored tone. "We're here because Queen Estel has important information to share with us. It's about our enemies."

"Or she's a spy," Queen Minuette says with a dangerous, airy hiss, her blue hair rippling behind her on an invisible wind.

"She has a point." Aspen narrows his eyes at Estel.

"Estel *is* a spy," Nyxia says. "She's been spying for *me*." Her eyes move from one fae to the next until she's burned us all into silence.

"For you?" King Aelfon's voice is low and gruff. He stomps a yellowed hoof, shaking his curled horns. "Why is this the first we're hearing of it?"

"Because I wasn't sure I trusted her yet," Nyxia says through her teeth.

"But you do now?" Aspen asks, tone skeptical.

"Enough to let her speak," Nyxia says pleasantly.

The Star Queen steps closer to the table, the particles of her face dispersing and rearranging until they form a stoic expression. "Queen Nyxia is correct; I agreed to spy for her. It is why I have yet to officially join your alliance. But the actions I must take next will pit me firmly against the opposition, and I will not be able to spy any longer."

King Aelfon crosses his thick, brown arms over his barrel chest. "What is this special information you have, then?"

"As you know," Estel says, "Irridae Palace has been vacant since Ustrin's death. He left no heir, which meant all who were loyal to him were displaced upon his death, including his household."

She's right; this information is known. Within a day of me defeating Ustrin, Nyxia urged me to send a pair of moon dragons to Irridae Palace—Ustrin's former home— to investigate the grounds. When they returned, they reported that the palace was empty, all entrances sealed, the grounds protected by some strange magic. I ordered them back to Irridae to remain nearby and report any changes, but I haven't heard a word since.

Estel continues. "What you don't know is that Queen Dahlia has been adamant that we hunt down members of Ustrin's former household for intel. She wouldn't say why at first, at least not in front of me. I think she suspected my hidden motives from the start. But she called a council meeting yesterday and told us what she's discovered."

Aspen runs a hand through his blue-black hair, sending a good portion of it spilling into his eyes. It takes all my restraint not to reach up and brush it off his brow. "What is it?" he asks.

"Dahlia told us she'd suspected Ustrin had a weapons stash hidden in his palace," Estel says. "She claims the informant she questioned confirmed it exists and that they aren't just any weapons. They are iron, the same ones Ustrin tried to use against his own kind."

I shudder, remembering how Ustrin's guard carried an iron sword during a peaceful exchange of words, then used it against Franco. He later threatened his own fire fae with iron-filled grenades, a weapon that would have obliterated his own soldiers in the process if used.

Estel continues. "With this new information, she set

forth a petition to send the council's newly appointed seelie king as Ustrin's replacement to take over Irridae Palace at once. She said it was to weaken Queen Evelyn's claim, but I know that isn't the real reason the Renounced are suddenly sending someone to occupy the abandoned palace. They want those weapons."

Flauvis mutters a curse-like growl, while Minuette lets out a low whistle.

"When are the Renounced sending the new pretender king?" Aelfon asks.

My attention snags on the word *Renounced*, having heard it twice now, but I'm more concerned with hearing the answer.

"I was supposed to escort him tomorrow evening. Instead, I'll be escorting Evelyn, solidifying my stance against the Renounced and with the Alpha Alliance."

"Wait," I say. "Renounced? Alpha Alliance?"

Nyxia lets out an irritated sigh. "We can't very well continue calling our enemies *the council*, can we? Not when we've deemed the Council of Eleven Courts disbanded."

"And we can't keep calling ourselves the rebels when we aren't in the wrong," Aelfon grumbles.

"The former fae council is now the Renounced, as far as we're concerned," Nyxia explains, "and we are the Alpha Alliance."

"Not that that's a much truer name," mutters Flauvis. "How many of you were appointed by the council as opposed to proving yourself the alpha blessed by the All of All?"

"That's not what matters right now," Aspen says, raising his voice. "What matters is that Irridae Palace contains dangerous weapons. We need to get to the palace first and make sure those weapons don't fall into the wrong hands."

"Exactly," Estel says in her soothing voice. "Queen Evelyn, it's time to claim your new palace."

6

My new palace.

Even though I've known I'll have to eventually claim Irridae Palace as my own to demonstrate the seriousness of my stake as queen, I've dreaded the thought. I can't imagine how something that once belonged to Ustrin could be considered my home. Not to mention, I've never set foot in the Fire Court. Never felt its desert heat.

But Queen Estel is right. The Alpha Alliance is right. If Irridae harbors iron weapons that could harm the fae I'm sworn to protect, I must do whatever it takes to keep the palace out of enemy hands. I'll get there first if it's the last thing I do.

As the meeting comes to a close, the fae royals begin to file out the door of the throne room. I'm about to follow suit when I notice Aspen hasn't budged from his place at the table. His body is tensed, eyes fixed on the obsidian surface before him. I groan internally. So this is where it will happen. This is where we'll have that dreaded talk he promised.

I cross my arms and lean my back against the table, watching the rest of the fae exit. The last is Nyxia, although she lingers by the door for a moment. Beneath the threshold, she glances at me over her shoulder. "A little owl told me the most delicious piece of news," she croons. "It seems a certain brothel in Grenneith burned down earlier this week. A brothel that has since been revealed to have housed fae merchandise." She looks me up and down, a knowing glint in her eye. "Well done, little foxy."

Aspen tenses even further, and I can already hear the growl building in the back of his throat. As Nyxia closes the door behind her, I whirl toward him. He does the same toward me.

Before he can open his mouth to speak, I say, "Aspen, I have something very important to discuss with you."

"As do I," he says through his teeth.

I ignore his venom, doing my best to feign a nonplussed air. "This is important. Timely, considering what's about to happen tomorrow."

Some of the fire seems to go out of him, which was my very intention. He furrows his brow. "What is it?"

"As I'm going to claim Irridae Palace, it's time I get serious about appointing my household staff. Primarily, I'll need an ambassador."

"I am sure Foxglove will be happy to serve you until—"

"No, Foxglove is your ambassador, and he's already done so much for me. I'd like to officially appoint someone to the position."

"And you'd like my advice on whom you should appoint?" Aspen almost looks pleased, which makes my heart sink.

"No," I say slowly. "I have someone in mind, but I need your..."

I hesitate. What exactly is it I need from him? Permission? His blessing? Honestly, this whole tangent was meant mainly as a distraction, despite the truth of the matter. I square my shoulders. "I want to make Lorelei my ambassador."

For a moment, he appears dumbstruck. "Lorelei?"

"Yes. And since she's employed by the Autumn Court, I figured I'd run it by you first."

He rubs a hand along his jaw, then shakes his head. "I don't think it's a good idea."

My mouth falls open. "Why? Do you think she should toil away as a lady's maid the rest of her life? Surely, she's worth more than that."

"She is," he rushes to say. "It isn't that at all, it's more... it isn't a good idea to appoint your friends as your staff. Especially to such powerful positions."

"Why not?"

"It makes things difficult," he says. "When your subordinates are your friends, it makes it harder to be firm with them."

I bristle. "For one, I don't consider Lorelei my subordinate but my equal, and for another, why should I ever need to be firm with her?"

"See, this is exactly why this is a bad idea. You don't understand—"

"No, *you* don't understand. I didn't bring this up because I wanted your opinion. I brought it up simply to inform you of my intention to remove her from your employ and into mine."

Aspen rolls his eyes. "Why did you even bother asking, then?"

"I thought you might support me," I say, "but clearly you don't trust me to make my own choices."

"Like I trusted you when you said you only needed space? That you promised you'd stay safe?"

I scoff. "Oh, here we go."

"As soon as I saw you in that human dress, I knew you'd lied. I knew you'd done something reckless. But never could I have imagined you'd do something so stupid as to return to Grenneith. Nyxia was right, wasn't she? You burned down that brothel, the one Henry Duveau tried to send you to."

I take an angry step toward him. "I put an end to fae torture. You don't know what it was like there. They had them cuffed in iron, forced to pleasure whoever came to pay them a visit. Some of the fae had their wings shorn. Worst of all, the brothel's madame sold half-fae children to be experimented on." A lump rises in my throat, but I burn it with fire. "I only saved two children."

His expression softens. "I'm not saying what you did was wrong, but doing it alone was reckless. You should have mentioned this was something you wanted to do. We could have brought it up to the Alpha Alliance. We could have taken the brothel down as a formal demonstration to the humans."

"I wanted to do it alone," I say softly. "I *needed* to do it alone."

"I understand you felt like you had to seek vengeance. Do you think I don't know what it's like to feel helpless when those who've wronged you are free? My own brother is living in my palace and I've yet to have the means to move against him."

My rage returns in a flash. "It's not the same. My mother died right in front of me."

"I know, Evie, and I'm so sorry. But what if Mr. Duveau had found you while you were in Grenneith?"

"I wanted him to find me!" I shout. "He was half the reason I went there. I hoped Madame Rose could be glamoured to tell me his location."

His eyes bulge. "Don't tell me you tried to glamour someone."

"I did, Aspen, and it worked. For the dress, at least." I purposely omit mention of glamouring the man who harassed me in the street. "And it would have worked on Madame Rose too, if she wasn't wearing rowan."

He throws his hands in the air. "This is what I'm talking about! That is reckless. That is the opposite of staying safe."

My fury rises higher and higher, and I let it burn around me. Let it melt my pain and emotions away. "You need to get it through your head that you don't control me. I am queen of my own court. I am ruler of my own actions. I will make my own decisions in all things, and that includes seeking vengeance where I please and making Lorelei my ambassador. You don't get to stand over my shoulder and operate me like a puppet."

His expression falls, wounded like I've never seen before. His words come out quiet, strained. "Is that what you think I'm doing here, Evie? Controlling you? I confess, I cannot help but try to keep you safe. I love you more than I can say, and it kills me to watch you run from your grief and instead put yourself in danger. And when it comes to your rule, I only gave you my advice because I thought you respected my opinion. I thought we were ruling together. As mates. Did you not mean what you said to Nyxia? That my household is your household?"

Something breaks inside me, and guilt swarms my heart. Suddenly, I feel the barbs of the words I said to Aspen pricking my chest. That was my fire talking, not me. And yet, I can't bring myself to reply when every truth I want to say teeters on the brink of the emotions that could destroy me, that could pull me into that black chasm of sorrow.

Aspen misreads my silence, eyes going steely. He takes a step back from me, then another, shaking his head. "No. When it all comes down to it, you're just a lying human."

He turns on his heel and stalks toward the door.

Agony, rage, and terror surge through me. "You don't mean that," I call after him, painfully aware of how my voice trembles. "Don't walk away from me."

He reaches the door without a second glance.

No, I can't bear it. I can't let him leave. "Aspen." The name rings out with power, and that bridge spans between us in my mind's eye.

He whirls back toward me, his gaze as sharp as a dagger's edge. "Don't you dare," he says through his teeth.

I burn him with a fiery glare. "By the power of your true name, don't walk away from me. Come back to me right now."

His shoulders tense, arms rippling with rage, but he's powerless against the command. With pounding footsteps, he returns to me, stopping just inches away. "How dare you use my name like this. I thought we—"

I crane my neck to look into his eyes. "I don't want to be mad at you."

"And this is supposed to help?"

I tilt my chin up. "Kiss me."

He narrows his eyes. "This is hardly the time for that."

Magic dances on my lips, emitting the power of our Bond. "Kiss me," I repeat, louder this time. "That's not a request. It's a command."

His mouth presses hard on mine, almost painfully so. I can feel his anger as if it were my own, and I meet it with mine, kissing him equally as firm until we both break away with a gasp for air. Then his lips are back on mine, the pressure still fierce, but with a more yielding quality. His hands slide down my shoulders, helping me shrug out of my coat. I tear the belted obsidian blade from my waist as one of his hands moves into my hair, the other down my back. After tossing the belt on the floor, my arms wrap around his waist, pressing him hard against me as if we could melt into one another.

His kisses are like fire, my lips an inferno as he burns against me. My mouth parts, and his tongue moves against mine, sending a wave of pleasure through my core, igniting heat between my thighs. His lips part from mine only to carve a trail of fire along my jaw and down my neck where they pause at the high lace collar of my gown.

"Evie," he whispers against my neck, the feel of his breath making me shudder against him. I can't tell if there's a command in the word or not, but I don't care either way. "Take off your dress."

I rake my fingers through his hair, paying no heed to his unwashed state. I press a kiss to his forehead, then his temple, until I reach the lobe of his ear. My teeth graze it, before I say, "Take it off for me."

At that, he spins me around. I brace my hands on the table as he rips the buttons free at the back of the gown. "I hate this dress," he says as the back opens. He slides the dress down my back and over my hips, and I step out of it. He gathers the black and white satin in his hands and tosses it onto the table. Then his fingers skate over the laces of my corset. One hand moves over my stomach while he brings his lips to my shoulder. I close my eyes and turn my head to let his kisses move to my neck, his body pressed close behind me. "How do I get you out of this thing?" he whispers.

I brace my hands steadier on the table as my knees threaten to give way beneath me, his breath on my skin unbearably pleasurable. "The laces in the back," I manage to say.

The hand on my stomach moves up the front of the rigid corset and over my chest where the tops of my breasts strain against the starchy linen. "I don't think I have the patience for that."

"Then rip the damn thing off already," I say. "I never want to wear it again."

That's all the permission he needs before both hands come to the bodice of the corset and tear it in two. I gasp with relief and can't help but laugh. "It's just like in the novels." I reach an arm behind me to grasp the back of Aspen's neck.

"What kinds of novels have you been reading?" His hands move over my bare skin, his palms warm against my naked flesh. I arch my back as he teases the crest of my breast with his thumb.

"The wrong kind, apparently," I say. In all honesty, it was Amelie who read the romantic stories, and I laughed at the few I tried to read. I was always more interested in academic literature. But why am I thinking about books when the real thing is right here? Aspen's thumb continues to elicit the most delectable sensations, while his free hand moves down, over my hips, my thighs, then to the place between them.

I return both hands to the top of the table, a moan escaping my lips. Despite the desire stirring inside me, I need more of him to fully quench it. I whirl toward him, dragging his mouth to mine, my fingers reaching for the waistband of his trousers. Before I can free the top button, his hand moves to my waist, lifting me until I'm propped on the table. With agonizingly slow kisses, he leans me back until my bare skin is fully upon my discarded dress he'd tossed there. I reach for his trousers again, but he intercepts my hands, pinning them over my head as his lips leave mine to trail down my neck. Then his mouth moves lower, across my chest, his tongue trailing over each mound, then further down to my ribs, my stomach, my hips.

I gasp as his lips continue even farther down, resting at the apex of my thighs. My body tenses at the unexpected caress of his tongue. As he elicits the most euphoric pleasure, the tenseness leaves every muscle and I succumb to the devious spell Aspen has put me under. The sensations reach an impossible crescendo. I arch my back and gasp. I'm limp and shuddering by the time Aspen's lips return to mine.

He pulls away, and our eyes lock. He brushes my hair from my sweat-soaked forehead as he catches his breath. "I love you, Evie. You devious, reckless creature."

My stomach sinks despite his passionate words, considering they seem to hint that our pleasure is over. "Not so fast," I say, voice trembling. "I'm not done with you yet."

Again, I reach for his trousers, but this time it's a sound that stops me—the throne room door opening.

"Is this what I left the two of you alone to do?" calls Nyxia's exasperated voice.

Aspen goes still over me, and I'm suddenly grateful one of us has kept their clothes on, as well as the fact that I'm fairly certain I'm hidden mostly from view by Aspen's form.

"I know from experience that this table works wonders for such activities," Nyxia says, voice dripping honey, "but it's mine. Go spread your passions all over your new palace and get off my damn furniture."

At the sound of the door shutting, Aspen and I burst into stifled laughter. "I suppose we should get you back in that dress." Aspen caresses my cheek with his thumb, which only reminds me of what his thumb was doing not minutes ago.

I find my hips moving beneath him, the heat returning to my core. "Can't we—"

The door opens again, just long enough for Nyxia to say, "Now."

7

My cheeks are warm as Aspen walks me to my room. We stop outside it, and I turn to face him, back pressed against my closed door. Aspen steps closer to me, one hand braced on the doorframe, the other winding around a strand of my tangled hair. The energy between us sizzles, and it takes all my restraint not to pull him inside my room and push him onto the bed so we can pick up where we left off.

I bite my lip as Aspen lifts his hungry eyes to meet mine. There's no doubt he's thinking the same thing. He lets out a sigh that almost sounds like a groan. "I should probably get cleaned up and changed."

With a reluctant nod, I force my fantasies to subside. "As should I. I must meet with the fire fae tonight and tell them of the plan to go to Irridae."

A cloud falls over his face, reminding me of our fight. He drops my strand of hair and straightens his posture.

I reach for his hand before he can take a step away. "I

didn't mean what I said," I say in a rush. "I let my fire take over. I've been...doing that a lot lately."

"It's all right," he says. "A lot of what you said was true. I can't control you, and I need to give you the space to make your own decisions as queen."

"That doesn't mean I don't want you at my side. I really did mean what I said to Nyxia when your refugees came here. Your household is mine, and I want them to come to Irridae. I want my home to be their home. Even once you defeat Cobalt, I want us to continue to rule side by side, if we can."

His expression brightens, lips pulling into a crooked grin. "Does that mean you want me to come to Irridae too?"

I lace my fingers through his, squeezing his palm with mine. "I thought that went without saying from the very start. I need you, Aspen. I love you."

He leans in and kisses me lightly on the lips, soft and slow. Too slow, for it gives me enough time to crave him again. I'm about to suggest we get cleaned up together, perhaps perform an encore of our time in the moon baths, but he pulls away. "I'll let you get on with your tasks."

My heart sinks, but I let him go. I turn toward my door and am about to push it open when Aspen's voice drags my attention back to him.

"It's a good idea, Evie," he says. "Making Lorelei your ambassador. She deserves the promotion, and you deserve someone you trust at your side." With a wink, he turns away and continues down the hall.

My eyes sting as I watch his back until he's out of sight. Although I would have gone forth with my plans regardless of his approval, hearing him vocalize his support moves me in a way I hadn't expected. Despite his stubborn streak—and mine, for that matter—I think we make a decent pair.

So long as we don't burn anything down when we're at our worst.

Then again, I burn things down when I'm at my best.

ONCE I'VE CLEANED AWAY THE GRIME OF MY TRAVELS AND changed into a gauzy indigo gown, I knock on Lorelei's door. Her eyes widen as she opens it and then throws her arms around me. I return the embrace, no longer surprised at Lorelei's warm affection. For someone as sharp as she is around most people, I'm honored by how freely she shows her care for me.

"You're back!" She pulls away to scan me from head to toe, as if checking for damage, then lowers her voice. "Nyxia told me what you did. Or at least what she suspected you did. Is it true? Did you burn down the Briar House?"

She steps to the side so I can fully enter her room and leads us to a set of chairs. She sits in one, and I sink wearily into the other, not bothering to maintain a regal countenance around her. "I did."

She lifts her chin approvingly. "Well done. Although you don't look too pleased yourself."

I sigh. "I am, it's just...I'm..." I consider telling her everything; the fae I rescued, Mikaela's scarred back, the fire, the escape, the way I got stuck in my unseelie form. But the thought alone exhausts me. Instead, I sit straighter. "Actually, I came to speak to you about something specific."

She leans forward, brow furrowed. "What is it?"

"I'll start by saying I've spoken to Aspen and he approves." Of course, I leave out the part where he at first *didn't* approve. "That is, if you agree. You may remain in his employ if you prefer, but—"

"Wait, I'm losing my job?"

"No. Well, yes, but..." Why am I so nervous to ask? "Lorelei, will you be my ambassador?"

Her mouth falls open as she leans back in alarm. "Me? Your ambassador?"

"Yes."

My stomach drops as she does nothing but stare at me for a few moments. Then finally, she says, "Are you sure? I'm not a fire fae."

"Is that important?" I ask, and my uncertainty is genuine. Now that I think about it, most of the ambassadors I've seen were easily distinguishable as belonging to a certain court based on their appearances. But is that simply due to clothing and style choice, or their actual heritage? "Must all ambassadors be native to the court they represent?"

"No," she says to my relief, "but I thought perhaps you'd want to establish a connection with the fire fae. This is an opportunity to elevate one of your own people and show your respect for them. Elevating me might... well, it won't be seen as a negative thing, but it will remove that possibility to connect with others you'd want to keep close."

My eyes unfocus as I consider what she said. She has a point, one I hadn't considered myself. Still, there's no one I can imagine doing a better job than Lorelei. "See, this is why I need you. What you're saying makes perfect sense. However, I don't know or trust any of the fire fae enough to make any appointments just yet. As my ambassador, you can help me navigate my relationships with them and find other opportunities to honor them."

"I could." The word comes out slowly.

"Will you do it?"

I wait with bated breath as she considers. For a moment, I worry that the offer has somehow offended her. Perhaps she prefers being a lady's maid or considers it a step down to work for a less-established royal like me. Then her lips pull into a wide smile. "Yes, of course I will. You know I am already loyal to you. I love Aspen, but I will follow you anywhere."

I can hardly contain my joy, and before I know it, we're embracing again.

When we separate, she puts her hands on her hips and smirks. "Besides, now I can finally get away from Nyxia." Despite the exaggerated relief in her tone, I can tell there isn't the same venom that used to be present when she'd speak about Nyxia. It makes me wonder if her heart is softening in regard to the fierce queen. I know her grief over her deceased lover will likely never fully disappear, but I can't help hoping there might be a second chance at love waiting in the near future for my friend. Perhaps even another shot with Nyxia.

"Do you think you can begin your ambassador duties tonight?" I ask.

She squares her shoulders with a confident grin. "I'm ready."

"Good. Then we'll visit the fire fae together."

"If you truly want me to start my duties now," she says, "then I have a better suggestion. You won't be *visiting* the fire fae. You will hold court and your people will come to you."

I flash her a smile. "I knew you were the one for this job."

AFTER EVENING FALLS, I MAKE MY WAY TO THE WISHING Tree at the edge of the lawn outside Selene Palace. Lorelei arranged everything to accommodate my makeshift outdoor throne room, including an elegant moonstone chair to act as my temporary throne. With the long skirts of my indigo gown flowing around my legs, I lower into the chair with as much grace as I can muster.

"Your people should arrive shortly," Lorelei says, standing at my right. "They have been briefed on your travel plans, so you won't have to go into much detail regarding that."

I'm surprised she informed them already, only because I hardly know the details myself. All I know is that Estel will be escorting me and a small retinue to Irridae. I get the feeling the Star Queen won't be acting simply as a guide, but using some sort of magic to take me there. "Do you know anything about Queen Estel's powers? Does she have control over travel or something?"

"Pretty much," Lorelei says. "The Star Court's magic is deeply connected to time and space. All courts are represented by some combination of the elements. Star magic has an affinity for air, which makes it easy for the most powerful star fae to utilize their magic for swift travel.

Queen Estel specifically excels at travel through time and space. Her technology created the axis line and the axis points in each court when the wall was built."

A chill runs up my spine. I had no idea a single fae could have such significant power. What other strange magics have I yet to learn about? "So when she said she's escorting me to Irridae Palace..."

Lorelei nods. "What she means is she will use her magic in the form of a portable travel device called a Chariot. It's hard to explain. You'll see it for yourself."

"Wow. All right. I had no idea that was possible."

"Her magic is rare, as are the devices she creates," Lorelei says. "That's why the Renounced wanted her to escort their fire king pretender. Taking you instead will be a huge slap in their faces."

"How many do you think Queen Estel can transport at once? I was told I should bring only a small retinue."

"I've never known the Star Queen to transport more than eight. We already know your retinue will include you, me, Aspen, and Foxglove, and I can guarantee the king will insist on bringing at least two guards. So that leaves two—"

"And Amelie," I rush to say before I have a chance to take it back.

Lorelei pauses, mouth hanging open. "You want to bring your sister with you?"

My pulse quickens. Talk of Amelie is dangerous territory, as I can't think of her without considering everything she's done. Betraying me for Cobalt. Missing Mother's trial which resulted in her death. Arriving at Lunar without warning, giving me the power of her name as the only tether to trust her by. My fingers curl around the armrest of the chair as I squeeze the cool moonstone. The distraction stabilizes me, helps me maintain even breathing as I say, "I can't leave her here."

"Can you trust her?"

"Of course I can't," I say, "but she's my responsibility. If she truly came here on some nefarious order from Cobalt, I can't leave her at Lunar to draw danger in my absence."

"What if this is exactly what he wants?" Lorelei's eyes are wide with fear. "What if he ordered her here, knowing you'd eventually take her to Irridae, to the weapons stash?"

I shake my head. "If that's the case, I'd like to see her try so I can catch her in the act and be done with her for good. Besides, I'd rather lead my enemies straight to me than put another court at risk." Lorelei opens her mouth to argue, but I speak first. "I'm sorry, Lorelei, but in this, I can't be persuaded otherwise. If Amelie is my enemy, then I must keep her close. And if she isn't..." I was going to say, *then I can protect her*, but I can't bring myself to voice it out loud. There's still too much fire in my veins when it comes to my sister. It will take a miracle for me to trust her again. To go out of my way to protect her when she already denied me once.

For *him*.

I squeeze the arms of the chair again, forcing my breathing to calm.

"Then you will have one opportunity to show favor to a fire fae," Lorelei says. "Appoint whomever you think you can trust most to travel at your side."

∼

DOZENS UPON DOZENS OF FIRE FAE BEGIN TO GATHER before me, screeches, yips, and yowls filling the air as they settle in. Once it seems everyone has arrived, I'm surprised to find there are even more now than there were in the caves. I see two more moon dragons, a few more varieties of kitsune, an entire family of the mushroom-crustacean fae, multiple flocks of firebirds, and all the others I remember from before—fiery sprites, glowing wisps, snakes, salamanders, and desert rodents.

These are my people.

I'm still intimidated by that fact, by the unseelie ways I'm still mostly a stranger to. But I'm no longer afraid of them.

As easy as it is to get lost in my curious study of the fae, I remind myself that I must present a regal facade. By now I've grown adept at adopting the regal bearings of the fae I've come to admire—Aspen's cold stoicism, Nyxia's powerful authority, even Lorelei's intimidating stare. I wear it all like a glamour. The mask of the Fire Queen.

I sit tall in my chair and lift a hand in greeting. "Thank you for coming to our makeshift court," I say, allowing my voice to carry over the lawn. "This will be the only one like it, as the next time I hold court, it will be at Irridae Palace."

The response seems positive, if I'm reading the wagging tails, barks, and slithering bodies correctly.

I continue. "As you have been informed, Queen Estel will be transporting me to the palace tomorrow afternoon. Those of you who prefer to remain in Lunar will continue to be welcome guests under Queen Nyxia's rule.

However, for those of you eager to return to your native court, you will now be safe to do so."

More wags, yips—and even a few human-like shouts of excitement—come from the crowd.

A blue wisp bobs forward, sinking into the semblance of a bow before hovering several feet before me. Her voice is light and airy. "I offer the services of my fellow wisps to guide our travelers to the palace."

A white kitsune with a blue flame over his tail pads forward. "No," he snaps at the wisp, "everyone knows you have a terrible sense of direction."

The wisp whirls around. "I do not. I am an excellent navigator. Ask any of my brethren."

"I offered the services of my tribe first," the kitsune argues.

"I witnessed no such offer."

"You weren't there!"

The two continue their argument while Lorelei leans close to my ear. "The kitsune is correct. Wisps should never be allowed to guide travelers anywhere, unless you're trying to sabotage them."

I nod to her, then address the crowd. "Be silent," I order, forcing my voice to be firm. As uncomfortable as I am with enforcing my new power, it's time to take control. "You," I say to the kitsune. "What is your name?"

"Dune, Your Majesty."

"Dune, I recall you did offer me the services of your tribe and I will grant you that honor now. You will be responsible for guiding all who wish to return to the Fire Court, taking them safely through the Star Court. You will not take the route through Solar, as they are considered my rival at present and cannot be trusted to allow safe passage."

Dune taps excitedly from paw to paw. "It will be done, Your Majesty."

The wisp pouts, bobbing low toward the ground.

"You," I say to her, "will seek out any fire fae who did not come to court tonight and relay the details they have missed."

She floats higher, her blue a shade brighter. "It isn't as fun as travel, but I will do as you say."

It takes no small effort to hide my amusement, but I remain the gracious queen as the two fae return to the crowd. Lorelei leans toward me again. "You should select your traveling companion now before anyone else tries to come forth."

"If only I knew who to choose," I whisper back, a flash of panic rising.

"Has anyone demonstrated budding loyalty?"

I scan the crowd until my eyes fall on a deep red flame. It's a fire sprite with a female figure, slightly larger than the blue wisp—about twice the length of my palm. She lets out a girlish gasp as she realizes she has my attention. Her eyes are wide as she fights to hide the squeal building in her throat, her tiny hands framing her face. I'm almost positive I recognize her, based on her unrestrained enthusiasm alone. "What is your name?" I say to her.

"Breeda, Most Esteemed and Beautiful Majesty!" Her voice trembles with her effort to keep her composure.

"Breeda, you will accompany me to the palace tomorrow afternoon. You will keep watch over me when we arrive and light any dark places." I don't actually know if there will be such dark places for her to illuminate, but I hope it sounds like an honorable job. And if she's the same sprite I remember, she'd asked to journey with me to Fire anyway.

She spins in a circle before facing me again. "Most Glorious Queen Evelyn, this is a great honor. I won't let you down."

I glance at Lorelei, seeking her approval. All she gives me is a subtle shrug and a slight grimace. "If you say so."

"You said budding loyalty," I mutter.

"That's more than loyalty," she whispers back, but I can hear the laughter in her voice. "That's more like idolatry."

She's right, but maybe that's exactly what I need. If I can hardly accept that I'm now queen of an entire court, the least I can do is surround myself with those who believe in me enough to make up for the faith I lack. And maybe—*just maybe*—my rule as queen will come to feel more than just an act.

Until then, idolatry will have to do.

8

The next day, I follow Nyxia down the dim obsidian halls beneath Selene Palace toward the dungeon. Shadows writhe up and down the bars of the dark cells that line the walls, each occupant hidden from view, likely cowering far away from whatever debilitating power said shadows contain.

My throat feels dry as Nyxia stops outside one of the cells—one I haven't visited since the day my sister arrived. I squeeze my hands into fists at my sides, relishing the sharp sting as my nails dig into my palms; it's a welcome distraction from the anxiety that builds in my chest at the thought of facing Amelie.

One of the dungeon guards, a wraith in flowing black robes, slides open the barred door. I uncurl my fists and shake out my hands, turning up a palm with the intention for light. After a few seconds, a pale blue flame sparks above my hand where it hovers steadily as I steel myself to enter.

"Are you sure this is wise?" Nyxia says, stopping me in

my tracks before I can step inside. Her tone is laced with irritation, but I can sense what lies beneath it—fear. The Lunar Queen, the powerful alpha capable of summoning one's deepest terrors to the surface of their mind is *afraid*. But I don't think she's afraid for herself; she's worried for me.

If I wasn't feeling so on edge, I'd be honored knowing Nyxia cares enough to consider the distinct possibility that Amelie could still be working under Cobalt's orders and will kill me at her first chance.

"Isn't that how the saying goes?" I whisper to the queen. "Keep your enemies close?"

She shakes her head dismissively and steps back to lean against the wall opposite the cells. Despite her casual posture, I can see her shoulders are tensed, body poised to leap to my defense if needed.

With the comforting assurance of the Lunar Queen's protection, I enter the cell with slow, cautious steps. It isn't until I'm at the center of the tiny room that my blue light falls on a form huddled in the corner of the far wall. Amelie appears to be sleeping, curled in on herself, back facing me. My chest squeezes as a wash of guilt tugs at my heart. When I first came to see her, I hadn't noticed how sparse her accommodations were. Now I see there's no bed, no chair, no table. Nothing but a few blankets, a chamber pot, and cold obsidian from floor to ceiling. *What have I done? How could I have kept her like this?*

I reach for my inner fire to steady me, calling forth my anger. *Remember what she's done. Remember what happened to Mother.*

My guilt burns away, and I square my shoulders. With

the tip of my shoe, I nudge Amelie in the shoulder. Once. Twice. Harder. "Wake up."

Finally, she stirs. Back still facing me, she shifts to her hands and knees, then sits back on her heels. She looks one way and another, then at her hands. Her shoulders begin to tremble and heave, and a wail escapes her throat.

"Amelie," I say.

She pays me no heed as she hunches forward, bringing her hands closer to her face. Her wail builds higher and higher until it's a shout. Only then does it shape into words. "What have I done?"

"Amelie!" I say again, taking her by the shoulder with my free hand and forcing her around to face me.

She tumbles to the side as she whirls around, but her eyes are still on her hands. "Whose blood is this?" The flame in my palm illuminates the terror on her face, pupils dilated as her fingers quiver before her. "What did I do?"

My gaze flashes to Nyxia, who watches my sister with a furrowed brow. "Are you doing this?"

The queen shakes her head. "Don't get me wrong," she says in her smooth voice, "her fear tastes delicious, but it needs no help being conjured forth by me. What-ever she's seeing is entirely her own making."

I have a hard time believing that, considering what I was told about the shadows blanketing the cell bars. Perhaps the human side of my sister has made her more susceptible to whatever mental powers this dungeon has over its prisoners.

I turn back to my sister and crouch before her. Again,

I take her by the shoulder, shaking her forcibly until her eyes meet mine. "Amelie, wake up!"

Her chest heaves as she blinks several times, body still convulsing. A look of recognition crosses her face, followed by relief. She lunges forward, arms outstretched.

I lurch back, holding the fire in my palm between us while my free hand flies to my obsidian dagger. Before I can slide it from its sheath, I realize Amelie's arms were reaching for an embrace, not an attack. At least, that's how it appears now.

Hurt replaces the relief in her eyes, but she seems to steel herself as she rises to her feet and pins her arms at her sides. "Evie, it's you," she says, her soft, familiar voice like a knife to my heart. How many times has that voice been my comfort, my companionship? "Are you taking me somewhere?"

I consider not answering her at all, but there wouldn't be much point, since she'll find out in a matter of minutes. "Yes."

"Are you punishing me?" Her voice comes out small, but there's a flash of something unexpected on her face— anticipation, perhaps. Whatever it is, it's a profane contrast to our topic of conversation. "Am I to be executed for my crimes?"

"Not yet. Come with me."

Just as I take a step away, she retreats toward the corner. "You should give me commands first. To protect yourself from me."

A hint of the terror I saw in her eyes returns, sending a chill up my spine. "Why? I thought you said you waited out any of Cobalt's commands that could hurt me."

"I did." She moves farther into the corner, as if she

could disappear into it, posture rigid. "But I don't know where you're taking me. If we're going to...if we see...if it's *him*, I..." She squeezes her eyes shut as her chest returns to heaving.

I'm rendered speechless as I take in her growing discomfort. How much of this is an act? All? None? Is this still the fear generated from the dark magic of the dungeon? Whatever the case, she's probably right. It would be stupid to let her leave this cell without commands.

"Amelie Fairfield." I let my voice fill the cell, waves of magic rolling off my tongue. "By the power of your true name, I order you not to hurt, harm, sabotage, or incapacitate me in any way."

My sister sighs, shoulders sagging as her breathing returns to normal. With her eyes still closed, she says, "If you're going to give me more commands than that, which I suggest you do, you should provide a time period in which I'm required to obey. Cobalt renewed my orders daily."

I remember her mentioning something about that the first time we spoke after her arrival here. "Why is that?"

She opens her eyes, and from the light of my flame, I can see her pupils have returned to a normal size. "He once gave me several long-standing orders at the same time and the results were debilitating for me. A single lifelong command will do, or several short-term commands. I suggest the latter to cover all your bases, and that you extend them to twenty-four hours."

"How convenient it is that you have such specific parameters for me to go by." My tone is flat, eyes narrowed as I study her for any hint that she's manipulating me.

"If you don't believe me, you may try and do what you wish." She says it without taunting or malice. It's more like resignation that fills her toneless voice. "You can see for yourself."

"Fine," I say through my teeth. "You will follow my commands for twenty-four hours—"

She shakes her head. "In order for it to work properly, you must specify that you are altering your first command. And then provide the time frame for each separate command you give me."

I curl the fingers of my free hand into a fist, jaw clenched tight as I consider whether she's doing this to stall me or sabotage the commands. Then again, I did command her not to sabotage me. "Amelie Fairfield, by the power of your true name, I alter my first command. I demand you will not hurt, harm, sabotage, or incapacitate me in any way for the next twenty-four hours. I demand that you remain by my side and in my sight at all times for the next twenty-four hours. I demand that you not hurt, harm, sabotage, or incapacitate anyone I consider a friend, ally, or subject for the next twenty-four hours." I pause, searching my mind for any other potential threats to protect against. "And you will not attempt to run away or communicate with anyone I consider an adversary, threat, or enemy for the next twenty-four hours."

"As you think of more, you may add them throughout the day," Amelie says.

I give her a pointed look. "Thanks so much for your permission," I say with venom, then turn on my heel. We exit the cell, Amelie remaining close to my side. Nyxia throws my sister a scowl, then starts down the dungeon hall. We follow in her wake, the wraith-guard trailing close behind.

After a few minutes of silence, Amelie edges closer to me. My body goes on high alert, fire flooding my veins as I prepare for any attack. "Don't hate me, Evie," she whispers to me. "I hope you can come to trust me again."

Her fingertips brush against my palm, and she inches closer, curling her fingers around mine. I flinch at the touch, the feel of her flesh conjuring images of Mother's hands grasping mine through the bars of her cell at the Spire. A bullet. Blood. Flames. A shiver of revulsion runs through me, and I snatch my fingers away to fold my hands at my waist. I can't bring myself to meet her eyes as I say coldly, "So do I."

9

After we leave the dungeon, I allow Amelie a short visit to the moon baths. My eyes don't leave her as she washes away the grime of her captivity, wrings the dirt from her hair, and attempts to smooth her matted tresses. I try not to focus on how her shade of copper looks so much like Mother's. Instead, I attune myself to the potential threat she poses.

Every muscle in my body is tensed, poised for attack. Part of me expects my sister will whirl around to face me wearing the head of her selkie skin—even though I know the skin is gone; Nyxia informed me it was disposed of as soon as Amelie arrived at Selene Palace. Still, I don't know if I'll ever forget the way she looked at me on the balcony at Bircharbor Palace, the way she told me she didn't want my protection, the way she pulled the sealskin over her face and leapt off the rail and into the waves below, leaving me for *Cobalt*.

His name is like a curse, even in my thoughts.

I force the memories from my mind, tapping my foot

impatiently for her to hurry up. Once she's done taking her sweet time, Amelie changes into a simple black gown borrowed from Nyxia, one to match my own plain, gauzy black dress. Considering our next destination will likely host temperatures hotter than I've ever felt before, I figure we should dress appropriately in simple, lightweight attire.

After she's dressed, I lead us to the throne room. That's when my stomach starts to roil. In a matter of minutes, I'll be transported to a new court. A new palace. My new home. The concept is still impossible for me to reconcile.

For the love of iron, I own a *palace!*

As we enter the throne room, I see everyone else has already gathered. Aspen grins at me, and my lips tug upward to mirror his, warmth stirring inside my chest. With all the arrangements that needed to be made last night, my mate and I have yet to finish what we started in this very room. I blush as my gaze snags on the table at the edge of my periphery.

I missed you last night, he says through the Bond, and with it pulses his desire. His eyes flicker to the figure at my side, and all heat is extinguished from his expression, gaze turning to steel. The same goes for Foxglove and Lorelei, who'd been engaged in animated conversation until we walked in.

I hazard a glance at Amelie, watching her face brighten when she sees her former fae friends. She opens her mouth as if to speak, only to shrink in on herself as Lorelei shoots her a seething glare. I almost feel bad for my sister. Almost.

A girlish squeal cuts through the tension in the room

as a red flame flutters over to me. "Your Most Incredible and Beautiful Majesty," Breeda says, folding into a bow before spinning in a circle. "I am so honored to serve you."

"I am grateful to have you at my side."

Her tiny mouth stretches into a wide smile, and she floats above my shoulder between me and Amelie as I join the others. Aspen stands at my other side and Queen Estel stands next to him. Two fae I recognize as Aspen's guards flank the group. Even Nyxia is here, although I know she won't be traveling with us.

"We should make haste," Estel says. "I want us to arrive well before the Renounced expect me to come to them. Once they realize I have shifted my allegiance, I don't know what they will do. We must all be on alert for any retaliation."

"They would be idiots to retaliate," Aspen says. "They've already lost Spring. Once they realize they no longer have Star, they'll see they're outnumbered."

"That may be the case," Estel says, "but they find it all too easy to replace those who've joined the Alpha Alliance with pretender kings and queens."

"Those pretenders have yet to prove competence or power," Nyxia says, lifting her chin.

While that may be true, there's an unvoiced concern I can't help but confront. What if Queen Estel can't be trusted? What better way to sabotage a threat to the Renounced than this? Our enemies could be waiting exactly where she takes us. She might not take us to Irridae Palace at all, but to a nest of blades and adversaries. Then it would be easy to overpower me and

Aspen, taking out two rulers at once. My heart races at the terrifying thought.

But fae can't lie, I remind myself, trying to steel my nerves. I pat the dagger at my waist for good measure, only this time, I wish it were iron like my old one. Iron, at least, would work on my enemies amongst the Renounced. Like Dahlia. Cobalt. Maybe even Estel.

That's when another nagging thought creeps up on me. There *is* a way for fae to lie. Cobalt discovered it. What if that's Amelie's true purpose? What if she gave a piece of herself to more than just him? What if she made similar bargains with all the Renounced and gave them the ability to lie?

Aspen's voice comes through the Bond, shocking me from my racing thoughts. *What's going on in that head of yours?*

I consider brushing him off, but if there's a chance I'm right...

With a sigh, I quickly relay my fears through our Bond. *Do you think it's possible?* I ask.

I watch his brow wrinkle as he considers the question. Part of me expects him to tell me I'm just being paranoid. If anyone knows about being a paranoid ruler, it's him. But instead of dismissing my concerns, he turns to Estel, interrupting her conversation with Nyxia. "Queen Estel, do you promise you are taking us to Irridae Palace and that no Renounced know of this plan?"

Silence falls over the throne room, a blanket of unease settling over us. The particles on the shimmering queen's face disperse and shift into a frown, but only for a moment. With grace, she faces my mate. "I promise I am taking you, your mate, and your companions straight to

Irridae Palace and that none of the Renounced know of this. I promise my allegiance is to the Alpha Alliance."

Aspen gives her a nod of respect. "Thank you."

A weight slides off my shoulders. I remember Cobalt confessing that he was still bound by direct promises, even with the power to lie. That should make me feel better. Shouldn't it?

Estel's gaze falls on me. "Are you ready?"

I swallow hard, shoulders tense. "Yes."

Queen Nyxia takes a step away from our gathering. "Good luck claiming your new palace," she says to me. "Try not to get yourself killed if things go badly, all right? If there really is a stash of iron weapons at Irridae, we need you alive to defend it."

I give her a wry smile. "I'll try not to inconvenience you with my death."

We exchange nods, and I watch as Nyxia makes her way to the door of the throne room. There I see a slim figure with silver hair leaning against the doorframe. Franco. The sight of him warms my heart, and I flash him a smile. He winks at me, then turns and enters the hall at his sister's side.

I return my attention to my companions, and Estel instructs us to form a circle around her. Breeda can barely contain her squeal of excitement, while Amelie trembles next to me, eyes on her feet.

Estel opens her shimmering palm, and a silver, hexagonal disc appears over it. With a flick of her thumb, two halves separate on a hinge. One half appears to be nothing more than a cover while the other is inlaid with several facets of quartz surrounding a small orb of golden light at the center. The light is so bright it looks like a miniature star. Estel's eyes meet mine. "This is the Chariot. It will take us to your palace."

I return my gaze to the disc, hardly able to blink. I'm so fascinated by what I see. *That's* the mysterious Chariot Lorelei told me about? That tiny object is a device to allow instantaneous travel? As I continue to stare at it, sifting through all the scientific knowledge I have to explain how even the concept alone could possibly work, the light at the center begins to glow brighter and brighter, spanning in a radius until it surrounds us all. Then it grows taller, encompassing us in a bright golden bubble.

The skin prickles up the back of my neck, and I'm forced to admit this goes beyond everything I know about science. It's beyond everything I know about *magic*, even. This is so unlike the magic of the axis line. There, the transition is subtle, imperceptible. Here, the power at work is unmistakable. The light seems to vibrate to my very core, humming in my bones as the throne room disappears, swallowed by the light. The humming increases, and for a moment I think it will tear me apart, as surely, I am no longer a solid being. Am I?

And then it's gone.

The golden light is absorbed back into the tiny orb, and Estel closes the cover over it. The next thing I'm aware of is a stifling warmth, a heat unlike anything I've felt before. It's different from the scorching glow of my fire; this comes from all sides with a weight that immediately makes sweat bead at my brow.

"We're here," Estel says.

Aspen's guards break from the group, unsheathing their swords as they flank us to investigate our environment. I turn in a slow circle, hand on the hilt of my dagger as I eye an enormous courtyard surrounded by a tall sandstone wall. The sun beats high overhead, blindingly bright with its glow. Peaks of mountains in shades of brown and gold hover in the distance far beyond the wall while fluffy green palms and spiky cacti decorate the sandy landscape.

Next, my attention turns to what's inside the walls of the courtyard, glimpsing the perfect symmetry spread before me. Two rows of palms stand sentinel along each side of the courtyard, lining two rectangular, crystal-blue ponds that flank a red tile walkway—and that's when I see what the walkway leads to.

A set of immense blue double doors decorated in gold filigree await at the opposite end of the tile floor, surrounded by a breathtaking palace that spans from one side of the wall to the other. Its base is of brown sandstone that gives way to slender white towers ringed with circular balconies. Some towers are peaked with tiled turrets while others end in bulbous white marble domes. Three larger domes are clustered over the center portion of the palace, each carved with intricate flames and floral designs.

My mouth falls open as I study the structure. If I thought Bircharbor and Selene were incredible feats of architecture, this puts them both to shame. I've never seen such beauty, such craftsmanship that defies the norms and seems to favor art over function. "It's beautiful," I say under my breath, shoulders relaxing as my hand finally leaves my dagger.

Amelie whirls to face me. "I've never seen anything like it!" Her expression is so bright, so much like the sister

I grew up with, that I forget for a moment the tension between us. Without realizing it, my grin has mirrored hers, and I'm about to grasp her hands excitedly in mine.

That's when I remember the wall I must keep firmly in place. I can't grow lax in my trust, not until I know the truth about her.

I clench my fingers into fists and avert my gaze, returning my attention to the palace. From the corner of my eye, I see Amelie lower her head, her disappointment at my rejection so palpable, it makes my heart clench.

Remember what she did to Mother, I repeat in my head, allowing my fire to replace my guilt.

A flicker of red hovers at my shoulder, and Breeda lets out a squeal. "We're home, Your Majesty! Do you just totally and completely love it?"

I stand tall and give her what I hope to be a regal and composed nod. "It's quite adequate."

Aspen snickers at my poorly concealed awe, and my lips curl into a smirk. He opens his mouth to speak, but movement near the front doors of the palace catches my eye. The others notice too, and silence falls over our group as one of the doors swings open.

Aspen's soldiers rush to the front of our retinue, standing between us and whatever is coming out to greet us.

Once the door opens fully, a bronze haze funnels outside. All I see is a vicious face and two gigantic hands thrusting forward before everything is replaced with a cloud of dust and sand. It builds before the door, growing higher, higher, blocking out the light of the sun.

Then it speeds straight for us.

10

I close my eyes and spin away from the dust cloud as it crashes into me. Gasping for breath, I fall to my knees, feeling sand barrel into my back. My first thought is that I was right. This really is a trap. Queen Estel betrayed us after all.

But it's her voice I hear, shouting over the din of my companions' coughs and the swirling of dust and sand beating relentlessly overhead. At first, her words are incoherent, but then I hear, "Stop! Queen Evelyn of Fire is here to claim Irridae Palace. Stand down before your queen!"

To my surprise, the dust storm abates. Once I no longer feel the sand pelting me, I rise to my feet, coughing through gasping breaths. I try to open my eyes, but grit stings them so badly, I dare not attempt to rub it away for fear I'll simply irritate my eyes further. Instead, I allow my tears to well, allow them to push the grains away. But it's no use. There's too much—

I'm struck by a sudden splash of water that drenches

me from head to toe. From the gasps I hear around me, I take it I'm not the only one. When I'm finally able to open my eyes, it's to Aspen's face, concern written in the crease between his brows as he takes me by the shoulders. His blue-black hair hangs limp around his antlers, dripping brown, sandy water.

"Are you all right?" he asks.

I nod. "What happened? Where did the water come from?" I glance around us. Everyone but Estel and Breeda —who were apparently immune to the attack, likely due to their less-corporeal forms—are covered in a mixture of sand and water. Amelie is slumped on the ground, blinking rapidly while Foxglove and Lorelei take turns brushing debris off each other's faces.

"I pulled water from the ponds to clear the dust," he says. "Can you see?"

"Yes," I say, looking from him to the two ponds flanking the palace, a sense of awe washing over me. Even though I know my mate holds power over water, I've never seen him use it before. It's a chilling reminder that there's still much about him I don't know.

"Which one of you is this supposed queen?" a voice calls out from near the palace, filling the courtyard with its deep, echoing resonance. I face it, finding Aspen's guards already edging forward, swords pointed at the figure standing before the doors. He wears no shirt, only loose, brown trousers that reveal a wide torso, broad shoulders, and thick arms roped with muscle. His skin is a deep bronze, his eyes dark and deep set below thick black brows. Strands of long, wavy black hair brush his shoulders. From this distance, I can't tell exactly how tall he is, but he appears even taller than Aspen.

Foxglove nearly trips in his haste to rise to his feet, grasping Lorelei's wrist for balance. "For the love of oak and ivy," he mutters, his tone full of fear...or is it awe?

I take a few hesitant steps forward, squaring my shoulders as I force myself into as regal a posture as I can, despite how haggard I'm sure the dust storm has made me. "I am Queen Evelyn of Fire."

The domineering fae crosses his arms over his chest. "Is that so?"

"Who is he?" I ask, quiet enough so only my companions can hear.

"He's a djinn," Lorelei says.

"He's quite angry," adds Breeda.

As one of the guards creeps forward, the djinn's face clouds over with a snarl and he lifts his hands. Dust and sand begin to rise at his feet.

Foxglove whirls toward me and Aspen. "Tell the guards to stand down or he's going to attack again."

"Then why should they stand down?" Aspen says through his teeth.

Foxglove wrings his hands. "He's clearly Bonded to the palace and trying to protect it. We must speak with him."

Two orbs of dust have gathered in the djinn's hands and are growing larger by the second. His eyes flash from one guard to the other.

Aspen lets out a grumble, then shouts at his guards, "Stand down!"

The guards falter, freezing in place. The djinn doesn't lower his arms, keeping the enormous orbs of sand hovering over his palms.

Foxglove swallows hard. "I'll go speak with him."

Lorelei whips her head toward her friend, burning him with a glare. "Why you? I'm her ambassador. I should speak with him."

He flushes. "My dearest Lorelei, while I respect your new position and am confident in your abilities, this situation must be handled with care."

She puts her hands on her hips. "What's that supposed to mean?"

"You aren't the friendliest with strangers," he says with a grimace.

She pops a hip to the side, narrowing her eyes. "As ambassador, I will be...*friendly*...just fine."

Foxglove raises a brow. "Really? Can you honestly say you're planning on going up to the very male who just attempted an attack on your queen and speak to him with courtesy and calm?"

The two are locked in an icy standoff, neither saying another word. For a moment, I worry my decision to appoint Lorelei as my ambassador may have created an unforeseen complication—pitting the two friends against one another. I'm about to intervene when Lorelei's lips pull into a smirk. "Good point."

Foxglove nods triumphantly. "Well, then—"

"Actually, I should be the one to speak with him," says Breeda, bobbing toward foxglove. "I am a fellow fire fae. He'll listen to me."

Before another argument can erupt, I say, "You both should go. Now." I then raise my voice and address the djinn. "I am sending an ambassador and a fire sprite to speak with you in a peaceful exchange of words."

For a tense stretch of silence, the djinn makes no move to lower his threatening orbs of sand. Then finally, he returns his arms to cross his chest and the sand crashes to his feet. "Very well."

Foxglove sighs and removes his spectacles, rubbing them on his burgundy jacket before replacing them. His efforts seem to have done nothing but smear a layer of dust over the lenses. With trembling fingers, he runs his hands through his damp, dirty, brown tresses, which only makes his hair stick up at odd angles. "How do I look?"

The hope in his eyes catches me off guard. "You look..."

"Flustered," Aspen finishes for me and grunts a laugh.

"Well, do you see his arms?" Foxglove says. "He could completely crush me in them." Despite his words, I'm almost certain there's wistful excitement in his eyes, not terror.

Realization settles over me; I've seen that expression before. "You fancy the djinn, don't you?"

Foxglove blushes, a sheepish grin tugging his lips.

"But I thought you fancied Franco."

He waves a dismissive hand. "Forget Franco."

"A motto to live by," Aspen mutters with a smirk.

I roll my eyes. "Just go."

Foxglove flashes me an anxious smile, then he and Breeda begin their slow approach toward the djinn, stopping several feet from him and the palace steps. Breeda speaks first. "Your Most Large and Powerful Servant of Irridae Palace, I represent your new master, Queen Evelyn of Fire."

Foxglove takes a hesitant step forward. "You may not have heard, but Queen Evelyn has defeated the former

King Ustrin. She has been blessed by the All of All and has come to claim the palace that is hers by right."

The djinn's eyes flash over their heads to pin me beneath his stare. "I will allow her to approach. If she truly is the new Queen of Fire, she may take my hand and let the palace decide the validity of her claim. If she is unworthy of the palace, she will burst into flame and burn until her bones are nothing but ash."

I suppress a shudder at the not-so-veiled threat. The blood leaves my face as I consider all possible scenarios. What kind of magic is at work here? Is it the magic of the All of All? Will I once again receive the proper blessing? Or is this some trick, some vile defense Ustrin had woven into the palace should his reign fall? Worse than that is the thought that the magic he speaks of is real and I will be deemed unworthy. Ever since I defeated the Fire King, part of me keeps waiting for everything to blow up in my face. For my people to turn on me, for them to realize I'm just a pathetic human—

Relax, Evie. Aspen's voice comes through the Bond like an invisible caress. It's then I realize how tense I've grown, my jaw clenched and hands balled into painfully tight fists. *You will pass this test. Just like you did in the Twelfth Court.*

I can only hope he's right, that he understands whatever ritual I'm about to participate in. With a deep breath, I call out to the djinn. "I will take your hand and prove to you my right. Allow me to approach with my guards and companions."

"Very good," he says. "The easier for me to kill them should you prove to be false."

I purse my lips to hide my snarl. *No, the easier for them*

to kill you should you make one wrong move against me, I think to myself.

As we make our way to join Foxglove and Breeda, I notice how Amelie lags behind, nearly dragging her feet with every step, eyes wide with fear. She's clearly struggling against the compulsion of my command that keeps her at my side at all times. In the presence of our foe, I can hardly blame her. Is this proof that my commands truly work as she claimed they would?

We pause once we reach the palace steps, and I make my way to the front of the retinue, the two guards crouched in defensive postures just a step behind me.

The djinn extends his hand. "Place your palm in mine."

I meet his eyes, summoning all the confidence I can muster. Now that we're close, I can see he is in fact nearly a head taller than Aspen, which places him significantly taller than me. I try not to notice the sheen of his bronze skin over his rippling muscles as I grasp his enormous hand.

At the touch of his flesh on mine, fire roars through my blood, rushing down my arms, my legs. Pink, purple, and aqua flames lap over my skin, adding to the unbearable heat from the sun. My flames, however, don't scorch me. Not like they did when Aspen carried me from the Spire, resulting in me burning the both of us in my unrelenting rage. This time, they are nothing but a warm glow.

My eyes remain locked on the djinn's, and his widen as my flames grow higher, extending toward him.

In one swift move, the djinn drops my hand and falls to his knees before me.

My flames extinguish, leaving me feeling invigorated and strong.

The djinn lifts his head to find my gaze. "Forgive me, my queen. My name is Fehr, and I am your humble servant. Welcome home."

11

My new home is even more breathtaking on the inside than it was on the outside.

Fehr leads us through the entrance hall to a grand foyer with towering ceilings and thick marble columns. The walls are made of sandstone interspersed with white marble panels carved with as much intricate detail as you'd expect from a painting or a tapestry.

"Soooo pretty," Breeda squeals, hands framing her tiny face as she flits from one wall to the next.

Our footsteps echo as we make our way across the tile floors. The hollow reverberations sing of how empty the palace is. There's no bustle of busy servants, no mutterings from guests and residents.

It's just like the moon dragons had reported; there's no one here.

Fehr comes up alongside me. "I pray you forgive me for the attack. I will take any punishment you see fit." His rich baritone is devoid of fear or remorse. In fact, I'm almost positive there's a hint of indignation laced into his words, as if he's speaking out of rote necessity.

I suppose I can't blame him for neither trusting nor liking me. The feeling is mutual. Distrust aside, logic has me recalling Foxglove's assumption regarding the djinn's motives. I adopt a formal bearing as I say, "I assume your actions were taken to protect Irridae Palace."

"You are correct. I was Bonded to the palace as its life-long steward long ago by King Caleos."

A ripple of surprise runs through me at the mention of my grandfather. "Why?"

"A punishment for my darkest deeds. A way to control my power." That hint of resentment returns, clearer now, but it doesn't linger. "I am loyal to the palace and am bound to serve the one who rules it. As steward, all household matters of importance may be given to me."

"And how does the palace know who the true ruler should be?" I can't help but think of the pretender king the Renounced had planned to send here. Would he have passed the test? Or burned to a crisp?

Fehr lifts his chin, expression turning haughty as he eyes me with a condescending smirk. "It is simply the palace's magic, Your Majesty. Ever mysterious, even to me." The last part is said somewhat under his breath, revealing more of his poorly hidden disdain. It's clear he's surprised I passed the test. Then again, so am I.

We reach the end of the foyer where it opens to an enormous atrium. At the center is a large circular table carved from fiery pink, orange, and red sunstone. On each side of the table are wide staircases; one leads to the upper levels of the palace while the other descends below. Several halls branch off from here, leading who knows where.

Aspen's hand brushes my arm. *Now that's an adequate table,* he relays to me.

I press my lips tight to hide my grin and wonder if my sudden blush is visible through the layer of grime that coats my cheeks.

"Do you know of a stash of iron weapons hidden within the palace?" Estel asks, facing Fehr.

Fehr's eyes narrow with suspicion, his expression hard as he assesses the Star Queen. "I do not answer to you."

I'm about to tell him it's all right, that he may answer the question. But again, I'm plagued with doubt. Estel gave us our promise that she is on our side, but now that I've experienced the trial required to enter the palace, I wonder if the Renounced needed me to come here, to reopen the palace, to show someone where the weapons stash is so they could be led straight to it.

I shudder, as Amelie's proximity feels heavy. What if Lorelei was right? What if *this* is why my sister is here?

"It's all right," Estel says, shaking me from my thoughts. "I will ask you something else. Will you protect Queen Evelyn and the palace until sufficient guards and household staff can be appointed?"

Fehr's jaw shifts back and forth, hand flying momentarily to his chest before he composes himself. "I will protect the queen and Irridae with my life now and even after she has proper guards. It is my duty, which is not to be questioned."

Breeda flashes the djinn a scowl, then mirrors his posture. "I will guard Our Most Beautiful Queen Evelyn as well. None will dare creep upon her while my light shines."

Estel's face shifts and rearranges into a look of amusement, then settles on a more serious expression. "I must return to my court in case there's any retaliation from the Renounced. I will return tomorrow with more of King Aspen's guards."

I furrow my brow, the thought of retaliation sending a shiver up my spine. What happens if our enemies retaliate *here*? Can Fehr truly protect us? As begrudging as he obviously is to serve me, his declaration of loyalty does little to strengthen my confidence in him. My only consolation is that what little tales I've heard about djinn have always told of their immense power. "Must you wait until tomorrow to bring more guards?"

Estel opens her palm, the silver disc that brought us here flashing beneath the light streaming in from the high windows of the atrium. "The Chariot only works twice before it must be charged by starlight. I've already used it once, which means I can only use it to take me to my palace."

It's strange that something so powerful would require a period of rest. Then again, I suppose even the strongest magic must have its limits. If the fae could travel through time and space at will and in unlimited quantity...the power is almost too incredible to imagine. The fae would be unstoppable.

Perhaps Estel's device was created with limitations on purpose.

The hair rises on the back of my neck at the thought. I hope, despite my doubt and suspicions, the powerful Star

Queen truly is on our side. I'd hate to see her power in the hands of our enemies.

ONCE ESTEL LEAVES, I ORDER AMELIE TO REMAIN WITH THE guards while I speak with Fehr out of earshot. I square my shoulders and force myself to ignore the way he narrows his eyes when he looks at me. "About the question Queen Estel asked," I say, keeping my voice level. "I need to know that answer myself. Is there an iron weapons stash?"

His lips curl in disgust at the mention of iron. "There is a vile room in the lowermost level of the palace, below the dungeon. It reeks of iron, strong enough to keep prisoners weak, although I've never been able to get close enough to the room to witness what is inside."

"Can you take us to it?" My eyes flash toward my sister, and I add, "After stopping at the dungeon first, perhaps?"

"It will be done," he says with a low bow.

We rejoin the others and Fehr leads us down one of the staircases. The lower we go, the cooler the temperatures become as open windows disappear and are replaced with solid mud-brick walls. Fehr conjures an orange flame over his palm to light our way, but it begins to shrink the farther down we go. His pace, too, starts to slow, and the breaths of my companions grow ragged.

I glance at my mate, seeing the sheen of sweat that now covers his brow. Even with only the light of Fehr's flame, I can tell he's grown pale. However, the others seem to be faring far worse—Breeda has dulled to a pale pink glow, the guards struggle to maintain their postures, Foxglove looks like he's on the verge of retching, and Lorelei appears worse than she did when Mr. Meeks used iron teacups against us. It seems only Amelie and I are immune to the iron we must surely be nearing.

The staircase opens to a narrow hall, where the mud-brick walls melt into a more natural formation, with curved walls pocked with tiny holes, like the lava caves I've only seen documented in encyclopedic sketches. As we leave the final stair to enter the hall, my companions slow to a halt. Fehr's flame all but sputters out. I open my palm and ignite my own light, blanketing us in a blue glow and revealing rows and rows of barred caverns. This must be the dungeon.

I turn toward the djinn, who sags against the uneven wall, glaring into the corridor. "Are there any prisoners currently kept here?" I ask.

"All were expelled along with the household," he says, voice hoarse. His eyes flick from me to Breeda, and his expression softens for the first time. "Although I doubt you would consider many of them a danger, if you keep company with the unseelie. Most were like her. Sprites. Wisps. Any who refused to take seelie form at his command."

My eyes widen. "He kept unseelie fae down here?" Fehr nods, and I step farther into the hall to examine the cells. Each room is small and rounded, providing no flat surface to lie down, not to mention the rough texture of the curved walls. The doors and bars of the cells are of dark green malachite. I see no additional defenses like Lunar's dungeons, no dangerous enchantments or writhing shadows. Then again, considering the degrading state of my companions, I doubt any added protections were needed with an iron store so close.

Fehr comes up beside me, his steps slow and lagging. "Was there a reason you wanted to see the dungeon first?"

I look over my shoulder where Amelie stands nearby. Her head is lowered, but she eyes the cells, shoulders trembling. When she suddenly lifts her head and meets my gaze, her expression goes slack. She gives me a subtle nod, as if to relay her resigned acceptance over why we're here.

I look from her to the cell, hating the way my heart lurches at the thought of her inside that cramped room, unable to stretch out or lie down. But why do I care? *Remember what she's done. Remember Mother.* Fire floods my veins, and I know I must make the command. If the commands truly work, then she can't leave my side unless I give the order. I open my mouth to do just that, but I stop myself as a slew of questions invades my mind. What if she can easily break free? What if there's an unseen tunnel hidden behind the cells, like the ones leading from the coral caves at Bircharbor? What if leaving her alone is exactly the opportunity she needs to escape?

My sister isn't weakened by iron, so if there's a way out, she can find it.

Evie, Aspen says into my mind, cutting through the chaos of my thoughts. His voice comes across barely louder than a whisper, expressing just how weakened he's becoming. *You don't have to leave her in there if you aren't comfortable with it.*

I bristle at that, even though I know my irritation isn't meant for him. I'm more annoyed at myself for wearing my internal debate so clearly that he could see it.

I sense Aspen's approaching presence before I feel the brush of his hand on my lower back. It soothes me, steadies my mind.

I turn to Fehr. "Thank you for showing me the dungeon. I think it will serve me quite well should anyone give me a reason to utilize it." I enunciate this last part, flashing my sister a warning glare.

Her eyes widen, and I'm not sure if it's from fear or surprise that I'm not locking her up. I hold her gaze, letting the veiled threat hang heavy between us so she understands what I'm trying to convey. I'll give her a chance to prove me wrong, but I'll be watching her every move, waiting for the moment she tries to betray me. And if she does, I'll be ready.

Fire burns inside me, so hot it helps drown out the hidden truth I refuse to acknowledge—that maybe I'm not keeping her close just to catch her in the act of betraying me. Maybe I'm doing it because, somewhere deep down, I want to trust her.

THE FIRST TEST OF THE STRENGTH OF MY COMMANDS COMES when I order Amelie to remain in the dungeon hall with the guards and Breeda while the rest of us make our way downstairs. Foxglove and Lorelei only make it to the bottom of the final stair before the scent of iron overcomes them. Fehr's flame has completely extinguished, leaving only my blue fire to light our way as the djinn, Aspen, and I make our way down the black hall. Our pace is agonizingly slow, considering the weakened state of my two companions, and only adds to the eerie quality of our surroundings. The hall is made of the same volcanic rock as the dungeon, but there are no caverns or corridors along the way. There's nothing but a winding black tunnel that makes my skin prickle amidst its eerie quiet.

"You're sure it's at the end of this hall?" I ask, my whispered voice creating an unsettling echo.

"Like I said, I've never been able to get close enough to see it for myself." Fehr's voice is even weaker than it was upstairs, for once devoid of its bitter edge. "I've glimpsed a door though. Also, I know this tunnel is where Ustrin often took his human allies."

His human allies must refer to Mr. Duveau, who I'm sure is responsible for providing these weapons in the first place. They'd formed a secret truce, one I'm not sure I entirely understand. They both seemed united by the need to maintain the treaty for the sole reason of hoarding the power it gave them. What exactly had they bargained?

With a grunt, Aspen doubles over. My heart races as I whirl toward him and bring my free hand to his cheek. A sheen of sweat coats his entire face, expression twisted in agony. My throat feels tight, and a sudden stab of pain comes through the Bond, pain that isn't mine. "I'm sorry," I whisper, although I'm not sure what I'm apologizing for. He insisted on coming with me as far as he could, and we agreed it's imperative to confirm the location of the weapons stash.

"It's all right," he says with a gasp. "This is as far as I can go."

"I won't be able to go much farther either," Fehr says,

"but I can at least make it to the point where I can see the door."

A rush of fear goes through me at the thought of approaching the end of a dark tunnel alone. All I can do is seek my inner fire to burn away my trepidation and hope Ustrin hadn't left me a trap to waltz into.

Fehr and I continue on farther down until he too doubles over and sags against the wall. With one hand grasping his chest, the other points down the hall. "You should see it," he mutters. "The door."

With a deep breath, I take a step away from the djinn and hold out my ball of flame. There's only a slight bend in the tunnel, and as my eyes adjust, I see the edge of something flat and metallic. With the door in sight, I hurry forward. Just like Fehr had assumed, the tunnel ends in an enormous wooden door. The metal I'd glimpsed is a bar that crosses it. I slow my steps as I approach, eyes flashing left and right for any sign of hidden threats. Finally, the door is within reach.

I brace my free hand beneath the bar, which appears to be solid iron, and lift.

Nothing.

I touch my flame to the ground, willing it to remain in place. Luckily, it obeys, illuminating the door as I struggle to lift the bar with both hands now.

It doesn't even budge.

With a grumble, I retrieve my flame and storm away from the door.

"Well, that was disappointing," I say to Fehr once I reach him. "The door is barred with iron and I'm the only one who can get close enough." Well, aside from Amelie, of course, but I don't say so. Besides, I'm not even sure the both of us could lift it together if we tried. "How was Ustrin able to use this room at all?"

"His human allies were the only ones who could enter the room itself," he says, pushing off the wall to right himself on unsteady feet. "I believe his use of these weapons was contingent upon compliance with them."

That explains why Ustrin only used iron weapons twice, to my knowledge. At least this serves as proof that none of the Renounced could reach the weapons room. If not even Aspen and a powerful djinn can, then I doubt there's any fae alive that could fare much better.

Then again, the Renounced aren't our only enemies, and our other foes have no problem with iron.

12

Night has fallen by the time we make it back to the atrium upstairs. Fehr snaps his fingers, bringing orbs of light over the sconces on the walls and throwing the area under a warm glow. The color seems to be coming back to my fae companions' faces, although the mood is significantly subdued. Conversation shifts to talk of meals, baths, and bedroom accommodations, which Fehr leaves to arrange for us. Breeda trails after him, insisting she must have final say over the best room for me.

As our guards move to stand watch at opposite ends of the atrium, and Foxglove and Lorelei leave us to lounge by one of the windows, I realize this is the first opportunity I've had all day to be somewhat alone with Aspen. As if he can sense my thoughts, he catches my eye with a grin. It pains me to see the effort he puts into the expression after so much strength was expended downstairs. I'm only glad the iron store doesn't affect him or my friends up here.

"Amelie," I say with the power of her name, "I allow you to leave me momentarily, only to remain where you are until I return to you, whereupon your order to remain at my side will recommence."

She nods, eyes downcast, and I take Aspen's fingers in mine. We make our way to stand by the table near the stairs, which is far enough from the others that we can speak privately. He faces me, bringing a hand to my cheek and brushing a thumb along my jaw. "What do you think of your new home?"

My heart feels warm as I luxuriate in the feel of his simple touch. Placing my hands on his waist, I tilt my head to meet his eyes. "I think it's only home because you're here."

He brings both hands to my face, cupping my cheeks. "I am here. For everything you need, the good and the bad."

For some reason, his words stir shame inside me as I recall how easily he saw through my inner turmoil over keeping Amelie in the dungeon. It also brings to mind something I hadn't previously thought of, something that makes my heart sink. And once again, he must be able to see my mood written clearly over my face.

"What is it?" he asks, brow furrowed.

"I can't stay with you tonight," I say with a grumble.

His concern melts off his face, replaced with a look of understanding. "You want to stay with your sister."

I groan. "I don't *want* to at all, but I should. At least tonight. I doubt I'll be able to sleep no matter where she is in the palace, not until I'm certain the commands will hold her in place. But tonight I want to keep her in plain sight."

"I understand."

"Is that because you're just as paranoid as I am?" I say with a teasing grin.

"No, it's because you're clearly just as smart as I am." His tone is smug, reminding me of how I perceived him when we first met. It's funny how easy it is to see through it now, how that vulnerable side of him is never far below the surface anymore.

"Your Majesty!" Breeda shouts, becoming a stream of red as she circles me and my mate.

I force myself not to roll my eyes in irritation as I separate from Aspen. "Yes, Breeda?"

She stops her circling to hover in the air before me. "You will never believe how beautiful the room I've picked for you is. It's the royal chamber!" Her words dissolve into a delighted squeal.

Fehr steps onto the landing from one of the staircases and offers a bow. "The bathing chambers and bedrooms are prepared."

"Ugh, delightful," Foxglove says as he and Lorelei saunter up to join us. "I haven't wanted a bath so badly in my life."

Fehr's eyes rove Foxglove as if seeing him for the first time. Beneath the djinn's stare, Foxglove blushes and looks sheepishly at his feet. I can almost hear the giggle he's sure to be suppressing.

"What about clothes?" Amelie's voice is so small and unexpected, it takes me a moment to realize she'd spoken. She remains where I left her, lifting the hem of her filthy black skirt, a grimace twisting her lips. Considering today is the first she's been allowed a bath and change of clothing after a week in a dungeon, I'm surprised she even cares. Then again, her preoccupation with fashion is so befitting the Amelie I once loved that my chest tightens.

I tear my eyes from my sister and return my gaze to the djinn. "Yes, Fehr, we will all require clean clothes, especially ones appropriate for this climate."

"In each bathing chamber, you will find towels and robes to change into," he says. "While you bathe, I will ensure each room is properly stocked with clothing. However, King Ustrin kept no concubines or female mates of status. There likely won't be much suitable for a queen."

"It will have to do," I say. Unlike Amelie, I have never been overly concerned with style, although that has changed much since coming to Faerwyvae.

"For now," Aspen adds, as if he finds my response lacking. "Once the new household staff has been appointed, see to it that Queen Evelyn has a royal wardrobe made up at once."

Fehr's gaze slides slowly from me to Aspen. "Am I to listen to his orders, Your Majesty?"

Aspen tenses, hands clenching into fists, but says nothing in reply.

"Yes," I say to Fehr. "King Aspen is my mate. His household will arrive here shortly, and you will allow them entrance onto the palace grounds. Same goes for the fire fae who will arrive from Lunar."

"Very well," Fehr says, expression hard as he bows to Aspen. "I will see that Queen Evelyn's wardrobe is made a priority by the palace seamstress. Shall I show you your rooms now?"

"Give me one more moment to speak with my mate."

Without a word, he returns to the bottom staircase, where Foxglove and Lorelei join him. Even Breeda seems to get the hint and joins the others, where they spark up casual conversation. All but Fehr, that is, who stands composed and slightly away from the group, unaware of how Foxglove's eyes flicker admiringly at him every few seconds.

I turn my attention back to Aspen. "I'll miss you tonight," I whisper. "I'll stay in a guest room with my sister. You take the royal chamber—"

"Just like that?" His lips pull into a devious smirk, making my stomach flip. "The woman who all but kicked me out of my own bedroom the night we became mates is forfeiting her right to the royal chamber?"

I put my hands on my hips, lips quirking up at the corners. "Were you hoping for a fight?"

"Why would I expect anything less? Especially when our last one ended so favorably."

Heat stirs in my core, and I tilt my head to the side. "Maybe I will fight you for the royal chamber after all."

His arm snakes around my waist and pulls me to him, then he presses his lips to mine. Not even the grit covering our faces or our nearby spectators can keep me from deepening the kiss, and I once again debate if I shouldn't just throw Amelie in the dungeon so I can take Aspen to bed here and now.

Too soon he pulls away, leaving my lips tingling for more. "You win," he says with a mock sigh. "Take the royal chambers tonight." With a wink, he turns away and joins the others at the staircase.

Unable to suppress the grin on my face, I go to retrieve my sister.

"So, it's true," she says as I reach her side. Her awestruck tone shakes me from my giddy daze. "You've truly come to find love with the Stag King."

Her words wipe the smile from my face. I try not to read too much into the tears that glaze her eyes. If I did, I might think she's genuinely happy for me.

THE ROYAL CHAMBER IS A SIGHT TO BEHOLD; NOT EVEN Aspen's bedroom at Bircharbor is this breathtaking. Its ample spaciousness contains all the accommodations I've come to expect from a palace bedroom—bed, bathing chamber, wardrobe, desk, dressing screen, sitting area— but the style is unlike anything I've seen. The walls are white stucco painted with intricate designs in gold, blue, and red, with orbs of pale yellow light hovering above red clay sconces. Arched windows line the expanse of the far wall, each with intricate gold shutters left open to invite the night air. The bed is draped in layers of cool linen sheets and topped with a heavy brocade blanket. Overhead, a canopy of gauzy chiffon hangs from the ceiling, tied off to the side on all four corners of the bed. Everything from the sheets to the canopy is a deep orange color.

The only thing that spoils my awe is the icy tension hanging between me and my sister. We've gone through the motions of washing and changing into robes without saying more than a word here and there to each other. Now we stand on opposite sides of the bed, sorting through piles upon piles of bland, brown dresses Fehr has brought us.

"You could have locked me in the dungeon," Amelie says, breaking the silence.

I purse my lips, tossing a dress that looks more like a shapeless sack to the floor. I must admit Fehr was right about Ustrin not having anything appropriate for a female royal to wear. The staff here must have been dressed quite plainly indeed.

Amelie seems to have given up on the dresses altogether and instead fiddles with the swaths of bright cloth the djinn brought from the former seamstress' room. Unsatisfied with my refusal to respond to her statement, she adds, "Why didn't you lock me in there? I expected you would, but—"

"I wanted to keep my eye on you," I say, tone firm as I toss yet another dress into the *absolutely not* pile.

"I can't disobey your orders," she whispers. "You can leave me by myself."

I lift my eyes from the dresses to study her with narrowed eyes. "Is that what you want?"

She shrugs. "I can tell you don't want to be near me. You'd rather be spending the night with your mate, would you not?"

"That's none of your concern."

"If you gave me commands to stay in my room all night, I would be bound to follow."

"You sure are keen on convincing me to leave you alone."

She meets my eyes for a moment, then lowers them back to the saffron spider silk in her hands. "I just don't want you to feel like you must watch my every move. I know I'm a burden to you, but I don't want to keep you from enjoying what should be a wonderful experience. You have an entire palace, a mate you love—"

"We're at war," I snap. "There's no such thing as a *wonderful experience* right now."

She gives another shrug, one that makes my blood boil. I burn her with a glare, studying her every move to see if I can decipher any hidden agenda written on her face. But she gives nothing away, her attention fixated on the length of russet chiffon she holds up to her chin, as if she's imagining it as a dress. Her brow furrows as she shifts it this way and that, the tip of her tongue visible at the corner of her mouth. In this moment, she bears a chilling resemblance to Mother hard at work on a new tincture or tisane.

My chest tightens at the sight, my throat constricting. I whirl away from my sister, eyes unfocused as I try to burn the dueling images that plague my mind. Amelie. Mother. Amelie. Mother.

How can I love one and hate the other?

Remember what she's done. Remember what her betrayal cost Mother.

I reach for my inner fire, let it burn the conflict from my mind until it clears, dissolves into nothing. The heat warms my insides, but I'm left realizing the skin on my arms has begun to prickle. I cross my arms over my chest and rub my shoulders, frowning at the open windows and the cool air they welcome into the room. At first, it was a relief to feel a drop in temperature, but now I almost wish we had a fire going in the hearth.

That's when I recall the red clay fireplace that lines one of the walls. I approach it, finding it empty of any source to burn. For a moment, I consider calling in

Breeda from the hall to have her fetch something. I'd ordered her to stand guard to give me a break from her chatter, and she's likely still out there doing her due diligence as if it were the most important job of her life. However, this might be something I can solve myself.

I extend my hand and think of heat. A spark of blue light flickers over my palm, then grows into an orb of flame. I'm about to reach inside the fireplace to set the flame down like I did by the weapons room, but I stop myself. I've seen both Aspen and Fehr summon light over sconces in an instant; surely, I can do something similar with a hearth fire. I narrow my eyes at the orb of flame, willing it to transport from my hand to the hearth. All it does is flicker in my palm.

I clench my jaw. How in the name of iron do I move a flame from one space to another, without simply transferring it by touch?

I'm suddenly reminded of Queen Estel and her power over time and space. Lorelei had explained it's the Star Court's affinity with the air element that gives her such an ability. Ustrin must have mastered at least a portion of air, considering he was able to send an orb of flame straight to Selene Palace. But how can I use the ability myself?

I close my eyes, recalling what little I know of the air element. I remember my first visit to the Twelfth Court, the ethereal, windblown pixie I met there. *We get along well,* she'd said. *Thought. Intellect.* How do I use either of those things to move my flame? Surely, I can't *think* it into moving.

What else do I know about air?

An instinctual nudge calls my attention to my firefox form. As soon as I give in to the train of thought, my body relaxes. Through my unseelie form, everything comes so much more naturally. My intellect is bound to my instincts, data is filtered at rapid speeds and turns into usable information. I call upon my inner firefox, ask how else she relates to air, aside from what goes on in her head. She shows me an image of me running through the woods, my paws taking me across vast stretches of land. Smooth, swift travel. Then she shows an image of me leaping from a tree to a boulder, then to another tree, gaining height with my momentum.

In that moment, it's clear to me. I can see how it all connects, how the elements weave together in everything I do. The way air meets earth in a strange and magical dance that creates gravity, acceleration, travel, motion.

With this awareness filling every part of my being, I will the fire to leave my hand and light inside the hearth. A sudden burst of heat pulls my eyes open.

There it is. My fire.

I watch the flame as it shifts from blue to orange, roaring quietly inside the fireplace. Sweat beads at my brow, dripping into my eyes, but it isn't from the heat. It's from the feat of concentration I just pulled, although I hardly realized I was doing it until it was done.

"You've grown so powerful with your magic," Amelie says, startling me from my awe.

A blush creeps up my cheeks. I shouldn't have let her see that. My gaze turns steely as I return to the bed where Amelie appears to have constructed several makeshift dresses from the bright fabrics. How she managed to do such a thing without a single stitch is beyond me.

She lifts a gown of flowing silk in a deep golden hue. "This one is fit for a queen," she says. My breath catches as she rounds the bed and approaches me with it. "Let me show you how it's worn."

I tense with every step she takes. Part of me wants to refuse to allow her close enough to help me dress, but I doubt I'll be able to figure out how to don the strange garment myself. With a sigh of resignation, I strip off my robe, and she drapes a swath of long, golden silk over my shoulders to drape over each breast down to the floor. Then she takes a separate piece of the same cloth and wraps it around my waist, tying it off just above my hips to form a skirt. The end result is light, breathable, and surprisingly elegant.

Amelie steps back to admire her work. "You make it look even more beautiful than I imagined." With a grin, she returns to the bed to pick out her own dress.

"How did you do this?" I ask, unable to suppress my curiosity as I stare down at the smooth silk. "You've never made a dress in your life."

"I examined the style of the others and made one like those, but more regal," she says. I'm about to return to sorting through the dresses, but after seeing what Amelie created, it seems futile. Silence falls between us again as I mindlessly push the dresses from one side of the bed to the other. Then Amelie says, "How do you make fire? Do you simply wish for flame and it happens?"

I press my lips into a tight line, debating if I should remain silent. Somehow though, this dress she's made has softened something inside me, for better or for worse. "I can conjure many forms of fire through intent, but the first time was an accident." There's much I leave unsaid with that statement, primarily the fact that I was with

Mother when it occurred. "I was angry, and it just happened."

She meets my eyes with a curious gaze. "Is that what helps you create fire? Anger?"

"Anger, rage, passion. There are many emotions that can spark it, but those are most natural for me."

Her expression turns to steel, hands wringing around the cloth she holds, lips pursed so tightly, they turn white. "I've felt more rage than I can stand, and I've never summoned so much as a spark, accident or no."

A flash of heat goes through me. I doubt she's felt anything close to my rage. Still, I keep that to myself, my own curiosity taking over. "You've been underwater, correct?"

"Cobalt had me locked in our bedroom in the coral caves." Her tone is cold, and I think I hear a hint of a tremble.

"An attack by water weakens fire," I explain. "There's a possibility that your proximity to water stifled any chance of recognizing your power."

She furrows her brow. "So, you think I could have the same gifts you do?"

I give a halfhearted shrug. "It's possible."

She lifts her palm, eyes narrowing to slits as she examines it. A hateful grin, one so unlike anything I've seen her wear, pulls at her lips.

My body is frozen as I watch her, trying to make sense of—

A red flame bursts over her open hand.

13

W ith a gasp of delight, she turns to me with a glowing smile. "Evie, look—"

"Amelie Fairfield," I say in a rush, the power of her name ringing in my voice, "I forbid you from using the power of fire."

The flame extinguishes along with her smile, all hope and pride draining from her eyes.

"For the next twenty-four hours," I hurry to add. My chest heaves, shoulders trembling. The terror of seeing my sister conjure flame like it was nothing strikes me harder and harder with every second that ticks by. It had been so easy for her. *Too* easy. How could that be?

"I'm sorry," Amelie whispers. "I never should have even thought of trying it."

I grit my teeth and stalk over to the sitting area. With my back to my sister, I sink into one of the chairs. "Put the dresses in the wardrobe once you're finished."

The tension in the room is so heavy, it makes my skin

crawl, and my mind continues to spin from the shock of what I just witnessed.

"Did Mother hate me?" Amelie asks, breaking the silence. Her words don't diminish my discomfort, however; they add to it. How dare she mention Mother? How dare she even ask?

I turn in my chair to burn her with a glare.

Of course she doesn't so much as flinch at my stare. She never was one to read a room, always saying the wrong thing in her sweet, naive way. Her next words come out tremulous. "Did she...die...hating me? Did you tell her the awful things I did?"

The air leaves my lungs as her words open a chasm of grief beneath me. I return to facing forward in my chair, fingers clenched tight around the armrest. I should silence her. I should forbid her to speak. But before I know it, my response is tumbling from my lips. "I told her the truth," I say through my teeth, tone dripping venom. Then, against all reason, I soften the blow. "But I didn't give her the details. I said you bargained away your name for love."

"Love." She scoffs the word like a curse. "I only bargained my ability to lie for love. We didn't exchange names until after I left Bircharbor."

Again, I clench the armrests. This time, it isn't grief I'm fighting against but the rage that threatens to explode out of every pore in a fiery inferno. "So, you're saying you gave him the ability to lie of your own free will? That he didn't compel you with magic?"

"Exactly." She says it as if she were speaking about someone else, a response to some juicy gossip regarding a foolish peer. From the corner of my eye, I see her carry an armload of dresses to the wardrobe where she begins to hang them. She's changed into one of her makeshift gowns, a pale orange.

But all I can see is red. "So, you betrayed me from the very start, and yet you wonder why I can't trust you."

She turns to face me, taking a few steps closer. "It wasn't supposed to be like this, Evie. He still had the power to lie back then. It was fading fast after the Holstrom girls' deaths, but he had it and he used it on me. I'm sure he used it on you too."

She's right. He did use that power on me, well before he stole my sister. "How is that supposed to make a difference? You still did what you did."

"I was misled." There's no pleading quality to her tone, only bitter resentment. "He said everything was supposed to be perfect. He and I would be together, as would you and Aspen. The four of us were supposed to be happy."

Another flash of rage heats my veins, and it takes all my restraint to breathe it away. "Does anyone look happy to you?"

Amelie returns to the wardrobe and continues hanging the dresses. Once finished, she approaches the sitting area with slow, hesitant steps. I can't bear to look at her as she lowers onto the couch nearby. "You looked happy," she whispers.

My gaze flashes to hers, a scowl burning in my eyes. "Excuse me?"

"When I saw you and Aspen together today. You shared a moment that was so potent, even I could feel it."

"You know nothing about me and Aspen."

She laces her fingers together, then smooths them

over her legs, an anxious gesture. "I knew he cared for you from the start. While you were unconscious after the incident with the kelpie, I saw a side of Aspen during our daily chats. It only came out when we talked about you."

"Is that when you began your secret tryst with Cobalt?" I don't bother hiding the malice in my tone.

"Yes." Her confession comes without hesitation. "All along, I knew it was wrong for me to desire your fiancé. I was selfish and cruel to do what I did, conspiring with him to find a way for us to be together. He promised me the four of us would be paired with the mates we were best suited with. He said as long as I did everything he told me to and followed his plan, everything would work out perfectly. Seeing how Aspen cared for you fueled my justifications that it was the right thing to do, even if I had to keep the truth from you. Now, I regret the day Cobalt ever looked upon me. I curse the moment he declared his secret affection." Her hands clench into fists at her sides, posture stiff as her eyes unfocus.

Her words weave conflict in my heart, reminding me what may have happened if she *hadn't* betrayed me. I could be the one in Amelie's position, and she could be Aspen's mate. There's no way I can regret what brought me and Aspen together. Right?

"Everything was supposed to be perfect," she whispers, tone wistful as she stares at her lap. "He promised me it would be, over and over. I believed him."

Fire turns in my stomach. "Shouldn't you have realized you were wrong when you abducted me from the palace and attacked me in the coral caves? How about when Cobalt had me trapped in a cage? Or when he stole the throne from Aspen?"

Her eyes are filled with tears when they meet mine. "I wasn't myself during any of those instances. You have no idea how many of my words and actions were controlled by Cobalt."

"I offered you my help. I told you I would protect you from him and you denied me."

Our eyes lock in an icy standoff, fury radiating from each of us. I can tell she wants to argue, wants to defend herself, but she purses her lips and returns her gaze to her lap, another agonizing silence blanketing the room. As heat prickles behind my neck, I regret lighting the fire in the hearth.

"Remember you love me." Amelie's words are so quiet, I question whether I heard them at all.

"What?"

"That's the only clear memory I have before everything becomes clouded beneath the haze of his commands. The last thing I remember him saying is this: 'In everything you do today, you will remember how much you love me. No matter what questions or angers or worries arise, you will brush them aside. You will return again and again to your love for me.'" A tear rolls down her cheek, but her expression isn't one of sorrow; it's anger etched across her face.

The image she portrays is like looking in a mirror. All that rage, all that fury—I never could have dreamed I'd see it on my carefree, confident sister. But is it true? Something in the deepest recesses of my heart tells me it is, that that kind of fury can't be faked. That same part of me begs to reach for her, to take her hand in mine and tell her I understand.

Yet I can do no such thing. Just considering it is

dangerous territory. In this moment, it feels so easy to give in and pity her. But what if she's lying? What if it's Cobalt who controls her emotions now, even in this confession? What if her Bond with him is the same as mine is with Aspen? What if he can travel in spirit to see her, the way Aspen has been able to do with me? He could be here right now. Watching everything. Hearing everything. Perhaps he's waiting to attack until Amelie can confirm the contents of the weapons room.

My stomach lurches as I jolt to my feet and rush to the door. I don't know where I'm going, but I know I need air, to get away from my sister and the tangled emotions she weaves inside me, at least for a minute. As I reach the arched doorway, I say her name.

Her eyes meet mine.

"Don't leave this room or speak to a soul until I return."

With that, I flee.

14

Breeda greets me in the hall as I rush out of the room, but I order her to remain outside the bedroom to guard my sister. My legs tremble as I make my way through the palace and out the front doors. I don't stop until I reach one of the rectangular ponds within the courtyard. There I collapse to my knees, gasping for breath as my conversation with my sister strikes me even harder. Free from her gaze, I can fully process the emotions she stirred—fear, pity, fury, sympathy, rage, love.

As fast as I try to burn it away, it grows and grows, rolling over me in waves, gathering momentum with thoughts of Mother, of iron bullets, blood, and flame.

Guilt floods me next, followed by crippling shame. How can I be queen if I can't even keep my emotions under control? How can I lead an entire court when a talk with my sister unravels me? How can I rule both seelie and unseelie when my seelie side is weak but my unseelie form threatens to trap me?

Every inch of me ripples with anxiety, the burden of everything I've faced and done burying me beneath its weight. I sink deeper into the ground beneath me, the cool sand digging into my knees and shins.

"Are you all right?" Aspen's voice snaps me to attention.

I face him, watch as he approaches from the tile walkway. The sight of him returns me to the present, reacquaints me with this moment, the feel of my breaths, so shallow in my compressed lungs. On trembling legs, I rise to my feet, sucking air deep into my diaphragm. I close the distance between us, pressing my face into his chest once I reach him. Strong arms close around me, holding me tight. "I had to get away from Amelie for a time," I say, my voice breaking on my sister's name.

"I sensed you through the Bond." His voice rumbles deep in his chest, a soothing reverberation against my ear. "Your pain was so strong, I could feel it as if it were my own."

We say nothing else for endless moments while he holds me, his rosemary cinnamon aroma filling my senses, calming my heart. The warmth of his bare chest pressed against my cheek helps drain the remnants of my anxiety until my breathing returns to normal. My fire returns, and I reach for it, let it flood my arms and legs with its steadying heat. Only then do I pull away to study him.

I quirk a brow as I take in the golden planes of his chest left bare where his cream linen shirt hangs open and unbuttoned. My eyes trail down to the loose brown trousers he wears, much like Fehr's. They aren't quite as neat and tailored as what he usually wears, but I must admit, he looks good in them.

"I like your outfit too," he says with a smirk.

My lips pull up at the corners, but my smile wavers when I'm reminded who made my outfit.

Aspen furrows his brow. "Are you sure you're all right? What happened?"

I release a heavy sigh. "It's just...hard being around Amelie right now."

"You don't have to stay with her. You can keep her in the dungeon tonight, or have Lorelei watch over her."

I bite my lip. Yet another conflict stirs in my heart. What is it I want from Amelie? To love her or hate her? To trust her or suspect her? Am I waiting for her to prove me right or prove me wrong?

With a shake of my head, I take Aspen's hands in mine. "I don't want to talk about her right now."

"Fair enough," he says, although his rigid shoulders can't hide his lingering concern. "Is there anything else you want to talk about?"

I force a grin as I grasp for a distraction. "Has there truly never been any other Bonded pair that can communicate the way we can?"

Some of the tenseness leaves his muscles. "Not that I've ever known. If there has, the pair has kept it a secret. But I have a theory why ours exists as it does."

Even though this tangent began as a diversion from more serious matters, I find my interest genuinely piqued. The word *theory* tends to do that to me. "You do?"

He nods. "You know how I told you that the Bonding ritual is performed as a sign of mutual fear and respect, most often used to forge alliances? That it's rare to be done in mate relationships? Well, I think that's why ours works the way it does. Because we are more than just allies Bonded by name. We love each other."

My heart flips at the word *love,* and with it comes a warmth spreading through my chest. Could he be right? Could only Bonded pairs who love one another form such a deep connection? A darker thought comes to mind: if that's the case, does it work that way with Amelie and Cobalt, just like I fear? Is there...love between them?

I shake the question from my mind. This is supposed to be my respite from thoughts of Amelie. This is about me and Aspen.

"I sensed you when you were away from me earlier this week too, after you went to Grenneith," he says. "Just like tonight, I sensed your pain. Even though I promised I wouldn't seek you through the Bond, my awareness of you and your emotions was strong."

His words toe the line before dangerous territory, the kind that could have me gasping for air and fighting back tears again. I have yet to give him the full details of my trip to Grenneith and the journey back to the wall with the freed fae courtesans. Eventually, I'll tell him all about it. Perhaps when I'm in better control of my emotions. But not today.

Needing yet another shift in subject, I tilt my head back and step closer to him, a wide grin on my lips. "You know what else is strong? Your ability to use water like you did today. I had no idea you could do that."

He says nothing for a moment, and I wonder if he'll let me get away with evading serious subjects twice now. Then his grin mirrors mine. "I suppose you haven't seen me use my magic much, have you?"

"Lorelei told me you had the power to fill the baths at Bircharbor at will."

"I may have done that for you a time or two," he says with a smirk. "Anything to encourage you to get naked."

A welcome heat warms my core, and I wrap my arms around his waist. "Is that so?"

"Can you blame me?" He leans down and presses his lips to mine. His warm mouth is like nourishment for my flesh. I yield to him, allowing our kiss to gently linger. When we pull away, I rest my head against his chest, letting my ears fill with the lullaby of his steady heartbeat.

"You can learn to wield water too," he says, returning to our previous conversation. "As a queen, you have access to all four elements now. It's only a matter of learning how to manipulate them."

I tilt my head to meet his eyes, a flash of excitement running through me as I recall the feat I accomplished with the fireplace. "I think I used air today." I tell him all about it, and of course, he exaggerates his pride in me.

"Combining two elements doesn't come easy," he explains. "Even the fae who've inherited more than one element tend to favor one as their primary. I take after my father's side and am much stronger with earth. And, as you know, I can also control water to a degree. I combined water with air to lift the water from the pools today and transport it to us after the dust storm. That's also how I was able to fill the tubs at Bircharbor. And Ustrin, like you've learned for yourself, used fire and air to transport flame."

"You really think I can learn earth and water too?"

"Of course I do. I know how capable you are. Not only

are you a queen, but you were strong enough to steal my cold, dead heart. If you can do that, you can do anything." His tone is teasing, his crooked smirk such a wicked sight it has my heart racing.

More aware now of the heat of his body pressed so close to mine, my thoughts turn devious as a much more enticing distraction comes to mind. "Do you realize this is the first time we've been completely alone since yesterday?"

He runs his palm down my hair, then trails up the length of my arm until his warm hand settles over my bare shoulder. I close my eyes at the sensation of the slow caress. "I'm aware of it."

I open my eyes and drink in the brown, gold, green, and ruby shades swirling in his irises. I run my hands up his chest, then grasp his collar firmly between my fingers. "You and I have unfinished business."

"What about your sis—"

"She can wait."

His eyes sparkle as his smirk matches the mischief in my heart. I tug his collar, and his lips are on mine again. My arms wind around his neck, pressing him closer to deepen the kiss. His hands rove the bare skin left exposed by the dress, then begin to explore every inch the sheer silk covers. My fingers tangle in his hair, then move to the branch of an antler, teasing a tine with my caress. He emits a hiss of pleasure, then moves his mouth down my neck. His fingers feel like fire through the silk of my gown as they trail the neckline. He tugs the neckline aside, and I arch against him, his warm hand full against my naked flesh.

My hands move down his back. When I reach the

bottom hem of his shirt, my fingers lift it so I can feel the heat of his skin. Our breaths grow ragged and our kisses move deeper, his tongue moving against mine, conjuring images of what his tongue did last time we explored our passions together. My legs nearly give way at the thought, and I move against him, rocking my hips to sate the craving for a deeper feel of him.

Then suddenly, Aspen tenses, and it isn't from desire. Completely still in my arms, his lips press into a tight line as a low growl rumbles deep in his chest. I pull away, brow furrowed. I study his face, but his eyes aren't on me. They're locked somewhere behind me.

Don't move, he says through the Bond.

But it's too late. I'm already whirling around.

At the center of the courtyard stands a shadowed figure. Dressed in a dark hooded cloak, all it reveals is a flash of teeth glinting in the moonlight, followed by the gleam of a blade.

15

Faster than I've ever seen Aspen move, he shifts his body in front of mine and lets out a hiss just as I hear a thud come from behind me. I whip my head to find a dagger stuck in the trunk of the nearest palm tree. Aspen slaps a hand over his shoulder where he was struck by the blade. My attention is torn between him and the menacing figure standing at the center of the courtyard.

The assailant reaches beneath his cloak, drawing another blade. I reflexively reach for my obsidian dagger, but I come up empty and recall I never put it back on after my bath. Still, I brace myself for the attack, preparing to dodge the assailant's next throw, but he falters as a roaring sound comes from near the palace doors. There, a funnel of sand begins to whirl and rise. I can vaguely make out Fehr's face at its center. The cloaked figure shifts his stance to face the djinn, and the glint of his dagger speeds across the courtyard, straight at the cyclone. It strikes its center, just below Fehr's face. I stifle a shout, but the djinn disappears, sand storm and all.

The assailant takes the opportunity to dart toward the palace. He obviously didn't come for Aspen and me. He came for something inside Irridae, and it isn't hard to guess what it could be.

I circle Aspen, seeking the site of his injury. "Are you hurt?"

"I'm fine," he mutters, already rushing toward the palace. "I'll go after him." Without another word, he shudders and tilts forward, as if he'll fall on his hands, but by the time he makes contact with the ground, his hands have become hooves and his body has been replaced with his stag form. The assailant races up the palace steps, retrieving the dagger he'd thrown at Fehr before charging through the doors.

Aspen tears across the tile walkway, hard on the figure's heels.

I spin back toward the palm tree, bracing one hand against its rough trunk while the other wraps around the hilt of the dagger. As the blade comes free, I note its composition. Iron.

That means the attacker must be human.

"Your Majesty." Fehr materializes before me, hand rubbing his chest, although I see no sign of injury. "The man has entered the palace. Shall I guard you or—"

"The weapons room. Now."

He nods and disappears in a puff of bronze smoke, leaving me alone in the courtyard. With the dagger in hand, I part my flowing skirts to trail behind me and pump my legs as hard as I can to race inside the palace.

Once I reach the atrium, a moment of disorientation stalls me. Which staircase leads to the weapons room?

I need my instincts, I realize. My fox.

Tucking the dagger beneath the waist of my overskirt, I close my eyes and give in to my fox form. With the fire of urgency roaring through my veins, it takes little effort to shift, body shrinking as my hands become paws. Almost as soon as the transformation is complete, my senses sharpen, and I become hyperaware of distinct aromas calling me to the staircase on the right. My mate passed by here, as did the human attacker, made clear by the smell of human sweat.

I take the stairs several times faster than I could on human legs, following the data that reaches me through my eyes and nose. Before I know it, I'm racing down a familiar hall of volcanic rock, the malachite bars of the cells, and then—

My heart leaps into my throat, threatening to shock me out of my fox form, as Aspen comes into view. He's no longer a stag; in his seelie form, he's hunched on the floor, head thrown back in agony as the hilt of a blade protrudes from his upper thigh. His hands frame the hilt, just inches from it, quivering with the resistance he's trying to fight in order to grasp it.

"Aspen." My voice wavers, and again I'm close to losing my unseelie form, yearning for human hands to grasp the dagger to free him from it.

"No." His voice is firm, and in his eyes is a command. "I'll be fine. Go."

I falter for only a moment, but my fox side swallows my fear, my pain, telling me the assailant must be nearing the weapons room, if he isn't there already. "I'll come back for you," I promise, and take off down the hall to the end of the dungeon and down the final staircase that leads to the winding hall. I speed down it, only slowing when I catch sight of Fehr. Several blades litter the floor at his feet, but he appears unwounded. His fight seems mostly with himself as he drags his body along the wall, struggling against the iron that keeps him at bay.

Fehr's eyes widen with momentary surprise as his eyes lock on me, seeing me in my firefox form for the first time.

"Where is the human?"

"He's already inside," Fehr gasps.

That's all I need to hear to surge onward, the door of the weapons room in sight. As I approach, I see the door is indeed thrown open, the iron bar that had kept it shut now on the ground. The figure stalks the room, shoving crates aside, prying open wooden lids, and tearing through dozens upon dozens of stands that hold iron swords, daggers, maces, and axes. I swallow my horror at seeing so many weapons, but the human doesn't seem to have eyes for them.

He's looking for something else.

This close, I can make out his face, his stature. He's tall and muscular, built like a warrior, his jaw set as he continues his frantic search. It's then I realize why I can see so clearly; at the center of the room, perched upon a wooden crate, rests a silver disc with a bright, golden light at its center.

A Chariot.

What this means, I have no time to consider, for the man's face brightens as he lifts a small, wooden crate. He brings it next to the travel device and opens the lid.

Whatever is inside illuminates the room like the sun. It's so bright, it's nearly blinding, and I'm forced to avert my gaze.

I blink rapidly, willing my eyes to adjust while I run through every scenario I could use to take him down.

The dagger.

For that, I need hands. Again, the urgency of the situation sends the fire rushing through my veins, burning away my firefox form and sending me stumbling as I rise on two human legs. The light coming from the box is still painfully bright, but it's dulled now. Terror seizes me when I realize it's because the light is no longer at the center of the room. It's muted by the man's fingers, the light cradled in his hand as if it's a solid ball he holds in his palm. His other hand reaches for the Chariot.

My fingers close around the hilt of the dagger as I lunge forward. With a flick of my wrist, the blade spins end over end. It doesn't meet its mark, which I'd intended to be his chest. Instead, it grazes the wrist that holds the Chariot. His eyes flash toward me, lips pulling into a sneer as the travel device goes clattering to the ground between two large crates.

With the orb of light still in his other hand, he dives to his knees. But I'm faster. I don't know when I shifted back into my firefox form, but paws are what reach the Chariot and send it skittering out into the hall. I dart after it, but the man clambers over the crates, leaping over my head, his cloak trailing after him. I snap my teeth, grasping the edge of his cloak and locking it in my jaw before he can escape. He whirls toward me and reaches his free hand toward his hip, but his eyes widen when he comes up empty. No more daggers.

Fire roars through me, and I let it rise, let my flame dance over my body, extending from my ears, my face, and the tip of my muzzle. Purple, pink, and aqua fire lights the edge of his cloak. I release him and my flames leap higher. He stumbles back, struggling with his free hand to release the clasp of his cloak, but I circle his ankles, igniting the hem of his trousers, the laces of his boots.

His cries assault my ears as he begins a frantic dance to stamp out the flames. It's no use. My fire is growing by the second. In a final bid to save his own life, he releases the orb from his hand. The fur stands up along the ridge of my spine, and everything inside me screams danger, even as the light of the orb blinds me once again. And yet, even without seeing it, I can sense the orb. The energy it emits hums through the corridor, a tangible weight against the air around it.

I close my eyes and leap forward. My paws make contact just as I realize they won't do the trick.

Once again, I need hands. Hands. Hands. It's all I can think.

My back slams into the hard floor, thrusting the air from my lungs. They're human lungs. And clasped between my human hands is the glowing orb.

ENERGY BUZZES BETWEEN MY FINGERS AS I RETURN TO THE weapons room. With trembling hands that beg to be rid of the chilling power radiating from the object, I return the orb to the small box and shut the lid. Only when the room returns to dark do I feel I can breathe again.

It takes me several breaths to compose myself before I can approach the man. He's gone still, and my flames have died down to a subtle flicker, seeking flesh and cloth that have yet to be charred.

I swallow the bile that rises in my throat as I look down at the man. His skin is blackened, chest rising and falling in shallow bursts. I crouch at his side, trying not to focus on his wounds—wounds I caused with my terrifying power.

"Who sent you here?"

His lips peel back from his teeth, the movement splitting the skin at the corners of his mouth, but he says nothing.

My mind reels to find a way to extend his life long enough to get the answers I need. He's most certainly near death. Then I remember the power I've hardly given much thought to ever since I learned I could wield flame. It's a power I've used many times without knowing it, something Mother and I were both able to utilize to help others heal—life force.

Ignoring my revulsion at the damage I've caused, I place my hands over his burnt chest. A gentle fire flows from my heart and down my arms, tingling my palms. "I will heal you if you answer my questions. Who sent you and what is the significance of that orb?"

He snarls again. "Don't touch me, vile half breed."

My entire body goes still. "So you know of me." Although, technically, I'm a quarter breed, but this isn't the time for asserting facts.

"Are you working with the Renounced? Queen Dahlia?"

"Fool," he mutters.

I clench my jaw and feel the halt in the flow of energy from my hands. "I will heal you if you tell me," I say through my teeth, "but you must tell me something."

"He will ruin you," he finally says.

My pulse races. "Who? Cobalt?"

The semblance of a grin stretches over his blackened face as his eyes roll back in his head. "He will ruin all of you."

I move my hands from his chest to his shoulders, shaking him. "Who? Tell me and I will heal you, you idiot!"

"The mainland army comes even as we speak. Warships by the dozen. The time of the fae is at an end."

My blood goes cold. I don't need to know the name he refuses to say. It could be but one person.

He grins, opening more fissures at the corners of his mouth. "Mr. Duveau sends his love."

I stare down at him, no longer able to feel the fire running through my palms. His eyes slide away from mine, his grin fading, lips going slack. That's when I realize the man is gone.

Another life taken by me.

16

My mate.

It's the only thing that snaps me out of my stupor, drawing my attention from the charred, lifeless body before me to recall the iron blade Aspen had stuck in his thigh. I turn away from the body, retrieving the human's Chariot and tucking it into the waist of my overskirt as I rise to my feet. I find Fehr slumped against the wall farther down.

"I failed you, Your Majesty," he gasps through his teeth. "You may punish me."

"Maybe later," I mutter. There's more ice to my tone than I intend, but all I can think about is Aspen right now. "The thief is dead and he's given us vital information. Come."

I don't wait to watch the djinn rise; instead, I race down the hall, up the stairs, and to the dungeon.

Aspen is where I left him, but this time, Foxglove and Lorelei are there too, faces full of concern. I brush them aside as I kneel before him, eyes locked on the dagger hilt, mind trained on nothing but the task at hand. My heart races, but I force my surgeon's calm to steady my hands.

"Tear a piece of cloth from my skirt," I command, voice level.

Lorelei rushes to obey. As soon as the cloth is in my hand, I pull the blade out with the other. Aspen bares his teeth but doesn't make so much as a sound as I throw the dagger to the ground and bind his leg with the cloth.

I wait for the pain to subside from his face before I allow him to stand. Foxglove and Fehr take up posts on each side of my mate as he favors his injured leg. With slow progress, we make our way up the stairs. Once we reach the atrium, we don't bother going any farther. All I need is to be far enough from the weapons room for Aspen's natural healing to kick in, so one of the couches near the windows will have to do.

"Bring wine," I tell Fehr, hoping the food stores weren't emptied when the household was expelled. After he brings a bottle of deep red liquid, I request cloth, needle, thread, and any other helpful tools from the seamstress' room.

My fingers fly as I go to work, ignoring the ache in my chest that burns at every wince on Aspen's face, every groan he suppresses while I clean and stitch the wound. Only a few tendrils of black branch off from the lesion, but his blood has yet to be tainted.

He will heal. He will heal.

The mantra keeps me sane, fuels my fire as I lay my hands over the bandaged wound, attempting to do what I failed to do for the human.

By the time I make it to my bedroom, my sister is already tucked into the bed, sleeping soundly. It was a struggle to leave Aspen's side, but he assured me he was well. He even managed—with the help of Fehr and Foxglove—to limp from the couch to the bedroom next to mine where he's staying. Still, I laid next to him for nearly an hour, hand resting over his steadily beating heart until I was satisfied with his condition.

Only then did I come back to my room, remembering my promise to myself that I would watch my sister's every move and renew her commands at my first chance. After the events of the night, my suspicion over my sister's anticipated treachery feels weak in comparison to the real dangers I faced.

Not bothering to change out of my dress, I crawl under the covers next to Amelie. The fire I created in the hearth still burns steadily, and the shutters have been drawn over the windows, blocking most of the chill. Never would I have imagined nights could be cold in the desert. Although perhaps the ice I feel is on the inside, left by the thief's chilling words.

The mainland army comes even as we speak.

Warships by the dozen.

The time of the fae is at an end.

I roll toward Amelie, burrowing deeper beneath the blankets as I try to shake the terrifying visions from my head. Seeing my sister's sleeping face, my mind goes still. Her expression is so soft and innocent. So much like the girl I grew up with.

If I let myself, I could pretend we're back home at the

apothecary, young girls snuggled up in the same bed after a nightmare. Back then, we sought comfort in each other, taking turns stroking the other's hair, depending on who'd had the bad dream.

It takes all my restraint not to nestle against her sleeping form.

~

WHEN I WAKE, IT'S TO SCREAMING.

Amelie thrashes in the bed, fighting the blankets, a blood-curdling wail tearing from her throat. It's just after dawn, meager light spilling in through the golden shutters to illuminate the terror that rips across her face. "What have I done?"

I bolt upright as she scrambles out of the blankets, backing away until she comes up against the headboard. She brings her hands toward her face, eyes wide as she stares at them. "Whose blood is this?"

A chill runs through me. This is how she was when I awoke her in the cell at Lunar. I'd attributed it to the terrible power of Selene Palace's dungeons, but now I can't fathom what could cause such a state of distress.

"What have I done?" Another wail escapes her lips.

I crawl toward her and grasp her shoulders in mine, shaking her the way I did before. "Amelie, wake up."

"No. No. This isn't happening. It wasn't me."

I shake her again, harder. "Wake up!"

She shudders, then her eyes meet mine. Her body trembles, but she sags as recognition crosses her face. Sweat coats her brow, and she brings her hands to cover her face and quietly cries into her palms.

I'm frozen in place as I watch her, uncertain of what to do. My hands leave her shoulders. Part of me wants to turn away and let her pull herself together on her own. But another part of me recalls the childhood memories I'd conjured last night, ones that make me want to reach for her, to brush the hair from her sweat-soaked brow and embrace her in a comforting squeeze.

Instead, I sit back and settle on words. "What happened just now?"

Silence answers, and I wonder if she'll ignore me. Then slowly, she lowers her hands and pulls her knees to her chest. Her eyes are distant as she subtly rocks back and forth. "I didn't know where I was. Or when I was. Maybe even who I was."

My heart lurches at the ghost of horror that lingers on her face. "What do you mean?"

"It's always like this." Her voice is small, breathy. "Every time I awaken from sleep. There's so much I don't remember. So much that plagues me."

"You remember nothing when you wake?"

She shakes her head. "I remember too much and nothing at all, all at once. My mind has grown addled ever since Cobalt first used the power of my name to glamour me, to force me to obey his commands. All I have left are snippets and images, and they haunt me. Today, I barely remember yesterday beneath the cloud of your commands. Tomorrow, I'll feel the same about today. The next day, I'll feel the same about tomorrow."

A lump rises in my throat, skin crawling at the thought. "How can you live like that?"

She meets my eyes, although hers are still haunted. "It's the only way I *can* live. You won't trust me without the commands, nor will I trust myself. Not until Cobalt is dead and the Bond breaks."

Again, I want to reach for her, comfort her until this stranger before me disappears and returns the sister I once loved.

Her gaze goes steely. "Don't feel sorry for me. Just promise me you will let me kill Cobalt." Like last night when I looked at her and saw my own rage reflected in her eyes, the fury in her tone feels like a mirror to mine.

It leaves me speechless.

"Promise me!" she shouts, making me jump. "Promise you will let me kill Cobalt!" She trembles with the anger coursing through her, so hot, I swear flames are dancing just below the surface of her skin.

My answer comes out a whisper. "I promise."

Then, with the power of her name, I trap her beneath another day's worth of commands.

As soon as I'm cleaned and dressed in another one of Amelie's makeshift gowns, I race to the room next door to see Aspen. I'm amazed to find him on his feet, standing before a mirror while he buttons a cream-colored linen shirt over his chest, similar to the one he wore last night. He wears another pair of loose trousers, these ones a deep burgundy, that hide all sight of the wound.

His eyes meet mine in the mirror, and a corner of his mouth quirks up. The golden color has returned to his skin, making him look very unlike a fae who suffered an iron injury mere hours ago.

My heart flutters with relief and I run to him. As he turns to face me, I throw my arms over his neck and draw his lips to mine. Fearing I'll hurt him, I don't let the kiss linger. "Are you all right?" I ask as I pull away.

He has the nerve to roll his eyes at the question, arm circling my waist to press me closer. "I'm fine, Evie. I told you I would be."

I put my hand on his chest to force distance between us. "Go lie down so I can change your bandages."

He takes my hand in his, removing it from his chest so he can place a kiss on the inside of my wrist. "I already took the bandages off myself," he says against my skin. "The wound has healed."

My eyes widen, although I shouldn't be surprised. The iron wasn't embedded inside him long, which means his own healing powers would have been free to do their work. "Then let me at least examine the site of the wound. I want to see for myself."

A wicked smirk plays on his sensual mouth. "Are you just trying to get me out of my trousers?"

My breath hitches as desire stirs inside my core, mind swimming with images of his body pressed against mine, his hands slipping beneath the layers of my skirt. Twice now, we've been interrupted from fulfilling the passion that's never far from the surface whenever we're together. Unfortunately, that thought reminds me of how we were interrupted last, bringing about an onslaught of sobering facts that must be attended to. I bring my lips close to his, and my words come out a little breathless. "I have every intention of getting you out of your trousers, Aspen."

He groans at the sound of his name and I take a few

moments to bathe beneath the hunger in his eyes, knowing I'm about to shatter it all with what I say next. "But there is much to do this morning, and there is much I need to discuss with you."

His next groan is one of disappointment. "Why must you be so intelligent?"

"Well, one of us must be if we're to win a war," I tease, taking a chaste step away from him, pinning my hands at my sides to keep from wringing them. "Has Breeda returned?"

He shakes his head. "I'm sure she'd have gone straight to you if she were back."

He's probably right. As soon as I saw her last night, still obediently guarding my bedroom like I'd commanded, I ordered her to go immediately to Lunar with a message for Nyxia. I bite my lip, eyes going unfocused.

Aspen's expression turns serious. "Why? What's wrong?"

I let out a heavy sigh. "I didn't just send her to relay what transpired last night. I also had her request that Nyxia call an emergency meeting of the Alpha Alliance at once."

"That's probably a good idea. Now that we've confirmed the weapons room exists, we must find a way to protect it."

"That's not all." My stomach sinks. He hadn't been in the best state last night for me to tell him everything that occurred. All he knows is that the human was able to enter the room and that I killed him before he could use the Chariot to escape. He has no idea about the strange orb, the final threat he made about the humans coming to destroy the fae.

He has no idea this is so much bigger than we'd thought.

So I tell him.

17

I t's terrifying how quickly the charred husk of a human being burns entirely to ash beneath my powerful flames. Almost as fast as the assailant's life was snuffed out, all that remains of him is contained in a bucket. My stomach churns as I haul it from the weapons room. Even once I reach the stair past the dungeon, the stench of burning flesh lingers in my nose, tickling the back of my throat. In addition, every step I take is haunted by what I left behind—the mysterious golden orb the human had tried to steal.

I'm so wrapped in my thoughts when I reach the atrium, that I almost miss the figures lingering at the far side. I pause, catching Fehr and Foxglove deep in conversation. Foxglove stares up at the much taller djinn, his smile brighter than I think I've ever seen it. They're too far for me to hear what's being said between them, but Foxglove laughs in response, covering his mouth with a demure hand. I've rarely gotten to see Foxglove so sweet and uncomposed, but more surprising is Fehr. Not only is the djinn rapt in their talk, but his eyes are crinkled at the corners, all traces of the resentful servant gone.

I feel like my heart might melt out of my chest, and I'm unable to tear my eyes away from the contented couple. However, I'm very much aware that this moment isn't meant for my eyes and my presence could shatter—

Fehr's eyes flash my way, and just like that, their sweet exchange is over. As they both straighten and offer stiff bows, I feel not like a queen but an interloper. I hide the heat that warms my cheeks as Foxglove excuses himself and scurries away.

Fehr approaches me, expression returning to its hard, familiar state. "Your Majesty, might I take your burden and dispose of it?"

It's then I remember the bucket of ash I carry. I extend it toward him, trying not to wrinkle my nose as the ash shifts with the motion. "You may."

He takes it from me and moves to step away, but I stop him with a word. "Fehr." Seeing him interacting with Foxglove has softened my heart, and I'm eager to be on better terms with my new steward. Or, at the very least, to understand him better.

He narrows his eyes. "How may I serve?"

"Why did my grandfather, King Caleos, bind you to the palace? You said it was a punishment, but what was the crime?"

The djinn purses his lips, jaw shifting side to side before he answers. "It was long ago. Long before humans came to the isle. Long before we knew humans existed. Our world was bigger then. Vast. My kind—the djinn— sought to control it."

His words send my mind reeling to comprehend what

he could mean. There are so many new questions, so much fuel for intellectual debate, but I still my eagerness and force myself to focus on the singular question I began with. "The djinn tried to take over the entire realm of the fae?"

He nods. "We were the most powerful of the fae, and we were tired of sharing rule with lesser kings and queens. We fought to overthrow those who tried to wrestle power from us. We refused to acknowledge those who'd obtained the blessing to rule over us by the All of All, so in essence, we fought the gods as well."

"And...you lost?"

He lets out a bitter laugh. "Indeed, we did. Very few of my kind remain, and those who survived were punished with eternal slavery."

"Even after all this time?"

"To the fae, time isn't forgiving, regardless of how long." He squints at me. "But you know so little of time, human that you are."

I know he means it as an insult, but I lift my chin higher. "I am part human, but I am also part fae, not to mention your queen."

He glowers, eyes locked on mine for an uncomfortable, endless moment. Then he averts his gaze with a resigned sigh. "Yes, the palace recognized your power. You are my queen and I am here to serve you."

"You aren't happy about that." It isn't a question.

"My happiness is of no concern. I do my duty without fail." He winces. "And yet, I failed to protect the weapons room last night. You may punish me."

I recall him saying the same thing last night. "Thanks

for the reminder." My words come out with a sarcastic bite. "How might I best punish you?"

"Death is suitable, although I'm sure you will deem such a punishment too kind."

My breath hitches at that, at the raw yearning in his eyes. "Do you truly find life so unbearable?"

"I have lived long and have lost much of what most consider a good and proper life." He states it not to evoke pity, but as a fact.

"What do you mean? Don't you have friends? Lovers?"

His expression softens, but only for a moment. "I can have no lovers without permission, and King Ustrin forbade me from getting too close to anyone, friend, foe, lover, or stranger."

My heart clenches, remembering the joy I saw on his face when he was chatting with Foxglove. As much as Fehr's disdain for me irks me, it probably isn't too different from how I felt about any of the fae when I first came to Faerwyvae. And despite the betrayal against his people, does he deserve an immortal life devoid of comfort and friendship?

The question sends my heart racing, as it evokes thoughts of my sister. *That's different,* I tell myself. She betrayed me personally.

I clasp my hands before me. "Fehr, I give you my permission to take however many friends and lovers you desire."

His eyes go wide, then harden with suspicion. "Aren't you afraid?"

"Afraid of what? That you'll actually enjoy your life beneath my rule and serve me out of respect rather than duty? Why, yes, what a terrifying thought."

He squints, studying me for a few moments. "King Ustrin ruled through fear."

"If you haven't noticed, I am not King Ustrin," I say, my inner fire heating my words. "I am not even my grandfather. That doesn't mean I am soft, however. I may be part human, but fire roars through my veins as hot as it did in my predecessors. I am my own queen, and I am dedicated to the Fire Court and the fae I now serve to protect. That includes you, Fehr. You'd do well to remember that."

He furrows his brow, as if puzzling over me and my words. "I will, Your Majesty," he finally says. His gaze moves to the bucket in his hand before returning to me. "I should inform you that this man has not been the first to try and invade Irridae Palace since Ustrin's death."

My pulse quickens, surprised at the sudden admission. "He isn't?"

"There were four other occurrences, all of them human, all using a Chariot. None were able to enter the palace, for its magic sealed it shut. Last night's assailant was the first who was able to enter."

"Because you opened the palace to me," I say under my breath. "Was it always the same man?"

"I believe so. The first time, however, he came with another, but they both disappeared almost as fast as they arrived. Ever since, there has been only one. We would battle in the courtyard, but he would always disappear before I could severely wound him."

I suppress a shiver as I prepare to ask the next question. "The first time, when two arrived...was it Queen Estel who brought the attacker?"

He shakes his head. "Both human."

I let out a sigh of relief. Even though the Chariot is clearly one of the Star Queen's devices, it makes me sick to consider she could be involved, that she could have been behind the attack to begin with. Not to mention, the chilling similarity the orb has to the much smaller light held within the Chariot. Until she explains how a human could have gotten one of her devices, my suspicion only hardens. Especially since she has yet to arrive with more of Aspen's guards like she promised.

"So long as you have the Chariot," Fehr says, stealing me away from my frantic thoughts, "the humans can't return."

"Unless there are more devices."

"They are rare, as far as I know," he says. "Only Queen Estel has access to them."

"That's what I'm afraid of," I mutter.

Fehr grimaces. "I should also add that, should the humans have more Chariots, and should any assailant manage to make it inside the palace without being apprehended, they will have the ability to return to any place they have already been in person. That is how the devices work."

A chill runs up my spine. Is that what would have happened if the attacker had gotten away? Would he have returned directly to the weapons room with a host of companions, only to storm the palace and turn their iron blades on everyone inside?

"We should destroy the iron," Fehr says, tone darkening. "So long as it remains, I cannot properly protect the palace."

I open my mouth to reply, but before I can consider his suggestion, a flash of red streams into the atrium and circles around my head before appearing as Breeda. She folds into a bow as she floats in front of me. "Your Most Beautiful Majesty," she says, sounding somewhat out of breath. "I have returned from my very important mission."

"You delivered the message to Queen Nyxia?"

"Yes! I told her exactly what you ordered me to. Then I rushed right back. Well, first I stumbled upon your retinue of loyal subjects on their journey here through Star. So, of course I had to make sure Dune was doing his job, for their progress seemed terribly slow. If *I'd* led them, they'd be here by now, but—"

"What did Queen Nyxia say?"

She spins in a circle. "Ah, yes. She said she has sent out notice to all the Alpha Alliance to come here for an emergency meeting. They will arrive by nightfall."

Nightfall.

My pulse quickens, anticipation mixing with equal parts dread. For who knows what this meeting will bring.

18

J ust as Breeda said, the royals of the Alpha Alliance all arrive by nightfall, which thankfully includes Estel. Knowing her guilt would be proven in her absence, I'd spent hour after hour of tense waiting, wondering if she'd even show up.

She was the first of the royals to arrive, and just as she'd said, she came with eight of Aspen's guards. One by one, the rest soon followed, and now the entire Alpha Alliance stands around the sunstone table in my atrium.

Aspen remains close at my side, and I feel his warm hand light upon my lower back. Warmth floods my chest with a steadying calm. *Are you ready?* he asks through the Bond.

Am I ready to tell them a fleet of warships is on its way to destroy all of faekind? Sure, can't wait. I wonder if my tone comes across as sardonic as I intend.

I'm here too, Evie. We're doing this together.

I nod, his words helping me keep my composure as I watch my guests settle in around the table. Nyxia, looking elegant in a black suit, stands slouched to the side with a hand on her hip, a casual posture that hides the tenseness I see in every muscle. Aelfon lowers into a chair, crossing his enormous arms over his chest as he watches me through slitted lids. Flauvis leaps onto a stool, tongue lolling from his panting muzzle. Minuette sways side to side, feet inches off the ground while her hair and the skirt of her thin blue gown blow behind her. Tris stands tall in her seelie form, lips pressed tight while her pink wings flutter against her back in clear agitation. Then there's Estel, looking as serene as ever, the particles on her face shifting and reforming, each expression as content as the last.

It's an effort not to let my suspicious gaze linger on the Star Queen, but I can't help wondering how she'll react when I confront her about the Chariot. My heart races, but I slow it with a deep breath. *One thing at a time.* With all eyes turning toward me, I greet the royals. "Thank you for gathering to meet me here."

"Yes, now will you tell us what this is about?" Nyxia asks in her smooth voice. Her expression reads a mixture of boredom and indignation, but her eyes are hard, keen. She knows I wouldn't have requested a meeting if it wasn't vital. She knows my vague message meant secrecy and tact were required.

"I too would like to know," Tris says, her impatience not feigned like Nyxia's. "I have a kingdom to run. I can't be called away on emergency meetings every other day."

"We're at war," Flauvis says with a growl. "If such things inconvenience you so, then perhaps you don't belong on our side."

Tris' lips peel back, the beauty of her tree-like face

transforming into a monstrous snarl that should belong only in nightmares.

"Yes, Flauvis, we are at war," Aspen says in his lazy drawl, "but not with each other. Cut it out so we can get on with it."

Flauvis runs his tongue over his muzzle, but begrudgingly averts his gaze from Tris. The Spring Queen pouts with a huff, eyes snapping to me.

"I summoned you here today for many reasons," I say. "Firstly, to say we have found and confirmed the existence, location, and contents of the weapons stash. There is indeed a room full of iron weapons here at Irridae Palace. My steward, Fehr, confirmed Ustrin had made a private alliance with the humans, particularly Councilman Duveau, which granted him access to these weapons. To what end, I am unsure."

"We know to what end," Minuette hisses. "To use them on his own kind. Disgusting."

"But what did the humans get in return?" Aelfon asks.

"That's what I'm not entirely sure about," I say, "but it leads me to my next piece of information. A human infiltrated the palace last night and went straight for the weapons stash."

Nyxia's eyes go wide, and Flauvis lets out a rumbling growl.

Tris scoffs. "Oh, so now that Ustrin is dead, they want their weapons back?"

"Not the weapons," I say slowly. "The assailant paid the weapons no heed. He was coming for this." I wave my hand at Fehr, who had been standing near the guards at the perimeter of the room. He steps forward and brings the small wooden crate I'd brought him just before the meeting and sets it on the table in front of me.

Gingerly, I remove the lid from the box, letting its contents fill the room. Even within the enormous atrium, the light is blinding. Squinting against its luminance, I grasp the orb of light in my palm. Considering my hands are much smaller than the assailant's had been, I'm only able to mute a minor portion of the light, but it should be enough to let the fae glimpse its shape. I hold it out for several silent moments before returning it to the crate and shutting the lid. Then I reach beneath the sashes tied around my waist to retrieve the Chariot and place it on the table next to the box. My tone sharpens as I pin Estel beneath a glare. "The human came here with this."

My indignation immediately dims as I take in the horror on her sparkling face. Her expression shifts again and again, eyes not on the Chariot but on the crate, and each new countenance she wears is only more terrified than the last.

Nyxia's face whips toward the Star Queen, rage heating her cheeks. "You have some explaining to do."

Estel brings a shimmering hand to her lips, the particles that compose her body buzzing faster than I've seen before. She takes a step back, and Aspen stiffens at my side. The nearest guards reach for the hilts of their swords and shift their spears. But she doesn't try to flee, eyes still trained on the crate. "It was supposed to be destroyed," she whispers.

"What was?" Aspen says through his teeth.

Estel's chest heaves. "The Parvanovae."

"*That's* the Parvanovae?" Nyxia's tone is shriller than I've ever heard, her composure shaken as she points a trembling finger at the crate. "The thing Queen Evelyn was just holding in her *hand*?"

Even Flauvis is unnerved, his hackles raised along his back. "It can't be."

Tris throws her hands in the air, shaking her head of cherry blossoms in confusion. "What is a para...parva..."

"It's a star bomb, Tris," Nyxia snaps before burning me with a glare. "A tiny, living star encased in crystal, and it could have killed us all, should it be dropped."

My mouth goes dry as the implications wash over me. I recall the chilling instinct I had to catch it when the assailant nearly dropped it. And I *held* it. A bomb. In my hand. "Blazing iron," I mutter.

Aspen runs his hands through his hair, shifting from foot to foot. "So, the humans are after a bomb."

"But what exactly is it?" Aelfon asks. "You say it's a star bomb, but why does it even exist? It isn't a human creation."

"No," Estel says with a breathy sigh. "It's fae. My sister created it."

"Queen Estora?" Aspen says, eyes incredulous. "She *made* this abomination?"

"You never knew my sister well," Estel says, her tone calm despite its defensive edge. "She was a brilliant inventor, even more talented than I am. She worked not only with time and space, but on the cutting edge harnessing the power of the stars. When the war with the humans began, she put all her efforts into creating something that could defeat our enemies. Just before the war ended, she invented this, the Parvanovae. It wasn't meant to be an abomination; it was meant to save our realm. It was...a mistake."

"My mother told me about it," Nyxia mutters, eyes fixated on the crate, shoulders tense as if she expects it to burst open at any moment. "The final, desperate move the fae were prepared to take before the treaty was made."

"This was the final motion the council was going to pass?" Aspen asks, mouth twisted with disgust. "The one to rid the isle of humans forever?"

Estel nods, expression grave as the shimmering particles tug her lips into a frown. "The very same. The council had gotten word that the mainland king was now involved and was preparing to send in armies to invade. Their weapons were said to be far more destructive than anything we'd seen used on the isle yet. The Parvanovae was our final defense."

Nyxia's eyes are glazed. "It would have killed everyone. Including the fae."

"Almost everyone," Estel corrects. "Some of the fae could have survived, but yes, most would die. Worse, the isle would take centuries to recover, leaving even the survivors with little to live off of."

Nausea churns in my stomach as I envision the carnage, the damage. If this star bomb can cause such detrimental effects, it must be far more powerful than any human explosive that exists today. The fact that the fae were willing to use it chills me to the bone. It's no wonder even the cold, cruel Melusine was willing to stop it. Despite the terrible mother she eventually became, my heart aches with the understanding that she alone saved the Fair Isle. Or perhaps I should say it was Aspen alone. For his birth was what swayed her heart, convinced her to shift to the seelie side and forge the treaty with the humans.

My gaze slides to my mate, taking in the distress on his face. I wonder if he's thinking about his mother too.

"It was supposed to be destroyed," Nyxia says through her teeth, eyes burning into Estel. "Why is it still in existence?"

Estel shakes her head. "Estora said—"

Her words cut off, and she closes her eyes. When she opens them, her expression looks puzzled. "No, I suppose she never did outright say it was destroyed. Only hinted that it was. Hinted it was no longer a threat to us."

"Did she give it to Ustrin, then?" I ask.

"I don't know," she says. "Even when I took her place as queen, she never said a thing about it. However, she was never the same after the war ended. She was bitter and weak, which was why I challenged her as alpha. She must have sided with Ustrin before she left us for the stars."

I furrow my brow. "Left you for the stars?"

"She died." Nyxia doesn't bother with any pretenses of sympathy.

"So, Ustrin has had the star bomb this entire time. But what about this?" I point at the Chariot. "It looks just like yours."

Estel opens her palm, revealing her own Chariot that she arrived here with. Setting it next to the other confirms they are nearly identical, aside from the scratches and signs of age on the one the human brought. "Yes, that is one of the first I ever made."

I bristle. "How did a human come to have it?"

She seems unconcerned by the suspicion in my tone. "When the war ended, one of my Chariots was given to the councilman who exiled King Caleos. It was an additional gift to ensure the balance established by the treaty. He never used it, nor any of his descendants, to my knowledge."

"That likely changed with Mr. Duveau," I say. "He must have used it to meet with Ustrin, to transport the weapons here with ease and without any of the other fae royals knowing about it."

"Estel," Aspen says, "is there a chance the Renounced know about the bomb? Is that what Dahlia truly was after?"

She considers this for a moment. "I don't think so. All who know of the Parvanovae know how dangerous it is. The seelie would never approve of using it."

"Perhaps they want it so it can be destroyed," Tris says.

Estel shakes her head. "Even if that were the case, not even the Renounced would be so careless as to send a human to retrieve it."

I bite my lip, eyes going unfocused. "Then that means Mr. Duveau is acting alone."

Minuette lets out a low whistle. "The humans want to blow up the isle."

Flauvis shows his teeth in a wicked snarl. "I say we use it to destroy the mainland. That will put the humans in their place."

My heart leaps into my throat. "What? No!"

"That is not what I joined this alliance for," Aelfon says, springing to his feet and stomping an enormous hoof.

"But Flauvis has a point," Nyxia says, and I burn her with a glare.

"I didn't come here to blow up humans either," Tris says, putting a hand on her hip. "I joined you to stand against the Renounced. Even though we must bring back the Old Ways, I remain seelie."

"As do I," Aelfon agrees.

"Pitiful." Flauvis shakes his wolf head with a canine grin. "We are gifted with the one thing that can silence our enemies forever, and you get cold hooves, Aelfon?"

Aelfon raises an enormous clenched fist and the wolf king crouches into a defensive posture, ready to spring off all four paws—

"Enough!" Aspen's voice rings through the atrium. "We did not call this meeting to divide our alliance."

Flauvis makes a muttering sound that mimics Aspen's tone in a high-pitched whine, but returns to his place at the table. Aelfon too stands down and lowers onto his chair.

Aspen continues. "We called you here because the threat from the humans is far more imminent than we originally thought." He turns to me, drawing the attention of the others.

"He's right," I say. "According to the assailant, the mainland has already sent warships. Even if we can keep the Parvanovae out of their hands, they're coming for us."

19

S houts and arguments roar across the table, so chaotic it makes my head spin.

"This is just like the last war, isn't it?" Tris puts her hand to her forehead, expression panicked.

"It's worse," Aelfon says. "The humans have far more terrifying weapons than they had back then."

He's right, but I can't bring myself to say so out loud. I've read about the latest weapons the mainland army has begun to manufacture, seen sketches in the broadsheets of tanks, rifles, machine guns, and mortars. Airships that soar through the sky like monstrous birds, dropping explosives on enemy soil. All things that make the swords, spears, and the occasional gun I've glimpsed on the isle seem like children's toys.

"All the more reason to use the star bomb," Flauvis says.

"No," Aspen argues. "We need more information before we can consider using the Parvanovae."

Heat rises to my cheeks. That wasn't the argument I'd

expected him to make. Fury radiates through my blood as I whirl toward my mate. "Are you seriously entertaining this idea?" I say in a furious whisper.

He doesn't meet my eyes as his response comes through the Bond. *I'm sorry, Evie, but we must discuss every possibility we have. Not only in terms of winning the war, but to make the Alpha Alliance fair.*

I continue to burn him with my scorn, fists clenched so tight I can feel my nails slice into my palms. It takes no small effort to wrench my gaze away, back to the arguing royals while tears sting my eyes. I'm surprised how protective I feel over the humans after everything they've done to me. But the truth is, for every corrupt councilman, soldier, or mayor, there are thousands of innocent lives. They don't deserve to die in a war they hardly understand. A war no human is ever taught the true history of. Until recently, not even many fae knew the truth—that the descendants of King Caleos had survived the very execution that sparked the first war.

Without realizing it, my voice leaps from my throat, quavering despite the fire that roars through it. "We cannot continue to perpetuate the same corrupt violence the humans began. If we annihilate their people, we are no better than the townspeople who burnt my grandmother at the stake."

"That's all very sunny and idealistic of you," Nyxia says, "but if a human army truly is on its way, we have no other choice but to meet that violence with greater violence."

"There must be another way," I say through my teeth.

"There is." Estel's voice is raw, quiet. All eyes turn to her. "We shift our tactic from violence to protection."

Nyxia cocks her head to the side, skepticism clear on her face. "And how do you suggest we do that?"

Estel sighs. "Before my sister shared her plans to destroy the Parvanovae, she'd had ideas to transmute the energy of the bomb to fuel an enchantment that would make the wall between Faerwyvae and Eisleigh impenetrable, keeping all humans from crossing over to our land. That, of course, went against the treaty."

Flauvis scoffs. "She should have done it anyway."

Estel ignores this. "If she discovered a way to use the Parvanovae to protect the wall, then I can figure it out too."

Aelfon stomps a hoof. "What good is a wall when warships could surround the isle and attack by sea?"

"We extend the wall around the perimeter of Faerwyvae as well," Estel says.

Nyxia rolls her eyes. "Yet another idealistic suggestion that sounds pretty but lacks execution."

"Nyxia's right," Aspen says. "Even if we could get the strongest earthen fae to begin construction at once, we can only do so in our own courts. How are we to ensure the wall gets built around the courts belonging to the Renounced?"

"I have a better idea," Flauvis says. "We destroy the wall, free our magic to flow over the entire isle. Then we kill all the pathetic humans and bomb the mainland."

I open my mouth to argue, but Tris speaks first. "How many times must I remind you I am seelie? I will not condone annihilating the humans on the isle!"

Flauvis ignores this. "In fact, Evelyn should leave for the mainland at once to detonate it."

"Excuse me?" I shoot the wolf king a scowl, hand on my hip. "You do know that would kill me too, right?"

"It's for the greater good." A malicious, teasing grin lifts the corners of his muzzle.

"It could kill more of our kind too," Estel argues. "The Parvanovae is untested technology. There's no saying how far the damage could reach, even if detonated solely on the mainland. If the blast radius reached the isle, only the fae with ethereal forms could survive."

"Then the rest of us burrow underground, just in case," Flauvis says.

Aspen puts his hands on the table and leans toward the Winter King. "Evelyn is not sacrificing herself to use the bomb."

Flauvis shrugs. "Then do it yourself."

Aspen growls, but Nyxia lifts a hand, shadows writhing around her shoulders and darkening the room for a split second. "This conversation is getting way off course." The royals quiet, but Aspen and Flauvis don't take their eyes from each other. "Estel understands the Parvanovae more than any of us, and if she says it isn't safe, then we cannot rely on it as our first course of action. I agree we must keep it as a last resort, at the very least as a potent threat to hold against the humans, but let us first consider the idea of extending the wall." She turns her gaze to Estel. "What is your plan?"

The particles on her face rearrange, shifting from worried to composed. "I'll need at least a few days to go through my sister's old blueprints. I know she recorded her original findings regarding the Parvanovae and the wall. In the meantime, Aelfon will organize builders to erect the stones around our courts."

"That still only gives us a partial wall," Nyxia says. "What do we do about the Renounced?"

Flauvis reveals his teeth in a chilling grin. "Let's turn those vile iron weapons on them. If they want them so badly, let's deliver them. We'll bury them right in their hearts so we need not concern ourselves with them any longer."

"No," I say. "We'd have to sacrifice our own—"

The wolf king bursts into maniacal laughter. "*Our own*, the human queen says!"

Aspen takes a forbidding step toward the wolf. "Evelyn is fae. She has proven herself worthy to the All of All."

"Ah, something not even you have done, little king."

Aspen clenches his fists, tensing as if he might leap across the table, but again Nyxia stops them with a flash of her shadows. "Enough with the alpha ego measuring contest. We can see they are both large indeed."

Aelfon snickers, but Aspen and Flauvis again stand down. I'm starting to think the wolf king lives for baiting others. He's worse than Franco.

I steel my nerves and take my opportunity to finish what I was trying to say. "I've seen what it's like when the fae are forced to use iron weapons. It's cruel and we cannot stoop to that level."

Flauvis mutters another high-pitched mockery, but I ignore him.

"But I agree something must be done with the Renounced before we face the human threat. We cannot fight two enemies at once, and we need their cooperation to extend the wall around Faerwyvae."

"Then what do we do?" Minuette asks, her blue hair fluttering around her head.

I ponder for a moment, pieces of a puzzle coming together in my mind. "We need to convince them to agree to a ceasefire until the wall is complete and the human threat is dealt with."

Tris nods her agreement. "They may be our enemies, but they deserve to be warned of what's coming."

"Will that be enough to get them to stand down?" Aelfon asks. "We can't tell them about the Parvanovae, in case they get any clever ideas, which means they can't know our plan for enchanting our proposed wall."

"We can tell them Estel has created the technology to protect us," Tris says with a shrug. "That's simple enough."

"If they were that easy to reason with," Flauvis says, "we wouldn't be at war in the first place."

"True," Nyxia says. "I doubt they'd even agree to hear us out. How can we convince them we're sincere? How do we get them to meet us for a peaceful exchange of words in the first place?"

Aspen shakes his head. "We'll have to offer them a compelling bargain."

"But what?" Tris asks.

My eyes unfocus as ideas shift and reassemble in my mind. A bargain. We need a compelling bargain.

Then I see it.

"I know what we have to do." All eyes turn to me, burning with curiosity, disdain, hope, fear. "Flauvis is right. If it's the weapons they want, we should deliver them."

Flauvis grumbles. "Why do I get the feeling it doesn't

involve the best part of my suggestion? The part about shoving them through their hearts?"

Aelfon shakes his horned head. "We cannot give them weapons they could use against us."

"We won't," I say. "Not exactly, at least."

Aspen turns to face me, brow quirked. "What are you thinking?"

"If they agree to a ceasefire, we will agree to deliver the weapons once the battle with the humans is resolved. What they won't know is that the weapons will be unusable by the time they receive them."

Aspen narrows his eyes, then his lips quirk into a devious grin.

I lift my chin and meet his approving gaze. "The weapons won't be usable because I'm going to melt them."

pparently, talk of fae deception was exactly what the Alpha Alliance needed to forge unity, for the rest of the meeting goes smoothly. Plans are finalized and our message to request a peaceful exchange of words with the Renounced is drafted. Nyxia promises to send it with one of her owls as soon as she returns to Lunar. By the time the meeting is adjourned, the mood in the atrium is far less grim.

As the royals begin shuffling toward the hall to exit the palace, Aspen turns to face me, taking my hand in his and bringing it to his lips. As he lowers my hand, his mouth quirks into a crooked grin. "You truly are a brilliant queen," he says. "Or perhaps it's your devious human side that is so wickedly clever."

His confidence in my plan makes my chest feel warm, but I can't keep my mind from spinning up the worst possible scenarios. I bite the inside of my cheek. "Do you think the Renounced will buy it? Do you think they'll even agree to meet?"

"The Renounced are losing allies by the day," he says. "They won't be able to refuse any chance at regaining the upper hand."

"I hope you're right," I say with a sigh.

He leans in and kisses my cheek, then trails his lips to mine. The nearby sounds of the royals chatting at the other end of the atrium keeps me from deepening the kiss, and too soon he breaks away. "I'll see the others out." His eyes flash to the side, a suspicious gleam in them, before he steps back and makes his way to join the royals. That's when I realize what—or whom—he'd glanced at.

Estel remains at the table, eyes trained on me while Aspen leads the others down the hall. Fehr comes up beside me, gaze shifting from me to the Star Queen. "Shall I wait with you or join your mate?"

I study my guest, her folded, shimmering hands, her serene expression. There's no threat in her lingering presence, only a silent request for privacy. Besides, she was the one most firmly on my side about not using the Parvanovae. "You may join my mate and see that the others are safely on their way," I tell Fehr.

With a bow, he follows Aspen.

Once we're alone, Estel slowly rounds the table to approach me. As she closes the distance between us, I'm forced to crane my neck to meet her eyes. As I do, the particles on her face shift into a somber expression, lips pulled down at the corners. "Thank you for supporting my stance regarding the Parvanovae," she says.

"I'm thankful for you as well. I agree with everything you said. The technology is untested and could have detrimental effects we can't even begin to imagine."

"And I agree that not all humans are our enemies."

I quirk a brow. "You're neutral unseelie, then?"

She nods. "My sister was not, but in the end, even she regretted creating the Parvanovae after the war ended."

"Then why didn't she destroy it like she said she'd planned?"

"I don't know. Perhaps she never was able to find a way to unmake it, only to transmute it like she'd planned with the wall."

"Do you really think it will work? Moving the wall and infusing an enchantment with the energy of the star bomb?"

"Once I find my sister's blueprints, I'll know for sure." Her gaze shifts from me to the crate on the table. "I will take it off your hands if you believe it is safer with me. However, I hate to admit I fear it being anywhere within reach of other fae. *Any* other fae."

Her words skirt around the truth, but I can read beneath what she's left unsaid. She's afraid of what would happen if even one of our allies got hold of it.

"I'll keep it here," I say, despite the nausea that turns my stomach at the thought of the bomb being in such close proximity for even a minute longer. "So long as you're certain no other Chariot is in possession by the humans."

She tilts her head at the two travel devices—hers and the one the human had—still resting next to the crate. "That was the only one. But are you certain humans won't try to take it another way?"

I bite my lip, considering that. As unlikely as it is that humans would try to infiltrate my court and palace on foot and without means of immediate travel, the possibility exists. And with all those iron weapons...

An idea forms in my mind, a way to prevent humans and fae alike from getting to the weapons room. Even better, it ties in so well with the deception we've planned for the Renounced. My lips pull into a tight smile. "I think I know what to do about that."

"Very well," Estel says. "I shall leave it with you." She reaches across the table and takes up the two Chariots, brow furrowed as she studies them. After a few moments, she extends a hesitant hand, palm up to reveal the slightly more beat-up Chariot, the one that had belonged to Mr. Duveau. "I think you should keep this as well."

My fingers tremble as I take it from her. "Why?"

"It was gifted to forge the treaty," she says. "It makes sense it should now belong to the one who has broken it."

I study the silver disc, flipping open the cover to reveal the golden light of the orb and the crystals surrounding it. "I don't know how to use it," I say as I snap it shut and try to hand it back to her.

She gives a dismissive shrug, making no move to take it back. "Like all magic, it's fueled by your intent. Simply open it and think of a place you've already been that you would like to go." Her face shifts into a smile. "Accept my gift, Queen Evelyn. I've come to trust you. I hope you trust me too."

As loathe as I am to trust much of anyone right now, I must admit this meeting has changed my suspicions about her. She might be the only one on the Alpha Alliance, aside from Aspen and Nyxia, that I trust at all. I match her smile and close my fingers over the Chariot. "Thank you, Estel."

~

I OPEN THE DOOR TO THE ROYAL CHAMBER, SURPRISED WHEN I find it empty. Before the meeting, I'd left my sister here with Foxglove, Lorelei, and Breeda. I hadn't ordered Amelie to remain in the room, only to stay at Lorelei's side. They must have found elsewhere to await the end of the meeting.

Just as well, I suppose, considering what I hold in my hand.

Safe from prying eyes, I stalk the perimeter of the room, looking for a place to keep the Chariot. When I accepted the gift, my first instinct was to hide it in the weapons room with the Parvanovae, but I remembered what Estel had said about it needing to be charged by starlight after it's used. If there's ever a chance I want to operate it, I need to place it somewhere beneath the open sky. But where won't it be in danger of being stolen?

I move to the windows and open the golden shutters. Leaning slightly over one of the ledges, a terra cotta window box catches my eye. I look down the row of other windows and see each hosts a similar rectangular box, all filled with tiny green succulents and miniature cacti with orange and purple blooms. I hadn't noticed them last night, but their inconspicuous design makes them the perfect hiding place for the Chariot. Carefully tucking the disc beneath a spiky, green limb—

"Oooh, what's that, Your Majesty?"

I jump back, sticking myself on several spikes in the process, as Breeda hovers before me. "Do not sneak up on me." My words come out much harsher than I intend, and I bring my tender finger to my mouth to soothe where I'd been poked.

The little sprite's expression falls, her red flames

dimming to a pink. "Oh, Most Beautiful Gracious Majesty, I truly didn't mean to! I saw the meeting was over and came to find you."

I sigh, forcing the fire to retreat from my veins. "It's all right, Breeda," I say with more composure. "Next time, state your presence if I've yet to acknowledge you."

Her color returns, as does her grin. "Yes, Your Majesty." She spins in a circle, then lifts her chin, eyeing the window box. "Is that a Chariot—"

"Please, Breeda, do not speak of it. You must tell no one. In fact, make it your duty to guard it." I curse myself inwardly, knowing I'll have to move it once I get the chance.

She nods. "I won't let you down."

"Where are the others?" I ask, mostly to change the subject. But also, I should relieve Lorelei from her charge. It can't have been fun to babysit someone she so thoroughly dislikes. I'll have to thank her with a bottle of Midnight Blush, if I can get my hands on some.

"I know just where they are," Breeda says. "Shall I take you to them?"

"Please." I follow the sprite out of my room and into the hall. She leads me away from where I know the sleeping quarters to be and into a part of the palace I don't think I've seen before. The doors are sparser, the hall wider. She pauses before an ornate pair of golden doors beneath an arched doorway.

I open one of the doors to reveal an enormous room, almost as vast as the atrium. The ceiling towers high overhead beneath a marble dome, moonlight streaming in through the long, wide windows. Orbs of light illuminate the room, their reflections dancing over the shimmering sunstone floor.

"Evie!" My sister's voice calls my attention to the perimeter of the circular room, where she, Foxglove, and Lorelei lounge in a sitting area near the wall. As I approach, I see evidence of half-filled glasses and decanters of wine. My sister rises to her feet, cheeks blushed pink, eyes alight like I haven't seen in such a long time. "It's a ballroom," she says, smile stretching from ear to ear. "*Your* ballroom. Isn't it incredible?"

"It is." My words come out stiff, despite the awe the room instills.

Foxglove lifts an empty glass. "Shall I pour you some? It's a Fire Court specialty. Agave Ignitus wine."

"It's so good." Lorelei's words are slow and slurred as she swirls the amber liquid in her glass. "You've got to try it."

Breeda flits in front of me. "It really is, Your Majesty."

I stare at my fae friends, the sprite, my sister, stripped of all words. A weight has settled into my stomach, and it takes me a moment to understand why. Then my gaze settles back on Amelie, and I understand.

Amelie is smiling, happy, as are her companions. Gone is the disdain Foxglove and Lorelei had first shown her when I brought her from the dungeon, as if it was never there at all. It's just like it was when we first arrived at Bircharbor. My sister, in her sweet and ever-likable way, has won their hearts all over again.

When I left my sister under Lorelei's care this evening, the wood nymph had grumbled. I hadn't expected to return and find them drinking amiably in a ballroom.

For reasons I can hardly comprehend, a lump rises in my throat, a feeling of betrayal sending fire through my veins. Before I can think, those flames are leaping from my lungs, weaving into my words. "I don't recall giving any of you permission to wander my palace or get drunk off my wine stores."

The smile slips from Amelie's lips. Foxglove and Lorelei stiffen, placing their glasses on the table. Lorelei rises to her feet, eyes wide and full of a trepidation I've never seen her wear for me. For Aspen, maybe, but never for me.

It's enough to cool my rage. Blazing iron, maybe Aspen had a point about the difficulties of appointing friends to positions of service when you're a royal. I hate the opposing forces that swarm inside me—anger at seeing them so at leisure, shame at the look in Lorelei's eyes.

With a deep breath, I do my best to compose myself. "Lorelei, can I speak with you for a moment?"

She nods and approaches me. Amelie follows, seemingly against her will.

Then I recall the order I gave her to remain at Lorelei's side. "Amelie, you may wait with Foxglove while I speak with Lorelei."

My sister nods and returns to her seat, while Lorelei closes the rest of the distance between us. She meets my eyes with hesitation. "Your Majesty?"

"I'm sorry," I say in a rush. "I didn't mean to react like that. I was just...worried."

Her shoulders relax, the frown smoothing from her face. "About what?"

My eyes flash from her to Amelie. "About..."

She turns to follow my gaze, then lowers her voice. "I owe you an apology too," she says. "I was wrong to be so firmly against you bringing your sister here. I think you were right about her. She...she seems sincere."

My throat feels dry at those words. I was *right* about her? No, this is all wrong. That's not what I'd intended to happen. I wanted to watch her, investigate her. Not open her to friends and dresses and ballrooms.

A life devoid of comfort and friendship.

My conversation with Fehr echoes in my head, creating a swarm of conflict in my heart. Again, I'm plagued by the same questions that fought inside my mind last night. *What is it I want from Amelie? To love her or hate her? To trust her or suspect her? Am I waiting for her to prove me right or prove me wrong?*

I still don't know the answer.

With a shake of my head, I burn the questions from my mind and return my attention to Lorelei. "She didn't say or do anything suspicious while she was with you?"

Lorelei shrugs. "No, she was silent. I admit, Foxglove and I gave her the cold shoulder until about an hour ago when we found the wine and decided to explore the palace." Her expression falls again. "I'm sorry we did that."

I wave a dismissive hand. "It's fine. But you're certain you found nothing suspect about her?"

She shakes her head, eyes turning down at the corners. "I think she's been through a lot more than I've given her credit for."

I grit my teeth, gaze trailing to my sister, who has already fallen back into casual conversation with Foxglove.

"Be careful," I say, my attention snapping back to Lorelei. "I may have been right to bring her here with us, but she's still a suspect. Do not let your guard down around her again."

The trepidation returns to her eyes at my stern tone, but this time I don't take it back.

If my sister wants my trust, she'll need to do a lot more than charm my friends to earn it.

21

The next day, I stand at the end of a river composed of molten iron. It spreads out before me, spanning one side of the hallway to the other, where the weapons room is. The room remains empty aside from the small crate containing the Parvanovae and the few weapons—explosives, primarily —that I wasn't able to safely incinerate.

I've spent the best part of my morning and afternoon melting nearly every sword, axe, dagger, spear, and mace the room contained. All but a minor selection of blades I've decided to keep for myself, of course. Everything else has now become a flowing stream of red-orange iron, kept in its molten state by my faintly glowing flames that dance over the top. At each side of the river, my flames are absent, leaving hardened metal to act as a barrier that keeps the river from entering the weapons room or from extending too close to the stairs at the other end.

I smile at the job well done. A tiring job, I must say, but one that will keep both humans and fae alike from getting to the Parvanovae. No fae could make it down the stairs to get to this hallway with how much iron now flows into the hall, and no human could brave a river of molten metal and flames. Only I can call my fire back. Considering my hearth still glows steady with the flame I conjured two days ago, it's clear my fire will obey my will and remain for as long as I intend it to.

That's my theory, anyway.

The heat of the fire is oddly comforting, despite the sweat that soaks my brow. I crouch down, balancing on the balls of my feet as I watch the beauty of my dazzling, tricolor flames. There's something hypnotizing about the way they dance and sway over the molten river's surface, making me feel an odd sense of calm. Or perhaps it's exhaustion I feel. Whatever the case, I can't help but admire my work. My fire. My magic.

Extending my hand, I reach for the nearest flame, letting its heat tickle the tips of my fingers. I open my palm, turning it upward, and the flame climbs over it, swirling until it shifts into a tiny orb. I let it dance and undulate, watching it until my eyes grow heavy.

Indeed, I should probably get some rest.

I lean forward again, about to return the flame to join the rest, when another thought crosses my mind, one that sharpens my senses and makes me feel suddenly awake.

Instead of rest, perhaps I should practice my magic.

I lift my palm again and focus on my orb of fire. Then, without touching it, I will it to rise.

It shifts and sways, moves and undulates. But for the most part, it remains an orb hovering just over my palm.

With a sigh, I close my eyes and try to summon the same elemental connection I felt when I lit the hearth—

the dance between air and fire. I created my river of melted weapons through touch, but now I want to hone the skill I've yet to master. With human armies coming our way, not to mention the meeting we hope to have with the Renounced, sharpening my fire magic as well as I can is more important than ever.

I breathe in, letting the dense, hot air fill my lungs, then breathe out, letting air whistle between my lips. Calm settles over me. I conjure thoughts of running, leaping, air brushing against my fur when I'm in my fox form, whipping my human hair the same way it constantly dances through Minuette's.

Eyes still closed, I focus on the heat of the fire brushing my skin, seeing the orb in my mind's eye. I envision the flame lifting, rising, sensing the balance between air and fire, the way it feeds it, raises it, encircles it, pervades it.

When I open my eyes, my orb hovers several inches above my hand.

Pride swells in my chest, but I try not to let it overcome me as I focus on the next feat. With my intention firmly in my mind, I will the flame to move away from me. I maintain my connection to the air and fire elements, watching as the orb floats higher, moves down the hall, following the river. Once it reaches the far end, I will it to lower.

As my flame disappears to join the rest, my chest bubbles with excitement. I did it! I moved my fire through space. Not just once, not just in a single flash of motion. I controlled its speed, trajectory, height, distance. My success should be enough to satisfy me, but it only fuels a deeper yearning for mastery. What if...

"Metal is earth, right?" I mutter as I squint at the river. "Earth is an element I should be able to control."

Again, I close my eyes, igniting my inner fire, reconnecting to air, and gathering all I know about earth. Rocks and plants are obvious. Logic and facts feel like they fit in here well. But I also remember what I learned from the goblin I met when I first visited the Twelfth Court. *Safety. Security,* he'd said. I wrap it all around me, picturing my fox paws padding over soft dirt, solid rock, lush grass. I see myself in the operating room, assessing facts and figures, using logic to dispense the proper amount of laudanum and chloroform. Then I imagine the halls of this palace, the walls of the apothecary that was my home, the composition of metal and stone that make up the weapons I've used to defend my sense of safety.

Once again, I lift my palm, and this time I picture it shaping an orb of the metal. My fire dances inside it, air envelops it, lifts it, helps it rise.

With a deep breath, I open my eyes. Just like the hovering flame, my orb of molten iron drifts above the river. My mouth falls open at the sight.

"You really are mastering the elements, aren't you?"

I startle at the sound of Aspen's voice so close to my ear, but I manage to maintain my focus on the orb. At once, logic tells me it isn't possible he could be here, not with the iron so close.

But as I turn my head to take in his form, the way he crouches at my side, studying my deadly river, I see the telltale violet aura that surrounds him. He's here through the Bond.

I grin, returning my gaze to my floating orb. With

control, I will the orb to slowly lower and return to the river. "I wouldn't say I'm *mastering* them. Not yet at least."

He faces me, eyes drinking me in. "No, I suppose you aren't."

I meet his gaze, brow furrowed. "You aren't supposed to agree with me."

"Then you shouldn't be so self-deprecating," he says with a smirk. He leans closer. Even though he's only here through the Bond, my awareness of his presence, his closeness, is as strong as if he were truly here. The energy sizzles between us just the same. "Besides, I meant it. Compared to how you've mastered my heart, that hovering orb is nothing."

I blush beneath his stare. "I don't know if I should swoon or roll my eyes at that."

His eyes fall to my lips. "I suggest you kiss me."

I place a hand on the side of his face, aware of the usual discrepancy of touch that exists between us when we visit through the Bond. Still, it's enough. Bringing our lips together, I luxuriate in the pressure of his mouth, the caress of his tongue. It stirs desire in my heart, in my core, and I want nothing more than to leave this hall to find him.

I gently pull away. "Where are you right now?"

"The bedroom next to yours," he says. He bites his lip, hunger heavy in his eyes. "Will I be joining you tonight? Or do you want another night with your sister?" There's no malice or judgment in his voice. Just a question.

Mention of Amelie sobers some of the passion heating my blood. I groan, considering what to say. So far, all evidence has proven her compliance with my commands, both with her own willingness and through the power of her name. Still, I hesitate to leave her alone at night. There are so many more what-ifs—what if I'm wrong? What if she isn't following my commands at all, but some lingering command of Cobalt's, forcing her to act as a spy? What if he comes for her in the night and takes her away again? What if I lose her again?

The last question catches me off guard, and I shake it from my head before I can analyze it too deeply. "One more night," I whisper. "That's all I need."

The disappointment is clear on Aspen's face, but he hides it with a crooked smile. "You can have as many as you need."

"But in the meantime..." I lean in and place a kiss at the corner of his jaw, sliding one hand behind his neck while the other moves up his chest, his torso, down his stomach to the waist of his trousers. He lets out a gasp as I slide my hand over the front of them. "I should come to you," I whisper, "so we can do this in person."

"Or," he says, snaking a hand around my waist and lifting me as he rises to his feet. My legs wrap around his hips, and seconds later I feel the warm volcanic stone wall press into my back. His lips crush into mine and I eagerly receive them, the caress of his tongue lighting a fire at my core. It feels so much like he's really here, but I crave every part that's missing. The heat is there, energy humming between our bodies. The rosemary cinnamon scent of his skin mingles with the smell of hot iron, and even his form feels solid. But there's something just slightly off about the pressure between our lips, the feel of his hands cupping my backside as I pull him closer.

It's enough to make me crave him harder than I ever have before.

Then again, there's something new and exciting about this, something enticing about the thought of being intimate across time and space. Perhaps in my normal state of mind, the idea would be unsettling, but right now, with him feeling so close, with his violet aura invading my senses...

"Aspen," I gasp as his lips trail down my neck. "Take me now."

With a groan, he presses me harder against the wall, lips returning to mine as one hand leaves my backside to grasp my knee, then trails up my thigh. Heat burns hot at my core, tingling at the apex of my thighs. I move against him, hating the linen of his trousers that creates a barrier between us. Unable to handle it a moment longer, I reach between us and slide them down—

I find myself suddenly on my feet, all warmth stripped from me as Aspen's body is no longer against my own. My chest heaves as I fight to catch my breath. Brow furrowed, I stare at the empty space where my mate just was.

There's no way I imagined all that.

"Well, that was incredibly awkward," comes Aspen's stilted voice. I whirl to find him standing next me, hands on his hips as he stares unfocused at the floor in front of him. His shirt and trousers are wrinkled but the latter are no longer pulled down. His golden cheeks are tinged with red and a sheepish grin seems to be hiding behind his pursed lips.

"What happened?"

He rubs his brow, his grin finally breaking through. "Foxglove has informed me our people have arrived at the palace. My household and your fire fae from Lunar."

I've never seen him so uncomposed; it's almost comical. And when I imagine what strange sight the ambassador must have just walked in on, I can't stop the laughter that bubbles in my chest and bursts from my lips.

He meets my gaze, trying unsuccessfully to look stern. "You think this is funny?"

"It is. Besides, I think you may have made one of Foxglove's lifelong dreams come true?"

He crosses his arms over his chest, lips quirked as he pins me with a teasing glare. "And what exactly would that be?"

I can hardly form the words through bursts of laughter. "A glimpse at your magnificent kingdom."

22

Aspen has regained his composure by the time we meet in the atrium. The only thing that betrays him is the embarrassed smile that continues to tug at his lips, and when he winks at me, part of me considers pulling him up the stairs to lock ourselves in the bedroom.

The thought doesn't linger long before Breeda soars into the atrium and hovers between us. "Everyone is here!" she squeals. "They're waiting in the courtyard for you to greet them."

"Fehr won't give permission for any to enter without your word," Lorelei adds, approaching from the hall that leads to the palace entrance. Foxglove follows just a step behind, cheeks crimson as he adjusts his spectacles, clearly avoiding Aspen's gaze.

My heart sinks as we close the distance between us and the ambassadors, and I'm worried that the awkwardness between my mate and Foxglove might not be easily undone.

"They're just outside," Lorelei says with an easy grin, oblivious to the tension. "Aspen's household too." She waves a hand forward, then pauses as if she's reconsidering her actions. Pursing her lips, her eyes flick to mine before she bends into a humble bow, arm extended for me to pass ahead of her.

Some of the day's mirth is stripped away from me at the sight, reminding me of the conversation we had yesterday. Instead of walking in front of her, however, I link my arm through hers. "Let's go."

Her eyes widen with surprise, but her lips pull into a grin. As we make our way down the hall, I hazard a glance behind me. Foxglove's neck is nearly swallowed by his shoulders as he shuffles at Aspen's side. My mate glances from me to Foxglove, then gives a resigned shake of his head. Slinging his arm over the ambassador's shoulders, he gives him a cajoling smile. "Did you like what you saw, my friend?"

Foxglove blushes deeper, eyes flicking up at Aspen as a grin stretches across his face. "I think it would be a treasonous lie to say I didn't, Your Majesty."

Aspen barks a laugh.

Foxglove's gaze meets mine and he lifts his brows, the tension seeming to melt from him as his shoulders relax. "Queen Evelyn certainly is a lucky lover."

Aspen squeezes the ambassador to his side. "As are yours, Foxglove."

Content that the awkward rift has been smoothed over, I return my gaze straight ahead.

"What was that about?" Lorelei whispers.

"I'll tell you later," I say under my breath, stifling my giggle. "If Foxglove doesn't tell you first."

OUTSIDE, THE COURTYARD IS FILLED WITH FAE TOO numerous to count. All of Aspen's refugees that had escaped Bircharbor are here, as are most of the fire fae from Lunar. Dragons dart across the sky, wisps bob in clusters, kitsune explore the paths and plants, and an entire family of the crustacean-mushroom fae settle in by one of the rectangular ponds. I catch sight of Dune amongst the crowd, tapping anxiously from paw to paw as he barks directions at some of his comrades, clearly trying to maintain order over his traveling companions. But the fae seem too relieved to have arrived at their destination to pay him much heed, as they continue to flit about the courtyard, awed by what they see.

Fehr watches them all through slitted lids, bronze arms crossed over his chest. "Do you approve of their presence here, my queen?"

I find myself momentarily taken aback. That's the first time he's ever referred to me as *my queen*, and not just Your Majesty. "I do, Fehr. Any who seek shelter indoors may also be permitted inside the palace. Those who would like to apply for positions within the palace may take it up with you and Lorelei. Same goes for all of my mate's household. All of his people will need rooms and positions in the palace."

He nods. "It will be done."

I scan the crowd again, which has begun to quiet now that most have noticed my presence. Then silence falls completely, and the fae—both Aspen's and mine—lower into bows. Our names are uttered, creating a wave of sound before they rise.

A tiny figure with brown skin hobbles toward us. "I hope you are still in need of a healer," Gildmar says.

Aspen and I make our way down the stairs to greet her. "Of course," Aspen says.

"You and all of Aspen's household are welcome here," I add, "and will be given appropriate positions."

She looks from me to my mate. "What will happen, Your Majesty, when you defeat Cobalt? Will you rule from Irridae together or reclaim Bircharbor?"

We exchange a glance, neither knowing how to answer. That's something we've hardly discussed. "We have two wars to win," Aspen says. "Only then will we finalize such plans."

Gildmar nods, her smile wide.

"Evelyn!" A familiar voice steals my attention as a human girl comes charging up the stairs. Marie Coleman, dressed in trousers and a linen tunic, stumbles into a last-minute curtsy before taking my hands in hers, a dreamy look falling over her face as she gives an exaggerated sigh. "Your palace is more beautiful than anything I've seen so far."

I stare at her, blinking rapidly before I find my voice. "Thank you, Marie, but...what are you doing here?"

She furrows her brow, her smile wavering. "I came with King Aspen's household. Did you not expect I would come?"

"No," I say. Then, lowering my voice, I add, "I thought you would go home as soon as you learned the treaty was broken."

Her expression continues to fall. "Why would I go home? This is where I belong now."

I shake my head. "Without the treaty, the Reaping is over. There's nothing keeping you here."

She studies me as if I've grown two heads. "I know that. I'm choosing to stay."

It's my turn to look at her in disbelief. "But why? We're at war with your kind."

"*Our* kind," she corrects, "and I'm well aware."

"Then you should also be aware how dangerous it is for you to be here. We don't know what's going to happen."

"Do you honestly think it's any safer back in Sableton?"

"Yes! Here, if things go poorly, there are fae who wouldn't treat you well."

She lifts her chin. "I've already dealt with plenty of prejudice from the fae, trust me. I can handle myself."

"It's more than prejudice." I sigh, searching for words that will help her understand the very real threats she could be facing. "Not all unseelie are kind and playful. There are some that will literally eat you. And there are others who could hurt you, if they think it would help their position in the battles that are to come."

She tilts her head to the side and gives me a pointed look. "How is that any more terrifying than returning to human parents who groomed you from birth to be a bride to a stranger?" I open my mouth to argue, but she continues. "Look, Evel—*Your Majesty*, I mean—this is the first time I've felt alive in all my life. Back in Sableton, every moment of my life was planned. All I ever wanted was to sail the seas on Father's merchant ships, but instead, I was forced into dresses, taught how to play the pianoforte, and how to snag a wealthy husband. In my free time, I was told how to please the fae, should I ever be chosen for the Reaping."

"Marie, Faerwyvae isn't a place for some lighthearted adventure."

She shrugs. "That's not how I see it."

"You are in very real danger. We are at war."

"We're at war in Sableton too," she argues. "Please, Your Majesty. I understand your fear for me, but don't send me back there. I'd rather live a short and dangerous life here where I can be free than a long one acting as a slave to my parents and husband."

My shoulders slump. I don't know why I should care. Before she came to Faerwyvae, Marie Coleman meant nothing to me. She was only Maddie Coleman's younger sister. And Maddie Coleman is lower than dirt, in my mind. Still, I can't help but feel responsible for Marie. Her words conjure something that makes my heart ache —a comparison between the meek, plain girl she was back home and the bold, reckless creature she's become here. Would sending her back to Sableton truly be in her best interest?

Her eyes are pleading as she brings her clasped hands to her heart. "Please, Your Majesty."

I purse my lips, jaw shifting side to side. "Fine," I finally say with a groan. "But don't say I didn't warn you."

She throws her arms around my waist and crushes me in a hug before abruptly breaking off and tumbling into an awkward curtsy. "Sorry. Thank you. I can't tell you how much I appreciate you."

With a flick of my wrist, I wave her away, but not before giving her a warm smile that expresses all that I wasn't able to say out loud...

That I completely understand her.

She skips back to the courtyard to join the others, the joy bursting from her face as she relays something to a companion—one I recognize as Vane, one of Aspen's handsome servants. Then she turns to another familiar figure, Ocher. Both males grin at her as she chats, and by the way her lips move, I can only imagine she's speaking a mile a minute. Her attention flips from one male to the other, totally oblivious to the way they look at her as if mesmerized by a fascinating painting.

I turn to Aspen, who has just finished speaking with a group of his soldiers. When he catches my eye, he comes to me and circles his arms around my waist. "Your empty palace just got very, very busy," he says with a smirk.

"Perhaps we should have savored our temporary privacy more."

"Not that it did us much good when we did." The blush I saw earlier returns to his cheeks, making me love him even more than I did before. It's funny the little things I discover about my mate that make my affections grow. Like the fact that he's easily embarrassed.

Aspen's irises glitter with their shimmering autumn color as they lock on mine. Then they leave me to light on something overhead. I follow his gaze, just as the sound of flapping wings beats the air. A white owl with black spots lands at our feet, quirking its head at us. Aspen and I separate, and my mate's expression turns to steel. "What is it?" he asks.

A male voice comes from the owl. "Two messages from Queen Nyxia. First, her owls have confirmed sightings of warships heading toward the isle. Second, the meeting with the Renounced is tomorrow."

THAT EVENING, I STAND BEFORE MY MIRROR IN MY bedroom, the blush of a pink and orange sunset lighting the room. Eyeing the length of my freshly donned gown, I shift side to side to see if any of my movements reveal the weapons I've concealed. My obsidian dagger is strapped to my thigh while an assortment of iron blades—the few I didn't melt—circle my waist.

The dress I wear is a deep red, another one of Amelie's designs. It covers my front and back from my neck to my ankles but remains open at the sides and is tied loosely at the waist. The dagger belts at my thigh and waist are covered by the design of the dress while still providing easy access for me to reach. I practice a few times, sliding my hand behind my back to retrieve an iron dagger from beneath the dress, then unsheathing my obsidian blade from my thigh.

"Are you going to tell me what's going on?" Amelie appears reflected in the mirror, coming up behind me as she wrings her hands. It's the third time she's asked since I came to add new commands that hinted at the need for travel.

I turn to face her, returning my weapons to their hidden sheaths. "I'll tell you when you need to know. If ever."

Her eyes are locked on my gown, as if seeking the invisible blades beneath it. "I'm worried about you," she whispers. "Whatever you're about to do..."

"Worry about yourself," I snap, turning away from her and moving to the bed where I stuff a few necessities into a bag.

"I'm worried about myself too," she says, following me. "You aren't...you aren't giving me back to *him*, are you? Please don't do this. Not unless you can guarantee me the means to kill him."

I pause and meet her eyes, surprised at the terror on her face. "That's not what we're doing."

"Then what is it?"

I ignore her and return to packing my bag. The Alpha Alliance will be meeting with the Renounced at midday tomorrow on the border between Fire and Solar. Fehr is in the process of allocating the best candidates to pull the coach Ustrin left behind so we can leave at once. My heart sinks at the thought of leaving the palace overnight, especially when Aspen's household and my own just arrived. However, we want to set up a proper camp and scope out the meeting place well in advance of the Renounced arriving. At least I trust the palace will be protected by Fehr, and the Parvanovae will remain inaccessible to anyone.

"Where's your bag?" I ask without looking at my sister.

With a sigh, she retrieves it from the sitting area, then places it on the bed next to mine. "Please." Her voice comes out with a stifled sob, stealing my attention to the anguish on her face. "Please tell me what's about to happen. I'm going out of my mind wondering if this is the end for me. If it is, just—"

"It's a meeting," I say through my teeth.

She furrows her brow. "What do you mean?"

I clench my jaw, hands on my hips as I shake my head in irritation. "I don't have to explain anything to you."

"If you're taking me too, it must have something to do with me."

I narrow my eyes. "Amelie, not everything is about you. I'm taking you because we won't be back by morning, perhaps not even by tomorrow night. It could take days to come to an agreement."

Her shoulders sag, relief ironing out the furrows on her brow. Then her gaze turns suspicious. "What's the meeting about?"

"What is it you don't understand? I don't have to explain a damn thing—"

"You can trust me, Evie. I've done nothing to show otherwise since I've returned to you."

Heat rises to my cheeks, a fiery rage flooding my veins. While she may be right, nothing will make up for what she's done. Still, there's that part of me that I hate to recognize. The part that softens with every day that goes by, the part that sees the sister she used to be. I let out a grumbling sigh. "We're meeting to establish a ceasefire."

"With whom?"

"Who do you think? With the Renounced."

Rage ignites on her face, transforming it in an instant. "You can't!"

I take a forbidding step toward her. "Is that so? Are you in any position to tell me what I can and can't do?"

Angry tears glaze her eyes. "The Renounced are our enemies. Cobalt is our enemy, and you promised me I could kill him."

"The ceasefire is temporary, only until we can defeat the human army that comes our way."

She doesn't seem surprised by this latter part, which tells me she's already heard about the oncoming threat.

I'm sure I have Foxglove or Lorelei to thank for that. She throws her hands in the air and turns her back to me. When she speaks, her voice comes out quiet. "Every day Cobalt lives is like a knife twisting in my heart. Not to mention what the ghost of his commands do to my mind."

My heart squeezes, a lump rising in my throat at her anguish. I find my walls unraveling around me, and I shudder at how vulnerable it makes me feel. How weak and small. "We will kill him, Ami."

She slowly turns to face me again. "You won't make me see him, will you?"

I shake my head. "During the meeting, you'll remain behind where we make camp. He won't even know you're there. Unless..." My blood goes cold, a question that I've yet to ask burning in my throat. "Can Cobalt...sense you through the Bond? Can you feel each other? See each other?'

She tilts her head back, perplexed at my words. "Of course not. That's not how it works."

I bite back my arguments that it very well *can* work that way. Maybe Aspen is right. Perhaps only Bonded pairs who deeply love each other can connect the same way my mate and I do. "You truly don't love Cobalt?"

A shadow darkens her expression. "I did, once," she says, tone flat. "That was before I realized what was going on. Before he started using my name to control me." Once again, her rage is a mirror to my own, as seen in her clenched fists, her steely gaze.

"How will you do it?" I ask.

She shakes the cloud from her face to meet my eyes. "How will I do what?"

"How will you use the power of his name to kill him?"

Her eyes widen for a moment, revealing fear and perhaps a hint of guilt. "I...I don't know yet."

Heat rises to my cheeks. "What do you mean, you don't know? When you first came to me, you said your power over his name could help us kill him."

"It can," she says in a rush, then lowers her eyes. "I just haven't sorted out how. I've never tried using his name like that before."

I shake my head with a roll of my eyes. "Great. A lot of use you'll be."

Indignation hardens her features when she lifts her head. "It's not like I had a chance to try. Once he began giving me daily commands, that was always one of the first. That I couldn't use his name or act out against him in any way. But trust me—"

"Trust you," I echo with a bitter laugh.

"Yes, Evie. When I get the chance, I will use Cobalt's name. I don't care if I have to force him to peel every inch of skin from his own body. I will do whatever it takes to watch the life fade from his eyes."

Her words send a shudder up my spine. One that tells me, perhaps her rage isn't as dark as mine. Perhaps it's darker than anything I've ever felt.

23

The sun beats high overhead as we make our way across the sandy dune to the stretch of land on the other side. The heat is so heavy in the air that I can see it, blurring the landscape in the distance. Still, I can make out rolling hills at the edge of the horizon. I'm surprised to see so much green beyond the invisible divide between Fire and Solar. I'd expected Solar to have more desert land like my court.

Aspen and I walk side by side with the rest of the Alpha Alliance, trailed by several guards. Each royal has brought two guards to the meeting, leaving another dozen or so at our camp to come to our aid in the case of an ambush. Amelie waits there too, with commands not to leave our tent. I wish there were more of us. I wish Foxglove, Lorelei, and Fehr were here. But our ambassadors remained behind to organize our newly arrived households, and Fehr of course can't leave the palace.

Aspen's hand lights on my back, and I turn to meet his gaze. A sheen of sweat covers his brow, and I can feel the same on my own face, as well as the gritty sand that seems to attach to my skin whenever I'm outdoors in the Fire Court. My mate gives me a reassuring grin, and I do my best to match it. I hate the thought of meeting the Renounced without absolutely obliterating them, but this ceasefire was my idea, after all.

It's necessary, I remind myself. *We have to do this.*

Our group slows its pace until Estel comes to a full stop at the head of our retinue. "This is it," she says. "The divide between Solar and Fire is just ahead. We will hold back and send my ambassador to meet theirs when they arrive."

My nerves only increase now that we've stopped, and the sun feels hotter. Oddly, I'm beginning to get used to the heat of the Fire Court, but I imagine not all the fae feel the same. While Estel and Minuette seem as content as ever, Flauvis looks downright miserable, panting rapidly. Nyxia glares up at the sky on occasion, as if she thinks it holds a personal grudge against her. Tris continues to shift between her tiny pixie form and her seelie form, as if she can't decide which one helps keep her cool.

Now in her larger form, her cherry blossoms seem to wilt beneath the heat. "Is it noon yet?" she whines.

Estel turns her shimmering face to the sky. "Not quite, but they should arrive—"

Something falls from the sky not too far away. When it lands, it takes the shape of a female figure rising on strong, heavily muscled legs. Her hair is golden with curls that rest above her shoulders, and she wears a gauzy white dress with gold trim that reaches just below her hips. Enormous golden-brown wings span out behind her. My heart races as I recognize her as one of the royals. I hardly noticed her at the council meeting where Aspen fought Cobalt for the throne, but now she's a formidable sight to behold. "Queen of Solar?" I whisper to Aspen.

He nods, his eyes narrowed at the figure. "Queen Phoebe."

The Solar Queen remains where she landed, arms crossed over her chest as she assesses us from afar. Movement behind her snags my attention, and I see a group marching to meet her.

"They're here," Aspen says under his breath.

My pulse races the closer they get, but as they come into full view, my nerves begin to calm. Their gathering is almost as large as ours, but not quite. The only other royal I recognize amongst the bunch is Queen Dahlia of the Summer Court. Her enormous yellow butterfly wings stretch out behind her as she joins Queen Phoebe. The rest of the fae are an assortment I can only imagine are their pretender kings and queens, some guards, and an ambassador or two. However, the only sea fae is a slender female with blue scales and coral-pink hair.

I whip my face toward Aspen. "Did Cobalt leave the Renounced?"

He studies the opposing crowd through slitted lids. "I can't imagine why he would have."

I return my attention to the sea fae. She stands next to Dahlia and the other supposed royals. Has Cobalt been replaced by a new royal? If so, why?

The question is stripped from my mind as Estel turns to face us. "I will send my ambassador now."

A fae who looks much like the Star Queen—an androgynous figure made of the same shimmering particles of light—bows low. "Your Majesty," the ambassador says in an airy, genderless voice, then turns away from us to make their way to the stretch of land that stands between our two groups.

Another figure—one I think I recognize as the Summer Court ambassador—does the same. The two ambassadors stop when they come within several feet of each other. From here, I can see their mouths move, but I hear nothing. My hands clench into fists, my anxiety returning in a rush. I'm desperate to hear what's being said, what arguments are made—

Then, just like that, the meeting is over. At least, it seems to be, for the Star Court ambassador is already making their way back to us. Aspen stiffens at my side. "It shouldn't have been that easy," he says under his breath.

I can't form a word as I wait with bated breath for what the ambassador will say. When the star fae reaches our group, their glittering eyes pin on me. "Queen Dahlia's ambassador claims her queen requests a one-on-one conversation with you, Queen Evelyn."

My throat goes dry. "Why me?"

The ambassador shakes their head. "She wouldn't say."

My gaze turns to my mate, then to the others. But wait. Why am I seeking permission? Validation? This was my plan to begin with and this is my decision to make. I steel my nerves, squaring my shoulders as I lift my chin. "If there is no argument from the Alpha Alliance, I will meet with her."

No royal speaks against my statement, so the ambassador nods and returns to the summer fae. When they finish speaking this time, both ambassadors return to their separate parties. I see Dahlia step to the front of the retinue, her gaze trained on me.

Aspen's fingers find mine. "Are you sure you want to do this?"

I tilt my head. "Am I sure I want to call a ceasefire, or am I sure I want to speak with Dahlia and try not to rip her head off her shoulders?"

He quirks a halfhearted grin. It's clear he's nervous for me; I can feel it rippling from his palm into mine. "Both."

I let out a heavy sigh. "It must be done." Returning my attention to our opponents, I give Aspen's hand a final squeeze and step away from our group. Dahlia does the same, mirroring each step of mine. Every inch we close between us feels like a mile, and my rage grows hotter the clearer she comes into view. It's impossible for me to forget everything she's done, starting with her poor treatment of Doris Mason and her cousin—the last two Chosen from the previous Hundred Year Reaping—and ending with her betrayal of Aspen, when she petitioned for Cobalt to take Aspen's place as king when my mate refused to marry Maddie Coleman.

We come to a halt several feet from each other, and my eyes narrow to slits, jaw clenched tightly as I fight the fury that radiates down to my fingertips. Every inch of me begs to release my fire, let it dance over my palms.

I could end this, I realize. I could attack Dahlia now, set fire to her pretty little wings. My allies could join me, and we could take down the Renounced before they even know what's happening. Now that I'm closer, the pretender kings and queens are in clearer view. They look meek compared to my allies. The only formidable opponents would be Dahlia and Phoebe.

That's all they have left.

Excitement rises within me at the realization, and I can feel my flames licking the surface of my palms.

Dahlia looks down her nose at me. "Whatever devious thoughts are running through your traitorous human mind, you can stop now," she says in her irritatingly smooth voice. "Phoebe's soldiers are on watch."

The queen glances up, and I follow her gaze. High in the sky, I catch sight of what appear to be birds. But I know better. They are winged fae like Phoebe. I return my attention to the Summer Queen, fire flooding my veins at the sight of her simpering smile.

"They could put an end to your pathetic life in seconds, should you try anything," she adds.

I grind my teeth, fighting the seething retort that begs to spring from my lips. However, I force my rage to calm to a simmer. This is a peaceful exchange of words. If I break it and everything goes poorly, it will be my fault.

Plastering an exaggerated smile on my face, I adopt a similar tone to hers. "Queen Dahlia, I will ignore that threat and instead tell you how lovely it is to see you again. You must feel the same about me to request such a close meeting between us."

She huffs. "It's only because I want to hear whatever nonsensical lies you've prepared straight from your lips."

I hold her gaze while I mentally prepare everything I must relay to the Renounced. Obviously, I hadn't planned on explaining it myself. It was agreed from the start that Estel's ambassador would be the one to do it. But now it must be me.

Clasping my hands before me, I begin. "We have

received intel that a human army has been sent from the mainland with the intention to wipe out faekind."

Dahlia pales, her eyes flashing with alarm before she steels her composure. Her words come out hesitant. "When you say you've received intel, does that mean you have proof?"

"Nyxia's owls have confirmed sightings of several warships."

"That could mean anything," she says.

"We've had an additional witness demonstrate the humans' desire to obliterate the fae as quickly as possible." I fill my words with enough emphasis to mask what I'm hiding—that the witness was a human who attempted to steal a bomb that could kill us all.

"Why should I believe you?" She gives a shrug, but the tenseness of her shoulders betrays how shaken she is.

"They're coming," I say. "If you don't believe me, let any of my allies confirm my statement."

"Am I supposed to believe this meeting is all an act of goodwill? A kind warning?" She scoffs. "I doubt that."

"No, it's to discuss the necessity of a ceasefire between us."

She barks a laugh, mouth falling open. "Why would we ever agree to that?"

"Because it's a matter of survival. We can't face a human army if we're divided, distracted by our civil war."

Dahlia's lips pull into a sneer. "Just because you and your pathetic allies will be distracted, doesn't mean we will be."

I bristle and force myself to keep my fury at bay. It takes all my control to hold my voice steady. "We'll be stronger together. Then as soon as the humans are dealt with, we can return to sorting out our grievances."

She doesn't even give it a second's thought. "I appreciate the warning, but no. We will not agree to a ceasefire."

I clench my jaw. Time to step up negotiations. "I have something you want."

Again, her composure falters, expression going blank. Her words come out clipped. "What would that be?"

"The very thing that made you try to take my palace," I say with a grin.

She studies me in tense silence before saying, "I don't know what you're talking about."

I put my hands on my hips, aware of their proximity to my hidden blades. "I think you do, Dahlia. Iron weapons. If you agree to a temporary ceasefire that lasts only as long as we must fight the human army, we will deliver the weapons to you once the army is defeated."

She pops a hip to the side, wings buzzing in agitation. "We do not agree," she finally says, although I swear there's a hint of regret in her tone.

Fire heats my cheeks at her easy dismissal. It wasn't supposed to go this way. I haven't even brought up the wall yet! No, this can't be how this ends. I must regain control over this conversation at once.

My gaze flashes to the gathering behind her. "I suggest you reconsider. Your allies are dwindling. All you have are pretenders. Without a united front, your little *council* won't survive the oncoming attack."

"That's what you think," she says with a grin that doesn't quite reach her eyes.

I study her, analyzing every tense muscle, the tick in

her jaw, seeking the truth beneath her feigned casual demeanor.

"How about this," she says, her mask of confidence regaining its hold over her features. "We will agree to a ceasefire, but we will not trade it for weapons. Instead, we will trade for something else, something we will claim at once. Otherwise, we will make no deal."

Dread sinks my gut, every instinct telling me whatever she has in mind can't be good. "What is it you propose we trade?"

"We will agree to this temporary ceasefire," she says, lips pulling into a devious smirk, "in exchange for you."

24

I stare blankly at the Summer Queen, blood draining from my face. When I regain my composure, I pin Dahlia with a glare. "What do you mean you want to trade for *me*?"

She looks at her fingernails, as if I'm no longer worth her attention. "It's exactly as it sounds. Give up your claim as queen, surrender to us, and we will agree to a ceasefire."

My fingers clench into fists as fire roars through my shoulders, my arms, my palms. "Why in the bloody name of iron would I surrender to you?"

She puts a hand on her hip, a scowl twisting her lips. "It's because of you that we're in this mess to begin with, Evelyn. You've already caused enough trouble, breaking the treaty and all. It's your fault this human army comes in the first place. Don't you think you owe it to your allies? To all fae? To the humans, even? For all we know, you stepping down as queen could be the very thing we need to repair the treaty or forge a new one."

My fire falters, draining from me at her words. Guilt sinks my heart, making my legs feel heavy. I feel how I did when I first learned my pairing with Aspen had been invalidated, then later when I learned my heritage was putting the treaty in jeopardy. All I wanted to do then was sacrifice myself. To do whatever it took to prevent war and bloodshed. The treaty was the only thing that stood between peace and war, and I was the only one who could stop it.

In this moment, it's like that all over again. Once again, I alone am responsible for the threat, and this one storms across the sea from the mainland. I feel like I'm the one at the helm of each of those warships, and only I can call them back.

It's just me. My life. My throne.

If I give it all up, the isle could be safe. All I've ever wanted was to save lives. That's exactly why I wanted to become a surgeon.

I can't deny this final chance for peace.

I open my mouth, my pulse racing at the words that nearly climb up my throat. But something tugs at my mind—a memory, one strong enough to give me pause. It surges through me with the echo of a voice. It's my mother's voice, fierce and strong and full of fire as she orders me not to make a deal with Mr. Duveau. Next, I hear Aspen's voice, posing the question of whether the treaty is worth saving at all. Then, it's my voice I hear, telling Aspen that Faerwyvae is my home, that I will sacrifice myself no more. Finally, I hear the words I said to the fire fae in the cave at Lunar, promising I would fight for the unseelie and to end the corrupt ways of both human and fae councils.

My fire returns to heat my blood as I remind myself who I am. I do not cower, I do not beg, and I certainly don't sacrifice my own life for my enemies.

I am Evelyn, Unseelie Queen of Fire.

"You had your chance," I say sweetly, "but I will agree to no such deal. Goodbye, Queen Dahlia." I turn my back on her and take a slow step away. I'm confident she'll call out for me to stop, to cave in and try to backtrack to my previous offer for the weapons.

But the words that come out of her mouth are not what I expect. "You won't agree? Not even to be with your sister?"

I freeze. I know she's bluffing, acting like they have Amelie even though I know better. But there's something about the bravado in her tone that chills my blood.

That's when I see it. Movement to the right.

I whip my attention toward it and see two figures skirting around the far end of the sand dune. They're far enough away from my allies that they haven't been noticed by the Alpha Alliance yet, but the direction they're coming from...

My blood goes cold. The camp.

I turn back to Dahlia, who wears a triumphant grin. "You think we didn't know your sister had returned to you?"

This is it. The moment I've been anticipating with both resignation and dread. The moment I get confirmation that Amelie truly has been lying to me, poised at every moment to betray me. Was every word planted by Cobalt from the start? Or was it her will all along?

Someone appears at my side, giving me a start before I realize it's Aspen. He's wreathed in the violet aura of the

Bond, eyes trained on the two figures that cross the stretch of land from Fire to Solar.

"What the bloody oak and ivy," Aspen curses between his teeth as Cobalt comes clearly into view.

I burn the traitorous male with a glare for only a moment before turning it on my sister. Cobalt grasps her around the waist, lifting her while her legs drag behind her. She's conscious, but the way she walks looks as if her legs have turned to lead, fighting gravity with every step. Her head lolls, face twisted, mouth open in a silent scream. It's enough to wipe the scowl off my face.

"This is a peaceful exchange of words," I say to Dahlia.

"And Cobalt has done nothing to compromise it," she says smoothly. "He simply reclaimed what was rightfully his. As Amelie is one of his mates, he has every right to take her back."

"She is not property."

She barks a laugh. "Oh? Is that why you kept her out of sight?"

I press my lips tight together, eyes flashing back toward Amelie. She truly appears to be in excruciating pain. That's when I remember the command I left her with: *do not leave this tent until I return for you.*

I reach for my fire to burn away the pity that sinks my heart. She may be in pain, but that doesn't mean she didn't betray me. "We're done here," I say. "You can have her."

"You're going to give her up that easily?" Dalia lets out a tittering laugh, then leans in, lowering her voice. "Cobalt may think we allowed him to seek her out for his own satisfaction, but he's wrong. His actions to harbor your sister when the treaty demanded both of you be exiled to the mainland is unforgivable. You may be the primary cause of the broken treaty, but he must pay a price for keeping her. And if it succeeds at punishing you too..." She doesn't clarify what she's hinting at, but her malicious smirk tells me enough.

I no longer know what to think, what to believe. Just moments ago, I was so certain Amelie was the traitor I'd always thought her to be. But now...

My hand moves slowly to my hip, fingers desperate to reach for the hilt of one of my iron daggers. Then my gaze moves to Aspen, still present through the Bond. He watches me knowingly.

If I react with violence, this peaceful exchange of words is at an end. Phoebe's winged soldiers will descend and chaos will break loose.

With a sigh, I begin to lower my hand.

"No," Aspen says, stilling me. His lips twist into a cruel grin that he pins on Dahlia. Of course, she can't see him, but the invisible threat fuels my inner fire. "I've already sent a guard back to our camp. If Cobalt didn't kill them all to take your sister, they'll be here any moment."

"Are you reconsidering my offer?" Dahlia says.

My fingers flinch toward my waist again. I send my words to Aspen through the Bond. *Are you sure? There will be no chance of a ceasefire.*

"There obviously never was to begin with," he says through his teeth.

I give a subtle nod. *Tell the others.*

In the blink of an eye, Aspen disappears. In that same moment, I reach for the nearest dagger on my weapons belt and lunge for the queen. Before she can react, I plunge the blade into her stomach. She calls out, eyes wide as she takes in the iron weapon protruding from her gut. I'm about to withdraw the dagger when I reconsider. The wound will only be fatal if it remains inside her long enough to poison her blood.

Footsteps pound behind me, the sound of the Alpha Alliance charging in. The Renounced surge forward as well, and I unsheathe two more iron daggers from beneath my gown. I advance toward Dahlia as she retreats from me, doubled over, face twisted in pain. Teeth bared, I prepare another strike of my blade, but a shadow swoops overhead, followed by the sound of flapping wings.

Winged fae descend from the sky, and one grasps long, curved talons beneath Dahlia's arms and lifts her high above me. In a matter of seconds, she's flown safely beyond my reach and out of sight.

Another set of talons is suddenly before me, and I have just enough time to lean back to avoid the deadly swipe. My fae opponent has a feline face with a mane of golden hair and wings like a falcon. She lets out a deafening roar before swiping out again. I duck under her reach and slice both blades across her ribs. She whirls back, hissing at the searing iron, but it only holds her back for a second before she charges again. This time, one of her claws grazes my left arm, opening the flesh over my bicep. I grit my teeth against the pain, fighting against the urge to drop the dagger from that hand.

Blood pours down my arm in rivulets of crimson, but I keep my eyes trained on my opponent as we circle each other. Sights and sounds of fighting surround us, but I don't let it distract me as I assess her height, her build, seeking weaknesses. Her talons seem to be her only defense, as she wears no armor, carries no weapon. Her body is composed of soft flesh covered in short golden-brown fur. If I strike her several times with iron, she'll eventually succumb to its effects. Grow weak. Heal slower. Even so, I hate to admit I'm at a disadvantage. Smaller. Shorter. Fleshy from head to toe.

But that's without my flames.

I let my rage fuel every part of me, let it surge through my veins, ignite my palms, and dance over my fingertips. It crawls up my arms, burns down my back. I feel it knitting the skin back together where I've been sliced open, stopping the flow of blood. The heat blankets me, but my flames cause me no pain. They feel comforting, strong. Like form-fitting armor made just for me.

My opponent's eyes widen at the sight of my tricolor flame, but she quickly replaces it with a glower. I fight my yearning to shift fully into my fox form, knowing human hands are needed to wield my iron blades.

"Is that all you have, human?" the fae teases. "Pretty little flames?"

I let my body form my reply, darting toward her with my daggers raised. As expected, she lunges with her talons, but I spin to the side, ducking under her arms, and grazing her forearm with the tip of one of my blades in the process. She hisses, and the momentary distraction gives me the opportunity to reach for one of her wings, letting the flames dancing over my arms ignite on contact. She swipes again, but I'm already retreating. She takes a step to close the distance but falters, her attention drawn to the fire crawling up her wings. The smell of singed feathers fills my nostrils, and as more of her wings are engulfed in flames, I suppress the wave of nausea that hits me. She begins to shout, spinning wildly to swat at the fire, but it's no use.

I'm frozen in place, torn over what to do. She's so distracted, I could charge in to make my killing blow. For a moment, I consider it a mercy, compared to the possibility of burning to death. Still, I find myself unable to move at all, consumed by a sudden horror at the thought of killing my opponent. I know I've killed before, but the others were personal or an act of self-defense. For the most part, I knew their crimes, their dark deeds. But this fae...

I retreat a step backward as my flames climb higher and higher up her back. My pulse races as I try to remind myself she's my enemy, but it's no use. Because the truth remains: for all I know, she could be like Foxglove or Lorelei. She could have been my friend or ally if the situation were different. It is only the queen she serves that pits her against me, not anything she's personally said or done.

I call back my flames, willing them to extinguish from her wings. As soon as they're gone, she falls to her knees in a wail of pain. I don't bother waiting to see the extent of the damage. All I can think to do is run, dodge the fighting pairs that surround me. Run from this field of growing carnage.

But there's nowhere to go. Nowhere safe from blood and blades.

Nothing to see but the bloodshed I've sparked.

25

When I resigned myself to break the treaty, I knew we'd go to war. I knew there'd be battles. Lives lost. But it's one thing to know and another to actually see it.

All around me the Alpha Alliance engage in bloody combat with the Renounced. My breathing is labored as I whirl around, daggers still clenched in my fists as I struggle to keep my wits about me. Half my attention is focused on preparing for oncoming attackers while the other half seeks a pair of antlers and blue-black hair amidst the chaos. Finally, I spot my mate in his stag form, fighting Queen Phoebe. The Solar Queen swings a gold-tipped spear in furious swipes, but Aspen meets each thrust and jab with his antlers. My heart lurches, seeing his fur matted in places with red, but my view of him is cut off as another fighting pair—King Flauvis, tearing his vicious fangs into the leg of the female sea fae—moves in front of them.

The sight chills my bones, but not because of the

blood that streams down the sea fae's scaly leg; it's because it reminds me of someone else.

Clenching my jaw, I steel my nerves and seek signs of Cobalt. My fire returns with every step I take, so strong I hardly register the soldier who charges me. It's another one of Phoebe's winged fae, this one far more humanlike, aside from his elongated beakish nose and tufts of feathers on the tips of his pointed ears. When he swipes out with his sword, I dodge back, blocking the tip with my crossed daggers. As he prepares another strike, fire encases my hands, dancing over my blades.

My intention wraps around the flame, shaping it to my will. Fire. Air. Movement. The fire leaves my daggers, hovering above them in a fiery, pink orb.

In a flash, I send the flame shooting to the curve of brown wings folded over the fae's shoulder. As it ignites the feathers, the soldier falters, slapping his palm in an attempt to stamp out the flame. I use the distraction to leave the fae behind, once again seeking Cobalt. I take hardly five steps before I'm forced to halt behind a writhing mass of bodies, groaning in agony. Above them, Nyxia, in her shadow form, reaches smoky black tendrils to each of their heads. She seems to grow larger and darker with every beat of my racing heart.

Keeping a wide berth, I skirt around the moaning fae to the edge of the battlefield. Finally, I see what I'm looking for.

Cobalt stands in the distance at the crest of a nearby dune, my sister locked in his arms. She still looks as if she's in pain, face twisted as she sags against him. I pump my legs and race toward them. Cobalt has the sense to look startled, stiffening as I draw near. He retreats a few steps, dragging my sister with him, then seems to think better of it. Instead, he stands his ground.

"Stop, Evelyn!" he shouts. "Can't you see she's being tortured?"

He doesn't say it like a threat, but his words slow my attack nonetheless. Keeping my daggers clenched tightly in my fists, I shift to a jog, only coming to a stop when I'm a dozen feet away. Everything in me wants to keep moving, keep closing the distance until Cobalt's neck is wrapped in my fiery hands. But even though he's refusing to join the battle, I must remember he's fought Aspen before and came out of it alive. He isn't harmless.

And now he has my sister.

"Did she give you her name?" he asks, pulling her tighter to his side. "Is that why she struggles to get back to your camp?"

I purse my lips, but it seems to be the only answer he needs.

"Renounce your command," he says, and there's a pleading quality to his voice. "Every moment she's forced to struggle against it is torture for her. You can't imagine the damage it could cause if it continues too long."

My heart squeezes as I go over the exact wording of the command I gave her. *Do not leave this tent until I return for you.* I gave no other expiration but my return. Is it possible her obedience would be enforced forever? I breathe in deeply to maintain my composure. "You should just let her go then."

"I will," he says, raising his free hand in a gesture of surrender. "Revoke your order and I promise I will let her go."

My eyes move from him to Amelie. She seems

completely unaware of all that's transpiring around her, eyes squeezed shut, face turning crimson as she screams soundlessly. He must have ordered her not to make a sound.

My hands begin to tremble. I can't let her suffer like that. I can't.

"Amelie." My voice fills with the power of her name. "I have returned to you. You are no longer required to wait in the tent for my return."

Just like that, her mouth snaps shut, tortured expression relaxing. As promised, Cobalt lets her go, and Amelie slides to the ground, limp, weak. Her copper hair hangs around her face and her shoulders heave as if she's sobbing.

When I return my attention to Cobalt, he's smiling. "Amelie," he says, dropping something onto the ground before her. It only takes a moment for me to realize it's a coral-bladed dagger. "Kill Evelyn."

My sister reaches a quivering hand to grasp the hilt and rises slowly to her feet. When her hair parts, her tortured expression returns. This time, tears stream down her cheeks, and her mouth moves, forming the word *no* over and over. With a heave, she lunges forward, movements wild and erratic.

Before I can consider it, the words leap from my lips. "Amelie, kill Cobalt!"

She halts mid-step, shoulders sagging as she whirls back toward him. His eyes widen for a moment before he points at me. "I gave the order first, kill your sister!"

Again, she turns to me, but she doesn't take another step. She begins to tremble from head to toe, subtly at first, then rippling into full-body convulsions. Her eyes roll back in her head and a stream of scarlet blood trickles from her nose, over her lips and chin.

"Revoke your commands," Cobalt says, eyes flashing from Amelie to me. "Revoke them now, or she dies!" Again, there's no threat in his tone, only mad panic.

"You revoke them first!" I shout back.

Amelie falls to the ground, convulsing in the dirt.

Cobalt puts a hand to his chest, his breathing labored as he watches my sister. Part of me knows this is the perfect time to attack Cobalt, catch him unaware, but the rest of me can't take my eyes off my sister. More blood continues to pour from her nose, her face turning a chilling shade of blue.

"Amelie, I revoke all orders." Cobalt's words come out strained, choked on a sob.

Amelie sucks in a deep inhalation, her convulsions calming back to a mild tremble, but she doesn't open her eyes.

Cobalt's gaze flashes to mine, his expression accusatory. "You must revoke yours too," he says with a sneer. "She's been overcome. She will not recover if you don't free her from your orders."

He could be lying. I know this. And yet, despite everything that's happened, every doubt I still hold about my sister's allegiance, I can't take the chance that my actions could be killing her.

"Amelie, I revoke all orders," I say.

Finally, she gasps again and goes still, the blue pallor already receding from her face.

"I'm so sorry." Cobalt steps toward Amelie, arms outstretched, but I leap forward, daggers raised.

"Don't touch her," I hiss.

His expression hardens, lips peeling back from his teeth as he meets my glare. "You could have killed her."

"Why do I get the feeling that would have been a mercy compared to everything you've done to her?"

"You know nothing! I love her."

My lips quirk into a cruel grin. "Well, she doesn't love you."

As if my words had been forged of barbed iron, he roars, head thrown back in agony as if struck by a fatal blow. He shudders. Once. Twice. Before my eyes, he shifts into his nix form, blue scales covering his body from head to toe, a crown of coral resting over his brow. His chest heaves with rage. "I will make her love me once you're dead." With that, he charges forward, sharp fingers outstretched with serrated webs in between.

I shift into a defensive posture, one dagger ready to swipe out in an arc, the other prepared to plunge straight into him, flames dancing over my body, hungry for his scales.

A flash of brown charges between us, knocking Cobalt down in the process. Aspen slashes his antlers into his brother. Where Aspen is ferocious, Cobalt is fast. He manages to roll out from under Aspen's enormous hooves, swiping a gash in the stag's leg in the process. Aspen doesn't falter, charging his brother with every retreat, pursuing him on and on until they take their fight to the other side of the dune.

My heart lurches, begging me to follow and see that Aspen is unharmed, perhaps even help him end Cobalt for good. But my attention snags on my sister's lifeless form. I return my blades to their sheaths and run to her side. Kneeling next to her, my fingers rush to check her pulse, finding it slow but steady. Then, taking her face in my hands, I slap her lightly on the cheeks. "Amelie. Amelie, wake up." There's no command in my voice, only urgency.

Finally, she begins to stir, eyelids fluttering open as she gasps for air. She mumbles, movements unsteady as she attempts to sit. It takes me a few moments to under-stand what she's trying to say. Then her words become clearer. "Where is he?"

"Cobalt? Aspen is fighting him. Are you all right?"

She succeeds at pushing herself up to sit and wipes the back of her hand across her mouth, smearing the blood that had dribbled down her face. Her chest caves in as she struggles to catch her breath, eyes unfocused. Then, with a snarl, her gaze narrows on me. "How could you do that to me?"

For a moment, I'm caught off guard. She's hardly shown an ounce of anger toward me since she first arrived at Lunar. I furrow my brow. "I'm sorry. I should have been the first to revoke my orders, but I didn't trust that he'd do so after I did."

"Not that," she says through her teeth. "You ordered me to kill him."

I lean back, fury heating my cheeks. "You're upset with me because of *that*? Because I ordered the very thing you've been begging me to let you do?" I rise to my feet and stare down at her. "After everything you said, you love him, don't you?"

"I *hate* him," she snaps. "And you had no right to rob me of the right to kill him with a clear mind. I told you, I want to see the life leave his eyes. I want to remember it forever. How can I do that if I'm trapped beneath the haze of your commands?"

My fury cools in the shadow of hers. In this moment, her rage is chilling, making her look so unlike the Amelie of my childhood. She's a feral creature, one hungry for blood and vengeance. It's enough to make my heart plummet. When I speak, my words come out strained. "Ami, this isn't the life for you."

"What do you know about it, Evie?" She rises angrily to her feet to face me eye-to-eye. "You've killed in self-defense. You've ended lives of terrible people. I've been *forced* to kill. For once, I want to kill of my own free will."

I shake my head. "It won't make you feel better."

"Is that why you tried to hunt down Mr. Duveau after Mother died? Why you burned down a brothel when you couldn't find him? Because it *didn't* feel good?"

A rush of guilt turns in my stomach. "How did you hear about that?"

She lets out a bitter laugh. "I may have lost half my mind, but I'm not stupid."

I clench my jaw, wondering if this is yet another piece of information shared by Foxglove or Lorelei. "Mind your own—"

"Oh look, you found each other," says a haughty, feminine voice.

I whirl to find Queen Dahlia, sauntering up to us, a tiny purple pixie hovering at her shoulder. The pixie carries a bright yellow flower that's almost as big as her, but my attention is pulled to the wound I gave the queen. The hilt of the iron blade I buried in her gut has been removed, the lesion bandaged. Her complexion is a little green, but she seems otherwise unharmed.

A rush of surprise washes through me. Who would have been able to tend to an iron wound so quickly? I figured the fae would have enough trouble removing the blade in the first place.

I reach inside my dress to retrieve a dagger, but a sudden puff of yellow dust obscures my vision. Gripping the hilt of my weapon, I blink rapidly to clear my eyes, seek out Dahlia. When the dust finally settles, everything around me begins to blur at the edges. Dahlia's pixie companion hovers before me, a mischievous smile on her tiny lips, flourishing the yellow flower in her hands.

That's the last thing I see.

26

I jolt awake into a world of agonizing pain. My mind feels slow, heavy, and all I can sense is cold. It burns my skin worse than any fire could, chilling me to my bones, my blood. My very soul.

My vision blurs as I pry my eyes open, blinking into whatever nightmare I've awoken to. When my sight begins to clear, adjusting to the semi-darkness of the room I'm in, I find the lower half of my body is submerged in icy water. It's contained in an elongated tub, like the troughs I've seen on the farms in Eisleigh. Ropes tie my ankles together and bind each of my wrists to handles on opposite sides of the tub. Panic surges through me as I whip my head from side to side. All I see are solid walls, a barred door, and my unconscious sister in the same predicament as I'm in, her tub just a few feet from mine.

It's clear now that we're trapped in a prison. A dungeon. And the ice-cold water tells me our captors have every intention of suppressing my powers.

My teeth chatter as I yank my wrists as hard as I can. It's no use, of course. I hardly have strength in my limbs to move, and the bindings are tied tight.

To my horror, my movement seems to stir a previously unnoticed presence, a dark silhouette leaning against the wall. I bite back a scream until my eyes fall on the shape of antlers. A sob of relief crawls from my throat as Aspen pushes off the wall and races to my side. "For the love of oak and ivy, you're awake." Warm hands move to my cheeks, and I nearly moan at the comfort they bring me.

"Get me out of here." My words come out weak, jagged through my chattering teeth.

His expression darkens, shifting between rage and sorrow as he brushes a damp strand of hair off my face. "I've tried. I can only touch you. Nothing else is affected by me."

Of course. Why didn't I see the violet aura before? Aspen isn't really here. "Did they take my daggers?" Not that they'd do us any good if Aspen's touch can only affect *me*. Still, I'd feel a lot better if I knew they were there.

Aspen leans in closer and slides his hand beneath one of the open sides of my sodden dress, running his fingers along my cold flesh. In any other situation, his touch would feel seductive. Right now, it only crushes me with disappointment. For if I can feel his hand flat against my back, then that can only mean my weapons belt has been taken. Damn.

"How long have I been..."

"Two days," he says, pulling back and moving his hands to my shoulders to warm them. "Do you know where you are?"

"The last thing I saw was Dahlia," I say. "There was a pixie with a flower. Some yellow dust. I'm guessing I'm in the dungeon at either Solar or Summer."

He shakes his head. "I've been to both palaces and seen both dungeons. This place is nowhere I've ever been."

A shudder runs through me that isn't from the cold. Where in the name of iron am I?

Aspen looks me over, taking in my violent shivers, my bound wrists, my damp cheeks, and pain lashes his face. Clenching his jaw, he rises to his feet with a roar. He stalks toward one of the walls and slams a fist into it. It makes no sound, creates no reverberation. "I can't stand to see you like this. I'm going to kill them all."

"What happened after I was taken?" I ask, each word a struggle while I fight the tremors that seize me. "Was anyone on our side injured?"

He leans on the hand that punched the wall, head low in defeat. "Not mortally. It was as if the Renounced were all waiting for something. Waiting for you to be taken." His eyes find mine, his gaze so full of rage and sorrow all at once. "Hardly any time had passed at all. One moment you were there with your sister, and I was fighting Cobalt. The next, a whistling call was made overhead, and the Renounced retreated."

"Cobalt?" I ask.

His eyes unfocus, a sneer pulling his lips. "He got away, taken to safety by one of Phoebe's winged soldiers. But not before I slashed out one of Cobalt's eyes."

"Where are you?"

"I've remained at the camp, along with Estel and

Nyxia. The others returned to their courts. As soon as we know where you are, we'll come for you."

I furrow my brow. "What about Estel's Chariot? Can't you use it to come here now that you've seen where I am?"

"I tried." His voice trembles with suppressed rage. "So many times I've tried. Visual reference of a place isn't enough if you don't actually know where it exists in the world. I need to know for certain where you are for my intent to fuel the device."

I mutter a curse under my breath, but mumbled words pull my attention to my side, where Amelie begins to stir. Her mumbles turn to moans and moans turn to screams. I lean as far toward her as I can within the restraint of my bindings. "Hush, Amelie!"

She pays me no heed as she thrashes in her tub. "What have I done?"

Aspen leaves the wall and darts toward us, eyes wide as he takes in the terror on Amelie's face, but of course there's nothing he can do. "What's wrong with her?"

"She always awakens like this," I say under my breath. Then, to my horror, the sound of footsteps pounding somewhere beyond the cell begins to draw near. "Amelie, quiet!" I hiss.

Her screams dissolve into sobs, head lolling to the side. The footsteps are closer now, just beyond the cell door.

I sharpen my tone, raise my voice just a little louder. "Amelie!"

At that, she goes still, blinking into the dim light of the room. She stifles a cry as she stares down at the water she's submerged in, the ropes binding her wrists and ankles. When her gaze turns to me, her breathing goes shallow, expression turning to panic. "Evie—"

A figure arrives at the door, cursing under his breath while he fumbles with the lock. "I leave for hardly any time at all…" The voice is unfamiliar, and I can't make out his face with the light coming from somewhere down the hall casting him in shadow.

Amelie's eyes flash from the figure to me. Her words come out in a whispered rush. "Order me not to obey any commands Cobalt might give me."

I don't give it a moment's thought. "Amelie, I command you to ignore any and all commands Cobalt might give you." I'm about to add a time restriction, but she shakes her head, making my mouth snap shut.

The figure enters the cell with an irritated sigh, every move stalked by Aspen, whose hands clench into fists at his sides. I can see his desire to pummel the male etched in the tic of his jaw, the fury in his eyes.

As the figure draws near, I make out his features. Tall, slim, with long white hair slicked back behind his pointed ears and falling far below his shoulders in silken sheets. He wears a long blue robe with silver embroidery, like something from a long-forgotten century. His eyes are slanted with pale blue irises, lips pursed with irritation. I think I recognize him from the meeting with the Renounced—one of the pretender kings. His appearance makes me guess he's from Winter.

"Where are we?" I force out, voice tremulous as my shoulders continue to shake from the chill.

The fae wrinkles his nose. "Some gods-forsaken place I've never desired to be," he mutters, then holds out a hand toward each of us.

I gasp in shallow breaths as the water grows notice-ably colder, a thin sheet of ice coating the surface.

Aspen slams a fist through the winter fae, but of course it's no use.

My words are even more of a struggle to bite out now. "Why...are you...doing this?"

"Why am I babysitting you when I'm supposed to be a king?" He seems to be speaking more to himself than either of us. "We're a joke. And two humans in exchange for thousands is supposed to make up for it." He lets out a bitter laugh.

Two humans in exchange for thousands. What's that supposed to mean? My mind spins to comprehend the implications, but all thoughts are stripped away when another set of footsteps sounds down the hall.

A whine comes from Amelie. She shakes her head, the sudden terror in her eyes telling me she recognizes those footsteps. It's no surprise when Cobalt's silhouette appears in the doorway.

What is surprising, however, is his appearance as he steps into the room; a leather patch covers one eye, so similar to ones I've used with Mr. Meeks when treating ocular damage. When Aspen said he'd slashed out one of Cobalt's eyes, I assumed it would heal and grow back. Then again, it makes sense that full removal of vital limbs and organs are unable to grow back. The evidence being the scars on Mikaela's back where the courtesan's wings had been shorn.

Aspen crosses his arms and glares at Cobalt. "It looks good, brother." His voice is thick with venom; I only wish Cobalt could hear it.

Cobalt falls to his knees before Amelie's tub, lips pulling into an agonized frown. "Amelie."

"Get away from me!" my sister shouts.

He blinks at her a few times, as if he can't comprehend her scorn. "I'm sorry, my love. They won't let me take you from here."

Amelie's lips peel back from her teeth. "Don't you dare use that word around me. *Love*. I am not your love and you are not mine. I hate you and you know it."

He puts a hand to his heart. "Dahlia deceived me. I never thought she'd trap you too."

I analyze his words backwards and forwards, hating how slow the ice-cold water is making my mind. What he's saying suggests he knew all along the Renounced were planning on capturing me.

"I promise you," Cobalt says, "I will get you out of here. I will free you and we will be happy—"

"Cobalt," Amelie hisses as she burns him with a glare. Even with the shivers that rack every inch of her body, her fury is palpable. She says his name again. Then again. "Cobalt. Cobalt." With every repetition, her pitch shifts, changes.

Her mate shakes his head. "What is it, Amelie? Why do you..." He freezes, face going pale.

"Cobalt." She says his name one more time, and this time, the hair on the back of my neck stands on end. I recognize the power wrapped in his name, her fury woven through each syllable. Even Aspen seems to notice, shoulders tense as he stares at my sister with wide eyes.

In a flash, Cobalt lurches away from her, scrambling to rise to his feet. His single eye bulges with terror as he backs away, tripping over his own feet. Before Amelie can say another word, he's gone.

Amelie screams, thrashing against her bonds, sending water and shards of ice splashing over the sides of the tub. "Come back here!"

The winter fae, unaffected by the tense exchange, lets out a bored sigh. "Quiet down." He approaches my sister, hand outstretched. The icy surface of the water in her tub begins to crack and ripple. I don't understand what's happening until I notice the orb of water in the fae's palm, growing larger and larger until it's the size of his head. Then it floats toward Amelie, which is threat enough to quiet her shouts.

Aspen stiffens and starts toward the fae, even though there's nothing he can do.

"What are you doing?" I ask, pulse racing as the ball of water hovers above her scalp. Then, with a snap of his fingers, the ball loses shape and douses Amelie, coating her hair, her face. She gasps for air, her shuddering more intense.

The winter fae turns a cruel grin to me. "Might as well teach you both a lesson."

Before I can react, a second orb of water crashes over my head, its icy shock turning my vision to black.

27

The cold. The cold is all I feel. Time loses meaning as I slip in and out of consciousness. The winter fae returns now and then to chill our water every time it grows even remotely comfortable. I only feel the slightest bit warm when Aspen visits through the Bond, rubbing his hands over my cheeks, my shoulders. Even if he were truly here, I doubt his actions would do much good.

For the love of iron, will this cold be the death of me?

Several times now, I've experienced what Mother once referred to as *an attack by water*. First, was when the kelpie took me under and Cobalt feigned his rescue. I must have come very close to losing my life by drowning, for I was unconscious for three days. Not long after that, Cobalt held me in a coral cage after pulling me underwater. I was sick and miserable afterward, but it wasn't nearly as bad as the first time.

This, however, is far worse than both combined because the attack is unrelenting.

And now I know how my mother felt.

This thought pursues me into wakefulness as I come out of my cold slumber. My nightmares were plagued with memories of Mother trapped in the icy tub at her trial, and now I wake finding that same fate cursed upon me. I blink into the dark, the only light coming from that same illumination from somewhere down the hall. I find no sign of Aspen or the winter fae. It's just me and Amelie, who sleeps in her tub, skin pale and tinged slightly blue. My heart squeezes at the sight, and a wave of terror writhes through me. Surely, this will kill her. Is it only our fae heritage that keeps us from succumbing to frostbite and death?

Again, I think of Mother. Mother trapped in a tub just like this one. Mother shaking and trembling at her trial. Mother with a bullet between her eyes. My breathing grows painfully shallow as a lump sears my throat as if barbed with razors.

I cry out, but it's stifled by another memory that ripples through me, one shocking enough to dispel my pain at once—Mother, flames dancing over her fingers despite the water that holds her. Mother melting her iron cuffs, fighting the guards with her fire.

It's the part I never recall. The part that always gets swallowed by the memory that follows this one. A bullet. Blood. Death.

This time, I push this latter away and linger on the former. Despite all odds, my mother was able to summon her flames to fight for her freedom. Could I possibly do the same?

My mind feels thick and heavy, but I seek my inner fire, searching for it buried beneath the depths of ice that tamp it down. Still, no matter how far I seek, it isn't there. For a flicker of a moment, I feel rage or anger, but it doesn't last. Each time a shiver runs through me, it's gone. Only cold remains. Water. Ice.

If only I were like the winter fae—

The startling realization is enough for me to feel a momentary warmth heat my core. I *am* like the winter fae. I may not have a natural affinity for ice or water, but I am a queen, which means I have access to all four elements. I've already proven my competence with fire, air, and even earth. Water can't be out of reach for me.

I shake my head to clear my mind, steel myself against the bitter chill that threatens to snap my bones. With the deepest breath I can take, I close my eyes and focus on the water that surrounds me. It hits me harder than before, as if I can feel the weight of every drop, every particle of ice that brushes my skin, that clings to my dress, the ends of my hair.

Focus.

I summon what I know about water. Hydration is obvious. Rivers, lakes, and streams. But if there's anything I've learned about the elements, it's that each contains layer upon layer of deeper meaning.

I recall my first visit to the Twelfth Court, and my meeting with the ethereal kelpie. He'd expressed his disdain over me and my kind, over our thoughtless invasion of fae land and sea. How did that relate to water?

My mind grows cloudy again, the chill threatening to drag me back to unconsciousness, but I bite the inside of my cheek to sharpen my thoughts. The pain brings me back into focus, and I home in on my memory of the kelpie.

Now I remember. We debated over whether the fae could feel emotion.

Emotion. That's it. That's the water element.

I sink into that, and an immediate rush of sorrow comes to greet me, swallowing me whole. The breath is stripped from my lungs as the moment Mother died plays over and over in front of me.

A bullet. Blood. Death.

It was over so fast, and it was all...

It was all...

It was...

"Evie?" Amelie's voice pulls me from the endless chasm of grief, returning me to the present. To my cold tub and the oppressive walls of the cell. It's then I realize I've been sobbing.

I swallow my tears and turn my head toward my sister to see her watching me with hazy concern, her lips a terrifying shade of blue. Memories of the sorrow that consumed me threaten to pull me back down, but I refuse to slip into them. Instead, I seek my rage, which slowly complies. No fire accompanies it, but it's enough to harden my heart, thrust the dangerous emotions away.

"Evie, what's wrong?" Amelie asks, voice weak and trembling.

I turn my anger—the only thing that makes me feel warm—on her. Narrowing my eyes to burn her with a glare, I speak through chattering teeth. "It was all your fault."

Her shoulders heave as a violent tremor rips through her. "What?"

"All of this. Everything." I swallow hard. "Getting caught. Mother's death. It's all your fault."

Her eyes widen for a moment, then she nods and turns her face forward. "You never told me how she died."

I let my rage grow, building a wall against her words. Even with the cold combatting all heat it could bring, the intangible barrier is an immediate comfort. "Yes, I did. Mother was sentenced to death because you refused to attend her trial."

Her shoulders sag. "I know. But how was she executed?"

My lips pull into a snarl. "Mr. Duveau shot her with an iron bullet and ended her life."

Silence stretches between us, and I wonder if she'll cry. Beg for forgiveness. But she does neither of those things.

"You're right," she whispers, lower lip trembling. "I don't think I ever admitted it out loud, but I am now. It's my fault. I killed Mother."

At that, I shudder, her unexpected confession far more chilling than the tub.

"I may not have had a choice in refusing to attend," she says. "I tried. I really did. I tried to get a letter to you after the one you sent me. Cobalt showed up just as my orders not to communicate were beginning to fade. I had a pen in my hand and ink had already begun to flow, but he stopped me. And yet, that's not when it began, is it?"

Her eyes meet mine, and I shake my head.

She continues. "It began when we arrived at Bircharbor. When I had my heart set on your fiancé. When I agreed to do whatever it took to be together. When I was stupid enough to fall for his lies and extend the very ability that allowed him to deceive me in the first place. To continue to deceive you."

Slowly, I nod, but my malice is beginning to fade. I can't help but recall the thought I've had many times now. If she hadn't betrayed me, I might be in her position right now. I might not be with Aspen.

Amelie's gaze turns to steel. "I did it. I killed Mother. And when this is all over, when I've killed Cobalt, I want you to take your final revenge on me. I want you to punish me. I want to feel every inch of pain you can give me until my dying breath."

Her face contorts, shifting from the sister of my childhood to the feral creature who lashed out against me for robbing her of the chance to kill Cobalt with a clear mind. The one who wants to watch the life fade from her mate's eyes, force him to peel his own flesh from his bones. I told her this isn't the life for her, but it's clear it's the life she's chosen. She wants revenge.

And not just on Cobalt. She yearns to have revenge on herself.

My heart feels like it's shattering in two.

Seeing the hatred in her eyes tells me she's already punishing herself more than I ever could. The realization unwinds me, melts my anger, freezes it in place like the water that surrounds me. Her permission to kill her makes me understand something else: I don't *want* to kill her. I don't want to hate her. Not really. Maybe I never did. I only want to hate her because it helps me hide the truth. That it isn't her I hate. It isn't her I blame. It's me.

It's *me*.

She is my mirror. We are one and the same.

The lump returns to my throat and with it comes a searing truth. It breaks through the shadows in my mind, battles the chains around my heart, and rises to the surface. A truth I despise more than any other.

"It isn't your fault," I say with a sob.

Amelie burns me with a glare. "Stop, Evie. I don't want your pity."

I shake my head, feel words rising from my gut like bile. Words I can't keep from either of us a moment longer. "You may have started this, but you never acted alone," I say in a rush. "You alone didn't kill Mother. At the very end, I had a choice that could have saved her life. A bargain was offered, one that would have defiled my body and shattered my pride. She told me not to accept it. She wanted me to fight. She wanted us to fight together. But even knowing what she wanted doesn't make it better, for the choice still rested with me. In the end, I refused the bargain, and it resulted in a bullet in Mother's forehead. That was me. I killed her."

I expect another lash of pain, for that chasm of grief to return to finish the job, for endless black to consume me until I'm nothing more than dirt and ashes. Instead, I feel empty. An emptiness that feels an awful lot like peace.

Amelie remains silent, her gaze neither accusatory nor pitying. There's only a dawning understanding in her eyes. I stare back at her, waiting for her to speak. When she does, her words are quiet. Weak. "Mother had a choice too. We all had choices. Some of them might have been wrong, but her choice not to let you sacrifice yourself wasn't a wrong choice."

"But I still must live with the part I played. I don't know how to get over that."

She attempts a shrug despite her bonds. "Do we ever

get over the choices we make that lead to another's death? Will I ever be able to look at my hands and not see Melusine's blood? What else can we do with our grief but let it eat us alive?"

The answer comes to me right away. It's what Aspen would say if he were here. *Take it to the Twelfth Court.*

My breath hitches, and I repeat it out loud. "Take it to the Twelfth Court."

Amelie furrows her brow. "What does that mean?"

I ignore her. Closing my eyes, I throw my head back with equal parts gratitude and irritation. Why didn't I think of this before? My flames may be thwarted but that shouldn't stop me from shifting. The Renounced don't know about my unseelie form; only Ustrin did, and he died before he could share what he knew. My unwitting captors put nothing in place to stop a fox.

The Renounced underestimated me.

Now I'll make them pay for it.

28

I t takes longer than usual to seek my fox form, like grasping water, only to find it shapeless and running through your fingers. I know it's there. I know I can reach it. If both Aspen and Franco were able to shift in Eisleigh, where the wall weakens fae magic, then I should be able to from this predicament as well.

"Evie, are you all right?" Amelie asks.

"Stay silent." My words come out harsher than I intend, but I can't afford the distraction right now.

I ignore my sister's worried protests and steel myself against the cold, trying to imagine the burning chill feels more like fire than ice. I let it wrap around me, ignite my rage. Focusing my mind's eye on the faces of those who've put us here—Dahlia, Phoebe, Cobalt, that infernal winter fae—I seek my inner fire, even just a spark.

There.

The flame is tiny, just an ember at the center of my core, but it's enough. Closing my eyes, I take that minuscule fire to the Twelfth Court.

At first, nothing happens. No violet haze, no buzzing particles of energy to swirl around me, shifting my form. I let my disappointment turn to fury, let fury turn to flame, let flames grow brighter, hotter.

Then it happens.

Violet falls over my vision, and just like that, my fox form feels near. I summon her forth, feeding her all my rage and sorrow, giving her the energy she needs to transmute it into physical change. I feel a buzzing in my hands, like flames dancing over my skin as my wrists grow narrow. The ropes that bind me begin to feel loose as my hands shrink to paws. A momentary pain shoots through me at the unnatural angle my fox limbs are being stretched, but as I shrink smaller, smaller, I slip from my bonds altogether.

Amelie cries out in alarm as I'm plunged beneath the icy water on my back. In a swift roll, I right myself and break my head above the water. As a fox, the chill is far more bearable, but I still can't call it pleasant. Lacking much grace, I scramble out of the tub and shake the icy water from my fur. I'm panting by the time I'm freed from as much of the water as I can, but the warmth that envelops me outside the tub is more pleasurable than anything could be in this moment.

"Evie?" The word is strangled, quavering.

I turn my attention to my sister, finding her startled expression fixed on me. "Time to go," I say to her and dart toward one of the tub's handles where her wrists are bound. Grasping the rope between my teeth, I gnaw, feeling each fiber snap as I work my way through the thick coil. When it comes loose, I run to the opposite side and free her other wrist.

Amelie shakes out her hands, eyes locked on me. "Is that really you, Evie?"

"Yes, Ami," I say. "Now hurry and untie your ankles. We need to get out of here."

Her gaze lingers on me only a moment longer before she leans forward to work out the knot binding her ankles together. When her cold fingers don't seem to obey, I have her swing her legs over the edge of the tub so I can chew the ropes apart.

Fully free, Amelie rises on unsteady feet, her dress dripping water on the floor of the cell. I run to the barred door, my heart sinking at the next obstacle that awaits. My fox form is slim enough to squeeze through the bars, but what about Amelie? I assess the length of the door, seeking a solution. It's then I realize the bars are steel.

Steel. An iron alloy. In a fae prison?

Even though iron alloys are only harmful to fae who have been weakened by pure iron, I can't imagine the fae would ever utilize something like steel. I remember how unbearable Aspen and Lorelei had found my steel surgery tools when they were recovering from iron injuries.

I shake the thoughts from my mind and refocus on my task. There's only one solution I can think of. But for this, I'll need hands.

Shifting back into my seelie form, I extend my palms toward the bars. "Stand back," I tell Amelie. I can feel her wide eyes burning into me, but she obeys. I seek my inner fire again, horrified that it remains hardly a flicker. Shifting forms seems to have dried most of the icy water from me, but still, my connection to my magic feels weaker than ever before. I know the detrimental effects an attack by water can have, but...

Steel bars. Weakened magic.

My stomach sinks at what these implications must mean, but again I train my mind on what needs to be done. Closing my eyes, I summon my rage and fury, my sorrow and grief. Cobalt's face flashes through my mind, then Dahlia's. Ustrin's. Duveau's. I recall Maddie Coleman's smug expression when she taunted me over taking my place as Chosen. I return to Mr. Meeks' underground lab, feel the searing pain as his knife cuts through my arm. Mr. Osterman's vile hungers. Madame Rose's cruel brothel.

I let my anger grow, let it rush through my veins until an inferno roars inside me, begging to be released. Finally, I allow myself to think of Mother. But not the moment of her death. The moment she produced flame when it should have been impossible. The moment she told me to fight.

In a flash, fire ignites over my palms. Its heat warms me like a lover's caress, soothing me, healing all remnants of cold and ice. I open my eyes, taking in the pinks, purples, and aquas of my flames before I return my attention to the barred door.

Air.

I breathe in deeply, feeling the air flood my nostrils, imagining it moving through my body and down my hands to join the flame. It surrounds it, moves it, sways it. I see where I want it to go, and the air obeys. My flames leave my hands to dance over a portion of the door. In seconds, the bars glow orange, reaching a molten state before my eyes. As the metal begins to drip and pool on the stone floor, I realize my plan is far from complete. While I may be able to leap over a pool of molten steel if I shift back into my fox form, Amelie cannot.

Earth.

Just like with my river of melted weapons, I connect to the liquid steel through the element of earth. Logic. Safety. Mixing with air, I lift what has spilled onto the floor, shaping it into an orb. As my flames melt what remains of the door, I gather the rest of the molten steel into my orb, letting it hover before me, my outstretched hands guiding it where I want it to go. I shift it from beneath the door, moving it into the hall.

"Come on," I whisper to Amelie. Slowly, we step out of the cell and into the corridor, following the orb. Once on the other side, I guide the orb back into the cell, preparing to set it down near the tubs. Before I do, I separate a smaller piece and call it back toward me. The larger portion I allow to dissolve into a molten puddle.

Amelie gasps. "How are you doing this?"

"Not now," I say, returning my attention to the hall. It is long, dark, and narrow with no windows. One side disappears into darkness, while the other ends with light —a single torch set in a sconce. We make our way toward it, past rows of black, empty cells. I keep my small molten orb before me, let it illuminate the shadows in the absence of torchlight. As we continue, the hall curves to the right, on and on. At first, I think it's going to bring us back around in a circle, but as the cells come to an end, the floor takes on an incline, then stairs. The walls are empty stone now, with only the occasional torch along the way.

Finally, one last torch illuminates the end of the hall. A door. And a slumbering figure dozing against the wall.

The winter fae.

I motion Amelie to stop, but it's too late. Our footsteps have woken him, sent him lurching upright. He blinks several times, as if he can't believe his eyes. Then he raises his hands, long, sharp icicles forming in each fist like knives. Maintaining focus on my molten orb, I move air around it, let it shape the metal into an elongated point. Pulling back my flames, the steel begins to cool until a red-orange dagger remains.

His eyes widen and he swallows hard, looking from me to the threat that hovers in the air between us. The icicles tremble in his hands.

He's scared. Of *me*.

As he should be.

I could kill him. With the flick of my wrist, I could direct the makeshift dagger straight to his heart. Even if I missed, I could still strike him, disable him, melt the steel and embed it so deep no fae healer could remove it. But just like with the winged soldier I fought on the battlefield, I hesitate. Why do I hesitate? Why is it sometimes so easy to defend myself and other times I'm weak?

But am I truly weak? Or is there a difference between self-defense and cold-blooded killing? A difference between justice and cruelty?

I take a deep breath, keeping my weapon hovering in place. "I don't have to hurt you," I say. "You can let us go."

He barks a laugh, but it doesn't diminish his obvious fear. "Let you go? Why should I do that?"

I recall the bitterness he's shown, the way he tended

to us as if the duty were an insult to him. "Because you're fighting for the wrong side."

"I'm fighting for the side that would make me king."

"And how's that going for you?"

He shakes his head with a sneer. "It's a joke. This is all a joke. Two humans for thousands. It's a disgrace."

There it is again. *Two humans for thousands.* "Let us go." I inch my dagger closer, my eyes locked on his. "Or I will have to hurt you."

Sweat beads at his brow as his gaze flashes to my blade. Silence wraps around us. One of us will have to make the first move, and it looks like it will be me.

"Fine," he says through his teeth. Lowering his hands, the icicles disappear. "Go ahead and leave."

I eye him through slitted lids, watch as he leans against the wall, arms crossed over his chest. The tip of my dagger remains trained on him with every move we make. Amelie and I inch forward, my sister pressed close to my back. Keeping a wide berth, we skirt around the winter fae to the door. When we reach it, I give him a reluctant nod of thanks.

He doesn't bother looking at me. "Letting you go isn't a mercy," he says with a smirk. "Wait and see. I've just had enough of this pathetic *council*." With a shudder, he shrinks, replaced a moment later with a sleek white ermine with a black-tipped tail.

Amelie bites back a startled squeal, and I push open the door. The ermine darts between our legs, disappearing into the night. We don't wait long to follow suit, rushing up the short staircase that opens onto a stone walkway. We pause once under the open night sky, the moon bright overhead. Grasping the hilt of my dagger, the metal still warm to the touch, I begin to turn in a slow circle to gather our bearings. Amelie's fingers grasp my free hand. I squeeze her palm.

The first thing I see is a towering structure. A lighthouse. Ancient and built from weathered stone, an undeniably human building.

My stomach sinks. The steel bars. My weakened magic. The reason Aspen has never seen the dungeon we were held in. It's because we aren't in Faerwyvae. We're in Eisleigh. But where? Why?

The next thing I see is the crumbling wall that extends to either side of the lighthouse—an old fortification. The sight is so familiar, although it's nothing I've ever seen in person. Perhaps in a history book? A painting? The smell of salt tingles my nostrils, followed by the rhythmic sound of waves.

Then it dawns on me. I know where we are. This is Varney Cove.

During the first war with the fae, the humans used Varney Cove as a naval base to defend against the sea fae, and the lighthouse was repurposed as a fort. But why in the name of iron are we here?

Amelie gasps, her grip on my hand growing suddenly tighter. I whirl to follow her line of sight. Behind us stand rows and rows of tents. Military tents, the kinds I've only seen depicted in the broadsheets.

I feel like my throat will close up from the effort it takes to suppress the scream that builds in my chest.

I can only think one thing. *They're here. They're here. They're here.* The mainland army is here and we're too late.

Aspen, I whisper down the Bond. *Aspen, I know where we are.*

I continue to take in the rows of tents, my eyes falling on the one at the far left bearing the scrolling *B* crest of mainland Bretton alongside a second symbol—the winged staff denoting a place of medical practice.

Now I know how Dahlia received such quick care from the iron injury I gave her. The Renounced have allied with the humans. And not just any humans. Soldiers from the mainland, sent by King Grigory—the King of Bretton—himself. But to what end? *Two humans for thousands.*

Movement catches my eye, sending my heart hammering against my ribs, but it's just Aspen, violet aura rippling around his form. He heard my summons.

Storming over to me, he grasps my shoulders in his warm hands. "Where are you?"

"Varney Cove in Eisleigh," I rush to say.

He repeats it under his breath, then looks around, as if committing each sight to memory. When his gaze falls on the army camp, he mutters a string of curses. "I'm coming for you, Evie." Without another word, he's gone.

I'm left blinking at the place he was, hoping against hope that he now has all the information he needs to use the Chariot. Then again, perhaps I should have waited until I got us farther from the camp. If Aspen comes here, it will be to the heart of a viper's nest, surrounded by a human army with human weapons. Weapons that could end his life in an instant.

At least the camp is asleep, I remind myself, willing my quavering breaths to go silent.

Amelie trembles at my side. "We should run," she

whispers. "Why are we still here?"

"Aspen's coming for us." Before the words finish leaving my mouth, another flash of movement enters my periphery. My pulse races, fueling a spark of hope. But it isn't Aspen that's returned. It's a human guard, marching along the inside of the wall, a rifle held against his side.

I grip the hilt of my makeshift dagger tighter, wishing I knew the first thing about creating an invisibility glamour. Perhaps another kind of glamour could work. If I can lock his gaze when he sees us—

There's no time. Before I can react, his rifle is leveled straight at us. "Prisoners escaped!" His voice rings out, shattering the silence of the night. Movement erupts in the camp, soldiers rushing from their tents while more guards close in from their previously unseen posts. Footsteps pound the stone behind me, spilling out from the lighthouse tower. I flash my dagger toward one threat then another while Amelie presses in closer. Closer. The barrels of countless rifles form a ring around us.

One dagger against an army. Not the best odds. Even if Aspen were to suddenly appear, even if he brought all the fae the Chariot could transport, could we even make it out of this alive?

"Evie," Amelie cries.

"I know," I bark under my breath. "I'll—"

"Who is that?" She nudges my left side, prompting me to whip my attention toward the lighthouse. There the soldiers have parted to reveal a smug-faced Queen Dahlia. But that's not who Amelie was inquiring about. For standing before the Summer Queen is my greatest foe.

Mr. Duveau.

29

"Evelyn Fairfield," Mr. Duveau says, taking a step closer.

Heat courses through my body at the sight of my mother's murderer. I grit my teeth against the urge to lunge for him, to plunge my blade into his heart. As much as the thought fuels my fire, I know I wouldn't live long enough to see it through. Not with all these rifles and armed soldiers surrounding us.

Instead, I burn him with a scowl. "Hearing you say my name doesn't quite have the same ring to it anymore. Do you know what I mean?"

His expression darkens, but he maintains his composure. He seems somewhat changed since I last saw him, as evidenced by the dark circles beneath his lower lashes, his bloodshot eyes, the slight dishevelment of his hair. Even his formerly slim mustache has grown unruly, stray hairs brushing the snarl of his upper lip. Keeping his eyes on me, he speaks to Dahlia through gritted teeth. "I thought you said she was contained."

"She was," the Summer Queen says, tight lipped as she eyes me with clear disdain. "How did you get out, girl?"

I turn my glare on her. "Wouldn't you like to know."

She opens her mouth, but a human guard rushes up the stairs from the underground cells and whispers something in Mr. Duveau's ear. Dahlia's eyes widen at whatever she overhears, but the councilman only looks amused.

"It seems you're up to your mother's tricks," he says to me.

"My apologies, Councilman Duveau," Dahlia says, a pleading quality in her tone. I'm shocked to see her debase herself even slightly before a human. "I will have her returned to her bindings at once—"

"No need," Mr. Duveau says sharply. "I know how to make her obey."

I brace myself, squeezing the dagger tighter as he reaches beneath his jacket and withdraws a familiar weapon. My eyes lock on the barrel of the revolver as he cocks the hammer. I've faced this weapon before, but without the power of his name under my control, I know I can't still his hand the way I once did. My heart races as I assess the distance between us, trying to calculate how fast I could throw my makeshift blade before he can fire the gun. Perhaps if I wield air to direct its momentum, ensuring a direct hit to—

My thoughts go still as he moves the gun. Not to fire it. Not to bring it closer to me. He aims it at Amelie.

My sister bites back a squeal, her fingers digging into my forearm as she grabs me.

"Don't move," Mr. Duveau orders. "Either of you."

Every inch of me is frozen, aside from my raging heart that pounds in my chest. With his gun trained on my sister, every reckless idea I have loses viability. I hate that he's using her against me. I hate that he was right.

I know how to make her obey.

Threaten someone I love. That's all he has to do. That's all anyone has to do.

And after everything I admitted, both to Amelie and myself when we were trapped in the cell, I can acknowledge that I do in fact love her. For the love of iron, I love her fiercely. I can't let anyone take her away from me again.

"What do you want?" I ask, feigning as much calm as I can. Surely, he can see the way my shoddy weapon trembles in my hand.

"First, release the dagger."

I hate to leave us defenseless, but what else can I do? The barrel of the revolver is aimed at my sister's head. Even if I could dive in front of her, she's taller than I am. He'll kill her just like he killed Mother. My fingers feel stiff as I open them one by one. Then, with a thud, the metal falls from my grasp to the ground at my feet.

Duveau nods to a nearby soldier, who rushes in to retrieve the discarded dagger. The soldier wrinkles his brow once he has it in his hand, clearly unimpressed by my workmanship. Mr. Duveau's eyes flash toward it, just long enough to see what I made. His gaze returns to me, a smirk on his lips. "Really, Evelyn? You thought you could take us down with that?"

I press my lips tight to avoid saying something I'll regret.

"You," he says, expression turning serious as his

attention moves to my sister. "Take a step away from her." When Amelie makes no attempt to obey, he waves the gun, emphasizing the direction he wants her to move.

With trembling steps, she inches away from me. Her fingers release my forearm, leaving my flesh cold in their absence. It takes all my restraint not to reach for her.

"Guards," Mr. Duveau barks. The soldiers shift, each step sure and calculated as some back away and others move in closer, until about a half-dozen men form a tighter circle around us. Revolver still trained on Amelie, Mr. Duveau's attention returns to me. "You will come with me willingly. Otherwise, these men pump you full of iron bullets. And that's after you watch me kill your sister. Agreed?"

I burn him with a glare. While I don't refuse, I don't argue either. "Where are we going?"

Duveau ignores me, motioning forth a soldier outside our ring of guards and whispering a string of orders. I hear the words *tub* and *water*, which tells me he plans on returning us to our former captivity. But when next he speaks, it isn't to order us back to the dungeon. "Turn around and walk," he says, nodding in the opposite direction, away from the lighthouse.

Dahlia's brow furrows as she eyes Mr. Duveau. "Where are you taking them?"

"You know where," he answers without looking at her.

"But...how? How will you get them there?" There's no worry for me and my sister in her eyes. It's something else that has her suddenly so flustered.

"On my new ship," Duveau says through his teeth.

Crimson rises to the Summer Queen's cheeks. "I thought that was supposed to be *my* ship."

"You thought wrong."

Her fingers clench into fists. "What about our deal? I have a war to win. We're giving you the girls. We promised you a new treaty."

Finally, he leaves my gaze to pin Dahlia beneath a scowl. "And I'm giving you an army."

Two girls for thousands. There's my answer.

There's still so much I don't understand though. All those dozens of warships the human assailant mentioned...they were coming to aid Dahlia? How can that be? The assailant said *the time of the fae is at an end.*

The fae. Not just the Alpha Alliance.

He will ruin all of you.

"We agreed to more than this," the Summer Queen says, an edge to her tone. "Not just a single garrison."

Duveau lowers his voice. "You will get more as soon as I send word to the rest of the fleet. Once I'm on the ship with the girls, I'll know you're worth your word."

Her eyes flash dangerously, but she makes no further argument. Finally, with a begrudging nod, she takes a step back. Mr. Duveau's eyes immediately find mine. "Move!" he shouts, thrusting his revolver at my sister.

Amelie jumps, and I whirl around, nudging her with my elbow to follow suit. We begin to walk in the opposite direction toward the other end of the crumbling wall. Progress is slow as each step is mirrored by our circle of guards, who maintain an uncomfortable proximity at all times. The only benefit to our pace is that it gives Aspen more time to find us.

Then again, do I even want him to find us? Now that

we've awoken the entire camp, there's no way he could make it out of here alive.

Aspen, I send down the Bond. *Don't come here.*

I hear nothing in response, filling my heart with dread.

As we reach the end of the wall, the ground shifts to a decline where old stone steps lead the way down the side of the cliff beneath the lighthouse. With the morning sun beginning to rise, I get my first glimpse of the sea. It spreads out below us, beneath the cliff. And not too far from the beach is a massive black shape. A warship. Additionally, dozens of soldiers pace the beach, some guarding a smaller sea vessel while others offload the crates it carries, crates of what I can only imagine are weapons.

I nearly trip on the next step and force my eyes to return to the crumbling stairs.

"What's going on?" Amelie whispers.

"No talking," comes Duveau's voice from behind. Even though I can't see his revolver, I can feel its presence all the same, nipping my heels, dragging invisible black claws down my sister's spine.

Once the stairs meet sand, I catch yet another sight of the warship, a hulking mass far more terrifying than the broadsheets depicted. Its body is long and angular, smoke billowing into the air while impossibly tall, slim towers pierce the sky. The deck is lined with turrets armed with enormous guns, ones I never wish to see fired.

I shudder at the sight. War on the mainland always seemed like a faraway thing, something that could only ever involve the larger landmasses and countries, never the Fair Isle. But here it is, lurking outside my isle. My home.

We continue forward, our guards ushering us toward the smaller boat. A pair of soldiers offload the last crate, leaving the sea vessel mostly empty, aside from two men who stand at what must be the helm. The levers and mechanical panels tell me this boat is unlike anything I've seen before; its technology is likely closer to that of the warship. At a nod from Mr. Duveau, one of the boat's operators turns to the controls, and the vessel roars with the deafening sound of a motor coming to life.

"Get on the boat," Mr. Duveau orders.

My heart races as Amelie and I obey, my mind spinning to find a way out of this. But every move I can think to make only ends in Amelie's death. And my own.

Once we reach the center of the boat, Mr. Duveau orders us to face him. I steel my nerves as we slowly turn around. Fury rushes through my veins at Duveau's triumphant grin.

"What will you do with us now?" I ask. To my credit, my voice somehow manages not to shake.

"You're coming with me back to the mainland," he says. "And don't even bother with fantasies of escape. Unlike your little friends, you'll find your new guards far less lax." Another reminder of the rifles still pointed at us, unwavering in the hands of the soldiers.

"What then?" I ask, if only to keep him talking. Anything to give me more time to think of something. Anything. I still have my fire. It may be weaker than I'd like, but it's there, hovering just below the surface of my skin. I know how to shape it with air. Know how to manipulate the metals of earth. That's got to be worth something, right?

Mr. Duveau hazards a quick glance behind him. My eyes flash over his head, where I see two sets of guards heaving our tubs down the steep steps below the cliff. He's waiting for them before we depart.

Good. That means I still have time.

"There I will present you and your sister to King Grigory, show him I alone was able to apprehend the two girls who put the treaty in jeopardy."

Half my mind analyzes his words, while the other half assesses our surroundings, the space between me and Amelie and our armed guards. I quirk my lips in a teasing grin. "Trying to save face for the blunders you made?"

His expression darkens. "Those weren't my blunders. Those were yours. You nearly ruined everything."

I bat my lashes, shaping my next words carefully. I know they'll put me on thin ice, but I need to rattle his confidence without inviting deadly reproach. "Sounds like *your* blunders, if a single girl could upend your standing with the King of Bretton so easily."

"Shut up," he says through his teeth, face flushing crimson. "You know nothing. I tried to fix everything a different way, but those attempts proved fruitless."

The memory of the thief sent to my palace comes to mind. "You mean the weapon you tried to steal? How was that going to fix anything?"

He purses his lips, studying me for a moment. "You do have it, don't you? It's still at Irridae just like I thought, isn't it?"

Heat flushes the back of my neck as I consider it may not have been the wisest to bring up the Parvanovae. A quick change of subject is in order. "And now you're making a deal with the fae in order to make up for your failures? How's that going to work?"

He regathers some of his composure. "Your enemies are my allies because we want the same thing. Peace on the isle."

I bark a laugh. "Peace? Is that what you call giving power-hungry fae the means to destroy their own people?"

"I don't care what the fae do to each other, so long as it serves the greater good of Eisleigh."

I study his face, the tick in his jaw. "There won't be a treaty with the fae, will there?"

"What are you talking about?"

"I wonder...does Dahlia suspect you plan to betray her? Will her gifted soldiers turn on her as soon as the other warships arrive, or after the armies have killed her enemies?"

He refuses to rise to my bait. "I have no idea what you mean."

I'm right. I know it. He didn't forge a deal between the King of Bretton and Queen Dahlia. He just found a convenient way to get human soldiers on fae soil without a fight.

"I don't know who disgusts me more right now," I say with a sneer. "You, for obvious reasons. Or Dahlia, for being a big enough fool to trust you."

His eyes blaze as he takes a step forward. "Watch your mouth. Don't forget whose life is at stake."

That silences me, but my mind remains active, fire coursing through my veins, gathering at my core in a fiery orb. It glows so hot with my rage that it takes all my restraint to keep it beneath the surface of my skin. I can't summon it forth for the others to see. Not yet. Not until I connect to the other elements, figure out how to send my flames outward in all directions at once—

Mr. Duveau takes a sudden step forward. All fire drains from me as he presses the barrel to Amelie's forehead. "Stop!" he shouts at me. "Whatever you're thinking, whatever you're doing, stop. I can see the calculations in your eyes."

"Evie," she cries, voice strangled.

I raise my hands in surrender, force my words out as calmly as I can. "I'm not doing anything."

Revolver still pressed firmly against Amelie's forehead, Mr. Duveau calls out to the soldiers still making their way across the beach with our tubs. "Hurry up! Fill them with the coldest water you—"

"Get away from her." The voice that rings out from the beach isn't one of the soldiers. It's Cobalt. Shimmering blue scales cover every inch of his nix form, chest heaving as he pins Mr. Duveau beneath a glare with his single eye. His empty eye socket remains hidden behind the leather patch he had on before. The soldiers on the beach turn their rifles on him, but he pays them no heed.

Keeping his gun in place, he whirls to the side to eye Cobalt. "What are you doing? We're in an alliance," he calls out.

"Amelie wasn't supposed to be part of it."

A guttural sound comes from my sister, and I turn my head to catch the hate twisting her face. She no longer seems to care about the revolver kissing her skin. "Cobalt," she mutters, then changes her tone, her pitch. "Cobalt. Cobalt."

My blood goes cold. This may not be the best time for Amelie to focus on vengeance. I hush her, but she continues to say his name again and again, her voice growing louder each time.

Luckily, Duveau seems too distracted by Cobalt to notice. "You're wrong," Mr. Duveau says. "This is indeed vital to my agreement with your people."

As the soldiers on the beach inch closer to Cobalt, he extends his sharp fingers, curling them as if he's preparing to swipe.

"Stand down or die," Mr. Duveau says. "I doubt your friends will be too upset if I kill you, considering they've all agreed what must be done."

Cobalt pauses, gaze locking on Amelie. His brow furrows as Amelie continues to speak his name.

Mr. Duveau whirls back to her, finally aware of her mutterings. "Why are you doing that?" He pulls back the gun just enough to tap it against her forehead. Fire lights the tips of my fingers, the orb reforming at my core. When Amelie doesn't stop, Duveau swings the gun away from her, as if preparing to strike her with it.

"Cobalt!" Amelie shouts, the power of his name ringing through her voice. "Kill these men."

At the same moment, calls of alarm come from the lighthouse, followed by gunfire.

30

Cobalt spins into action in a whirl of blue, darting toward the nearest set of soldiers. Gunfire rings out all around, both above and below the cliff. From here, I can't see what's going on at the lighthouse, but I can feel it. I can feel my mate's proximity. He actually came.

Which means those bullets above the cliff are for him.

My heart lurches over Aspen's unknown fate, but I force my attention back to the scene before me. With the chaos of gunfire, the beach falls under a haze of disrupted sand, leaving only a vague image of the action taking place, of several dark shapes and one blue. The human shouts I hear are far more telling.

Amelie's smile is vicious, eyes fixated on the beach. She takes a step forward as if to join the mayhem, sidestepping Mr. Duveau's revolver while his attention is drawn away.

"Stop!" one of our guards shouts, and Mr. Duveau

whirls back around, stopping Amelie in her tracks. Some of the fight leaves her eyes as she seems to remember the very real threat before her. Slowly, she lifts her hands in surrender and takes a step back.

"Go!" Mr. Duveau calls above the din.

Vertigo seizes me as the boat lurches into motion. Amelie grabs my arm as we both struggle to keep our feet beneath us.

"Get away from each other," Duveau orders, and we rush to separate.

With my legs somewhat stabilized against the motion, I return my attention to the beach, feeling my heart sink at how far away it already is. My eyes flash to the lighthouse, watching it shrink with every second. *Aspen, please tell me you're alive,* I think to myself, not daring to use the Bond in case it distracts him from protecting his life. I squint, wishing I could see what was going on up there.

Something above the lighthouse snags my attention, a small, dark shape making lazy circles in the sky.

A raven.

Do I dare think...

Its circles spread out farther, over the beach, over the sea. Then the bird suddenly changes course, heading straight for us.

I suppress a smile.

Mr. Duveau flashes a glance over his shoulder, trying to glimpse what has me so amused. When he whirls back to me, he snaps his fingers with his free hand, eyes wild. "I'm getting tired of you girls not taking me seriously."

I curl my lip in a mock pout. "Aww, you poor thing."

He shakes his head with a smirk, then nods at the nearest guard. "Knife."

The soldier lowers his rifle, exchanging it for an iron blade.

"Take one of her fingers," Mr. Duveau says, tilting his head toward Amelie.

The blood leaves my face as the soldier lunges forward, grasping my sister's wrist between his fingers. "No!" I shout.

"From this point on, she'll lose one for every smart retort you make," Duveau says. "And for every instance of even mild disobedience, I'll have one of her toes. Until I have your full compliance, I'll continue to carve up your sister until there's nothing left."

I should stand down, I should beg for Amelie's safety, but my rage is so hot, flames return to my core, reforming the fiery orb. I can feel my skin growing hot, fire tickling my palms, begging for release.

The soldier lifts Amelie's hand as she screams and struggles to pull away. Gone is that reckless girl who used Cobalt's name to order him to kill, replaced with the sister I always swore to protect.

"Stop struggling, or he takes two," Duveau says in a bored tone, thrusting the barrel of his gun at her to remind her just how many dangers there are. "And don't worry. This will be very, very slow, considering we don't have a proper chopping block."

Amelie lets out a wail, tears streaming down her cheeks.

The soldier singles out Amelie's forefinger and brings his blade toward it.

My eyes flash to the sky, to the dark shape hovering just overhead.

The orb of flame burns hotter at my core, and I begin to shape it with air, preparing to send it flying outward.

The soldier with the knife looks to Mr. Duveau, who nods. "Do it," he says. The edge of the blade bites into her skin just as a dark shape drops into the boat, landing near the motor's controls.

"Hey beautiful," says a familiar voice.

Our guards whirl toward it, leaving Franco in full view, perched on the control panel in his seelie form. Two dark, smoky tendrils spiral from his fingers to the heads of the navigators, holding them immobilized while their mouths are open in silent screams. Shadows are leached from them, flowing into the prince.

Mr. Duveau starts forward, but Franco burns him with a scowl. "I wasn't talking to you," Franco says, then lifts his chin with a charming smile, eyes on me. "Hey there."

"Fire!" Duveau shouts.

"Bye now." With a flutter of his fingers, Franco leaps to his feet and shifts back into his raven form. But not before he kicks out against two of the levers on the control panel. The rifles fire just as the boat's momentum is thrust back by the sudden loss of power, making the soldiers' aim go wild. Several bullets strike the boat's controls.

The man with the knife loses balance and releases Amelie from his grip.

I reach for her, pulling her close to my side as I unleash my flame, letting it shoot out in every direction from my core, lashing the guards in a fiery inferno. Flames erupt from my skin, and it's an effort to keep them from scalding my sister. Screams roar along with my growing fire, and I charge the nearest guard, who spins in a circle, desperately trying to beat the flames from devouring his uniform. Lifting my knee, I aim a kick at his gut, sending him curling inward. I shove him to the side and pull Amelie forward as we rush to the edge of the boat. With every step I take, I leave fire in my wake, coating the floor of the boat, raging up soldier's legs. I hear splashes as soldiers jump from the other side. I exchange a glance at Amelie. She nods, knowing what must be done.

Squeezing each other's hands, we take a deep breath and jump.

WAVES PULL ME UNDER AT ONCE, SWALLOWING ME INTO A world of cold and darkness. Sound is muted in my ears while pressure builds in my head, my lungs. I open my eyes, feeling the sting of salt as I struggle to orient myself in the raging current. Spreading my arms, I realize with horror that Amelie's hand is no longer in mine. I whirl one way then the other, my movements painfully slow, but I see no sign of her. All I see is dark water with no indication which way is up or down.

Panic seizes me as my lungs constrict, the last of the air being pressed from my lungs.

This is the end. This is it. I'll drown in the one element I was never able to master.

My movements go still. Not with fear; with realization.

The elements.

I may be under water, but the other elements aren't lost to me.

My first need is air. I imagine a pocket of air, forming from the oxygen molecules that help make up water. I envision it growing into an enormous bubble, one large enough for me to swallow a lungful of breath. I can feel it. It's so close.

But why can't I see it?

Pain sears my chest. I won't make it much longer. I need to breathe.

I close my eyes, thinking of Minuette, the wind that constantly writhes around her. I imagine the feel of a breeze against my human skin, then rustling my fox fur as I run through the windblown forest. I focus on what the air element represents. Thought. Imagination. Innovation. I know air. I *know* it.

With calm certainty, I open my eyes.

Then I see it. A shimmering bubble of air unlike any ordinary bubble I've ever seen. It's enormous and round, maintaining its shape as if it were a solid thing, not one composed of air. It floats slowly through the black water, just feet from where I am. Jolting into motion, I kick out my legs, pull my arms, swimming toward the bubble. My vision fades with every inch I close between myself and the air I so desperately need, and I fear I'll lose consciousness before I reach it. Still, I keep going, focusing on my connection to the element of air, imagining it filling my lungs long before it truly does.

Then finally it's there. My lips press against the bubble, and I suck in an enormous breath. My chest still aches, but at least I've given myself more time.

Now how to reach the surface?

I immediately know the answer, and it surrounds me like a shroud. Water. I must connect to the element of water. Work with it. Make friends with it.

Face it.

I already know what it will bring, but I have no other choice. Closing my eyes, I allow myself to feel the icy sea against my skin, taste the salt on my lips, feel its pressure squeezing me at all sides.

Then I open myself to it, using all my will to take it to the Twelfth Court.

There I fall into a chasm of grief.

31

A bullet. Blood. Death.

I'm back in the courtroom where Mother's death plays out before me. The violet haze of the Twelfth Court does nothing to take from the pain of this memory, and the emotions that accompany it swallow me whole. Pain and regret. Guilt and shame. Sorrow. Sorrow. Endless sorrow.

I want to open my mouth and wail, but a small part of me remembers where I truly am, knows what will happen if water rushes in through my lips.

My next instinct is to pull away, swallow the painful emotions or burn them with my fire. I can do neither of those things, for my fire is tempered by the water around me, and the only way out of this is through it. I don't know how I know that, but I do.

Mother's death plays again and again. I watch the life leave her eyes as a bullet strikes her forehead. Blood streams down her face, filling the tub she's kept in. She sinks lifeless into the crimson water, the color bright against the violet haze that falls over everything else.

Gone. She's gone.

Dead.

And it was all my fault.

I admitted as much to Amelie, and once again, I confess it to myself.

It was all my fault. All my fault. All my fault.

I'm so sorry, Mother.

The pain that drags me down is too much to bear. I can feel it sinking me deeper, deeper toward the ocean floor.

A bullet. Blood. Death.

A bullet. Blood. Death.

Again.

Again.

Mother's lifeless form sinks into a tub of her own blood—

"Stop!" The voice freezes the scene, crimson water suspended midair in the moment it was about to splash over Mother's head. Everything else in the image is frozen as well—the guards, the councilmen, the jurors, Mr. Duveau—but all is blurred aside from the tub. "Stop this, Evelyn," the voice says, and I know who it belongs to. It's a voice I never thought I'd hear again.

Mother.

I blink at the frozen scene just as movement begins to stir inside the tub. With equal parts joy and terror, I watch as Mother rises from the bloody water. "Why do you always return to this scene?" she asks, eyes pleading as rivulets of scarlet trail down her face.

"Because it haunts me," I whisper. "It's the moment I saw the consequences of my choice."

She shakes her head. "It wasn't just your choice." With a flick of her wrist, the image begins to reverse, the blurred shapes of the guards returning to their posts, Mr. Duveau's gun swinging away from Mother and instead to me. Mother's arms are outstretched, wrists locked in the iron cuffs. Her expression is defiant.

I recalled this moment in the cell with Amelie. The moment Mother sought her flames when she should have been at her weakest. The moment she wanted me to fight.

The rest of the image returns to stillness, but flames ignite over Mother's hands, turning her cuffs a molten orange. "I chose to fight here, Evelyn."

"I know." My voice comes out with a tremble. "But then...I tried to use the councilman's true name. Tried and...failed. That's why he shot you. To punish *me*."

"No, my love," she says. "I chose my death before he pulled that trigger. And I would choose it again and again if it saves your life. If it saves your sister's life. You cannot take that moment from me, Evelyn. It is mine, not yours."

Tears stream out of my eyes, but they float from my cheeks like twinkling violet stars floating through a stream. No, an ocean. Part of me remembers where I truly am, knows that I'm drowning, while the rest of me remains in the violet courtroom, eyes locked on Mother's face.

"I could stay here," I say, voice small. "With you. This could be the end of all my pain, all the fighting."

Mother's face falls, eyes turning down at the corners.

"You cannot stay here with me. There's so much more for you to do. For you to live for. Love for. And yes, fight for."

Aspen's face flashes through my mind, then Amelie's, Foxglove's, Lorelei's, and Nyxia's. I see Franco's face and Breeda's. Dune's face and Marie Coleman's and Fehr's, and all the other people and creatures I'm sworn to protect. "But I'm running out of time. I don't know how to get out of this."

"You do." In a flash, Mother's chains are gone. She exits the tub and comes to me, her steps slow and swaying, trailing water with every move. Just like my tears, the water doesn't remain in place but lifts into the air in glittering droplets. When she reaches me, her hands come to frame my face. "You are a queen. This element is yours. Even if you weren't a royal, you would still have access to it. Do you know why?"

I shake my head, eyes glistening as I luxuriate in the feeling of her gentle, familiar touch.

"Because water is the element of emotion. And the most powerful emotion of all is love, which you are no stranger to. All you have to do is open to it. All of it."

"But it brings so much pain."

"I know. But you're stronger than the pain. You are stronger than you know. You'll never see just how strong you are, though, if you don't allow yourself to."

I continue to study her face, memorizing every crease at the corner of her lips and eyes. The violet haze lifts from her, revealing the emerald shade of her glittering irises, the bright copper of her hair, the peachy hue of her skin.

"It's time for you to go," she says.

I want to argue, but I know she's right. I can feel the

compression of my lungs, my single breath of air already running out. With a sob, I nod.

My heart lurches as she takes one step away, then another, retreating from me. The water from the tub begins to rise, spilling over the edges. Mother smiles as she backs up another step, paying no heed to the water that floods the courtroom, darkening it. I watch as she continues to back away from me, watch her smile even as we both go under the rising tide, until we hang suspended in the cold, dark sea.

I love you, Evelyn, she says straight into my mind.

I love you too, Ma.

You can do this. It's the last thing she says before she disappears.

My heart feels like it will break in two, and I sink into that feeling, noticing how similar it feels to drowning. But it won't drown me. Not this time. For alongside that grief lies every memory that uplifts me—Mother brushing my hair from my head after a bad dream. Mother kissing my wounds and laying her hands over scrapes and bruises, telling me her love will mend them. Then I see Amelie and me laughing, playing, fighting, then making up over mugs of warm tea that Mother offers us.

The memories bring equal parts joy and sorrow, and I accept them, giving both emotions equal places in my heart. Allowing the memories to wrap around me, hold me, lift me, I open my awareness to the feeling of water. I know I'm nearly out of air, but I manage to keep my panic down, manage to fight the urge to control the water, and instead surrender to it. Grow one with it. Flow with it. Become it.

The pressure begins to ease around me, giving way to

a sense of rising, floating. A shimmer of light in the dark sea draws my attention. Is that the surface? I kick out, my arms stroking through the water as I reach for hope. Air. Safety. Drawing near, the light begins to grow brighter. Brighter. And at the center of it is a figure with dark copper hair streaming around her like a halo.

My heart leaps. It's Amelie!

I swim faster now, and she swims toward me. Her movements are far more elegant than mine are; her limbs cut through the water with ease, propelling her forward to close the distance between us in seconds. Her hand grasps mine, and she pulls me toward her, circling an arm around my waist as she turns us back in the direction she came. Swimming with one arm, she guides us up, up, closer to that shimmer of light. Then finally, our heads breach the surface into the light of the morning sun. I gasp, coughing up water as I suck in the most delicious breath I've ever tasted in my life. A second later, a wave crashes over our heads, but another gulp of air is on the other side.

Amelie sputters, skin pale and cheeks ruddy. "Can you swim to the shore?" she asks, voice hoarse.

I look in one direction and then another, finally spotting the lighthouse. We're a good distance away from the shore, and I've never swum so far in my life. "I...I don't know. Can you?"

She nods. "Selkie experience." Steel flashes over her expression.

Another wave douses our faces, leaving me gasping in its wake. "I'll try." My words come out with a cough.

"Perhaps I can help." A shadow blocks out the light overhead, and I look up to find Franco, partially shifted between his two forms—mostly seelie but with an enormous set of raven wings spanning out on either side of him. His lips quirk in a crooked grin as his outstretched arms reach for me.

I cast a glance at Amelie, who eyes Franco with suspicion. She may have seen his diversion on the boat, but they aren't well acquainted yet. I attempt a smile, despite the seawater dripping over my face. "We can trust him," I tell her, lifting my arms for Franco to grasp beneath my armpits.

Amelie's gaze locks on mine as Franco hoists me into his arms. "I'll see you on the shore," she says with a nod, then dives beneath the waves.

32

I barely have time to secure my arms around Franco's neck before he takes off toward the shore. As it comes into view, all I see is smoke and sand, but the closer we draw near, the more obvious it is that the fighting is still underway. However, most of the commotion seems to be coming from near the lighthouse. I try to lift my chin to see over the wall, seeking any sign of Aspen, but just as the fighting becomes visible, the sight drops from view.

"No!" I cry, fighting against the arms that secure me. "Take me to the lighthouse."

He shakes his head. "You don't want to go there right now."

"Is Aspen there?"

He gives a short nod.

"Then that's where I want to be."

"He told me to get you to safety so you can get out of here." Ignoring my protests, Franco continues our descent toward the beach where the fighting has condensed to the far end. Several soldiers remain locked in physical combat with what is unmistakably Cobalt, still in his blue nix form, as well as a few other sea fae who look like the guards I've seen in his employ. Franco's momentum slows as we near the ground on the abandoned end of the beach, where only carnage remains. My stomach roils as I take in the blood that coats the sand, along with dismembered body parts of dead soldiers. I'm momentarily stunned with the realization that Cobalt likely did all this. But as soon as we land, I remember where I need to be.

I'm barely out of Franco's arms before I round on him. "Bring me up to the lighthouse."

"Your mate can take care of himself," he says. "Nyxia and Estel are there too, as well as four of my sister's soldiers. We need to wait here."

I furrow my brow. "For what?"

He turns his eyes to the sky, squinting through the smoke that hangs in the air. Then a smile tugs his lips. "For that."

I follow his gaze, unsure of what he's looking at. There's nothing there. Nothing out of the ordinary, at least.

Then I see it.

A red light hovers in the sky, darting this way and that as if in search of something. Franco waves his arms wildly in the air until the light pauses. After only a moment's hesitation, it shoots down toward us. As it draws near, I see the unrestrained joy on Breeda's tiny face. "Your Most Beautiful Esteemed Majesty!" she squeals, flying around my head with dizzying speed. When she stops, she extends her arms, revealing a silver disc. "Look what I brought you."

A Chariot. *My* Chariot. The one I hid in the planter outside my bedroom window.

I open a palm and she sets the device upon it, then brushes her hands together. "That was heavy."

"We have what we need," Franco says. "Now it's time to leave."

I close my fingers around the disc and narrow my eyes. "I'm not leaving without Aspen or Amelie."

He grasps me by the shoulders, desperation in his eyes. "Aspen and the others have their own Chariot, Evelyn. As soon as we're away, Breeda will fly up and give the signal. The others will follow us."

My heart sinks at the thought of leaving without Aspen. But if he's only stalling for me to get away…

"We at least need to wait for my sister." I turn to where the waves lap upon the bloody shore, my eyes seeking any sign of life between here and the wreckage of the boat, where flames and smoke continue to rise into the sky. Behind that, the hulking warship remains. With the sea so wild, I can't make out much else at all. Then finally, I see movement halfway down the beach.

Amelie falls to her knees as she fights her way out of the waves to catch her breath. She made it.

I rush toward her, Franco close at my side. "Amelie!" I call out.

She turns to face me, her eyes lighting with relief. But it's short lived as her attention is drawn to the other end of the shore.

Every muscle in her body stiffens, and I watch as her fingers curl into fists.

The air leaves my lungs when I realize what has her so distracted. It's Cobalt and the sea fae, fighting more human soldiers. I see now that some of the humans have built a barricade to hide behind, revealing their faces only to take aim with their rifles. The rest of the soldiers engage the sea fae in close physical combat. Cobalt's blue scales are shredded in places, revealing bloody gashes. Some lesions go as far down to the bone. And yet he fights just as fiercely as if he were unwounded. There's almost a madness to the way he dodges the blasts of the guns, falters for only seconds when struck by an iron bullet. He presses on despite every wound.

Fueled by Amelie's command. *Kill these men.*

My gaze returns to my sister, but she continues to watch her mate. Without taking her eyes off him, she reaches into the sand, retrieving a discarded blade. Then, to my complete horror, she charges into the fight.

"Amelie, no!" I halt, my scream shattering the air, yet it doesn't reach her.

"Evelyn, watch out!" Franco yanks me roughly by the arm as a figure nearly barrels into me. We stumble back as Mr. Duveau rises clumsily to his feet, dripping seawater. He's lost his jacket and waistcoat, his shirt torn and stained crimson. He darts forward again, but a red flame sears his face, making him lurch back.

"Stay away!" Breeda shouts, brandishing a tiny fist. "I am charged with protecting Her Most Beautiful and Gracious Majesty."

Duveau blinks, eyes unfocused in the heat of the fire sprite. Then, with a shout, he swipes his hand through the air, right through Breeda's flames, and sends her spiraling through the air.

Franco pushes me behind him, and shadows begin to writhe around his shoulders. As he grows taller, the skin prickles on the back of my neck. I don't need to see his face to know what he looks like. I've seen how terrifying he can be, how he can transform his features into those of a nightmarish monster at will. The true origin of the haunting vampire tales of my youth.

I back up a step, catching a glimpse of the councilman.

Duveau, however, seems nonplussed. He grimaces but shows none of the terror the drivers of the ship revealed. "You forget, princeling. I've been dealing with the fae my whole life." In one swift move, he reaches for the waistband of his trousers to withdraw his revolver.

Fear floods me, but I know the gun is wet. Surely it won't work...

Mr. Duveau swipes out, and that's when I realize he hadn't pulled out his gun at all, but a blade. Franco doubles over and staggers back, grasping the left side of his torso. Blood flows through his fingers, and I can only hope the cut sliced over his ribs and not into his heart.

My preoccupation with Franco is all Duveau needs, and he lunges for me yet again. He tackles me to the ground and crawls on top of me, straddling my hips. I expect to feel the edge of his blade strike me next, or for his fingers to wrap around my throat. But all his efforts are thrown into grasping my right hand. He twists my wrist, making me cry out. Then his weight releases me, and I scramble to my feet.

Duveau retreats, flashing me a wild gaze before turning his attention to what he holds in his hand. My Chariot. With a grin, he opens the lid, the bright golden light wrapping around him in an instant. I dive forward, but in the blink of an eye, he's gone.

I stand staring at the empty air for a few moments, until more pressing concerns steal my focus. I whirl toward Franco and Breeda. The prince's face is pale as he grasps his wound, but he shakes his head.

"I'll be fine," he says. "It isn't deep and there's no iron embedded in me. I'll heal once we return to the other side of the wall."

I then study Breeda, who seems dazed but unharmed.

My next thought is Amelie, and I take off running. Franco tries to call me back, but I let his voice die out behind me, focusing on the fighting at the other side of the beach, seeking a glimpse of copper hair amidst the spray of sand and gunfire. The scene has become clouded by a smoky haze, making it impossible to see much of anything. Then a blue-scaled sea fae clears the haze, darting toward the ocean. Just before he reaches it, an explosion strikes right where he was about to step.

I stop in my tracks as what was once a sea fae is now a radius of flying debris. Bile rises in my throat as pieces of gore land just feet in front of me. I look wildly about, but there's no sign of my sister. "Amelie!" I call her name again and again, but my voice is drowned out by another explosive blast.

Then I see her.

Near the base of the cliff, she clears the wall of smoke and sand. Cobalt limps after her, no longer a blue nix. In his seelie form, his wounds look far worse, skin a sickly green, his shirt a darker shade of red than Mr. Duveau's was. What little is left of his collar is grasped in Amelie's fingers. She squeezes the cloth so hard, her knuckles are white. Once they're far enough away from the barricade, she releases him, pushing him to the ground. He falls to his knees as he struggles to right himself, hands clasped as if in prayer.

I run toward them, but neither seem to notice my approach.

Amelie looks down her nose at Cobalt, a cruel smile twisting her lips. Then she extends her hand, pointing her dagger at her mate. He hangs his head, but she shouts something at him. With trembling fingers, he accepts the weapon. Not bothering to lift his gaze, he raises his forearm, one already torn to shreds. Pressing the tip of the blade to a patch of ragged skin, he makes a cut.

Words she spoke just days ago ring through my head. *I don't care if I have to force him to peel every inch of skin from his own body. I will do whatever it takes to watch the life fade from his eyes.*

She's doing it. Despite the violence and danger around her, she's pursuing vengeance like it's the only thing that matters.

It makes my stomach turn with dread.

Then something else makes my gut drop even deeper. A cylindrical object flies from the haze and lands at Amelie's feet.

Cobalt's gruesome ministrations go still, his attention fixated on the grenade. Amelie's eyes find it next, going wide, draining all the deadly malice from her expression. She retreats a step away from it just as Cobalt lunges forward. Grasping it to his chest, he darts toward the haze.

It explodes.

Again, I stop in my tracks, the sound of the explosion ringing through my ears. This one, however, isn't the same that ended the life of the sea fae. For Cobalt's body isn't obliterated at once. Even so, he lays unmoving, face buried in the sand. I pump my legs to close the distance between me and Amelie, reaching her just as she grasps Cobalt and rolls him onto his back.

I come up behind my sister, recoiling at the sight of the male below her. The damage caused by the explosive may not have been immediate like the other grenade was, but this blast is just as lethal. Cobalt gasps for breath, chest gaping open, his skin coated black. Tiny shards of what I can only imagine is iron pierce everything from his face to his arms, as well as every open lesion.

I'm reminded of the grenades Ustrin had threatened to use against his fire fae when he confronted us in the cave. These must be the same. Cruel, human weapons technology crafted for the fae.

And Cobalt took the entire brunt of it himself to save Amelie.

Amelie's sobs come out short and heavy, her hands shaking as she attempts to touch him but can find no place uninjured. I want to reach out to comfort her, to pull her away, but I can't bring myself to move, nor can I bring myself to look away.

He's dying. Even without the iron puncturing his insides, I doubt even a fae could heal from this type of wound. Especially not on this side of the wall. While the thought of him dead should come as a relief, the sight before me only makes me feel empty.

Amelie's shoulders slump. "I was supposed to kill you," she whispers.

His face turns toward her, but I can't tell if even his good eye remains intact. "And I was supposed to love you," comes his raspy voice. "I was supposed to bring peace to the isle with a radical seelie reign. I failed at everything. Everything."

Amelie hangs her head. "Your blood was mine to spill. How dare you take that from me!"

He attempts to lift a hand but doesn't make it far. "Instead, you have my heart. Always."

Amelie convulses with the weight of her sobs. "I don't want it, Cobalt. Do you hear me? I don't want it."

"And yet..." He takes a few strangled breaths. "It's yours."

His body goes still.

Amelie throws her head back and wails, and a light begins to shimmer over her skin. Then it turns to a deep red flame that dances over every inch of her, rising higher and higher. Her skin begins to blister beneath the heat.

Driven by urgency, I allow myself to place a hand on her shoulder. I ignore the sharp bite of flames that are not my own, and when she whirls to face me, a snarl pulls her lips. Then recognition crosses her face, and she reaches for me. Her flames settle to a gentle roar as I wrap my arms around her, igniting my own flames alongside hers as I fall to my knees at her side. With my fire protecting me from hers, I brush the tangled, blood-soaked hair from her brow and let her rest her head in the crook of my neck.

33

I know we should get up. I know we should run. We've already seen one grenade reach this far. We're defenseless, should the army throw another. But I also know what Amelie is feeling, this debilitating pain that drags her down. Whether it's from the loss of Cobalt or her vengeance, I can't say. All I can do is hold her, be here for her.

And yet, we need to move. Retreat. Find Aspen and the others.

"Amelie," I say, my words coming out quiet, strangled. "We should get to safety."

She only wails harder, grips me tighter.

"I'm here, Ami," I whisper into her hair, although it dawns on me she might not be able to hear me. Our proximity to the blast has left my ears ringing, my own voice muted. But as my flames dance over my skin, fueling my healing, my ears begin to clear.

Yet it's still quieter than it was before.

Too quiet.

Gunfire still rings out in the distance, but the beach is almost silent. No...there *is* a sound. One that sets my heart racing, my flames retreating.

Marching footsteps approach, and I whirl around to face the human soldiers who close in on us, rifles raised. Amelie must realize the threat too, for she stills, clinging to me as she turns in my arms, her fire extinguished.

Six men spread out in a semi-circle around us. My eyes flash from them to the barricade, which now seems empty. Are these the only survivors? Two look vaguely familiar, dripping seawater. They must be guards from the boat I set aflame, those who were able to swim to shore like Duveau. I hazard a glance at the other side of the beach, seeking Franco and Breeda, but I see no sign of them.

"Stand up," orders a soldier, one of the guards from the boat.

Shakily, I rise to my feet, pulling Amelie up with me. Keeping my breathing steady, I reconnect to my flame, readying it. Until the end, I will fight.

The man who spoke steps closer. "Hands where I can see them."

As we raise our hands, I assess the distance between us and the soldiers, process scenario after scenario of possibilities to take them down. There are only six of them. Two of us. And we both wield fire.

"What are we doing with them, Averson?" asks another soldier, expression wary.

The man before us, Averson, narrows his eyes to study us. "Mr. Duveau wanted these two brought to the king."

"But they're creatures," says another. "They have no place in Bretton."

Averson's lips curl into a cold smile. "I agree. Besides, we don't take orders from Duveau."

"Then we—"

"Yes." Averson nods. "Execution."

I flinch as he raises the barrel of the rifle to my forehead, but my fire burns hot inside me. Locking eyes with him, I seek to draw in the imagery of the bird in the cage. At such a close distance, I could glamour him. But no matter how long his eyes remain on mine, the imagery doesn't come.

The soldiers must be wearing rowan.

"Turn around," Averson orders.

Keeping my voice steady, I say, "I'd rather look at you while you shoot me." But I'm not looking at him. Not anymore. My attention is now fixated on his gun, the metal that formed it, shaped it from elements of the earth. Elements I can control.

"Fine," Averson says, then nods to the soldier on his right. Another man steps forward and levels his gun between Amelie's eyes.

My inner fire falters. Damn. I can't focus on two guns at once. "Kill me first," I say, voice trembling. If I can keep his attention, keep his gun from firing just a few seconds longer...

"Very well." Too soon, Averson reaches for the trigger.

But it isn't a trigger he finds.

Averson bites back a yelp as the metal that was once a trigger melts onto his finger, burning red-orange. He pulls his finger away, but the barrel too begins to glow. Then it...bends. With a shout, he drops the rifle and takes a step back. The soldier with the gun on Amelie trembles, his own weapon glowing hot in his hands. Just like the first gun, the barrel melts and bends toward the sky. The man drops it just as it fires overhead.

The other soldiers watch their guns with terror in their eyes, retreating several steps. Theirs too begin to glow, and the two soldiers the farthest back are lost in a fiery blast, their guns exploding in their hands.

I'm stunned as I watch all this unfold.

This isn't me. I'm not the one doing this.

I glance at Amelie, but she seems just as dumbfounded as I am.

Then the four remaining soldiers all seem to see the same thing. Their eyes grow wide, mouths agape as they retreat farther. Farther.

Grasping Amelie's hand in mine, we whirl around.

There, coming down the steps from the cliff is the most terrifying yet beautiful sight I've ever seen.

My mate.

His arms are outstretched, his feet barely touching the stone steps as he glides down, drawing nearer. His blue-black hair swirls wildly around his face, pupils so dilated, his eyes look black. His golden skin is paler than I've ever seen, every vein visible beneath his flesh, lips peeled back from his teeth. He flicks his fingers this way then that. Behind me, I hear another gun explode, then another. Then the sound of waves rising to a roar. A gurgling scream. Despite my curiosity about what's happening to the soldiers, I can't take my eyes off Aspen.

Aspen in all his terrifying, haunting glory.

This is the creature I was raised to fear.

And I've never loved him more.

At the base of the cliff, his feet meet sand. I watch in awe as he stalks across the beach, past the bodies of the dead soldiers, to the edge of the shore. There he pauses, water lapping up his legs as if in praise of him. Not too far out I see two figures, frantically swimming out to sea, making a desperate bid to reach the warship which appears to be retreating as well.

Hands raised toward the water, palms facing the sea, he thrusts outward. In answer, the water recedes, gathering in a wave. It swallows the two swimming men, drowning them in its depths as the wave grows higher. Higher.

All reason tells me this wave can only crash back into us, but instead, the water shifts, rising, twisting, lurching in an impossible direction. Away from the shore. Toward the warship.

An eruption of sound startles me, and Amelie squeezes my forearm. What follows is a deafening crash into the face of the cliff, rocking my feet beneath me. Ducking from flying debris, Amelie and I scramble to the far end of the shore, to the abandoned barricade built from large bags of sand. We kneel behind it as another blast strikes the cliff.

My heart hammers in my chest, and I hazard a glance over the top of the barricade, seeking Aspen. Once the rubble clears, I find him, still at the edge of the shore. His wave continues to build, rushing toward the warship.

Another blast.

Biting back a scream, I duck, covering my head with my hands. Amelie's arms wrap around me. But as soon as the trembling begins to fade, I leap back up again, eyes darting immediately to Aspen.

Still unharmed, his arms tremble as if pushing an incredible weight.

He opens his mouth in a scream that doesn't reach my ears over the raging wave. Gathering speed, his wave finally reaches the warship, dousing it in a roaring crash. The ship goes under, disappearing beneath the sea. To my horror, it reappears seconds later, rocking erratically. It has ceased firing its enormous guns, but the ship remains whole.

Aspen staggers his legs and thrusts again, gathering another wave. The ocean grows wilder, darker. His arms, however, begin to tremble more, his shoulders starting to sag.

That's when I notice the blood dripping down his torn calves, the puncture marks in his side, his arms.

He looked so strong when I first saw him coming down the side of the cliff; I hadn't seen how wounded he'd been.

Without a second thought, I leave the safety of the barricade and run to his side.

"Evie, stay back," he shouts through his teeth. The veins in his face and neck are more visible than they were before, and even worse than that—black tendrils spiral up the skin on his arms, and dark threads mingle with the blood that seeps from a few of the lesions. He has iron embedded in him.

A painful lump sears my throat. "I'm not leaving you."

"Go!" he roars, sending his newest wave crashing over the warship. Again, the ship goes under, only to reappear.

I don't know why he's so adamant about destroying the ship, especially when it clearly taxes his strength. I want to argue him away, force him to abandon his mission so I can tend to his wounds.

But something stills my heart, fills me with a profound calm.

I do know why he's doing this. Safety. Protection. Love. Vengeance.

We can't let them get away.

Planting my feet firmly beneath me, I stand at his side and raise my arms. I open myself to love and grief, connecting to the element of water. With rage and fury, I connect to fire. My duty as queen to protect my people links me to earth. And my mind, piecing all of this together with precise thought, connects me to air.

Like Aspen, I thrust out my arms, giving strength to his wave, shaping it into something more. The water builds higher than ever before, then separates, reaching for the warship like two monstrous hands. Fire heats the metal hull of the ship, a crack forming at its center. Then, in tandem, Aspen and I curl our fingers into fists. The two waves mimic our motions, wrapping around opposite ends of the ship. With a final thrust downward, the waves snap the warship in two.

Lowering my hands, I watch as smoke barrels into the sky. Smaller waves continue to pummel the broken ship, forcing the two halves to drift apart. One begins to sink. Then the other.

Terror surges through me as I watch the shattered warship sink and become swallowed by the hungry waves. I shudder, shoulders trembling at the sight.

Aspen's fingers brush against mine, and my racing pulse begins to calm. Together we watch the sea, watch the roiling waves toss and rage, all signs of the warship gone.

I take his hand fully in mine and lift my chin. We may have done an ugly thing, but it needed to be done. There may be dozens more, but this enemy warship won't be coming back to take out the fae. My people. My home.

It's one thing. One small, infinitesimal feat in a much larger war.

But we did it.

And we did it together.

34

W e continue to watch the sea as the waves subside, satisfied in the wake of its meal, until footsteps sound behind us. I turn to find Amelie approaching. Behind her, Breeda flutters down from the cliffside.

Aspen shifts to face them as well, but his legs give out beneath him. Gasping, he falls to his knees, face contorted as he clenches his chest.

"Aspen!" I shout, lowering to his side.

"The iron," he bites out, teeth bared.

My throat goes dry as my gaze falls on the black tendrils spiraling up his neck, his arms. If he wasn't already weakened by the iron embedded in his wounds, he certainly is now. Any feat of magic is nearly impossible on this side of the wall. For him to do what he did...

To do what *we* did.

"What's wrong?" Amelie asks, eyes wide.

"He's taken several iron injuries." My hands fly frantically over him, assessing what little I can through the grime and blood.

"You can help him," she says, a flicker of hope weaving in between her furrowed brows.

"I need tools. I need..." My breath hitches as I recall the medical tent I spotted in the camp outside the lighthouse. I rise to my feet to intercept Breeda as she draws near. "Where are the others?" I ask her. I can no longer hear fighting anywhere, not just on the beach.

Her color is muted, her characteristic joy absent from her face. "Prince Franco and I went to warn the others that we lost the Chariot," she says, her voice so much slower and weaker than usual.

The blood leaves my face. "Was anyone hurt?"

"There was hardly anyone who wasn't hurt," she says. "So much blood. So much...death."

"Where are the others?" I ask again.

"Pursuing the retreating army. Franco joined the fight, and I came to you."

"What about the camp?"

She shrugs. "It's empty. Unless you count dead bodies." Her color goes a shade paler. "I don't suggest you count the bodies."

I spin toward Amelie. "Help me. Please."

She nods, then lowers to the other side of my mate. Aspen lets out a pained groan as we help him to his feet. We make our way across the beach and to the stone stairs. It's slow going as Amelie and I help Aspen climb, but we eventually make it to the top, sweat soaked and gasping for breath.

We assist Aspen, guiding him toward the wall of the fortification where he can lean his weight. Once he's settled, I race to the medical tent with hardly a glance at the blood and carnage Breeda had mentioned. I pull open the tent flap with force.

I startle as I enter, finding a human woman doing the same. She whirls to face me, her hand flying to her mouth. My eyes move from the cases of supplies she's gathering, then to the symbol of the winged staff on her tan uniform. She's a nurse. And not just any nurse. Considering how quickly Dahlia's injury was treated after I stabbed her, the nurses in this camp are trained to treat the fae. Sliding my gaze to her left wrist, I find a strand of red beads. I lurch forward and grab her forearm tightly in my fingers, nails digging into her flesh. With the other hand, I rip the strand of rowan beads from her wrist and toss them to the floor. She cries out with alarm, cowering away from me, but I grab her by the shoulders and shake her into silence. Bringing my face close to hers, I lock her gaze with mine. The imagery of the bird in the cage comes at once. Her face goes slack, pupils dilating.

Just like that, I have her under my control.

"You will tend to my mate at once."

It isn't until his surgery is over that I feel I can finally breathe again. After tedious hours spent helping the human nurse remove every bit of iron embedded in his skin, all we can do is wait for the others to return. Luckily, laudanum proved effective on him, easing his pain and allowing him to slip into unconsciousness. I now watch him sleep, taking in the rise and fall of his breaths. The tendrils of black have ceased their spread, although I doubt they will begin to recede until we return to the Faerwyvae side of the wall.

But he *will* heal.

I place my hands over his chest, willing my inner fire to strengthen his, to speed his healing.

The nurse stands at his head and checks his pulse. "He's stable," she says. Still under my glamour, her moves are precise, her tone even.

I lock my eyes with hers. "You will continue to tend to him until I release you."

Her face slackens further than it already is. "I will."

I return my attention to Aspen. I don't know how long my glamour over the nurse will last. I've always known a mental glamour isn't nearly as strong as using one's true name. But in case my friends return wounded, I'll need all the assistance caring for them that I can get.

Sudden commotion comes from somewhere outside the medical tent—several sets of footsteps and what sounds like sobbing. Fear prickles the back of my neck as my thoughts immediately go to Amelie.

"Stay here," I order the nurse. Then, with a final glance at my dozing mate, I dart from the tent.

My eyes find Amelie at once, rushing from the door of the lighthouse tower, followed by Breeda. The two had gone to the top to keep watch for the return of our friends. But the commotion comes from the far end of the camp. Amelie joins my side as we eye the spaces between the tents. Flames erupt from my fingertips, shaping into an orb, but my sister stills me with a touch. "It's them," she says. "Estel and the Lunar Queen. I saw them from the lighthouse."

Relief washes over me, and a second later, I see Nyxia

leading the party. Shadows writhe around her, but she remains in seelie form. Her black trousers and tunic are torn, and nearly every inch of her skin is coated in blood. But that's not the most shocking sight. Wailing and sobbing at the Lunar Queen's side is Dahlia, stumbling while Nyxia drags her forward. The normally composed Summer Queen is covered in dirt, blood, and grime, one of her yellow butterfly wings bent at an unnatural angle. "Phoebe," Dahlia cries out, shoulders heaving.

"Phoebe is dead," Nyxia says through her teeth.

Estel follows closely behind Nyxia, her shimmering particles a dull glow, although she seems otherwise unharmed. Franco limps next to her, but the fact that he's alive tells me the wound Mr. Duveau gave him wasn't too bad after all. The only other figure is a single fae soldier —one of Nyxia's wraiths. His robes flutter on an invisible wind, but I can't help noticing the trail of blood he leaves behind. Is it his? Or that of his enemies?

"There are less than we came with," Breeda says, fluttering by my ear. "I am most certain we traveled with four guards."

My heart sinks at that. When they finally stop before us, Nyxia shoves Queen Dahlia, who falls to her knees, her sobs never ceasing. "You know what to say," Nyxia says, her tone thick with venom.

Dahlia flashes a miserable look at me before sitting back on her heels, mumbling something unintelligible?

"What's that?" Nyxia prods. "It doesn't count if she can't hear you."

Dahlia takes several shaking breaths. This time, her words are clear. "I accept and acknowledge your rule. You are the rightful Queen of Fire."

Nyxia's lips peel back in a triumphant grin. "The Renounced are defeated. Phoebe is dead and Dahlia has surrendered on behalf of the rest."

My mouth falls open, but I'm not sure what to say. In light of the devastation of battle, I hadn't given a moment's thought to how we fared against the Renounced. With Cobalt's death and Dahlia's surrender, there's no other fae to stand against us. Unless the pretender kings and queens count, which I'm certain they don't. We've won. "And the human army?"

"Retreated," Estel says. "We pursued as many as we could, but we couldn't stray too far south. We're already far enough from the wall as it is."

"Wait, where's Aspen?" Nyxia asks, looking around the camp.

"He's stable. He went under surgery to remove the iron bullets embedded inside him, but we need to get him back to Faerwyvae. Do you still have a Chariot?"

Estel nods. "We'll depart at once."

"What are we doing with her?" Nyxia tilts her head toward Dahlia. Then her gaze falls on my sister, and she wrinkles her nose. "And her?"

I exchange a glance with Amelie and reach for her hand. She places her fingers in mine, and I give them a squeeze. "Amelie has proven herself trustworthy, and her loyalties will no longer be questioned."

My sister lets out a heavy sigh.

Releasing Amelie's fingers, I put my hands on my hips and watch Dahlia through narrowed eyes. "But I too want to know what we plan on doing with this one."

"We could present her to the rest of the Alpha

Alliance," Estel says. "We can let her acknowledge the rest of us the same way she did with Evelyn just now. Then she can send out an official declaration urging her allies to acknowledge our rule and a return to the Old Ways."

"Or we can execute her here and now," Nyxia says. Her eyes find mine. "What do you think?"

I clench my jaw, recalling all that she's responsible for.

Dahlia's eyes are wide with terror as she looks up at me, hands pressed together in supplication. "Please," she says. "I've already lost everything."

I take a slow step toward her. "You tried to trade me and my sister to Mr. Duveau in exchange for a human army. You were going to let our enemies onto fae soil."

"It was my last chance to defeat you," she says, tears streaming over her cheeks. "My final opportunity to secure peace with the humans. We would have drafted a new treaty—"

"No, you wouldn't have." I let out a bitter laugh. "Do you still not get it? Mr. Duveau was using you. He needed me and my sister to save face with King Grigory, but the alliance you made with him was a farce. You were a pawn to get human armies into Faerwyvae without conflict. After they destroyed us, they would have destroyed you too."

She pales, shaking her head. "No. No, we made a bargain."

"Not a watertight one, obviously," Franco mutters under his breath.

"He's right," I say. "You made a joke of a bargain. When I met with you to arrange a ceasefire, I meant what

I said. We had proof that the humans sought to obliterate the fae."

"You mentioned the warships," she argues. "I already knew they were coming. They were sent for my aid."

"You honestly believed that? They were invading whether you let them in or not."

She opens her mouth, but she can't seem to find the words. Instead, she purses her lips, regaining some of her haughty air. "How do you know? What is this proof you claimed to have that revealed the humans wanted to destroy all fae and not just the rebels?"

I crouch down, balancing on the balls of my feet. It takes everything in me to control the rage that comes from being this close to her. "Have you heard of the Parvanovae?"

She leans back, hand flying to her chest. Her voice comes out barely above a whisper. "It's a myth."

I study her expression, the way her eyes widen in fear. Up until now, I wasn't entirely convinced she hadn't known about it from the start. There was still a chance she'd been after it when she sent her pretender king to occupy my palace. After learning about her alliance with Mr. Duveau, the possibility remained that they were working together to find it. But the look on her face tells me, despite her claim that the star bomb is a myth, she's terrified of it.

No, she wouldn't have worked to bring the bomb to the humans. She may be a fool for believing Mr. Duveau's promise of an alliance, but she's not stupid enough to put the most dangerous weapon known to man and fae alike in human hands.

Reading the truth on my face, she shakes her head. "It can't be. It was supposed to be destroyed."

"It wasn't. But you will be if you make one more move against me and my allies. Say even one thing against us, and I will tear the wings from your body shred by shred. Then I'll burn you alive."

She swallows hard and gives me a short nod.

I rise to my feet and address the others. "I agree with Estel. She can come back with us alive, so long as she works with us and acknowledges our rule. I doubt the broken bargain will stop the warships from coming, but at least we can face the armies as a united front."

"Does even a united front stand a chance against a dozen warships?" Franco asks. "I'm not sure we would have survived a single army, if they hadn't retreated."

"I don't know," I say, "but we must try. Besides, Aspen and I were able to destroy the ship in the cove before it could get away."

Nyxia assesses me from head to toe, eyes alight with appreciation. "Nice work."

"Thanks. Now, we need to get back to Faerwyvae so everyone can heal and we can make a plan. Aspen is still unconscious. Can he travel by Chariot in such a state?"

"No," Estel says. "He must be awake."

I turn around and start back toward the medical tent. "I'll see if I can wake him, but he has laudanum in his system—"

"Wait." Estel's voice freezes me, and I whirl to face her. The particles shift rapidly over her face, her expression lost beneath the movement.

"What is it?" I ask.

The particles go still, revealing a look of deep concern. "Franco said you lost your Chariot."

I nod. "Mr. Duveau stole it from me."

"Where did he go?"

Dread fills my stomach, but I don't know why. "To safety, I assume. Once I destroyed the transport boat, he knew he couldn't get me to the warship. It was over for him."

"But you aren't certain where he went?"

"Of course not." My heart hammers in my chest as the particles begin to shift and swirl over her face again. "What are you getting at, Estel?"

With a quick stride, she closes the distance between us and thrusts out her palm, revealing a silver disc. "Take this and return to Irridae at once," she says, voice trembling as she presses the Chariot into my hand.

I accept it, although I don't understand the urgency. My eyes seek hers, then the others, who all look equally as perplexed as I feel. "Me? Alone? You already used this once to get here, haven't you? That means it only has one more use left tonight. Shouldn't we use this to return together?"

"Go to Irridae right now. Let the Chariot charge by starlight and return to us at dawn."

"But why?"

Estel releases a shuddering breath and lowers her voice. "Go to Irridae. Travel straight to the weapons room."

"The weapons room," I echo. Then the horrible truth dawns on me. My legs tremble as I grasp the source of her fear. "You think Mr. Duveau used the Chariot to take the Parvanovae."

She nods. "Your Chariot was not used to arrive here, which means it has two uses. Mr. Duveau has been to Irridae. He's very likely been inside the weapons room itself. Now that Fehr has opened the palace, the councilman won't need to attempt an invasion from the courtyard. If he wanted, he could travel straight to the bomb. In the next second, he could be safely back home."

My stomach churns. When I stalled him on the boat with my questions, I all but confirmed I had the Parvanovae at my palace. That's why he didn't kill me when he had the chance. That's why he grabbed the Chariot instead. "No, no, no."

"Go," Estel says, voice firm as she ushers me forward "None of us can come with, not as weak as we are right now. Your molten river would debilitate us."

"I'll go," Amelie says, coming up beside me and lacing her fingers through mine.

I nod. With the Chariot in my free hand, I flip open the cover with my thumb. Recalling everything I know about using the Chariot, I focus on the golden light as it grows around me, the energy that pulses and hums through my bones.

Estel steps out of the radius's light, just as it blocks my view of everything around me. Closing my eyes, I picture the weapons room at Irridae Palace, fueling my need to go there with every ounce of my will. I repeat the name of my destination to myself over and over. When I open my eyes, the light grows brighter, brighter. In a blink, the light goes out, plunging us into darkness.

I squeeze Amelie's hand to confirm she's still with me.

"I'm here," she whispers, returning the squeeze.

As my eyes adjust to our new surroundings, the glow

of my molten river illuminates the weapons room. I stand at the center of the room with a few boxes of explosives to my left. Those were the only weapons, aside from the selection of daggers I claimed, that I hadn't melted. I turn in a slow circle, seeking any sign of a small wooden crate.

But there's nothing else there.

The Parvanovae is gone.

35

I don't sleep a wink that night, opting instead to stare blindly out my bedroom window, waiting for the first light of dawn to creep over the horizon. Amelie sleeps in my bed while Lorelei dozes on my couch, her soft snores falling upon my ears.

After discovering the star bomb gone, I barely had the energy to carve a path through my molten river for Amelie and me to get through. Once we made it to the atrium, I collapsed, both from exhaustion and grief. That's where Lorelei found Amelie and me, covered in blood and sand and looking near-death. She's refused to leave us since.

She wasn't the only one worried. After Lorelei coaxed us into the bedroom to get cleaned up, Foxglove and Fehr peeked in on us, asking the same questions Lorelei had.

What happened?

Is everyone all right?

Are you *all right?*

They each got the same answer. *It's over. It's gone.*

Whether Amelie explained more, I hadn't had the energy to notice or care. All I could think about was Aspen. The bomb. Aspen. The bomb.

It's still all I can think about now as I wait for dawn to arrive.

No sooner than I catch the first blush of sunlight creeping behind the distant mountains, I'm on my feet. I cast a glance at Lorelei and Amelie. I don't bother waking either of them before I retrieve the Chariot from my planter box and flip open the lid. I fill my mind with thoughts of the lighthouse. Varney Cove.

The light of the Chariot wraps around me, energy buzzing, humming, and growing. Seconds later I'm at the army camp. A gentle breeze carrying the tang of salt washes over me, bringing memories of fighting. Blood. A broken warship.

The camp is quiet, and seemingly empty, aside from the raven who flies overhead. Franco must be on guard duty. He caws down at me, but I can't bring myself to offer so much as a halfhearted wave.

Lowering my head, I start toward the medical tent. As I draw near, movement rustles the tent flap, stealing my attention. A pale hand emerges first, then a heavily bandaged forearm. Finally, Aspen slowly limps out of the tent. His eyes find me at once. At the sight of my mate, my heart awakens for the first time since I found the bomb missing. There's still a heaviness upon it, but my love for him releases me from the overbearing numbness I've felt all night.

With a strangled sob, I rush to him, closing the

distance between us. His arms wrap around me, and I press myself to his chest, careful not to squeeze him too tight. He brushes a hand down my hair, saying nothing as I cry onto his bandaged chest.

When I think I can manage to find my voice amidst my sobs, I pull away and meet his eyes. There's sorrow in them, something that tells me Estel has already warned him of her fears. "It's gone," I croak out.

He nods, shoulders drooped in resignation.

"It's gone," I repeat.

He lifts a hand to brush my cheek, lips pulling into a feeble smile. "Let's go home."

THE FOLLOWING DAYS PROCEED WITH TENSE SOBRIETY. After returning to Irridae with the rest of the party from the lighthouse, the other royals leave for their own courts. Luckily, as soon as we settle in at home, Aspen's wounds immediately begin to heal at a much more rapid pace, the tendrils of black receding from his skin more and more each day.

It's the only thing that brings me comfort in all this. However, not even that can take away from the sense of doom that falls over me with every day that goes by, knowing any moment could bring the detonation of the Parvanovae. The end of everything I love.

On the sixth night since Mr. Duveau stole the bomb, Aspen convinces me to join him in the bath. I don't know if he thinks I need to relax or if he's noticed how badly I've been neglecting my bathing habits. Whatever the case, I follow him to our bathing chambers and into the enormous sunstone tub. The aromas that invade my senses bring me a comforting feeling of nostalgia—rosemary, marigold, cinnamon, and cloves. It smells like fall. Like Aspen. Like the baths he used to draw for me at Bircharbor Palace.

I bite back tears of gratitude as I recline at one end of the tub, the warm water reaching my shoulders. Aspen climbs in after me, watching me carefully as he lowers down at the opposite end.

I hate the way he eyes me like I'm made of glass. Somehow, he's managed to handle the news of our impending doom with far more grace than I have.

"Do you like it?" he asks.

"I do." I force a weak smile, although I can't meet his eyes. Instead, I watch as sprigs of rosemary float over the surface of the water. Then a thought tugs my heart. "We should have a bath like this drawn for Amelie. She loved the ones at Bircharbor."

"Already done," he says.

This surprises me enough to bring my eyes to his. "Really?"

"Lorelei's taking care of it."

I blink a few times, taking in the sincerity on his face. "Thank you."

Ever since our return, Aspen and I have had the royal bedroom all to ourselves, and Amelie has taken residence in the guest room next door. I must admit, part of me feels she's still too far away.

For the first time, it isn't distrust that makes me feel that way. After everything we've been through together, I feel closer to Amelie like never before. My heart is linked to hers. Not only that, but I worry about her. She's been almost as withdrawn as I've been this past week. How will she recover from everything she's done? From the loss of her vengeance? The loss of a mate she once loved and hated to equal degrees?

Then again, how much time will she even have to recover? How much time do any of us have?

Aspen's touch brings me back to the present as he leans forward and runs a hand over one of my arms. "Are you all right?" he asks.

I meet his eyes again. "I should be asking you," I say. "You're the one still healing from iron injuries."

He looks down to examine his naked torso. Puckered skin remains over his chest, abdomen, shoulders, forearm —plus many other places hidden by the water—where incisions were made to remove the bullets. But nearly every tendril of black has disappeared. "Almost good as new," he says.

"Any updates from Lunar?" I swallow hard, not sure I want to know the answer. I saw one of Nyxia's owls arrive at the palace hours ago. Could she have discovered when and where the bomb will be detonated?

He steels his expression, which shows he's equally as unsure about whether he wants to tell me.

"It's all right," I say. "I've already resigned myself to our fate."

He sighs. "It isn't over, Evie."

I lean back further, letting the water come up to my chin. "Mr. Duveau has a weapon that could end all life on the isle. If it isn't over one way, it will be over in another. Now tell me what Nyxia said in her message."

"Her owls reported seeing the warships turning course back toward the mainland."

It doesn't come as a surprise, nor is it particularly encouraging. "That makes sense, considering the entire isle is about to be obliterated. King Grigory might as well get his expensive warships safely out of harm's way."

Aspen leans forward again and reaches a hand to my cheek. "Evie," he says with some force. "It's *not* over."

Tears well in my eyes as I take in all the hope he holds in his. "He has the bomb," I say, voice strained. "What better gift to give the king he so disappointed?"

"They might not even use it here," he argues.

"They will."

"They might not."

"They. Will." A lump rises in my throat, but I make no effort to swallow it down. I'm done ignoring the truth. "And it's all my fault."

Aspen pulls me closer, cradling me against his warm, sodden chest. "It's not your fault, Evie."

"I'm killing everyone on this isle."

"Enough," he says, tone firm yet gentle. "I don't want to hear another word of that."

I lift my head to meet his eyes again. "But it's true."

He shakes his head. "We don't know that. Until I see a blinding blast coming to end my soul, I will assume my lengthy lifespan will continue on as ever before."

The way he speaks so casually, so free, lifts some of the burden from my heart. "This is a strange time to be stubborn," I say through my tears.

"I could say the same to you."

I lower my head back to his chest, sinking deeper into the warm water. "If I knew what was coming—*when* it was coming—I would fight. It's the not knowing that is killing me. Draining my will."

"Don't let it do that to you, my love," Aspen whispers against my hair. "Don't let an unknown evil take you away from me before it's even time."

"I'm still here," I say with a sigh.

"No. You're already slipping away from me. It crushes my heart to see you like this. To see the fire extinguished from you."

I shrug a shoulder. "What else would you have me do?"

He reaches a finger for my chin, tilts it back until I'm looking at him again. "Live. If these truly are our last days, why aren't we living them to the fullest?"

"Because it isn't realistic."

"Evie, I don't give a centaur's bare ass what's realistic right now."

A corner of my lips quirks up against my will. "Is that so?"

He nods. "Meeting you has made me enjoy my life for the first time. You've made me feel like I *deserve* to enjoy it. With you. I'm not going to give that up just to sulk in the doom and gloom of reality."

"I think Nyxia would say that's all very sunny and idealistic of you."

He grins. "And yet it doesn't lack execution."

My lips mirror his. "So, what do you propose?"

"Let's pretend it never comes."

"Pretend? I never thought you'd be one to play pretend."

"Then you must know very little about your own

kind. The fae excel at playing pretend. Isn't that all a glamour is?"

His oddly light mood has mine lifting as well, even though I know it won't last. I suppose the least I can do is humor him. "What are we pretending, then?"

He sits up straighter, and I return to my place across from him in the tub. "Let's pretend this is a year from now," Aspen says.

"A year from now?"

"Yes. All that nonsense with the bomb—an entire year has passed since then. Agreed?"

I shrug. "Fine. I'll play. Where are we a year from now?"

"Well, first of all, remember when that idiot Mr. Duveau took the Parvanovae to the mainland and accidentally blew it up in the king's face? Remember how the blast destroyed Bretton, but we had our wall up in time to protect against it? Then Estel found some crazy solution that protected the isle better than our original plans? Remember that?"

My heart sinks. "If that were true, everyone on the mainland would be dead. That's only slightly less depressing."

"All right, let's not talk about the bomb at all," he says. "That was almost a year ago, besides. Let's talk about now."

"And what are we doing *now*?" I roll my eyes on the last word, my tone full of mockery.

"Right now, we are living in our new palace."

"Oh, we have a new palace?"

"We do," Aspen says. "We built it on the border between Fire and Autumn. There the weather is warm, but only perfectly so. The red leaves of Autumn mingle with the warm breeze of fire. And we have a lake for swimming. An ample bathtub even larger than this one. Oh, and an enormous table that rivals Nyxia's."

I bark a laugh. "What do we use this immense table for?"

"Certainly not meetings," Aspen says. "Only sex. Same goes for every viable surface in our palace. Our household staff knows exactly when to make themselves scarce and which rooms they should vacate at once."

"How do they know?"

His eyes unfocus as he thinks for a moment, a devious smirk tugging his lips. "We have a bell."

"A sex bell?"

"Yes. It warns all those within our vicinity that no surface is safe from us and all eyes must be averted at once."

"I'm guessing we pay our staff very well."

"They have a handsome salary indeed," he agrees.

"All right, so we spend our days fornicating all over the furniture. What else do we do?"

He waves a dismissive hand. "Tedious royal business of course. Signing papers. Holding court. Making appointments and ironing out conflicts. But no matter how taxing the day was—"

"From all the sex, of course."

"—I end my night laying at your side, thanking the gods that you came to the wall all those months ago and stole my heart."

My chest fills with warmth, tears glazing my eyes. I inch closer to him, and his hand finds my calf. He runs it idly over my skin, eyes drinking me in. When I speak, my voice comes out quiet. "What do we do after?"

His eyes sparkle with mischief as he reaches forward, grasping me beneath my hips and hoisting me into his lap. Water splashes over the side of the tub at the movement. "I think you know what we do after," he says, a teasing growl in his voice.

I lean closer to him, bracing my hands on the rim of the tub as I rock my hips over his. Once. Twice. I feel him stiffen against me. "Is tonight any different, then?"

He brings his lips to mine in a soft brush of a kiss. "Tonight is only a little different, for I must be gentle with you."

I quirk my brow. "Why is that?"

He gives me a shy smile. "Well, we've just begun to suspect you might be carrying my child."

I freeze, my body going still. "Your child? How do you know I even want children?"

Heat flushes his cheeks. His voice is hesitant as he asks, "Do you?"

I allow myself to ponder it before pulling my shoulders into a shrug. "Maybe someday. Not right now."

His expression regains its previous mischievous humor. "Well, we have hundreds and thousands of years to decide about children. If that isn't part of your one-year plan, then I suppose I don't need to be gentle with you after all." He grips my waist tight, then nips playfully at my neck. I squeal, but his bites dissolve into kisses, his lips trailing my collarbone.

Passion returns to my core. I tip my head to the side to allow him to nuzzle closer. My hips begin to rock again, and I bring one hand to his chest. I feel every hard muscle beneath my palm as I trail my hand down his torso, reaching his lower stomach.

"Are you sure you even want to?" he whispers against my neck, a hint of jest in his tone. "I mean, we've been doing it twice a night for a year now."

I pull back and look at him, my lips stretching into a grin. "Twice a night?"

"Ok, you're right. Most nights it's thrice. And that does not include what we do on the furniture." His face contorts with a pretend grimace. "But aren't your hips beginning to ache? Besides, at this rate, you're sure to be with child far sooner than you're ready."

I bring both hands to his shoulders. "Shut up and kiss me."

"Whatever you say, my dearest mate. My wife."

Again, I'm taken aback. "Wife?"

"Yes, my *wife*. Have you already forgotten our wedding? I seem to recall you being owed one when you were named my Chosen."

"That was a term of the treaty, *remember*? And we broke the treaty."

"Ah, but I am still a man of honor. I wasn't going to defile your human side too long without trapping you beneath the bonds of wedlock."

I roll my eyes. "How romantic."

"It was romantic. After all that business with the bomb, we settled down in our new palace, enjoyed a very human wedding, and even exchanged human wedding rings. You wore a hideous human dress which you glamoured from some poor, unsuspecting dressmaker. That was a night where we made love *four* times, if I remember right."

"Four? My, my, I think we have a record to break."

"Surely, we've broken it at least once this year."

I lean in close, planting a kiss at the corner of his jaw. "Nope."

"Well, the night grows late. We should get started trying to break it."

I place a kiss on the other side of his jaw, then pull back just enough to meet his eyes. "Aspen?"

"Yes?"

"Did you just propose to me?"

His lips curl into the most beautiful grin I've ever seen him wear. "I suppose I did. Do you accept?" He runs a hand up and down my spine, the touch eliciting a shudder of pleasure. Fire heats every part of me, my heart, my flesh, the apex of my thighs. It mingles with the joy that wells in my chest, the love that radiates to every corner of my being.

I don't care if it's pretend. I don't care if this year we're imagining never comes to pass.

In our minds and in our hearts, we're living it now.

"Yes, Aspen. I'll marry you."

His lips crush into mine, and a second later, I feel myself being lifted from the tub. Wrapping my arms around his neck, we kiss with every step he takes from the bathing room to our bed. He lays me down on our warm blankets and presses himself close. Before he can get too comfortable, I shift my legs, then roll my weight over his. He complies, allowing me to turn him onto his back. I climb upon him, arching my back as one of his hands caresses my hips, the other lighting over my breast. There he teases another wave of pleasure. A moan escapes my lips and I fall forward, catching myself on my hands.

"Always and forever, Evie." Aspen's voice comes low and rough. "No matter how many days that is."

I claim his lips with mine, then lower myself onto him. "Always and forever, Aspen."

36

The next morning, I wake in a tangle of sheets and limbs with Aspen's arm sprawled over my naked chest. Hazy morning sunlight peeks through the shutters in our bedroom, bringing with it the desert heat, already warming my skin. I shift beneath Aspen's arm to roll toward him, settling my hand on his side and bringing my face just below his. A smile comes to my lips as I study his slack expression, feel his soft breaths brush my cheeks. His antlers hang over the back of our mattress, his hair in tangled disarray, curled from last night's sweat and our time in the bath. Memories of our passion rise to my mind, as well as the playful words we exchanged. I can't say if we made love four times or not; it's hard to say for sure at this point. Even lying still, my body aches from our time spent together, engaged in our game of pretend. Pretend that also wasn't pretend.

Aspen begins to stir, and as he blinks his eyes open, he catches my gaze. A wide grin plays over his lips, and he immediately nuzzles closer, bringing our mouths to touch. "Good morning," he says, between kisses.

I wrap my arms around his neck, and he shifts his body slightly over my upper half. Pulling away, his eyes wander every inch of me, drinking me in with clear pleasure in his eyes. One hand is propped beneath my neck while the other explores my skin in a soft caress, roving lazily from my neck to my torso, then down my legs.

Just like that, fire ignites inside me. "If you aren't careful, we're never getting out of this bed," I say, voice husky.

He leans in for another kiss, his tongue dancing against mine. When we separate, he snags my lower lip gently between his teeth. "I can think of far worse fates."

The blood leaves my face at the mention of worse fates, and Aspen's expression turns apologetic.

"I could have phrased that better." His hand finds mine and laces our fingers together.

With him so close, with his body so warm against me, it's impossible for the flash of dread I felt a moment ago to linger. Our game last night taught me something valuable—that if we must face certain doom, I don't want to do it sulking and living in fear. I want to face it without regrets. I want to live my last days to the fullest because they matter.

I smile up at him, breathing in the scent of his skin. "How do you do it?"

"Do what?" His smile mirrors mine, and it's his sweetest one, the kind that crinkles his eyes, free from mischief and teasing.

"How do you know exactly what to do to get me out of a mood?"

He shrugs. "I think you would know how to do the exact same for me."

I ponder that for a moment. Is he right? If the tables were turned, would I know how to get him out of the darkest humor? "I'd probably just fight with you."

Now the mischief melts into his grin. "Exactly. We work well together, you and I." He brings our lips to meet once again, and this time, we let our kisses linger, deepen. I'm almost certain we're nearing an encore of last night when a knock sounds at the door.

We pull away, breathless and smiling. "We slept late," I whisper. "I suppose we should attend to our duties."

"Must we?"

I ignore him and shout toward the door, "Coming!"

"She's actually not," Aspen adds, "thanks to you."

I swat him playfully as I extricate myself from his arms. He steals several kisses in the process, and by the time I'm at the door, wrapped hastily in a crooked robe, my cheeks are flushed with heat and happiness. However, the face I see on the other side of my threshold has my brow furrowed. It's Marie Coleman.

"Your Majesty," she says with a clumsy curtsy. She's dressed in loose slacks and a cropped, sleeveless linen top, its drape flowing in several folds gathered from a wide, bronze ring around her neck, revealing a flash of skin over her stomach. Although it isn't a dress, I'd know an Amelie design anywhere now. And I'd say Marie seems comfortable in her new Fire Court attire if it weren't for the way she wrings her hands, shifting from foot to foot.

"What is it, Marie?"

Aspen's footsteps approach from behind, and I feel him place a comforting hand on my lower back.

She looks from me to my mate and back again. Finally, she withdraws an envelope from her pants pocket. "My uncle sent me a letter," she says, a guilty look passing over her face.

I take the envelope, unsure why she's handing it to me. "Your uncle knows you're here?"

She lifts her chin in defiance, although the guilt remains in her eyes. "I wrote to him so he can tell my parents I'm safe. I may not have wanted to go back to them, but I didn't want them to worry either."

I bite back my argument. I'd already warned Marie it isn't safe for humans in Faerwyvae when we're at war. Informing her relatives of her whereabouts could create major complications I don't have time for. Especially when her uncle is the Mayor of Sableton. Someone not entirely fond of me, at that.

I turn the envelope over in my hands. The seal has already been broken. "How did you even get a letter to or from him?"

She wrings her hands again. "I may have used an ambassador's seal. I was with Lorelei when she found the one belonging to the former Fire Court ambassador. Once I had my letter, I sent Dune with it. I didn't expect him to bring one back."

"Dune took a letter to Sableton?" My voice comes out sharper than I intend. How did this happen without me knowing? The answer comes to me at once. I've paid very little attention to much of anything this past week, focusing only on my dread. With a sigh, I soften my tone. "That was reckless, Marie. Dune could have been in danger going to Sableton like that. There's no telling if the humans will even honor an ambassador's seal right now, especially one borne by an unseelie."

"I know. I'm sorry."

"So, what did your uncle say? Is he demanding your return home?"

She shakes her head. "The letter he sent back isn't about me at all. He wants to meet with you."

"About what?" Aspen asks, stepping closer.

"He says he has information regarding the safety of the isle."

I exchange a glance with Aspen. His expression is equal parts suspicious and intrigued. I lower my voice to a whisper. "Do you think he knows about..."

Aspen shrugs. "Can you trust him?"

I recall my last interaction with Mayor Coleman at Mother's trial. While he may not have shown the same cruelty as Mr. Duveau, he did make it quite clear he was against me in every way. My pulse races as I pull the letter from the envelope. Aspen leans forward and we read the letter together.

It contains very little more than what Marie has already said. Mayor Coleman claims to have vital information pertinent to the safety of the Fair Isle and requests an urgent meeting with me to discuss it. The only other statement the letter contains is a promise that he offers this conversation in peace, even going so far to use fae verbiage of a *peaceful exchange of words*.

I return my gaze to Aspen, who runs a hand through his hair. "I don't know," he says. "This could be a trap."

He's right, but I don't think I can pass this opportunity up. If there's even the slightest possibility Mayor

Coleman knows anything about the Parvanovae, I have to take the chance. "This could give us the ability to prepare. To fight."

He stares at the letter in my hand as if he could decipher the mayor's intents between the inked words. Finally, his expression softens, gaze meeting mine. "I already know you're going to go, so I'll go too."

"He might not speak with me if you're there."

"If he's desperate enough to reach out to you, he will. And if it's indeed a trap...I can protect you."

There's no use telling him I don't need protection. If Mayor Coleman hides some devious plan, I might need all the protection I can get.

I return to face Marie, who eyes us warily. She seems unsurprised by our whispered conversation, although she can't be fully aware of all that Aspen and I know, either. We've only made public to our people the news that we won the war against the Renounced but still face an even greater threat from the humans. One we might not be able to win. "What do you think, Marie? Can we trust your uncle?"

She shrugs. "I can't say for certain. I know he resented you becoming King Aspen's Chosen instead of my sister and me after the Holstrom girls died. And yet I think you might be right about his desperation. He seems worried about something." Her eyes unfocus as she goes silent for a moment. Then excitement crosses her face. "I know! Bring me. Use me as a hostage in case he tries anything."

"Marie, no—"

"He'll make no move against you if I'm there."

I cross my arms, giving her a pointed look. "Somehow I doubt he values you quite as much as you suggest. If he was eager to ship you off to Faerwyvae, I can't imagine you'd make a great hostage."

"You don't understand," she says. "He's always been fond of me. He may not love the fae, but he considers the marriages forged from the Hundred Year Reaping to be a great honor for human families. Promoting and protecting his family is all my uncle cares about."

"That still doesn't make you a good hostage," I say. "Besides, I think that goes against a peaceful exchange of words."

She rolls her eyes. "We won't call me a hostage. I'll come under the pretense of wanting to see him. My presence will merely be a veiled threat." Her grin glows with mischief as she presses her palms together. "Please, Your Majesty. Let me be useful for something."

I look to Aspen, who shakes his head as if to say he's not the one to ask. I'm probably not the best to ask either, for as much as I want to protect the girl, I must admit her presence could provide just the right amount of collateral to ensure the mayor behaves.

"All right," I say, much to Marie's morbid delight. "You can act as my sort-of-hostage."

"Thank you, Your Majesty," she says, standing straight. I almost expect her to salute. "I'll be the best hostage you could ever hope for."

I shake my head in amusement. Never in all my days could I have expected to hear those words. "Go find Dune," I say. "Since he's so fond of delivering messages, let him take my response back to your uncle."

37

Three days later, after sundown, Aspen, Marie, Dune, and I make our way through the Spring axis toward the wall near Sableton. Dune lights the way, the blue flame hovering over his tail creating a soft glow as he pads quietly across the forest floor. Marie nearly skips with excitement, her enthusiasm unhampered by the exertion of our journey. Luckily, our travels haven't been too strenuous, for Queen Tris granted us permission to transport our party directly to her Spring axis from my Fire axis, something I previously hadn't known we could do.

Marie lifts her face to the night sky, arms spread out before her as she breathes in deeply. "I could get used to this. Everything smells like cherry blossoms in the Spring Court."

"Enjoy it now," I say. "Once we cross the wall, it will be very much fall." I tug my newly made cloak around my shoulders in anticipation of the cool weather that awaits. I can already see the telltale fog that lines the Faerwyvae side of the faewall, telling me we'll reach our destination in a matter of minutes. My heart races at the thought.

I feel Aspen's gaze on me, and I turn my head to meet his eyes. "Are you ready for this?" he asks.

I nod, although I know I can't hide the trepidation I feel. Despite the mild weather of the Spring axis, my nerves have me sweating. None of us know what to expect from this meeting with Mayor Coleman. His reply to my acceptance of his offer to meet was brusque at best. I pat my hip and the dagger strapped around my waist— my newest blade forged from the molten river. It may not be as elegant as my obsidian blade was, or the daggers I took from the weapons room, but it is far more carefully crafted than the one I made at Varney Cove.

We slow our pace as the wall of fog draws closer. Only when we are beneath its blanketing quiet does Marie's enthusiasm begin to wane. "What is the purpose of the fog?" she asks, wrapping her cloak around her.

"Privacy," Aspen says. "To keep humans from crossing the wall."

"Not that it kept them out completely," I add, remembering Mr. Osterman—the Butcher of Stone Ninety-Four —and his vile traps. Even Amelie and I once crossed it when we were younger, driven by a bold dare made by Maddie Coleman. That was a night that changed everything, solidifying my hate for the fae, and my distrust for my mother. My heart sinks with regret. I was wrong about so many things back then.

With the thought comes a chasm of grief, but I allow it to open beneath me, let my body sink into it. Tears prick my eyes and I breathe past the lump in my throat. Instead of swallowing me whole, the grief washes over me, moves with me and through me. Then its power diminishes, turning it into more of a companion than a threat.

Aspen's fingers find mine, and I catch his reassuring smile through the dense fog.

"Foxglove told me the fae are extending the wall around Faerwyvae to protect us from human attack," Marie says. "Is that true?"

I mutter a curse. I really need to have a chat with Foxglove about spreading gossip. Even when it's true. "Well, we were."

"We still are," Aspen says, and I flash him a surprised look. I hadn't realized the efforts were continuing now that the Parvanovae is gone. Then again, maybe I shouldn't be surprised, considering not everyone else reacted to the theft with the same level of apathy as I did. And to be honest, I haven't had much communication with the other royals since then. We've had only one meeting of the Alpha Alliance since our return from Varney Cove, and that was primarily to present Dahlia to the others so she could make her surrender known. When talk turned to the subject of the Parvanovae, and Flauvis began growling insults over my incompetence, I left the meeting. But not before tossing him a rude gesture.

Aspen continues. "The process is slow going, but now that the Renounced have been defeated, King Aelfon has been able to coordinate building efforts in all courts.

"To what end, though?" I ask, lowering my voice. "Without the ability to infuse the wall with an enchantment..."

He shrugs. "Who says it can't be infused with an

enchantment? We may not be able to proceed with the one Estel's sister had designed long ago, but that doesn't mean we can't protect the wall."

Hope begs to rise in my chest, but it doesn't go far. Even if we could find a new enchantment to protect Faerwyvae, will we be able to finish the wall before the next attack? And if we are...what if the humans detonate the bomb in Eisleigh instead? Is there any enchantment strong enough to protect from the blast of an exploding star?

"I sense a human," Dune says from up ahead, shaking me from my thoughts. His blue flame is muted by the mist, and I can barely make out the kitsune as more than a white shape. He pauses for us to catch up. "Stone Eighty-Five, I believe."

"Do you sense only one human or multiple?" I pat my dagger again, wrapping my fingers around its hilt.

"One," he says to my relief. That lessens the chances that this is a trap.

I let my fingers leave the dagger. "Take us to him."

Dune leads us through the mist, the towering stones of the wall now in full view. Aspen's hand remains locked in mine as we make our way between two stones and onto human soil.

The chill is the first thing I notice, the bite in the air sharp against my skin, even through my clothing. My previously warm cloak now feels threadbare, making me wish for a heavy winter coat instead. The next thing I notice is the smell of the forest on this side of the wall, the aroma of dirt and rotting leaves, of waste and pollution in the villages beyond. Finally, I spot the human figure stepping out from behind one of the trees. The sight of the heavy-set mayor sends my mind reeling back to the night of Mother's trial, igniting fire in my blood, but I do my best to keep my rage under control.

Marie nearly starts forth when she sees her uncle, but I place a warning hand on her shoulder to hold her back. If she's going to serve as a warning to keep the mayor in line, I can't have her skipping around without a care. "Somber, remember?" I whisper.

She nods in understanding, slowing her pace to remain close at my side.

We come to a stop several feet from the wall and wait for Mayor Coleman to close the remaining distance. He narrows his eyes at my companions, going a shade paler at the sight of Dune. It's rare for a human to come into contact with a fae who isn't an ambassador, and it's an even rarer thing for them to see an unseelie. When they do, it almost always ends in trouble from one side or the other.

"I thought you'd come alone," the mayor says as he halts before us.

I keep my posture erect, my chin lifted in a regal air. "You thought wrong, Mayor Coleman."

He turns his gaze to his niece, offering her a curt nod. "I certainly didn't expect to see you here, Marie."

She gives him a small smile. "I wanted to see you, Uncle. Her Majesty was so kind as to offer me the chance."

He shifts his jaw, making his bushy mustache twitch. "Are you being treated well?"

"Of course I am," she says. "That's why I've chosen to stay with Queen Evelyn and King Aspen."

I put my arms around her shoulders and pull her

close to my side, doing my best to appear domineering despite the fact that Marie is nearly my same height. "We've been given no reason to treat her with anything but kindness." My words come out slow to emphasize the feigned threat beneath them.

"Right," the mayor says, and I can see in his eyes that he understands completely.

I withdraw my arm from Marie's shoulders and bring it to my hip. "So, why did you ask me here to talk?"

"I said in my letter. I have vital information regarding the safety of the isle."

I pin him beneath a glare. "You're going to need to be more specific than that."

With a deep breath, he takes a step closer, flashing a wary glance at my mate. "Eisleigh's council has been given a twofold warning, straight from King Grigory," he says. "First, that the isle will be under attack by the king's own army coming from the mainland. And second, that only the most prestigious families are to be given notice and urged to vacate."

Dread sinks my stomach, but I do my best to appear aloof. "This news isn't surprising. The fae already know we're at war with the humans. It was only a matter of time before the King of Bretton got involved with the matters on the isle."

"There's more." His expression darkens. "I looked into this matter, spoke to someone I thought would know more. Turns out he knew a great deal more."

From the way he speaks, I already know who he's referring to. "And what did this dear friend of yours say?"

The mayor opens and closes his fists, his cheeks turning crimson. "The king is in possession of a weapon that could destroy all life in a matter of seconds. Not just the fae. *All* life here on the isle."

Marie bites back a cry of alarm, pressing a hand to her mouth to stifle it. It's obvious this is the first she's heard of the Parvanovae and its threat.

I can't keep the steel from my gaze. Even though the news is of little surprise to me, it confirms Mr. Duveau gifted the bomb to King Grigory. Not just that, but he did so fully aware of the power the weapon possesses. Part of me has kept a flicker of doubt over whether he sought it without understanding how powerful the bomb could be, but now all doubts are erased. He knew all along that the bomb would destroy the isle, and he gave it to the human king.

The king who now seeks to kill his own people just to end the fae.

The mayor's eyes go wide. "You knew about this too."

I press my lips tight.

"Do you know when the king plans to unleash this weapon?" Aspen asks.

The mayor looks from me to my mate, shaking his head. "No, but I'm sure it's soon. The last of the covert ships transporting the elite to the safety of the mainland depart from Eisleigh tomorrow night." He opens and closes his fists again, forehead wrinkled. "Do you know what the weapon is?"

There's no use denying it now. "A bomb," I say. "One created by the fae at the end of the first war. I was tasked with protecting it from being used until it could be destroyed, but your dear friend stole it from me."

Mayor Coleman scowls. "Mr. Duveau is no friend of mine or the council's."

I raise a brow. "Is that so? It seemed at my mother's trial he had all of you wrapped around his finger."

"That was before the treaty broke," he says. "We may not know what happened, but we know he failed to keep the treaty intact. And now I know he's directly responsible for this newest threat."

I release a frustrated sigh. "Well, I appreciate the warning, Mayor Coleman, but if you have no more specific intel on the king's plans to attack, then I must bid you a goodnight."

"Wait." He takes another step closer, lowering his voice. "That's not the only reason I requested we meet."

"What else could we have to say to each other?"

He brings a hand to his face, rubbing his mustache as if it will help him find his words. Then his gaze falls on his niece, eyes turning down at the corners at the sight of her flushed cheeks, her unshed tears. He goes still. With a resigned grumble, he pins his arms stiffly at his side. "I need your help. *We* need your help."

I pull my head back in surprise. "Who's we?"

"The humans, Miss Fair—I mean, Your Majesty."

I'm so shocked to hear my honorific coming from his lips that my mouth momentarily falls open. I hurry to hide my astonishment behind a look of skepticism. "Why is that?"

He clenches his jaw as if it pains him to answer the question. "King Grigory has forsaken us, left his people to die just to be rid of a powerful nuisance."

I bristle at hearing the fae referred to as a *nuisance* but clench my jaw to keep from interrupting.

He continues. "He's willing to sacrifice an entire

population to wrest total control from the fae once and for all."

"He won't have much to rule over when he blasts the entire isle to smithereens," Aspen mutters.

The mayor nods. "I think he'd rather lose the isle than face possible defeat."

"Why come to me?" I ask. "What is it you expect me to do about it?"

"You're one of them. One of the fae. You have the ear of the other royals. Not only that, but I trust that you care about the fate of the humans."

"The fae are already doing our best to prepare for it. We will defend Faerwyvae at all costs."

"I know," he says, "but we need you to defend Eisleigh too."

I'm dumbstruck, words stripped from my throat as I stare at the mayor in disbelief. "You've got to be kidding. You want the fae to protect the *humans*? The humans who we are at war with?"

"We will set our squabbles aside."

"So, what? You're offering a temporary ceasefire?" I scoff at that, remembering how poorly my last negotiations over a ceasefire ended. "That's not good enough. We need your total surrender."

The mayor throws his hands in the air. "We have no king anymore, Evelyn. Eisleigh is broken. If you want our surrender, you can have it. It's nothing more than the plea of dying men."

Aspen and I exchange a glance. *He's desperate,* he says through the Bond.

Suspicion has my gaze returning to the mayor. "Why are you so willing to bargain with me? In fact, why are you even on the isle still? You said the king sent word to the council with a warning for the elite families to vacate. Shouldn't that include you?"

His voice comes out small. "I have more than just my household here. Yes, I have my wife and children. But also brothers and sisters." He waves a hand toward Marie. "Nieces and nephews."

"All of whom are among the wealthy elite," I say, narrowing my eyes. "Marie's parents own the most prosperous trade ships on the isle. Their ships could take your entire extended family to safety."

"Every one of their ships is out on trade," he says through his teeth. "As soon as the treaty was broken, the king sent word to all the ports, forbidding ships from returning to Eisleigh. That's when he launched his warships."

I frown. "None of the other ships would take you?"

"I'm not leaving my family," he says. "My wife won't leave her sisters. My brother won't leave without his daughters." His gaze turns to Marie, and his face falls. "Maddie won't leave Bircharbor, awaiting the return of her husband."

I bite back my urge to break the news that Maddie Coleman will be waiting indefinitely. With Cobalt dead, she's no longer the wife of a fae king.

The mayor gestures at his niece. "I doubt this one will leave the fae, for whatever godforsaken reason has her enamored with your kind. Please, I'm begging you. Tell me there's something you can do for the humans."

I close my eyes and bring my fingertips to my temples, my mind whirling with thoughts, questions, solutions. It's already an impossible enough task to come up with a way to protect Faerwyvae. How can we possibly make a plan that could save Eisleigh too? And if I agree to defend the humans myself, is there anything I can do to get the other royals to join me? I can already imagine Flauvis trying to convince the others that we should take this opportunity to eradicate the humans.

Aspen's voice comes through the Bond like a smooth caress. *What are you thinking, my love?*

I think you know, Aspen.

You want to protect everyone on the isle. But is it possible?

I open my eyes to find his, my answer pulsing through the Bond. *I don't know, but we have to at least try.*

Then you know what needs to be done, he says. *We must craft a bargain. One tempting enough for the other royals to accept.*

He's right. Already, I know what I must offer.

Marie comes up to me and Aspen, tears streaming down her cheeks. "Please help them."

"I will," I whisper to her. It's more than a statement. It's a promise made from the bottom of my heart. Even if I fail, I know I must at least try.

I face the mayor. "We shall make a bargain. If we save the humans, the Fair Isle falls under fae rule from then on. Agreed?"

His expression darkens. "You have the surrender of Eisleigh's council. We will not fight you. We will set all grievances aside and forge a new treaty. But turning rule over to the fae is too much. It's asking me to give up my position as mayor. My livelihood."

I let out a bitter laugh. "Oh, so your job is worth dying for?"

He mutters a curse under his breath. "No. But why would you require such a sacrifice?"

"It's the only way the rest of Faerwyvae will agree. I can only do so much on my own. To save the isle, we need all fae—seelie and unseelie alike—fighting for the same cause."

He shakes his head rapidly. "They'll eat us alive. Literally."

"Not if it's part of the bargain," I say. "Humans surrender to a fae rule. The fae in turn work to save the isle from the bomb. No humans rise against us, no humans are harmed."

His chest heaves as he studies me, a sheen of sweat coating his face.

"Do you agree?" I ask.

He gasps a breath, and with it comes another string of muttered curses. "Fine," he bites out. "On behalf of Eisleigh's council and people, I agree to this bargain."

A sob of relief escapes Marie's lips, but my own comfort is short lived. This bargain brings even more challenges. More to lose.

"Will you spread the word?" I ask. "Assure us no one will rise against the fae or our efforts to do what must be done?"

"I will."

"Good. Then I promise I will do whatever it takes to save the isle. However, it would be a lot easier if we knew when or where the bomb will be detonated. If we can steal it back, we could destroy it the same way we'd previously planned. You're sure there's nothing else you can tell us?"

"No," the mayor says, a dark glint in his eye, "but I know someone who can."

My heart races. I already know exactly who he means. "Mr. Duveau?"

The mayor nods. "I can tell you where to find him."

38

I've never run so fast in my life. Even with the increased swiftness my fox form allows, I know I'm pushing myself to the limit. Still, I run on and on, fueled by necessity. Need. Hope. With every panting breath, I keep my destination fixed firmly in my mind.

Port Denyson. Port Denyson.

That's where I'll find Mr. Duveau, catching the last ship from Eisleigh, leaving under the veil of night. Why he's taking a ship off the isle when I damn well know he has my Chariot, I cannot say. All I can do is pump my fox legs as fast as they can go, skirting around the most populated cities and towns in favor of forests. When towns can't be avoided, I rush through cobblestone streets, fully aware that my glowing fur won't allow me to pass as a regular fox.

Luckily, very few people catch sight of me, and those who do make no move against me. What could they do, anyway? To them, I am the unseelie beast they were taught to fear. Until Mayor Coleman's message about our bargain circulates the isle, that's all I and the rest of the fae will be.

There is one tangible threat to my progress, and that is exhaustion. At first, my flames are sufficient fuel to revitalize me just when I'm about to slow down. But the farther I get from the faewall, the weaker my fire becomes, and the more often I must stop for rest. With Port Denyson being at the southeastern end of Eisleigh, so distant from the wall and the magic of Faerwyvae, my travels grow more taxing as the hours drag on.

Hours. I've been running for hours and still have several more to go. My journey began soon after the meeting with the mayor, once I'd convinced Aspen to take Marie and Dune back to Fire so he can round up the other royals for an emergency meeting when I return. It took a bit of arguing to get him to agree to part ways, but he eventually conceded, knowing Duveau is our best shot at gaining an advantage over the coming threat.

But only if I make it in time.

Despite my aching paws, I continue to run.

ANXIETY RUSHES THROUGH ME AS THE SUN BEGINS TO lower in the sky. Mr. Duveau's ship is set to sail after nightfall—a coward's escape. I hate that the elite families of Eisleigh get to flee to the safety of the mainland while the unsuspecting villagers sleep, no clue what terrors await them. Not yet at least. If the mayor keeps his side of the bargain, the humans will know what's coming soon enough. They'll know they've been betrayed by their king with no one but the fae to save them.

My muscles are screaming as night fully falls over the forest, but still I press on. Just when I'm starting to lose hope that I'll ever find the port, the tang of salty air begins wafting in on the breeze, a sure sign my destination is near. Finally, the trees of the forest give way to a small seaside town. I slow my pace as I enter its sleeping streets, trying to orient myself. The sound of waves falls on my ears, but I'm not just looking for the sea. I need to find the port. The docks. The ships.

I attune myself to every sound, every smell, my fox instincts sharp as they take in every bit of data that filters through my senses. Then I hear it. The low hum of a boat's foghorn. I dart forth again, listening deeper, seeking the telltale sound of waves lapping against the hull of a boat.

I reach the beach, docks in sight. Racing forward, I search for signs of Mr. Duveau's ship. Yet all I see at the end of each pier are small fishing boats. I locate the larger docks where trade vessels and cruise ships would be. They're all empty. I run to the end of one, rich with recent scents of human bodies. One distinct, familiar aroma stands out above all the rest, turning my stomach. He was here. I can smell it.

I sit back on my haunches and stare out at the dark water. There, hundreds of meters out to sea, sails the last ship to the mainland. I'm too late.

Disappointment lashes through me, so strong it has me shifting out of my fox form and into my human body. I stumble back, catching myself on my forearms to keep from toppling over completely.

No, no, no, no. I can't have missed it. I ran as fast as I could.

My mind whirls with calculations, recalling every minute I wasted on rest. I now regret letting myself catch my breath, rest my paws. If only I'd pushed harder. If only I'd...no. There's still a chance.

I rise to my feet and undo my cloak, letting it fall to my feet as I assess the distance between here and the ship. I could swim to it, couldn't I? Or harness the element of water and get it to propel me to the ship? But even if I somehow could catch up, could I board it somehow? Pretend to have fallen off and call for a life raft? Then what? Do I question Mr. Duveau on the ship and then swim back here before it can take me too far?

No, no, none of this is logical.

My anxiety rises higher and higher with every inch of space that grows between myself and the ship. I know I must take action. Do *something*, logical or not. I must jump, swim.

I reach a hand out to the water, connecting to its element. Depth, emotion, sorrow—

Nothing.

I feel nothing.

I try to connect to my flame, my rage, my passion, but it's hardly more than a flicker inside me. This is the farthest south I've ever been from the wall—farther than Grenneith, and way farther than Sableton or Varney Cove. All I feel is aching muscles, blistered toes. My exhaustion is so heavy, I doubt I could shift back into my fox form if I tried.

Sinking to my knees at the edge of the dock, I stare down at the black water. It's over. Our last chance to get answers from Mr. Duveau. My last shot at vengeance. Gone. Gone.

"Please," I mutter, although I know not who I beseech. The Great Mother above? The All of All? "Please!" I call out again, louder now. "He doesn't deserve to get away."

The water has no answer for me. Nothing but the steady rise and fall of waves rippling from the motion of the departing ship. The ship bearing my enemy.

"He doesn't deserve safety," I say through my teeth. Then, closing my eyes, I throw my head back and shout into the night, "He doesn't deserve to live!"

"I say that about most humans."

I startle at the voice, drawing back from the water and the equine head that breaks above its surface, eyes red like rubies. Its fur is midnight black, dark mane floating around it, tossed by the waves. The rest of its body is hidden beneath the water, but I don't need to see it to know what creature this is.

Kelpie.

In a flash, I reach for the belt at my waist, retrieving my iron blade. "Stay back."

"I do not come to hurt you," he says, though his tone is far from comforting.

I assess the kelpie through slitted lids. "How are you even here?"

"I swim," he answers without humor.

"We're too far from the wall. There's no magic out here."

The kelpie rumbles with hissing laughter. "No wall can separate magic from the sea. It is everywhere."

I shake my head. "I can't feel it. No matter what I try, I don't feel connected to the elements here."

"That's because you are not of the sea."

"Perhaps," I say, "but fae are never seen this far from Faerwyvae, not even sea fae."

"Melusine forbade us," he says. "Although I prefer to think I have no master, no king or queen, I obeyed this order. It was for our protection. Sea fae do not like it on the human side of the sea. We can hardly stand to swim through the polluted waters, and when we do, the iron nets and barbed hooks are enough to keep us from coming back."

"Then why are you here now? I am not lost. I am in no need of your services."

"No, I suppose you are not." His tone holds a hint of regret. "Although, I hoped you would find yourself lost today, for you owe me a life. Yet every time I spied you running past my rivers and streams, you were a fox. And the fox knew the way."

A chill runs down my spine. The kelpie has been watching me? For how long? I saw no sign of him during my travels here. Then again, my focus wasn't on seeking out other creatures; it was on finding the port.

When I say nothing in reply, the kelpie releases an equine snort and begins to rise from the waves.

I take one step back, then another, keeping my blade between us as the kelpie pulls himself onto the dock with a sinuous agility a normal horse would never possess.

Righting himself on four enormous, ebony hooves, he pins me with his ruby stare, paying no heed to the threat I hold in my hand. "I saw what you and your mate did to the vile ship."

I furrow my brow; it takes me several moments to comprehend what he's referring to. "You were at Varney Cove?"

"The seelie rat who called himself king summoned my kind to his aid. Very few obeyed. The rest of us came only to watch."

"I'm sure it was great entertainment for you," I say, a bitter edge to my voice. Aspen and I could have used some assistance on the beach that day. If the sea fae weren't going to help Cobalt, they could have helped us instead. Especially considering Cobalt's death makes Aspen Regent of the Sea Court until another sea fae can gain the blessing of the All of All.

"We approve of your actions against the ship."

I put my free hand on my hip and toss him a sardonic glare. "Thanks for your approval."

A stretch of silence falls as the kelpie continues to watch me with his unsettling gaze. I'm considering the best way to extricate myself from the conversation when the kelpie speaks again. "You call yourself unseelie."

"I do."

"And yet you do not hate all humans."

"I do not."

The kelpie's eyes burn a shade brighter. "And yet you hate the one on the ship."

I shudder. "Yes."

"Would you like to speak with him? I could bring him to you."

The hair rises on the back of my neck. As much as I want to say yes, I can feel the threat of a bargain hanging in the air. I squeeze my dagger tighter. "What will it cost me?"

The kelpie's long, serpentine neck curves to the side, allowing him a glance behind him at the ship. When he returns to face me, his serrated teeth are bared. Whether the expression is supposed to be a threat or a smile, I know not. "A life."

I shake my head. "I will not give you my life."

"You need not," he says. "The life of the one you hate will do."

My pulse pounds rapidly, my eyes flashing to the ship. It's so far out now, it's nothing more than a dark shape amidst the equally dark night.

"Do we have a bargain?"

I swallow hard. "Yes."

39

The kelpie leaps off the dock and into the sea, disappearing from view. All I can hear are waves and the pounding of my own heart as I watch the ocean, the ship, unable to see anything taking place on it from here.

With bated breath, I stand vigil as several anxious minutes pass. With every inhale I take, doubts creep in, and I begin to wonder if the kelpie had been tricking me. He only insinuated that he'd bring Mr. Duveau to me at once, but a specific timeline wasn't part of the bargain. In fact, we never even agreed on who exactly I sought. Then again, the kelpie must have some strange ability to track travelers. He found me when I called for help in the coral cage, then located Aspen soon after on his rampage toward Sableton.

Sweat pools under my arms, behind my neck, despite the chill in the air. Several more agonizing minutes pass and there's still no sign of the kelpie. I begin to pace, ready to curse the kelpie and myself for making such a reckless bargain. Then motion stirs in front of the dock, sending my heart into my throat. I inch forward for a closer look, only to leap back as the kelpie suddenly breaches the surface. I stare open mouthed as he pulls himself onto the dock with a male figure locked on his back.

Terror and delight mingle in my gut as I watch Mr. Duveau gasp for breath from the kelpie's back, sputtering water from his blue lips. His elegant evening attire is dripping seawater, his hands and neck red where the kelpie's mane strangles his flesh.

"I brought you the one you hate," the kelpie says. His mane begins to shift, slithering from around Mr. Duveau like the coils of a snake. Once freed from the kelpie's bonds, the councilman falls to the dock at my feet.

Mr. Duveau coughs up water as he pushes himself to his hands and knees. Before he can do anything else, I'm upon him, my blade at his throat as I push him onto his back. His eyes are wide as he blinks the water from them, holding his palms out in surrender.

"Miss Fairfield?" His tone is laced with surprise, his voice rough from swallowing so much saltwater.

I press the blade closer until it knicks his flesh and heave myself over him. With my free hand, I reach beneath his jacket and retrieve his revolver. I chuck it over the other side of the dock and return to my search, bringing up two knives, which also make it into the sea. Further digging proves fruitless, as his pockets are empty of the one thing I'm looking for. "Where is the Chariot?"

"Please don't hurt me," he gasps.

"Wrong answer." I press the dagger closer, drawing a stream of crimson to trail down his throat. I avert my gaze, seeking something else of the same hue. Then I find it—a strand of red rowan beads circling his left wrist. Lifting my blade from his neck, I slice the bracelet off and toss it behind me.

Now the fear truly shows in his eyes as I lower my face toward his. He blinks rapidly, his chest heaving with his sharp, shallow breaths.

"Stop blinking or I'll cut your eyelids off."

"I'll tell you anything," he says, lids still fluttering. "Do anything."

"I know you will." I bring the dagger to the corner of his eye, letting the tip pierce his skin. "Now. Stop. Blinking."

Trembling, he obeys, face going a sickly shade paler.

I lock my eyes with his, drawing his attention to me. The imagery of the bird doesn't come, which makes me wonder if he's hiding rowan elsewhere on his body. Then I recall my difficulties connecting to the elements, the magic of Faerwyvae. Does that mean I can't glamour him?

No. I have him. He's not getting away.

I bring my face even closer until our noses nearly touch. His pupils grow so wide, they devour his irises. I focus on that black void, summoning my rage, my fury, my inner fire. The flame I touch is barely a flicker, but it's there. I call it forth, let it wrap around me, move through me, growing as large as it can despite this world without magic that threatens to tamp it back down.

Maintaining a steady awareness on my inner flame, I again seek the imagery of the bird in the cage, drawing his eyes to me, locking his attention in my grip...

There.

His consciousness becomes a bird, and my will is its cage, grasping him tight within my hands.

I have him.

His face goes slack, but his body remains rigid. My control over him feels tenuous at best, but at least it's something.

"Where is the Chariot you stole?" I ask.

His body trembles beneath me, but he answers without hesitation. "I gave it to King Grigory."

Fury courses through my veins as my lips peel back from my teeth.

"It won't work from Bretton anyway," he adds, as if that makes his treachery any better.

"And the Parvanovae?"

"I gave that to him too."

"And what is he going to do with it?" I already know the answer to this, but I want to hear it from his lips.

"He has ordered it to be detonated on the isle."

"When?"

"Five days from now."

"Five days?" My heart leaps into my throat. It takes all my effort to keep hold of the glamour. "Where will it be detonated?"

"Just beyond the wall in Faerwyvae."

I'm a little surprised at this. I'd assumed the army would try to detonate the bomb on the Eisleigh side of the wall, especially now that Mr. Duveau's broken alliance with Dahlia removes their opportunity to enter Faerwyvae unfettered. "How will the army get into Faerwyvae?"

"A warship."

"The warships were sent back to Bretton."

He gives a subtle shake of his head, but his eyes remain involuntarily locked on mine. "Not all will truly return. Tomorrow, one of the warships turns course and heads straight to its destination."

"Which is where?"

"Here. The warship will dock in Port Denyson."

My mouth goes dry. Of course the warship would come here, to one of the farthest points from Faerwyvae. That way, even if the fae were able to intercept the army, they'd be too far from their magic to do much harm. Still, it's a reckless plan. It will take the humans days to get from Port Denyson to the wall, especially with such precious cargo demanding a careful pace. There must be more to it than that. "How are they transporting the bomb?"

"I don't know."

Rage courses through me as I raise my voice to a shout. "How are they doing it! Tell me!" Just like that, I'm stripped from my concentration, severing the glamour. My body feels weak in its absence, but I force my limbs to remain steady as I bring the blade back to Mr. Duveau's throat.

Free from the glamour, he closes his eyes and whimpers like a broken animal. My lips curl in disgust; the sight of him so helpless makes me feel cold, sick, empty. Somehow, seeing my enemy brought to his knees is far less satisfying than I expected it to be. I can't help but think of Amelie sobbing over Cobalt's remains.

"Thank you," he says, snapping my attention back to the present. "Thank you for releasing me."

I purse my lips. If he wants to believe I released the

glamour on purpose, I'll let him. But that doesn't mean this is over.

Reconnecting to my inner fire, I remind myself of everything he's done. All the pain he's caused. Rage courses through my veins. "I'll ask you one more time," I say through clenched teeth. "How are they transporting the bomb?"

"A...a tank. I think."

A tank? I curse under my breath. I've only seen the armored vehicles depicted in the broadsheets. From what little I know of them, they're strong and deadly.

"Let me go," Mr. Duveau says, voice trembling. "I must catch up with that ship."

"Perhaps you should have thought twice before condemning the isle to death."

He shakes his head. "I never wanted this to happen."

"Oh, is that why you stole the Parvanovae from me and gave it to King Grigory?"

"I didn't think he'd use it *here.* I thought he'd use it on a distant enemy, not the Fair Isle."

I clench my jaw. "If that's true, then you're a bigger idiot than I ever thought before."

"You left me with nothing," he says. "The treaty stripped me of my position, my pay. My wife was made a social pariah. My sons—"

"Sons?" The blood leaves my face. All this time, I never imagined Mr. Duveau as anything other than a monster. Never could I have imagined him as a husband or father.

"Yes, my sons," he says, desperation straining his voice. "They're on that ship with my wife. Please, just let me return to them. They're only five and eight."

Darkness crawls into my heart, turning my voice cold and cruel. "Why should your sons' father live when my mother had to die?"

His eyes go wide, shoulders trembling. "I was following the letter of the law."

My lips peel back from my teeth. "No, you weren't. You were saving your pride."

"I was saving the treaty," he argues. "For my family. For peace. I never sought the isle's destruction. Giving the bomb to the king was wrong; I see that now. For all I know, the blast will reach Bretton and my family will die there too. Just let me be with them when it happens. That's all I ask now."

Despite my burning rage, watching him plead sends the darkness draining from my heart, leaving only emptiness in its wake.

He must see my resolve faltering, for the color rushes back into his cheeks. "Please, Evelyn. I'm so sorry."

With a heavy sigh, I toss my iron blade to the side, letting it skitter a few feet away. Then I pull myself to my feet.

Mr. Duveau scrambles back, eyes wide as if he can hardly believe I'm letting him go. "Thank you."

"Don't thank me," I say, turning my attention to the kelpie waiting silently at the edge of the dock. "It's all up to you now, Mr. Duveau."

He slowly turns his head to follow my gaze.

"Miss Fairfield," he whispers. "Please don't."

"I'm sorry." I take one step back, then another. At the same time, the kelpie inches toward its prey. "But I made a bargain."

Mr. Duveau's gaze flashes to my discarded blade. The kelpie takes another step forward.

"At least you can swim," I say, tone flat. Just as the kelpie lunges at him, I turn around, squaring my shoulders as I retreat down the dock.

The last thing I hear is Mr. Duveau's strangled scream cut off by a thunderous splash.

40

The journey back to Fire takes almost two days. I push myself nearly as hard as I did getting to Port Denyson, but as exhausted as I am, I force myself to rest far more often. As I cross the faewall, I find Aspen waiting for me in his stag form, and together we run the rest of the way to Fire, utilizing the axis line for the fastest travel. Once we make it back to Irridae Palace, I barely have time to clean myself up and change before I'm rushing back down the stairs to the atrium where my fellow royals await.

I slow my pace at the final staircase before the atrium, taking in slow, deep breaths to compose myself. With each breath comes an awareness of the magic flowing through my veins. After being nearly stripped from it at Port Denyson, I don't think I'll ever take this feeling for granted again. Nor will I curse the heat of the Fire Court. The heavy warmth that envelops me as I make my way across the atrium feels like a luxury after the bone-deep chill of a human autumn.

I approach the sunstone table, where all the other royals gather, some seated, others standing. Aspen turns to face me, a comforting smile on his lips, contrasting with his furrowed brow. On our journey from the wall to Irridae, I relayed to him all the details I'd learned from Mr. Duveau, but neither of us are looking forward to sharing the news with the others.

Squaring my shoulders, I take my place at Aspen's side. All of Faerwyvae's royals are here, not just the Alpha Alliance. However, with Cobalt's death leaving Aspen as Regent of the Sea Court, the only newcomers at my table are Dahlia and an ambassador from the Solar Court. Aspen told me earlier that Phoebe's heir has yet to be established, considering our victory over the Renounced brings an official return to the Old Ways. The radical seelie courts will have the hardest time adjusting to this, I'm sure.

The Solar ambassador bends in a bow of respect, while Dahlia gives me a tight-lipped nod. I offer her a saccharine grin, silently praying that someone gains the blessing of the All of All to dethrone her as soon as possible. My gaze moves around the table to far more welcome faces—Nyxia, Estel, Aelfon, Tris, Minuette, and...well, compared to Dahlia, I suppose Flauvis' wolfy sneer is a welcome sight too.

Aspen's hand brushes mine, and he gives my fingers a squeeze. The warmth of his skin makes my chest feel light, and my breaths come easier.

"Thank you for gathering for this urgent meeting," I say. "We have much to discuss, so I'll get into it at once. I know when the Parvanovae is set to strike."

Flauvis rumbles with a mocking growl. "You mean the weapon you let some pathetic human steal from you—"

"Flauvis!" Fire ignites over my body, rippling in tricolor flame from my head to my toes as I fix the Winter King with a furious scowl. "If I hear one more asinine comment from you—*one more*—I will leap over this table and tear out your throat with my teeth."

He opens his mouth, and I expect his high-pitched imitation to follow. Yet, to my surprise, he says nothing. His lips curl at the corner of his muzzle in a canine smirk...but he doesn't speak.

I return my attention to the others, waving my hand across the table. "The same goes for the rest of you."

Aspen snickers at my side and Nyxia struggles to hide her grin behind an air of boredom.

I extinguish my flames. "The Parvanovae comes in three days. It is set to strike just beyond the wall in Faerwyvae. One of the retreating warships will be turning course, if it hasn't already. It will then dock at Port Denyson, and the army will take the bomb north to the wall. If my intel is correct, the Parvanovae will be transported by an armored weaponized vehicle called a tank."

The table is silent as all eyes stare unblinkingly back at me. I expect gasps, shouts of alarm, arguments. But there's nothing. Nothing but quiet trepidation humming across the table.

"This means we still have one more chance to steal the Parvanovae back and use it to enchant the wall," I say, then face the Star Queen. "Estel, did you find your sister's blueprints for the enchantment?"

The particles shift and sway over Estel's face, obscuring it. She hesitates before finally saying, "I did."

I frown. "And?"

The particles continue to shift until they settle on a well-composed smile. "And it can be done. If we expand the wall around Faerwyvae, I can transmute the Parvanovae to fuel the enchantment. No one but the fae will be able to cross the wall, whether entering or leaving. To any human, it will be as if a solid barrier exists."

Hope flutters in my chest, making me want to bounce on the balls of my feet. Reeling in my excitement, I turn to the Earthen King with every ounce of grace I can muster. "Aelfon, how is the progress going with building the wall around the perimeter?"

"Now that the fae are no longer fighting amongst themselves," he says, "I've been able to send builders into every court that touches the sea. They've made progress, but it would be impossible to finish their work in three days."

My stomach sinks at that. "What about fae from other courts? Can we get all fae with an affinity for the earthen element to aid their efforts?"

Aelfon tilts his head one way, then the other, considering my suggestion. "That could help. I still doubt we could build an entire wall around Faerwyvae by then, but with more fae on the job, it's possible."

I bite back a grimace. "There's more. We don't just need a wall around Faerwyvae. We need it around the entire isle."

Nyxia's eyes go wide as she throws her hands in the air. "Why would we do that?"

"It wouldn't be possible," Aelfon says. "Our magic is too weak on the other side of the wall."

"Not if we first destroy the border wall," Aspen says.

I'm grateful my mate already knows my plan, my ideas. Knows what a daunting task it will be to get everyone else on board. At least someone here is already on my side.

Flauvis leans forward, panting, eyes glinting with enthusiasm. "Yes! We will break down the wall, unleash our magic, and destroy the humans! Finally, an idea I can support."

"No," I snap. "We aren't breaking down the wall to destroy the humans. We will free our magic so we can face the soldiers at Port Denyson with our full strength. But also..." I resist the urge to wring my hands, clenching my fingers into fists instead. "I've made a bargain with the humans."

Gasps and growls rumble from around the table. Even Nyxia looks murderous as she stares daggers at me.

"They've surrendered to the fae," I say. "The isle belongs to us now. All of it. But only if we protect it from the bomb. That means we must protect the humans too."

Minuette lets out an angry whistle through her teeth. "You never should have bargained without coming to us first."

I put my hands on my hips. "Would you have chosen differently? Would you have given up the opportunity to regain control over the land that first belonged to the fae?"

"No," Nyxia says, arms crossed over her chest, "but I may have worded things differently."

"Yes, how exactly did you word it?" Tris asks.

"And who will rule the portion of land that is now Eisleigh?" Dahlia asks, her voice like razors down my spine. "Are you claiming it yourself?"

I narrow my eyes at the Summer Queen. "No."

"Can we make the humans our slaves?" Minuette asks.

Flauvis runs his tongue over his muzzle. "Can we kill them after we save them?"

"Excuse me," Tris adds. "Must I remind you *again* that I do not support the extinction of humans? However, I don't want them living too close to me, either. Not with their...smells." She wrinkles her nose. "What will we do with them after we save them?"

Aelfon clears his throat, a sheepish look crossing his face. "I agree we shouldn't kill them, but I do think we should take the land back from them."

Dahlia leans forward with hunger in her eyes. "But how will we divide it?"

"Pardon," the Solar ambassador says, "but I do not think a conversation regarding land ownership should happen until the Solar Court has an official ruler blessed by the All of All."

"—*blessed by the All of All*," mimics Flauvis. "I say only those who were part of the Alpha Alliance should have rights to the new lands. The rest of you can—"

"Enough!" Aspen shouts, his voice ringing through the atrium.

That silences the others, but fire heats my core. "This is not what I called this meeting to discuss," I say through my teeth. "I don't know what we will do with the isle after we face the human army, but first we need to survive this war. This isn't the time to fight over land and power. We need to come up with a plan."

Nyxia runs a hand over her silver tresses, smoothing them away from her face as she releases a grumbling breath. When she speaks, her words are strained with poorly hidden animosity. "A plan would be far easier to come up with if you hadn't bargained the isle in exchange for more work from *us*."

"It may be more work," I say, "but it's in our best interests."

Nyxia raises a skeptical brow. "How so?"

"Well, returning the isle to the fae, for one."

Aelfon nods his agreement and Dahlia runs her tongue over her lips, as if she can already taste the extra land she hopes to claim.

I continue. "For another, this gives us a chance to free Faerwyvae's magic all over the isle. We won't be trapped on this side or drained of power on the other. With the humans' surrender, we can enter Eisleigh free of reproach. We can go *anywhere*. We can face the troops who invade at Port Denyson as soon as they touch land. We can meet them on our terms."

Nyxia lets out a resigned sigh. "All right. You have a point."

"There's still the issue of the wall," Estel says. "If we are to extend it around the southern half of the isle, we must first break down the border wall to release our magic. Then we must gather enough builders to finish the job before the invasion. With only three days, I don't know if it can be done."

"She's right." Aelfon leans back in his chair, arms crossed over his wide torso. "These aren't just ordinary stones. Each one is crafted with earthen magic, forged from crystals, rock beds, and soil. Not only must we destroy the thousands that make up the border wall, but we'll have to craft hundreds of thousands more. I don't know if it can be done in three days."

"Not to mention," Tris says, "even those of us with powerful earthen fae in our courts will need to reserve a fighting force."

Minuette nods. "We'll need to defend our courts, send soldiers to fight the men from the warship…"

"Prepare to defend the area beyond the border wall in case the army gets through our fighters," I add, my stomach sinking.

Aspen faces me, lips pulling into a frown. "That's a lot to prepare for in three days."

I look from him to the others. "There must be a way. Even if we can't finish the wall, we can at least pour all our efforts into stealing back the bomb. Then we can finish the wall once we have the Parvanovae."

"The human king will only send more warships to harry our efforts," Nyxia says.

"Then we'll keep fighting," I say. "We'll keep fighting and building until the wall is complete and Estel can perform the enchantment."

The responses uttered from around the table are mostly halfhearted mumbles of agreement.

"There is another way." The voice that speaks doesn't come from the gathering. I look toward the source and find Fehr watching us from the other end of the atrium. With slow steps, he approaches. His face is unreadable, but I see apprehension in the tense set of his shoulders.

"What is it, Fehr?" I ask.

"The wall. It can be built in three days."

"How?"

"You can use a djinn."

41

"Adjinn?" Flauvis falls into a fit of howling laughter. "You mean, like you? You've got to be kidding."

I ignore the Winter King, keeping my eyes on Fehr. "You think you can move the wall?"

Fehr lifts his chin. "The djinn are the most powerful of the fae, and I am no exception. Fire may be my primary element, giving me the power to create, but the earthen element obeys my command nearly as well. My strong affinity for air lets me move swiftly through time and space. I could break down the border wall and build one around the perimeter of the isle before the earthen fae can so much as fortify a single court."

Excitement rises inside me, but an obstacle remains that keeps his plan from being sound. "But you can't leave the palace."

"No," he says, "I cannot."

"He wants you to free him," Flauvis says, still shaking with mirth. "The creature who rose against his people wants release from his Bond so he can do it again."

Fehr turns a slow scowl to the Winter King. "My kind are all but extinct, and not one lives outside the bonds of slavery. There will be no uprising from us again."

Minuette watches the djinn through slitted lids, her blue hair rippling wildly about her face. "You just admitted the djinn are the most powerful fae. If you can singlehandedly build a wall around the isle, you could turn on us."

"I could," Fehr admits, a haughty smirk tugging his lips before he returns his gaze to me. "But I won't. If you free me from my Bond to Irridae Palace, I will build the wall. I will fight against the human army. Then, when the battle is won, I will return to serve you of my own free will."

"Do I smell a bargain?" Nyxia lifts her brow, assessing the djinn.

Fehr's jaw shifts back and forth. "Yes," he says through his teeth. "I will make a bargain."

I study Fehr, seeking signs that he plans to betray me, manipulate me. Abandon us when we need him the most. I recall how cold he was with me when we first met. How reluctant he was to serve me. But things have changed between us. He may not laugh or smile or chat at ease with me the way I caught him doing with Foxglove, but...he doesn't hate me.

"All right," I say. "We'll craft a bargain."

The table goes still, silent, with my breathing as the only sound. Each set of eyes watches me with anticipation; those on the far end of the table lean forward with keen interest.

I toss a glare at the royals. "We shall craft our bargain *after* the meeting and do so in private."

Rumbles of disappointment circulate the table as I return to it. Fehr bows low and steps back.

"So, we have a plan," I say. "Fehr will aid Aelfon's earthen fae in building the wall. The rest of us will prepare our soldiers. As soon as the border wall is down, we'll march to Port Denyson. There we'll fight the human army with the primary target to steal back the bomb. We must fight them with care, however, so we don't accidentally detonate it."

"Then when we have it," Estel says, her shimmering particles once again swirling rapidly to obscure her face, "I'll transmute it."

I can't help but feel there's something she isn't telling me. Or perhaps it's just because her particles keep hiding her expression. Is she simply nervous? She has every right to be, I suppose.

My gaze leaves hers to fall on the others. "Are we in agreement?"

"Are you sure we can trust the djinn?" Flauvis asks, teeth bared.

"I'll deal with him myself," I say. "Now are we in agreement or not? I need a yes or no so we can get to work."

Nyxia huffs. "When I said I'd support your claim as queen, I never anticipated you'd be so bossy."

My eyes lock with hers, and I lift my shoulders in a casual shrug. "You aren't the only one who's had to learn not to underestimate me." My gaze slides to Dahlia for a moment, and I let my lips peel back from my teeth until the Summer Queen blanches.

Nyxia's mouth quirks into an approving grin. "Well then. I agree to your plan, little foxy." She turns her gaze to the others. "And you? I've got places to be, you know."

The rest of the table adds their agreement.

Just like that, we stand a fighting chance.

WE FINALIZE THE DETAILS OF WHAT TO DO OVER THE NEXT three days, and then the royals begin to funnel out of the atrium to return to their courts. Fehr follows them into the courtyard to see them off.

Aspen lingers behind, turning to face me. His arms wrap around my waist and I bring my hands to his shoulders. Tilting my head back, I look into his eyes, finding true joy in them. Even though he hadn't fallen into the pits of apathy like I had last week, he hadn't seemed convinced we'd actually come out on the other side. He seemed more...at peace with death than anything else. But the expression he wears now contains true conviction. Optimism. Hope.

He smiles down at me. "Have I told you lately what an incredible queen you are?"

My lips turn up at the corners. "Well, that's the first time I've heard it today."

He brings his lips to mine, our first kiss since I returned from Port Denyson. Every second since has been clouded with anticipation of today's meeting, but now that it's over...

I retreat a step until I feel the edge of the table come up against my back. "You know, we've still never tested out this table. To see if it rivals Nyxia's?"

His irises glitter and his lips curl with mischief. "Important research. I agree it must be done. Do you think the royals have all left yet?" Pressing his body close, he places his hands on the table, framing my hips. His lips return to mine, his kisses slow and teasing. I lean back, drawing him against me.

A throat clears, and I find Fehr has already returned from escorting the royals.

"We really need that bell we spoke of." Aspen's voice is a husky growl in my ear.

I giggle and reluctantly push him away. "You might be right. But I should speak with Fehr. I'll come find you later."

After claiming my lips in a final kiss, my mate leaves me alone with Fehr.

I straighten the skirts of my saffron gown—another Amelie creation—and approach the djinn.

"We should craft the bargain sooner rather than later," he says. "That way I can get to work on the wall at once. I'll begin tearing down the border wall tonight."

"Very well. So, how do I release you from your Bond to Irridae Palace?"

He frowns. "Shouldn't we craft the bargain first? That way you can ensure I return to your service like I said I would?"

"Fehr, we're not making a bargain."

His eyes widen, then narrow with suspicion. "You aren't releasing me." He shakes his head, lips pursed tight. "I understand your concern, Your Majesty, but this might be the only way to finish the wall in time."

"I'm releasing you, but not into a bargain."

He blinks at me a few times. "I don't understand."

"You've been trapped beneath the Bond since before humans knew fae existed. I can hardly comprehend how long that has been. You may have rebelled against the fae, but I think you've paid the price for that already."

He assesses me through slitted lids. "No one would dare free a djinn, much less release one without a bargain. Most fae consider us monsters. Traitors. Murderers."

"You aren't the only one in this room who could claim those same titles." Mr. Duveau's chilling scream before he was taken by the kelpie rings through my mind. "I've killed my share. I've fought those whom I once considered my people. Used my magic for harm."

"No one would deem your crimes equal with mine."

"You know what, Fehr? I don't care. I don't care what the other royals would choose if they were in my shoes. Nor do I care what you've done to deserve your punishment. I told you from the start. I'm not Ustrin. I won't force you to serve me."

His breathing grows rapid, dark eyes glittering with hope. "You're truly going to set me free?"

"Yes. However," I lift my chin and I burn him with a steely gaze, "if you betray me at any point, I will hunt you down and kill you with every bit of strength I have. Understood?"

Swallowing hard, he nods.

"Good. Now, how in the bloody name of iron do I free you?"

～

ONCE MY BUSINESS IS DONE WITH FEHR, I MAKE MY WAY through the palace halls, searching for a head of copper hair. Finally, I spot Amelie where I should have thought to look first—in the seamstress' quarters. There I find her hunched over a swath of gauzy crimson fabric spread out before her. My newly appointed seamstress—a fae with tan, fuzzy skin and eight long, dexterous limbs—bends into a graceful bow, then returns to her work at a loom nearby, weaving yards of pale blue spider silk. I yearn for a closer look at the fae, for I'm almost positive she's making the silken strands from her own body, but I'll have to save that for another day. One where I'll have time to ask a lot of questions.

Instead, I approach Amelie, watching as her hands fly over the fabric, creating a row of neat stitches. It didn't take long for Amelie to find her way here after we returned from Varney Cove, and she's been here nearly every day since, working alongside her new mentor.

She looks up, grinning when she sees me. Her face is bright, making her look so much like she did when we were younger. But not quite the same. Dark circles hang under her eyes, and there's a density to her energy that not even the biggest smile can hide. At least she's found a way to channel that energy and whatever else lurks within her heart in the wake of Cobalt's death.

She rises to her feet, showing off the length of the gown-in-progress. "I'm making this for you."

I eye the ruby silk and the row of golden jacquard that lines the bottom hem. "It's beautiful, Ami."

She returns to her seat and immediately gets back to sewing. "How did the meeting go?"

I cast a glance at the seamstress, who'd paused her

work to watch us. Averting her gaze, she seems to get the hint and scurries out of the room on all eight legs.

Once I'm sure the spider fae is out of earshot, I perch at the edge of the table Amelie works at. "It went well," I say, struggling to maintain a casual air. I'm still trying to sort out how to speak to Amelie without a figurative wall between us. It doesn't feel quite natural yet, but I know we'll get there. "We have a plan. There's a chance we can intercept the Parvanovae."

"Good," she says. "There would be a lot of nice dresses going to waste if we all end up obliterated." She says it with a sardonic laugh, but I can't bring myself to join. There's a very real chance this plan could fail, making it all too real to joke about.

Bringing my hands to my lap, I anxiously pick at a fingernail. "I also released Fehr from his Bond to the palace."

Amelie looks up from her work, eyes wide. "Why would you do that?"

"He's going to help build a wall around the isle."

She furrows her brow but returns to sewing. "That's helpful, I suppose."

"Yes, it was interesting how I was able to free him. There's something he never told me—something I probably could have guessed if I'd thought about it."

"What's that?"

I bite the inside of my cheek. "He told me I've had the power of his true name all along. Since he was Bonded to Irridae, he was essentially Bonded to its ruler as well. When I took his hand that first time he confronted us outside the palace steps, the power of his true name was given to me."

Her stitches begin to slow. "So, then you released him?"

I nod, feeling a lump rising in my throat. "He told me how."

She stops sewing altogether, her gaze slowly lifting to meet mine.

I can hardly see her through the sheen of tears that glazes my eyes. "Amelie Fairfield, by the power of your true name, I release you from our Bond."

Something snaps inside me, and a tangible weight is lifted from my heart, my shoulders. Amelie leans back with a sharp inhale, as if finding her lungs suddenly larger than they were before. We stare at each other for several seconds, both trembling as we orient ourselves in this moment. One where my sister is no longer my slave, my subordinate, and I no longer carry the burden of her name.

Then her face crumples. No sooner than she rises from her feet, I close the distance between us, wrapping her in my arms. Tears stream from our eyes as we sob into each other's hair, taking our first steps at returning to what we were always meant to be.

Sisters.

42

Later that night, I pace alongside one of the ponds in the palace courtyard, pulling my cloak tight against the chill in the air. I'm still getting used to how cold the desert can be at night, but the coolness helps counteract how badly I'm sweating.

Sweating and avoiding sleep.

A dark shadow swoops overhead, making me jump, but one glance tells me it's just Venitia the moon dragon. The shadow of his mate glides over the mountains in the distance. Earlier, I ordered the dragons and firebirds to establish sky patrols. Even though we still have three days before the risk of invasion, I want to be prepared. I want eyes on every stretch of land from here to the faewall, in case the humans manage to break through our forces at Port Denyson.

With a sigh, I return to my pacing. It's the only thing that seems to keep my heart rate from skyrocketing. Perhaps I should have joined Aspen in preparing our soldiers. They'll be working through the night to ready themselves to march to Port Denyson. And since my nerves won't let me find sleep...

"Are you going to do this all night?" comes a voice from the palace steps. It's Lorelei. I whirl toward her, finding Foxglove at her side. The two ambassadors slow as they draw near, and Lorelei raises a questioning brow at me.

"No," I say. "Just until I feel tired enough to sleep."

Foxglove lets out a low chuckle, shaking his head. "Sweetie, we all know that's not going to happen. Might as well enjoy your insomnia." He thrusts a cup toward me, then reveals two more.

Now I see Lorelei holds two bottles in her arms, cradled like twin infants. "You never did try Agave Ignitus wine. It's the Fire Court equivalent of Midnight Blush."

I make to return the cup to Foxglove, but he pointedly ignores me. "I don't want to drink anything," I say.

Lorelei sets one of the bottles down and wrestles the cork out of the other. "Sure you do. It will settle your nerves." Refusing to hear my protests, she fills my cup, then hers and Foxglove's.

"Drink up, Your Majesty," Foxglove says with a wink.

I shake my head. "You two enjoy it without me. I can't indulge tonight. We could set out to march at any moment."

Lorelei barks a laugh. "Evelyn, you've already been marching for an hour."

Foxglove's eyes turn down at the corners. "We saw you pacing from the window."

"And it isn't helping a thing," Lorelei adds. "The best thing you can do right now is relax."

I stare at the amber liquid in my cup. "I'm not in the mood to get drunk."

"Drink," Lorelei says, lifting her glass. "Don't get drunk. If I can manage a clear head and a couple glasses of wine, so can you. Let's enjoy what might be one of the last nights of our lives."

At those words, my heart leaps into my throat, and wine just might be the only thing to coax it back down. Besides, she's right. If everything goes wrong, this could be one of my last calm moments with my friends. One of my last calm moments *ever*. And what did Aspen teach me about living each day to the fullest? I doubt pacing counts as that.

"Fine," I say, "but I'm only having one cup."

I HAVE THREE CUPS. FOUR.

But the wine is unlike any other I've had. The flavor is sweet, warming my stomach in the most comforting way. My mind remains strangely clear while my body is completely and utterly relaxed.

Foxglove, Lorelei, and I lay on our backs in the sand next to the pond, staring up at the stars. I can't help but miss the view from the telescopes at Lunar, but the sky is still impressive from here.

Foxglove lets out a dreamy sigh. "What do you think Fehr's doing right now?"

"Breaking down the wall," I say. I expect a rush of anxiety to wash over me at the mention, but it doesn't.

Lorelei rolls onto her side, propping herself up on her elbow to face Foxglove. "Has he kissed you yet?"

"Stop, you're embarrassing me," he says with a giggle, although I can tell he's relishing the attention to his love life. "Powerful beings are delicate creatures to seduce, all right? Maybe after all the doom and gloom is over."

My heart clenches. Of all the things that could upset me right now, the thought of Foxglove and Fehr never seeing their budding relationship through is oddly painful. Yet another reason why we must win this war. "Do you really think we can do this? Steal the bomb back?"

Lorelei sits upright and points a forbidding finger at me. "No, Your Majesty. We are not talking about war right now. We are relaxing."

"I'm relaxed," I say, and it's true. Even though my worries remain in the back of my mind, they don't send me pacing like they did earlier. "Just humor me. Is our plan crazy?"

She purses her lips with a glare, then finally relents. "No," she says with a sigh. "It isn't crazy. We're going to meet a single warship with the full might of Faerwyvae and its magic. There's no way they'll make it past us."

"We'll have to hold back, though," I remind her. "We can't do anything too reckless in case we jeopardize the bomb."

A corner of her mouth quirks up. "Is that a warning to me? Will I have to reel in my roots?"

"I'm more worried about the winter fae. Flauvis is bad enough."

Foxglove sniffs. "I'm glad I'll be away from the fighting altogether. I'll be perfectly content keeping things running here at the palace while you bloodthirsty warriors go do your fighting." He waves a fluttering hand.

I laugh. I can't even imagine Foxglove in combat. Verbal combat, perhaps. But physically fighting another? No way. It does make me wonder, though...

"Foxglove, what's your unseelie form?" I ask. "You once told me you're a flower fae, but I've never seen you shift into anything else. Nor have I seen you manipulate the elements in any visual way."

His expression falters, and Lorelei bites her lip, a warning in her eyes. Blazing iron, did I say something wrong?

I'm about to apologize when he releases a sigh. "I'm not too fond of my unseelie form," he says, shoulders slumped.

"Why is that?"

"Let's just say, I was never a very pretty flower. My parents were quite unimpressed with me. That's why I'm so fond of human things and the ability to maintain a seelie form. This way, I can be anything I want, look however I want. I get to shape my own beauty."

I can't help but smile at that. While he may not be tall, and he's neither slim nor muscular like most other fae males I've met, he *is* beautiful. Inside and out. "What powers do flower fae have?"

"We create beauty," he says with a shrug. "Each flower fae expresses that in a different way. Some create the most exquisite glamours. Others build impressive gardens. I haven't explored my own abilities too much, but I think I may start to one day."

"You are really good with hair," I say, recalling how he'd styled Amelie and me when we first came to Bircharbor.

"I am," he admits. "But I'm thinking even bigger than

that. Palaces, perhaps."

Warmth fills my chest at the mention of palaces, bringing to mind the game of pretend Aspen and I played. "When this is all over, Aspen and I may have something in mind."

He opens his mouth to reply, but a rushing sound, like a bellowing wind, enters the courtyard, drawing our attention to the tile walkway. There, a whirl of sand barrels toward the front doors. Foxglove is on his feet before anyone else, smoothing the front of his burgundy jacket, then adjusting his spectacles and hair. "Fehr," he says, a blush of color rising to his cheeks.

The cyclone pauses outside the palace doors, then dissipates to reveal the djinn. His dark hair is wind-tossed, bare chest rippling with more muscles than I can count. I'm not sure if it's the wine, or if freedom has made Fehr look more majestic than ever, but Foxglove isn't the only one blushing as the djinn approaches us.

Fehr spares a glance at Foxglove, lips pulling into a subtle smile, before his eyes lock on mine. "Your Majesty, I have broken down the border wall."

"Already?" Seeking my inner fire, I summon my flames to flood me, burning away all remnants of the wine. Euphoria slips away, leaving my pulse racing in its absence.

"That was the easy part," he says. "Now the building begins."

That's not all that begins, I think to myself. If the wall is down, that means it's time.

I curl my fingers into fists to keep my arms from shaking. "All right then. Go to the other royals. Tell them it's time to march."

43

Standing at the edge of a bluff just outside the docks at Port Denyson, I look out at the dark shape that crosses the Channel of Bretton. Dawn is barely a blush on the horizon as the warship makes its journey, still just a tiny speck in the distance. My eyes dart from the ship to what lies beyond—the mainland. From this high up on the bluff, I can just make out a sliver of land on the other side of the channel. It's strange to think that such a sight would have once inspired longing. Now it only fuels my rage. For there lies the seat of King Grigory, the man who would annihilate my people.

I rest my hand on the comforting hilt of a dagger—one of several obsidian blades gifted from Nyxia that now ring my waist. The weapons belt is cinched around the slim black tunic I wear beneath a bronze, lightweight breastplate, while thick leather trousers hug my legs. My hair is braided tight in a coronet around my scalp.

I steal a glance at Aspen, who stands at my side. His clothing is nearly identical to mine, aside from the belt of knives. He seems to think his antlers will suffice. His breastplate is also much larger and heavier than mine is, carved with maple leaves. Sensing my gaze, he turns and meets it. His eyes reflect everything I feel—rage, anticipation, trepidation. Fear. Neither of us can find smiles in this moment, but a look is all we need to express all that must be said—that we will fight to the death if we must, but first we shall fight to live.

A raven caws overhead, making its descent to the bluff. As it lands, Franco takes its place and makes his way to his sister, who stands in tense silence next to Lorelei. Aspen and I join them, as does Estel. The rest of the royals and fighting forces await down below, hidden just out of sight from view of the beach.

Lorelei gives me a tight-lipped smile as we approach, her usual swagger gone. She's outfitted in black trousers and bronze armor as well, which makes me realize I've never seen her in anything but a dress. It somehow makes her look even smaller than she is, and with that comes a wave of panic over her safety. But even though her presence puts her in mortal danger, there are few others I'd rather have fighting at my side. I've seen what she can do with her powers. Petite or not, I know how fierce she can be.

"I got a closer look at the warship," Franco says, shoulders rigid.

"Anything unusual?" Nyxia asks. Like always, her appearance is stunning, with shimmering black slacks that look unlike any fabric I've ever seen, and armor made from scales of moonstone and obsidian.

"What's unusual is the warship isn't alone. There are three smaller ships with it."

"Three!" Nyxia rounds on me. "You said a single warship. You mentioned nothing about three more."

"Neither did Mr. Duveau," I say. "I compelled him under a glamour. If he didn't mention the three ships, then he didn't know." Either that or my glamour wasn't strong enough, considering how weak my magic was. Of course, I don't say this out loud.

"The three smaller ships may be a naval guard for the warship," Estel says. "Were they armed?"

"Not like the warship," Franco says. "They seemed heavily armored and staffed, but they don't look like fighting vessels."

"Then we wait and see what they do," Aspen says. "They aren't expecting an ambush, so the warship won't attack until prompted."

"Won't they see the wall?" Franco asks. "I saw the stones on my return from spying. They'll know something has changed when they see it."

I look out at the beach and docks where Fehr has yet to complete the wall, then at the rows of stones that begin farther down. We know the warship will simply blast down any stones that interfere with its ability to dock, creating more work for Fehr, so we've decided to save this portion of the wall for last. As soon as we have the Parvanovae, we can destroy the warship without hesitation. Until then, we must treat our enemies like glass.

But Franco's right. With the rising sun illuminating the port, they'll see the stones once the ship draws near. They may not know an ambush is coming, but they'll be wary of attack.

A rush of wind swirls over the bluff, revealing Fehr when it comes to a stop. "The wall is finished," he says, chest heaving as he catches his breath. "I just erected the last stone, aside from the port. We're ready."

Relief has my shoulders dropping, chest open with an easy breath. "Thank you, Fehr."

"Finally, some good news," Nyxia says.

I turn to Estel. "Will you be ready to perform the enchantment once you have the Parvanovae?"

Like at our last meeting, the particles disperse over her face to hide her expression. This topic must truly make her nervous. "Yes. All I need is contact with one of the wall's stones."

I nod. "Good. Once we're in possession of the Parvanovae, you get to the wall. We'll destroy the warship—"

"I wish I could do it right now," Aspen says through his teeth, fingers clenched into fists as he casts a dark glance at the channel. "It will take all my restraint not to rip it to shreds as soon as it docks."

I suppress a chill, visions of the broken ship at Varney Cove flooding my mind. With his full strength and all the magic he needs at his beck and call, there's no doubt he'll be able to destroy it on his own.

"As soon as we get that bomb, it's all yours," I say. Then I turn to Fehr. "After the warship is destroyed, you will build the final stones."

The djinn nods. "I'll await the signal."

"And when the last stone is in place, I'll perform the enchantment," Estel says.

Nyxia lifts her chin with a smirk. "Then the isle will belong to us."

～

MORNING ILLUMINATES THE SHIPS AS THEY DRAW NEAR THE port. We remain on the bluff, crouched down to keep out of sight. Just when I think the warship will pull in toward the dock, it slows and turns starboard. My heart races when I consider it might be leaving and returning to the mainland. I can't tell if I'm angry or relieved, for we still need to regain possession of the Parvanovae. So long as it's in human hands, no one is safe.

But the warship doesn't change course; it remains in place with its port side facing us. The three smaller ships proceed forward, leaving the warship in the channel.

Panting breaths and the heavy padding of enormous paws tells me Flauvis has arrived. Not bothering to keep out of sight, he runs to the edge of the bluff. "Is the beast too scared to get close?" he says with a teasing laugh.

"Don't let your arrogance make you comfortable," Nyxia says. "The smaller beasts still come."

"Perhaps they're scout ships," Lorelei says. "Come to scope out the territory before they bring the troops in from the warship."

She might be right, but the sight of the smaller ships unsettles me. They may not be heavily armed like the warship, but there's still something terrifying in their design. What's even more unsettling is that the three ships don't head for the docks; they close in on a long stretch of beach beneath the bluff we're hiding on. Which means, if they hadn't noticed the new wall before, they must now, for Fehr left off his progress at the far end of the beach.

"Why are we hiding up here like fools?" Flauvis asks. "Why aren't we swarming these humans as soon as they touch land?"

"You know why," Aspen snaps. "We can't do anything reckless until we know who has the bomb. Trust me, it's making me crazy to do nothing too."

Flauvis grumbles in response, but he doesn't argue.

With bated breath, I watch as the three ships come in closer to the beach, expecting them to run aground at any moment. But instead, the bow of the three ships moves easily from water to sand, revealing a flat keel that keeps the ships upright as they ground.

"What kinds of ships are these?" Franco mutters.

I shake my head. "Nothing I've ever seen. They're amphibious. At least, partially so."

Flauvis' hackles rise and he begins to pace. "These ships bring death. We need to attack."

The same trepidation has the skin prickling on the back of my neck. Everything in me wants to keep whatever is on those ships at bay, wants to destroy them before a single soldier can emerge. But one of these ships could have the bomb. Destroying them could detonate it. "Just...wait."

Voices ring out from below, commands too distant to hear. Then, to my horror, the bow of one of the ships splits, swiveling outward like two doors. Once open, a ramp is lowered from inside. The other two ships follow suit, bows gaping wide. I can't help but imagine the ramps they spew as tongues lolling from the maws of great iron beasts. I expect fire, teeth, a guttural growl, but the inner belly of each ship remains dark, hiding what it contains.

"I don't like this," Aspen says next to me.

I don't either, but I can't find my words. I can hardly

blink as I watch those platforms, sound roaring to life from inside each ship. Then movement.

From the first gaping mouth comes an ironclad vehicle, rolling down the platform on two rows of elongated tracks. Its front is mounted with an enormous gun.

My blood goes cold. It's a tank.

Another one follows as the first drives down the beach, crawling over sand and driftwood with ease. Then the other two ships deploy their cargo, and soon six tanks are driving toward the docks.

That's when the soldiers emerge from the ships, crawling over the beach like a swarm of ants.

I turn to the others, heart hammering against my ribs. "The Parvanovae is in one of those tanks."

"We need to get to them," Nyxia says.

"Without blowing them up," Lorelei adds.

Flauvis paces anxiously at the edge of the cliff. "Well, isn't that just great," he growls. "They're made of pure iron. I can smell it from here. No one is getting inside one of those *unless* we blow it up."

"No one except me," I say. "I'm the only one who can get close enough."

Aspen clenches his jaw, and I can see the worry in his eyes. But he knows what must be done. "I'll cover you."

"As will I," Lorelei says.

"Those tanks are armed with guns, and possibly other explosives," I say, voice trembling. "I can't use my fire on them."

Aspen exchanges a glance with Lorelei. "We'll use earthen elements," Aspen says.

"Good idea," I say. "Let's get to our forces. Tell them

the plan. Engage the soldiers but focus our efforts on keeping those tanks from breaking past us. Estel—"

"I'll remain here," she says. "So long as I have this vantage, I can watch for the Parvanovae. If I discover which tank is carrying it, I'll come to you."

"And I'll await the signal to finish the wall," adds Fehr.

Aspen and I lock eyes, and I feel an invisible embrace reach down the Bond. Then I meet the gaze of Franco, Nyxia, Lorelei, and Flauvis. Terror, hunger, and rage swim in their eyes, echoed in the pounding of my blood.

With a steadying breath, I curl my fingers around the hilts of my daggers as flames heat my core. "Time to fight."

The fae stream down the abandoned streets of the port town, racing for the beach. Guttural cries fill the air, mingling with animal sounds and the roar of the approaching tanks. My blood throbs in my head as I run, Aspen and Lorelei on either side of me. Gunfire greets us as we arrive at the street outside the docks. My two companions extend their hands, reaching toward the earth. They draw out enormous roots that tear through cobblestones to block the bullets. The three of us huddle behind a wall of roots as we steal glances of what lies ahead, ducking behind the roots just in time to avoid another blast. Other fae rush past us, deftly dodging bullets. Human screams follow, then more gunfire.

I glance around the edge of the root wall, splotches of crimson catching my eye. I don't let my gaze linger long enough to see whether it belongs to human or fae. Instead, I seek the first tank, eyes locking on it as it draws closer. Soldiers march on foot ahead of it, keeping anyone from getting too close. Just as I retreat back behind the roots, I catch sight of a brown, shaggy wolf taking down one of the soldiers.

"It's coming," I say. The roar of the tank draws closer. Closer. Footsteps pounding ahead of it.

Aspen looks around our barricade, then back at me. "Now!" He leaps from behind the roots and runs toward the tank, Lorelei and I following just behind. We split formation to avoid the eye of the tank's enormous gun, Aspen running to one side, Lorelei and I to the other. Reaching for the ground, he sends several coils of roots springing up, lashing at the soldiers surrounding the vehicle. An enormous, gnarled limb sweeps their legs out from under them, sending gunshots wild. The tank's gun swivels toward Aspen, but he closes in and under its reach, its fiery blast soaring overhead. Another tangle of roots erupts from the ground to pummel the bodies of the men still standing.

Lorelei and I race to the other side. With a roar, she pulls up a network of roots to wrap around the tracks of the tank. The tracks grind against their bonds, while another set of roots—either hers or Aspen's—rise from the ground to wrap around the barrel of the gun, locking it in place.

More fae join the fight, tackling any soldier who moves in to defend the tank. The fae fighters carve a path straight to the side of the vehicle, which Lorelei and I rush to take advantage of.

"I need to get inside," I say once we reach it, gasping for breath as I press in close to the side of the tank.

"How?" Lorelei grimaces, her skin ashen as she struggles to maintain such a close proximity to the iron beast.

Craning my neck, I eye the top and spot the rungs of a ladder set at the back of the vehicle. "There. We need to move around back."

As if in answer, a wall of roots shoots up at the rear of the tank, and Aspen dives behind it. His tunic is already torn, bronze armor dented in places, forearms splattered with blood. At least the blood doesn't appear to belong to him. "Go!" he shouts.

I race to the back of the tank and hoist myself up the rungs. Keeping my flames burning hot within my core, I utilize their power to fuel my strength, moving me up the ladder which was clearly designed for a much bigger person. At the top of the tank, I find a circular hatch with a handle shaped like a wheel. Grasping it with both hands, I turn it with all my might. It doesn't budge. Does it lock from the inside? I pause my efforts to stare at the hatch, pondering how I can break through. I could try and melt it, but I'm hesitant to use fire around a vehicle that carries explosives. And possibly the Parvanovae itself. I'm about to shout down at Aspen for assistance from his powerful roots, when sound splits my right ear. A wall of roots shoots before me, just in time to block the bullet. Even so, I feel the sting of something sharp graze my shoulder. Ignoring the feel of hot blood raining down my arm, I ignite a layer of flames to heal my torn flesh and return my efforts on the handle. Then, to my surprise, I find it shifting easily in my grasp.

I leap back as the hatch pops open, and out from it emerges a soldier, rifle leveled at me. Fire leaping to my palms, I duck beneath the barrel of his gun and grasp the front of his uniform, fire lapping up his chest. I realize my mistake too late; if he falls back into the tank, the flames could ignite whatever is inside. My fear is short lived, however, as a sharp root climbs up the side of the tank and spears the man through the chest. Then it lifts him from the shaft, taking him and my flames from the tank and tossing the man through the air. From the ground, Lorelei meets my gaze with a nod.

I don't hesitate a second more, leaping through the hatch and down the shaft. As my feet meet the floor inside, I reach for the hilt of one of my blades and send it soaring toward the figure who stands at the tank's enormous scope. I connect to the element of air to control the trajectory of the blade. My dagger meets its mark, striking his gut, and the soldier collapses with a grunt. I see no one else in the main chamber, so I race toward the front. There I find the driver, trying desperately to move the vehicle past the tangle of roots. Before he can react, I unsheathe another dagger and bring it to his throat. His eyes meet mine, pupils dilating as his mind bends to my will.

So, not all the soldiers here are outfitted with rowan. Good to know.

"Where is the Parvanovae?" I ask.

"I don't know what that is." His voice is flat, toneless.

"Where is the weapon your king sent you to detonate?"

"I don't know. It's covert. Only the troop that carries it knows."

"Is it on this tank?"

"No."

"Are you sure?" My heart pounds so hard in my chest, I feel like it will explode.

"I'm certain. We're a diversion."

I curse under my breath. Even though I knew it was unlikely I'd find the star bomb so quickly, I can't fight the crushing disappointment. Keeping my eyes on his, I say, "Stop fighting. It's over. Abandon your tank and raise no more arms against the fae."

He gives a subtle nod, and I release him. I then return to the man I stabbed, finding him still alive, hunched over on the floor beneath the scope. With a groan, he pulls the blade from his gut. When I reach him, my fist moves into his hair, pulling his head back until his eyes lock on mine. Trapping him beneath my compulsion, I repeat the same orders I gave his companion. Then, retrieving my bloody blade, I return it to its sheath and scramble up the shaft.

Once on the ground outside the tank, I fight to catch my breath, seeking signs of Lorelei and Aspen amidst the chaos. The roar of another tank sends the ground rumbling as it skirts around this one. I clench my teeth and run after it. *Please let it be there.* My nerves are already frazzled after infiltrating just one tank. There are six in total. Six that could be carrying the bomb.

Roots reach for the tracks, lacing between them. A man emerges from the top hatch, shooting at the ground. I dance back to avoid the spray of gunfire. Lorelei pursues the tank with more roots. A second man joins the first at the top of the tank, blasting the roots with his keen aim. Each time one root gains hold, it's blasted in half. And it doesn't take the men long to realize an even faster way to deal with their woes—one of the men lifts the barrel of his gun and points it at Lorelei.

With a shout, I dive for her, pulling her back. Her body lurches, and she lets out a cry. Her roots uncoil, freeing the tank and it takes off down the street. Lorelei moans, grasping her bicep. I pull her toward me, ushering her into the shadow of the disabled tank, and inspect the wound.

"Were you shot?" I ask, voice trembling.

She throws her head back with a hiss, but says, "It doesn't feel like iron." Finally, she pulls her hand away, revealing a gash but nothing embedded in her flesh.

Relief washes over me. The bullet must have ricocheted off her breastplate.

"I'll heal," she says. "The iron in the air is making it worse, though. I'm not as strong as Aspen in that sense."

I look around, past fighting pairs, blasts of sand and gunfire. "Where is he?"

"He went to disable the tanks still on the beach," she says. "But you need to get after the one that got away."

"Can you stand?"

She pushes to her feet, and I can see the skin around the wound has already begun knitting back together. We're about to take off when another tank barrels toward us. Lorelei reaches for it, and again roots shoot from the earth to wrap around the tracks. She turns to lock eyes with me. "Go!"

With a nod, I turn in the direction the runaway tank was heading and find it's nearly reached the end of the street. To catch up, I'll need speed. With a shudder, I shift into my fox form, taking off on all fours. In a matter of seconds, I close the distance between myself and the tank, but without Aspen or Lorelei, how do I stop it?

The ground rumbles beneath my paws, then the cobblestones ahead seem to come to life, rising from the ground in front of the tank. Aelfon rounds the corner, flanked by dozens of earthen fae, some with horns and hooves, others with limbs like gnarled trees. The tank fires its gun, blasting a hole in the barricade, but in its place sprouts another stone. Another. As I race toward the tank, the hatch opens and out pour three men, storming from the tank to engage the surrounding fae on the ground. If each tank holds only three men like the first, that means the tank is empty.

This is my chance.

Skirting behind the fighting men, I leap onto the tank and scurry up the rungs, through the open hatch, and down the shaft. Inside, the belly of the tank is empty. I pad around it, seeking any sign of the Parvanovae. Tuning into my senses, I sniff for anything familiar, listen for the strange hum that always accompanies the presence of the bomb, feeling for its vibrations. But there's nothing. Unless it's well hidden, it isn't here.

Damn. Two down, four to go.

I race back to the shaft, paws on the lower rungs, when a shadow darkens the opening above me. The soldier freezes when he sees me, and I give him a warning growl. Then, tossing something down the shaft, he slams the hatch shut.

Shifting back into my human form, I climb the rest of the way up the shaft and grasp the handle. But as my hands close around it, I remember the object the soldier had thrown.

The skin prickles at the back of my neck as my eyes lock on the cylindrical object beneath my feet.

A grenade.

45

Biting back a scream, I wrap my hands around the handle of the hatch and turn with all my might. Just like it was outside the first hatch, this one is impossible to turn. There must be a locking mechanism I don't know about.

Sweat beads at my brow as I cast another glance at the grenade. My inner fire can sense the spark devouring the unseen fuse inside the device, and I know I only have seconds before it reaches the detonator.

My lungs collapse as fear locks me in an iron grip. How do I get out of this? How? I could melt the iron walls, but will that be fast enough? If I wrap myself in my flames, will they protect me from the blast? I may be strengthened by fire, but I can't see how that will help if my body is blasted to tiny pieces. The memory of Cobalt and the other sea fae I saw obliterated by a grenade has me trembling.

I need to be invisible. No, ethereal. If I could walk through walls like a wraith...

I sense the spark racing toward the detonator.

This is the end. It's here.

And all I feel is fear.

Take it to the Twelfth Court.

I don't know whose voice it is—is it Aspen's? Mine? — but I obey. Gathering all my fear around me, I close my eyes and wait for the blast.

WHEN IT DOESN'T COME, I BLINK INTO A WORLD OF shimmering violet.

My first thought is that I'm dead.

The grenade exploded, and in my journey to the Twelfth Court, I avoided pain but not the physical blast. However, if I were dead, I'd like to think the afterlife wouldn't leave me in the same place I died. And that's exactly where I am now, inside the tank with a grenade below my feet. The only thing that has changed is that all matter is now composed of shimmering particles of violet light.

I study the grenade, surprised that I can see through its outer shell to the inner spark that has slowed to a snail's pace. Like the first time I visited the Twelfth Court, time neither moves nor stands still. Everything around me is in motion, alive, active, and yet seconds and minutes and hours don't seem to exist. Neither do walls. Although the tank surrounds me, its particles shift and sway, and the longer I look at them, the less substantial they become. Soon the walls appear paper thin, a mere layer I can peel back with my thoughts, providing a view of what's on the other side. Squinting through the particles, I see a soldier suspended in midair, as if he were leaping from the tank. Another is doubled over as an earthen fae's horned head rams him in the gut. Other fighters are nearly frozen in battle.

I pull my attention back to the inside of the tank and examine myself. I too am composed of violet light, still clinging to the top rung of the shaft. My body feels weightless, as if I could float away if I simply let go of the rungs. The rungs seem both firm and weightless at once, given shape only by my hands. As if...

My heart has grown calm since entering the Twelfth Court, my mind steady. With my intent fueling each move, I lift a hand from the rung and press it against the vibrating particles that form the wall nearby. It feels firm beneath my hands yet yielding at the same time. Shifting my attention to the layers of swirling light outside the tank, I extend my hand. As if the tank were made of air, my hand slips through it. Angling my body away from the rungs, I slip both hands through the walls, pushing out as if swimming through slow, murky water. With my body fully outside the tank, my feet seek the ground, touching down just as a bone-chilling vibration rattles the air behind me. Moving faster than the other figures in my proximity, I run, tackling the nearest earthen fae in the process, hoping I can push him as far from the tank as I can. Each step I take feels heavy and yet strangely buoyant. I'm halfway down the street by the time the tank explodes, sending slow, violet flames and debris unfurling incrementally outward.

I turn to watch, hypnotized by the deadly dance of flame and shards of iron, but more pressing concerns urge me on. Surging into the mass of languid fighters suspended in battle, I race back to the beach. There I see Lorelei, frozen in time, her roots wrapped around a tank like a cocoon. Willing my sight beyond the walls of the tank, I see three human figures, electrical wires, mechanical panels, crates of guns. But no orb of powerful, dangerous light that I'd expect from the Parvanovae. I continue on, to where Aspen stands before the last three tanks. The closest one is nearly buried in sand, while the farthest one back is tangled in ropes of seaweed.

I gaze through the violet particles that compose each tank, beyond every layer, but I see no sign of the Parvanovae.

It isn't here at all.

WITH THIS REALIZATION COMES A RETURN TO SOUND, TO color, to substance. The Twelfth Court vanishes, leaving me in the midst of chaos. Fighting rages all around me as I struggle to orient myself with this new location and the flow of time. I only have a moment to gape over the fact that I truly escaped the exploding grenade through the magic of the Twelfth Court. But now that I'm here, new dangers await. Igniting my flames over my skin, I race to Aspen.

"I don't think the Parvanovae is in any of these tanks," I shout over the din once I reach his side.

He looks at me, temples pulsing as he thrusts outward, pushing the nearest tank back, burying it deeper in the sand. "How do you know?"

"I just do." At least I hope I do.

The tank struggles to climb from the sand, but it gains just enough purchase for the barrel of its gun to swivel toward my mate. Before it can fire, Aspen flicks his hand, and the enormous gun twists and bends, like the rifles he manipulated at Varney Cove. With a blast, the gun backfires, imploding the tank with a modest burst of flame.

"Well, it wasn't in that one, that's for sure," Aspen says.

"They all must be diversions," I say. "There must be another tank. Perhaps they sent another landing ship farther down."

"One of the fliers would have seen it," he says.

I turn my eyes to the sky, but only a few members of the aerial team remain there. Most must have joined the fighting on the ground. But that gives me an idea. "I'll go back to the bluff," I say. "Ask if Estel has seen anything unusual."

"Be careful," he says. "I'll take care of the rest of the tanks."

With a nod, I shift into my fox form. Racing on all fours, I take off back to the cobblestone streets, dodging blasts and bullets as I head for the bluff.

WHEN I REACH THE BLUFF, I FIND ESTEL AT THE EDGE. SHE looks out at the fighting below, perfectly still. All that moves are the particles on her face, crawling rapidly and blurring her features.

Shifting back into my human form, I stand at her side

and look down on the chaos. Flames dance into the sky above two of the tanks, while another sinks into the sea, strands of seaweed pulling it deeper down until it disappears from view. The beach is coated in blood and debris, the air clouded with smoke. I look away, seeking signs of any other evasive force at work. But there's nothing.

"I don't feel it," Estel says.

I turn to look at her, watch as her expression settles into one of concern. "Feel what?"

"The Parvanovae," she says. "I thought I would be able to sense it, but I can't."

"Have you ever sensed it before?"

"The day you brought it to the meeting of the Alpha Alliance, I sensed something. Before you even presented it to us, I felt it shifting the weight of the air. However, I never noticed it before, in all those years it was kept at Irridae Palace. Perhaps it wasn't always in the weapons room. Perhaps when it was, the iron clouded my senses. That's what could be clouding them now."

"Estel, none of the tanks are carrying the bomb."

She sighs. "It could be on the warship. They might be holding back just to see if they can wear us out fighting the tanks first. For all we know, a greater force awaits."

"Maybe I can find out." From this vantage, the warship is in full view. If I can return to the Twelfth Court...

With a deep breath, I close my eyes, fueling my intent with a need to see beyond the limitations of physical form. Just like before, the world returns to shimmering violet when I open my eyes. Time slows down once again, while the particles composing everything both dead and alive move rapidly over my vision.

I immediately look to the warship. It's difficult to see anything except the ship itself at first, but then the layers begin to split, revealing what lies beyond. I see human bodies, pulsing and shifting. Their numbers are far less than I expect, perhaps only a fraction of the men one of the landing ships brought. The brightest, most vibrant lights represent motors and sources of massive energy, but there's nothing to suggest the Parvanovae.

Breathing out, I let the haze of the Twelfth Court fall away and come back to the present moment. "I don't see it on the warship, either."

Estel turns to me, shimmering brow furrowed as she studies my face. "You can see beyond time and space?"

I'm not sure how to answer that, so I shrug. "I journeyed through the Twelfth Court."

Her eyes go wide, a small smile curling her lips. "You truly have been blessed by the All of All, haven't you?"

I open my mouth but can't find my words. It's never occurred to me that my experiences in the Twelfth Court are anything but ordinary to the fae. It's through the magic of the mysterious realm that the fae learn to shift forms. But I remember what Foxglove said when I first prepared to journey there to fight for Aspen's throne. *Going there is a rare thing. A sacred and dangerous excursion.*

Estel lifts her chin. "The All of All wants us to win."

"Then we need to steal back the Parvanovae. But where the blazing iron is it?"

Estel only shakes her head, lips pulling into a frown. "I don't know, but I think something's wrong."

Her words chill me. I'm about to ask her what it could be, when something draws my attention from the corner of my eye—a dark shape hovering in the sky. At first, I think it's Franco, or a dragon perhaps, but it looks impossibly large for how far away it is.

I skirt around Estel, squinting into the sky. There, stark against the canvas of cloudless blue floats an enormous, wingless beast.

46

The object is hardly more than a speck at this distance, but there's no mistaking what it is.

An airship. A great and terrifying master of the skies.

Just like the tanks, this is something I've only seen depicted in the broadsheets, and everything I've read about them does little to comfort me. Filled with hydrogen gas, its shape is long and cylindrical, tapered at both ends with fins at the rear. It's able to soar at impossible heights, evading enemy reach to drop bombs from the sky.

Estel turns and follows my line of sight. Her words come out breathless. "What is that?"

I shake my head, my heart pounding against my ribs at an agonizing tempo. "This is all a diversion," I say. "All of this. They have our fighting forces concentrated far from where they intend to drop the bomb. It doesn't matter that we've released magic. It doesn't matter that we're overpowering all of their tanks. The Parvanovae isn't coming by sea. They're sneaking it in by air."

I can't help but wonder...did Mr. Duveau know all along? Did he fight my glamour and feed me the lie that played us right into King Grigory's hands? Or did he not know the truth?

Estel squints at the sky. "It's coming in from the south of Eisleigh. I...I think I can sense something."

"It's there, isn't it?"

"I can't be sure unless I get closer. But I swear I can feel it."

Her words give me an additional idea. "If we can get close enough, I can try and glimpse it through the Twelfth Court, see if there's any sign of the Parvanovae. That way, if it's there, we'll know exactly where it is onboard."

Estel walks forward, as if a few feet closer could provide a better vantage. The truth is, we're about as high as we can get in Port Denyson, and the airship is already heading away from us toward the center of Eisleigh. "We must get closer. If we can confirm the Parvanovae is on the flying beast, we can send word back to our fighters to destroy the warship at once."

"Then Fehr will finish the wall."

Estel nods. "And I'll cast the enchantment."

Sweat beads at my brow as I watch the airship slip farther and farther from view. "How do we get close enough to the airship for a better look?"

She opens her palm, revealing a Chariot. Where she stores items on her shimmering, ethereal person, I'm not sure I'll ever know. And this isn't the time for such questions. "We must get somewhere along the flight path that isn't in Faerwyvae. If they reach beyond the border, it will already be too late."

I pace a few steps, mind reeling. "I can take us to Grenneith," I say in a rush. "If the airship plans on dropping the Parvanovae, they'll target a central location after they cross the border into Faerwyvae. Based on the ship's trajectory, it's sure to pass over Grenneith."

Without question, she hands me the Chariot. "Let's go."

I TRANSPORT US TO THE STREET RIGHT OUTSIDE THE SPIRE, to the very place I once stood with Aspen, Franco, and Foxglove while we plotted how to infiltrate the prison so I could visit my mother. One look at the building has me suppressing the shudder that writhes through me, but I know I must be strong. There is a proper time to sit with my grief, and this is not one of them. Not when the isle is at stake.

Pocketing the Chariot, I summon my inner fire to strengthen my will and lead Estel up the steps through the doors. Inside, the building is eerily quiet. Now that I think about it, even the streets outside were oddly empty for so early in the day. Word of the fighting must have traveled the isle, either from the people at Port Denyson who we evacuated, or from Mayor Coleman. Whatever the case, we don't encounter a single soul as we run through the building and enter the staircase that leads up the central column of the Spire. It isn't until we reach the lower level of the cellblocks that we meet company.

Rounding a corner to the next flight of stairs, we

come face to face with a pair of guards. They startle, hands flying to the hilts of their swords. I'm so used to seeing guns that I'm flooded with relief as one draws his blade and advances forward.

"Stop!" I shout, lifting my palms and letting blue flames dance over my fingers. "We are your new queens, and you will let us pass. Otherwise, I will have to hurt you." Or glamour them, I suppose. But right now, violence feels like the fastest solution.

"Queen," the guard echoes, eyes flashing from my face to my flames, then to the shimmering fae at my side.

"Yes, your new fae queens," I say. "Here to save the isle from complete annihilation. Now, let us pass or you will regret it."

The guard sneers, taking a step forward. "I'll bow to no fae." It seems violence will be the answer after all, until the second guard grasps his comrade by the shoulder, pulling him back. The two exchange a tense glance, and the second guard gives a subtle shake of his head. Chest heaving, the first guard considers his friend's silent warning before reluctantly returning his weapon to its sheath. Then, with another nudge from the second guard, they both step aside.

Estel and I brush past them and continue up the ring of stairs. We pass cellblock after cellblock until we finally reach the highest point in the tower. There I lead us to the end of the hall where one of the old, glassless windows welcomes a chill of autumn air. I lean forward, searching the sky for any sign of the airship. I know we beat it here. Only minutes have passed, and we crossed a great distance by Chariot. However, the airship was already far north of the port by the time we saw it. It must be nearly—

Then we see it.

It starts as a speck in the sky, then grows closer, crossing the east side of the city at a diagonal and heading straight our way. The nearer it comes, the more detail I can make out, from the gondolas suspended beneath the airship to its engine carts and motorized propellers.

"The Parvanovae is there," Estel says, eyes fixated on the approaching threat. The conviction in her voice is unwavering. "I can feel it with every speck of my being."

Even though I believe her, I want to see for myself. Turning inward, I close my eyes and seek the Twelfth Court. When I open them, the airship is beneath the violet haze, vibrating with shimmering particles. I don't even need to deepen my investigation, for there near the rear of the hull is an orb of blindingly bright light. I spare the rest of the ship a brief study, counting a dozen living figures, spread mostly between the rear and control gondolas, with a few figures lingering in the keel corridor.

I pull back from the Twelfth Court, blinking into the present. "I saw it. I know where it is."

"We must retrieve it. Now."

"Let's return to the port, gather an aerial force—"

"We can't attack the airship," Estel says. "If we destroy it, we destroy the Parvanovae. Even if it detonates from the air, it would be just as destructive as it would be on the ground."

"Winged fighters could invade the ship and take the Parvanovae back."

"No," she says. "I will not risk anyone but myself retrieving it. One wrong move could send it careening to the ground, resulting in our doom."

My eyes go wide. "How do you expect to get up there? You'll at least need someone to fly you up."

"No, I won't." Her palm flicks out, another Chariot appearing.

I check the pocket of my trousers, finding the one I used to bring us here still there.

"I brought a second," she says, eyes fixed on the sky. "It is my last. I will use it to transport myself directly to one of the gondolas."

I look from her to the airship, brow furrowed. "You're going to try and travel from here to a soaring object? One you've never been on? Can you even do such a thing?"

She nods, expression somber. "It's dangerous, and no one but a star fae should ever attempt such a risk with a Chariot. But if I can fixate on what those gondolas look like, and a specific space in the sky, I can transport myself there."

I want to argue, but time is running out. The airship is already at the center of Eisleigh. If we return to Port Denyson to gather an aerial team, we might not intercept the ship before it crosses into Faerwyvae. And even if we do, the crew could decide to drop the Parvanovae earlier if they sense our attack.

"Fine," I say, "but you're taking me up with you."

"No," she says with stern calm. "I already told you that using the Chariot without a clear mental picture of where you're going is dangerous, if not impossible. There's a chance I could miss my target."

"Then you better take me, because if I try it myself,

you can be damn sure I'll miss my target, then you'll have my death on your hands."

She burns me with a scowl, an expression I've never seen her wear. "I could have your death on my hands if I *do* take you."

I ignore her. "If you're transporting yourself to one of the gondolas, you still have to make your way into the ship's hull. There are a dozen men on board. You'll need me to cover you."

"Aspen will have my head."

"He'll probably have mine too. Now, let's go. Oh, and aim for the center gondola. It's vacant."

Her expression disappears behind a buzz of particles, demonstrating her irritation, before they settle back down to reveal pursed lips. "Very well. But when I say it's time to leave, open that Chariot I gave you without question. Understand?"

I nod.

She takes a long look at the airship, now passing overhead, then flips open the lid of the Chariot. "Are you ready?"

I swallow hard, my pulse pounding in my ears. "No. But we should probably go."

47

The light of the Chariot encircles us, buzzing around our bodies with its bright golden illumination.

In the next moment, the breath is stripped from my lungs as a rush of air has me reeling backward. Orienting myself to our new location, I find that we are not in the center gondola at all, but on the narrow gangplank that connects all three. My feet slip on the metal grate, sending me sprawling toward the side. I bite back a scream as I clasp my hands around the slim guardrail, scrambling to regain purchase on the gangplank.

Estel seems far more composed, arms outstretched to maintain balance. "Are you all right?"

Vertigo seizes me, my stomach churning. "If I don't look down," I shout over the rushing wind.

She looks over her shoulder toward the rear of the ship. "I can feel it. It's over there."

"That's where I saw it too." With my hands closed around the guardrail in an iron grip, I force myself to study the rear gondola. It's barely more than a boat-like metal box, partially enclosed at the far end where most of the crew are preoccupied with their tasks. Just above the middle of the gondola is a hatch that opens to the hull, a shaft of metal rungs leading to it from the gondola. "We need to get to the ladder—"

Just then, a figure rushes to the end of the gondola, shouting something I can't hear. I have only a second to react before he levels his gun and aims.

The sound of bullets striking metal rings out around me as I fight my terrified reluctance to move. With a deep breath, I let go of the guardrail and dart toward the center gondola, away from gunfire. Just before I dive behind the safety of the gondola's wall, something sharp slices into the back of my thigh. I've been shot. Collapsing to the metal floor, I press myself as close as I can into the side walls, safe from the blasts. I look for Estel and find her crouched on the opposite side.

Pain sears my leg, and I call forth my flames to combat it. The pain lessens, but I know it won't fully heal until I remove the bullet. And now might not be the best moment to try and do that.

"What now?" I call to Estel, but the wind and gunshots eat my words. There's a sudden break in gunfire. I pull myself onto all fours, prepared to dart across the gondola to Estel's side, but the appearance of a sudden figure has me retreating against the wall. The figure, however, joins me there. That's when I see it's Aspen, rippling with the violet aura of the Bond. His eyes are wide as he presses himself against the wall, arms splayed against it. "Where the bloody oak and ivy are you?"

"Aspen!" I shout, scrambling closer to him. "What's happening at the port?"

He stammers for words, looking wildly about, then finally manages to speak. "The warship has begun firing at the beach. We've destroyed all the tanks, and their soldiers are overpowered, but there's still a lot of fighting. The iron is growing thicker in the air and the fae are getting weaker."

I clasp his hands in mine. "We know where the Parvanovae is. We're about to steal it back."

"By flying in the air on a moving beast? This is madness."

I ignore him, giving his hands a tight squeeze. "Listen to me. Destroy the warship. Destroy everything. Then have Fehr finish the wall."

Finally, he nods, then his expression turns serious. "When this is all over," he says through his teeth, "I'm going to murder you for putting yourself in danger like this."

"Looking forward to it," I bite back. "And I love you too."

His lips pull into a subtle smirk, then he's gone. When I return my attention to the space between me and Estel, gunfire rains down from both sides. It seems we've drawn the attention of the forward control gondola too.

Estel crouches on all fours, looking both ways between blasts. Then, with a leap, she darts across to my side of the gondola. Bullets fly toward her, but I swear the particles of her body part to let them pass through the other side. She squeezes in tight next to me, appearing unscathed.

"Estel, can you die?" I've never seen her or any other

ethereal being mortally wounded by a physical attack. I've often wondered if it were even possible.

"I can shift and reform my mass at will, which helps me avoid most injuries," she says. "However, if iron strikes me before I can avoid it, my form will become more solid and I'll be vulnerable to further injury."

"So...I'm not the only one in mortal peril right now."

"I told you this would be dangerous."

I clench my jaw, trying to put on my bravest face despite the pain lashing the back of my thigh. "What do we do now?"

She cranes her neck to peer over the side of the gondola, ducking to avoid another bullet. "I must get to that shaft and into the hull at once. They could decide at any moment that we're putting their mission at risk and drop the bomb early. I have an idea, but it's a risk. We might not make it out before getting caught." She releases a sigh. "This would be so much easier if the wall were complete."

"It should be any time now," I say. "Aspen is destroying the warship as we speak. After that, Fehr will finish the wall."

She eyes me with curiosity. "How do you know?"

"Aspen and I can communicate through our Bond."

"Ah," she says. "He told me about your mysterious connection before we came to rescue you at Varney Cove."

Just then, Aspen returns, eyes bulging as he struggles to keep his balance amidst the rushing wind. "It's done," he says, crouching down before me. "The warship is destroyed, and the wall is complete."

My pulse races at this news. "Thank the Great Mother," I say under my breath.

Aspen's expression turns hard again. "Now get out of here, Ev—" He doubles over, clutching his side while blood streams between his fingers. Then, with a lurch, he closes his eyes and begins to stumble back. In the blink of an eye, he's gone.

"Aspen!" I lunge for the place he was, but Estel pulls me back, just in time to save me from a flying bullet. My mind reels to comprehend what I just saw. One moment he was there, and the next he was...he was...

He couldn't have been injured by the bullets here, for he traveled through the Bond. That means...

I shake my head. No, I can't think of that. He must be all right. He must. Surely, I'd feel it through the Bond if he were...

I swallow hard.

Estel takes me by the shoulders, shaking me gently.

Trembling, I meet her gaze. "The wall is complete." My voice is hollow, my throat dry.

Her eyes widen. "You're sure?"

I nod.

She rises into a partial crouch, as if ready to spring back into the fray. "Then I need to transmute the bomb here. Now."

Her words clear my mind, and it takes all my will to force myself back to the present. Everything in me wants to travel to Aspen through the Bond to ensure he's all right, but I committed myself to this job. One that is the difference between life and death for everyone on the isle. Swiping errant tears from my cheeks, I take a deep breath and refocus on our task.

"We need to get to it first," I say. It takes me a second longer to comprehend what else she said. "Wait, when you say *now*, do you mean *now* now? As in from the airship?"

Her expression turns hard, determined, fixated on the rear shaft. "Yes."

"Don't you need to be at the wall to transmute the bomb?"

"No. This is actually better, and I know exactly what I must do."

Pulling myself upright, I glance at the rear gondola, still teeming with armed soldiers. Half the crew is there, guarding the gangplank, our only path to the shaft. "What will you do?"

She lifts her hand and the Chariot within. "I'm going to transport myself straight to the shaft and pull myself into the hull. I'll need you to distract the crew so they don't see me."

"Wait," I hold out my hands as a better idea comes to me. "I can enter the Twelfth Court and go myself. Time slows when I'm there. I can make it past the soldiers before they see me coming."

"No." I've never seen Estel look so stern; not even when I manipulated her into bringing me up here. "I must be the one to get it. As soon as I touch the Parvanovae, I'll begin the enchantment. You must distract them only long enough for me to climb up. Once I'm out of sight, use the Chariot and get back to the bluff. Don't wait a second longer. Understand?"

I open my mouth to say yes, but a chilling thought dawns on me. "If I use my Chariot to return to the bluff, how will you get back? You're going to utilize your

Chariot to transport yourself to the shaft, which means you'll have used it twice."

Estel's eyes turn down at the corners. "I'm not coming back, Evelyn. Not from any of this. I never was."

Suddenly, it all makes sense—how ambiguous she's been at every mention of the enchantment, masking her expression behind her swirling particles. She was never planning on surviving this. "I don't understand."

She gives me a sad smile. "I discovered why my sister didn't destroy the Parvanovae like she said she would. I can't transmute the bomb unless I detonate it. To guide its transmutation, I must absorb the blast, become one with it. My final act of consciousness will be to fuel the energy with my intent, transmuting it into protection. It's the only way the enchantment will work."

"And that...will destroy you?

"It will, but I'm ready. I've *been* ready."

I shake my head, eyes wide. "You can't! You should have told us. We never would have agreed to let you do this."

"This is my choice, Evelyn. You can't take this from me. I'm sorry."

All further arguments are stripped from my throat as her words resonate deep inside me, echoing against ones said by my mother when I spoke to her in the Twelfth Court beneath the sea.

You cannot take that moment from me, Evelyn. It is mine, not yours.

Acknowledging them both, I nod.

Her eyes glaze with shimmering light as she places a hand on my shoulder. "I'm glad to have known you, Queen Evelyn of Fire."

I nearly choke on a sob. "I'm glad to have known you too."

"Promise me you'll leave as soon as I enter the hull."

With a deep breath, I force the words from my lips. "I promise."

Without another word, she opens the lid of the Chariot and disappears into golden light.

I turn around and face the rear gondola, glancing above the edge of my hiding spot. A flash of light ignites inside the shaft over the gondola. One of the men makes to turn toward it, but I rise to my feet with a roar. Filling my palms with fire, I draw their attention to me, connecting to the element of air to send orbs of flame down the gangplank. My diversion has them thoroughly preoccupied, and I only have a second to duck before they return my attack with gunfire.

When I peek back over the side wall, I catch only a glimpse of a shimmering foot. Then nothing; she's inside the hull. It takes everything in me not to charge the crew and follow her up that shaft. To respect the promise I made. Breaths harsh and shallow, I crouch back down behind the side wall and reach into my pocket. My fingers tremble as I flip open the lid of the Chariot and fill my mind's eye with the bluff.

The golden light swallows me whole, vibrating, humming, growing, then blinks out, leaving me surrounded by salty air at the edge of the bluff. Heart hammering against my ribs, I turn away from the sea to the northwest, where Grenneith should be. I find no sign of the airship from here, but still search the skies. What I'm looking for, I don't know...

Then a shudder vibrates through me, through everything, like a wave of sound washing over the land. A blindingly bright light appears in the sky, brighter than the sun.

My stomach drops.

No.

All I can think is that it didn't work; Estel detonated the bomb but wasn't able to transmute the energy. Or perhaps she was caught before she could.

I'm transfixed as I watch the light grow, awaiting with cold dread for the end.

But the end doesn't come.

Instead, the light retreats, pulling back to a single point in the sky. Its radiance shifts from a blinding golden hue to a collection of shimmering white particles. Then, with another wave of vibration, the particles blast outward, spanning in every direction until it curves up, out, and toward the ground. For a moment, the light of the sun is hazy, filtered through a dome of shimmering particles surrounding all that I see.

Then it's gone.

Invisible.

But not broken, for I can feel it humming all around.

Estel's enchantment is complete.

48

As a fox, I make my way down the bluff, following a violet tether in my mind's eye. Shifting into my fox form is the only way to make the journey bearable, with the bullet still lodged in my thigh. I summon my fire again and again, which helps keep me conscious, but at this point, I've lost a lot of blood. On three legs, I hobble down the hill, the violet tether pulsing like an artery, guiding my every step.

Only when I reach the first buildings of the port town, does the silence reach my awareness. There's no gunfire. No blasts. No shouts. And yet the evidence of battle lies all around, blood and bodies and discarded weapons. I refuse to look too closely, not wanting to recognize any faces amongst the dead and, instead, fixate my attention on that violet tether, padding after it on silent paws.

When I reach the main street near the docks, I finally see movement, hear sound. The first thing I hear are whimpers, cries, mingling with the hollow ringing in my ears. Then I begin to pick up strands of solemn conversation. The fae are here, gathering the dead, tending to their injured comrades.

What's strange, however, is the presence of humans. Humans that were not fighters. A dozen or so men and women, dressed in the clothing of regular townspeople, weave about the fae, kneeling next to the broken, conversing with the strong. Those who kneel have boxes at their sides. Boxes full of cloth, blades, bottles, and herbs. They're healers. Nurses, perhaps. And yet, they wear no uniform, no insignia to represent a specific medical practice. I furrow my brow. These people are... helping us? Of their own accord?

Of course, not all fae receive them with warmth. Nearby, a white wolf lies on his side, the bottom half of his body coated in blood. It takes me a moment to realize the wolf is Flauvis. Despite his injuries, he snaps his teeth when a human woman tries to come near. She holds her hands out in a sign of peace, saying something I can't hear, but Flauvis only bares his teeth. Part of me wants to go to him, shift back into my seelie form and inspect his wounds. But there's someone else I need to see. More than anything in the world.

Following the tether, I continue padding down the street, skirting around bodies as I reach the site of the first disabled tank. I hazard a glance at the beach, which makes me pause. The shore is littered with debris and the remnants of the ruined tanks. The three landing ships, now crushed as if squeezed by an enormous hand, sink into the channel beyond the row of stones that make up the new wall. There are more dead here, but the living gather too. On one of the docks, I spot human soldiers, survivors of the battle. They cluster at the center of the dock, just before the pair of stones that flank it. More of the human healers move about there, tending to the injured.

Evie.

My heart hammers at the sound of my name. The feel of it. A lump rises in my throat, a sensation so human I'm thrust from my fox form. With a cry, I stumble to right myself on my good leg, then return my attention to the violet tether, feeling it pulsing stronger now.

I limp forward. One step. Another.

Evie.

Faster I move, summoning my flames to burn the pain from my leg, fueling my pace as I continue down the street, past melted guns, more broken bodies, shattered cobblestones, mangled roots.

"Evie."

My breath hitches in my chest, a sob building there alongside it, as my mate steps into view. His breastplate is gone and there isn't a part of him not covered in blood, but he's standing. Standing on two feet. Standing and alive.

I rush forward, but he's faster, closing the distance between us and shrinking the tether that links us with every step. Then finally, he's here, wrapping me in his arms. I press myself into him, cry into his chest, let my weight sag into his.

"I was so worried you were gone," I whisper.

He strokes my hair, lips pressed against my forehead. "I was. For just a second."

I lift my face to study his, assessing every scratch, cut, and bruise beneath the dirt and blood. "What happened?"

"I was shot in the side, and another soldier struck me in the back of the head."

My eyes go wide. "Struck you?" My fingers tremble, yearning to reach for the back of his head, but terrified of what I'll find.

"With the butt of his gun. His bullets were out."

"That's not all the story," says a voice nearby. It's Franco.

My heart lifts as I whirl to face him, although my arms don't leave my mate. He lowers to the ground with his enormous raven's wings, arms crossed over his chest. He too is coated in blood, his silver hair slick with it.

Aspen purses his lips and releases a warning grumble. "We're kind of busy here."

"Busy leaving out the best part of the story," Franco says. He turns his gaze to me, lips curled into a haughty grin. "I saved your dearest mate here."

Aspen shakes his head. "I would have crushed them with my bare hands."

"Not if you're unconscious."

"I was only out for a second."

"And it would have been forever, if the armed soldier came in for another shot. However, I took the human for a little flight."

With a roll of his eyes, Aspen says, "Fine. You might have saved my life. Do you want a medal?"

Franco winks. "I just wanted to hear you say it." With a shudder, he leaps into the air in his full raven form, then calls overhead, "We might become dear friends after all, Aspen." Then he's out of sight.

I return my gaze to Aspen's. "Where are the others?"

"Nyxia is tormenting the soldiers who wouldn't stand down after they'd clearly lost. Aelfon and Minuette are with their troops. Lorelei is helping one of the humans bind fractures with her roots. Flauvis is, well..."

"I saw. He doesn't look too good, and he's not accepting help from the humans." I furrow my brow. "Who are these healers, anyway?"

He pulls back just enough to lift the hem of his bloody tunic to reveal his bandaged side. "They came to our aid as soon as the fighting stopped. They called themselves *veterinarians*." He says the last word slowly.

I quirk a brow. "Veterinarians came to our aid?"

"The one who tended me said Mayor Coleman sent word to them days ago, urging them to come to the port."

"Mayor Coleman sent animal doctors to tend fae wounds? Of course he did." I shake my head. Whether he did it as an insult, or if they were the only healers he knew would aid my people, I suppose it matters not. With this many wounded and with so many of the injuries being from iron, these tasks would have fallen on my shoulders alone without their aid. "I should probably go tend to Flauvis. I doubt the veterinarians will have any luck with him."

I make to pull away, but my injured leg gives out beneath me. Aspen catches me in his arms, brow furrowed with concern. "You're hurt."

Pain sears the back of my thigh again. "It's fine," I say, voice hoarse, summoning my flames to ease the agony.

"It's not fine. You need to see one of the healers at once."

"No, I need to help—"

Aspen grasps me by the shoulders, voice firm. "Evie, take care of yourself first."

I want to argue, but he's right. No matter how much fire I summon to regenerate my blood and weave my flesh, the wound won't heal until the bullet has been removed. And I'm in no condition to try and remove it myself. "All right. I'll...go to the vet."

"Good," he says with a nod. Then his lips curl into a crooked grin. "Besides, Flauvis should probably suffer just a little longer."

As soon as the bullet is removed and my wound is tended and bound, I go to the wolf king. He still snaps his teeth at me like I saw him do to the veterinarian, but after a few stern words, he gives in and lets me approach. My stomach sinks when I take in the severity of the wound. His entire back leg is mangled, torn to shreds by what looks like numerous rifle shots.

He'll need amputation. And from what I know about fae healing, the leg won't grow back. He, of course, does not take the news well. Luckily, chloroform seems to suffice in shutting him up.

"If I can hobble on three legs, so can you," I whisper as he slips into unconsciousness. "Perhaps it will humble you a bit too."

The veterinarian who tended my wound assists me now, lending me her tools for the amputation. When it's

over, I examine my work, running my hands over Flauvis'
filthy fur in search of any other minor injuries. But now
that the amputation is complete, taking with it all
remnants of iron, the rest of his wounds begin to heal on
their own.

"We should probably be out of sight when he wakes
up," I tell the veterinarian. "He's not going to be happy
about being a three-legged wolf."

She blanches and rises to her feet.

"Thank you," I say to her. "For helping him, me, and
all my kind."

"You're one of them," she says. "Your ears are
rounded, but...you're fae."

I lift my chin with pride. "I am."

"You're the one we've heard about, then. The human-
fae queen. The one who bargained for our protection."

I'm taken aback as I contemplate her words. Is this
what Mayor Coleman has told the people of Eisleigh? Or
has rumor spread on its own?

When I don't reply, she speaks, voice trembling.
"What happens now? You...your kind...rule us. What
does that mean for humans on the isle? For our cities and
towns? Our way of life?"

Her words echo questions of my own, questions I
have no answers to. So I give her honesty. "I don't know
what the future of the isle looks like. Yes, it belongs to the
fae now, but it is still your home. We won't hurt you."

She studies me, shoulders rigid. "Do the others feel
the same as you do?"

The truth will frighten her, but it's all that I have to
offer. "No, but I promise that I will fight on your behalf." I
can feel the promise ringing through my bones, and I

know it's one I can keep. I will fight for the humans, and I will fight for the fae. I will fight for a fair way of life for all people. Seelie. Unseelie. Human. I may not know what that balance looks like yet, but I will work to build it. And I know Aspen will too.

I extend an open palm to the human. After a moment's hesitation, she takes it in hers and gives it a squeeze. "Fae promises are binding, right?" she asks.

I give her a solemn nod. "They are. I will not break this one."

With a small smile, she dips into a curtsy, then turns away in search of more work to be done.

I too scan the street, looking for who I can help tend to next, but the sight of someone at the corner of my periphery has my heart leaping in my chest—Lorelei. She grins wide when I meet her gaze, and we both run to each other. As soon as she's in reach, I fling my arms around her, squeezing her petite frame close. Tears stream down my cheeks, and from the way her shoulders heave, I can tell she's crying too. When our sobs turn to laughter, we pull away, although our arms remain linked.

"The wall works," she says, eyes bright as she bounces on the balls of her feet. "Nyxia tested it on the soldiers."

"What do you mean?" I ask.

Her words come out faster than I've ever heard her speak, as if she can hardly contain them. "Nyxia glamoured one of the soldiers to attempt to pass between the stones near the dock. He couldn't. No human can, neither on nor off the isle, not unless accompanied by a fae. It's like a tangible barrier exists, one only the fae can cross. No weapon can pierce it either. Now Nyxia is escorting the surrendered soldiers onto fishing boats so we can ship them back to the mainland. They're never coming back. Ever."

This sends a rush of excitement to my head. My relief is so overwhelming, I have to squeeze Lorelei's arms to keep from swaying where I stand. Even though I already knew the enchantment had been completed, hearing that it's been tested and proven successful is a much-needed comfort amidst the grim aftermath of battle.

Lorelei's eyes sparkle as she bounces on her feet again. "She did it, Evelyn. Estel's enchantment works."

My face falls at the mention of the Star Queen, fresh tears pricking my eyes. "Yes, it does."

Lorelei's smile melts off her lips. "Where is she, anyway?"

My chin quivers as I summon the words from my heart. "Estel has returned to the stars."

Lorelei's shoulders droop, her hold on me growing slack. Her eyes are keen, telling me she knows there's much more to this story.

But it isn't one I want to tell right now. Not when there is still much work to do. Hearts to soothe. Wounds to tend. Dead to burn or bury.

When we're done, I'll tell them. I'll tell everyone.

Not a single soul, neither human nor fae, will go without knowing that Estel, Queen of the Star Court, saved the Fair Isle.

THE DAYS THAT FOLLOW ARE SOLEMN ONES.

We remain at the port while our wounded are tended to by myself and my fellow healers. When we run out of supplies, we go to town and get more. When we grow tired, we rest, only to wake up a few short hours later and return to our duties.

It takes two days to heal what can be healed, mend what can be mended. In the physical sense, at least. Then some of our fighters begin to leave. Traditions are followed for every court regarding the care of the dead. Some bodies are wrapped in cloth and taken away with their comrades to return to their families. Others are burned on the beach. Still others are feasted on. While the latter turns my stomach, I've already learned from my fire fae subjects that life and death are treated differently by each court, each culture, each species of fae. The seelie and unseelie will always handle things differently, as is their right. A right I'm determined to see is never stripped from either side.

On the third day after the battle, Aspen, Lorelei, and I guide our troops back to Irridae Palace.

On the fifth day, we're home.

The moon illuminates the courtyard as we enter the palace gates, cool night air brushing my skin. We hardly take two steps down the tile walkway before Foxglove and Amelie rush out the front steps to intercept us. As soon as Amelie is in my arms, we dissolve into tears, falling on our knees while we hold one another. I hear a similar reunion between Foxglove and Lorelei taking place nearby. When Amelie and I can finally bring ourselves to separate, I see Aspen has joined the two ambassadors, arms draped over their shoulders as he brings them to his chest.

Rising to my feet, I wipe the tears from my cheeks as more figures stream out of the palace—Marie Coleman,

Dune, the spider seamstress, and then Breeda with a girlish squeal. Then other fae funnel into the courtyard— the mushroom crab and his family, blue wisps, firebirds, dragons. The courtyard erupts in cheers and yips and excited conversation. Amelie runs to Lorelei and Foxglove, Breeda flutters around my head, speaking too fast for me to hear, and Dune taps from paw to paw, asking if I brought any dead for him to feast on.

As the commotion grows wilder around me, my attention is drawn to a figure who stands silently amongst the crowd. It's...Fehr. No one has seen him since he finished the wall. I'd expected he'd take his freedom and make himself scarce for a while, but he's...here.

He steps forward and takes a knee before me. "I'm sorry I didn't come directly to you, Your Majesty. I sensed unrest growing near parts of the wall in Eisleigh. Humans were rioting, trying to take down the stones."

The news fills me with dread. It's not that I hadn't anticipated some rebellion from the humans. I doubt everyone is so willing to accept a fae rule, no matter what we accomplished for the greater good. Still, hearing unrest has already begun to stir makes my bones feel tired.

"Even though the enchantment prevents harm from coming to the stones, I've dealt with the rebels," Fehr says. "I ushered them to the other side of the wall where they can either rot or try and make it to the mainland."

"You did well," I tell him. "We will find...other ways to deal with rebels in the future."

He rises to both feet. "I have returned to your service, Your Majesty."

I lift a brow. "Of your own free will? You know we have no bargain."

The corners of his mouth quirk up, and I see his gaze flick to a certain bespectacled ambassador in the process of uncorking a bottle of Agave Ignitus. "Of my own free will. I shall go where you and your mate go." He bows low, then disappears into the crowd.

I sense Aspen long before I feel him. His arm circles my waist, and I turn to him, pressing my head against his chest, silent as I watch our people celebrate our return home. With the sparkling lights coming from the wisps, fire sprites, and kitsune flames, it feels like the start of a revel.

As tired as I am from our journey, I hesitate to give in and join. But after everything we've been through, after all we've lost and won, perhaps a revel is what we need. Perhaps it's what *I* need.

I lift my gaze to my mate's, arms circling his neck. Our Bond pulses between us, saying everything we don't have words to express. Joy, gratitude, exhaustion, sorrow. Beneath it all is that which links us whether near or far, regardless of tether or Bond, life or death. It's the same element that connects me to my people, my sister, my friends. My mother. Estel. Those I've lost and those I still have near. It's that which makes me fight. Protect. Risk my life.

It's love.

With it comes waves of grief, chasms of pain and longing. And with it comes passion and joy. It's what it means to be human. What it means to be fae. Seelie and unseelie alike, whether they admit it or not, feel love.

Humans and fae, despite their differences, are bound by the same element of love.

I am bound by love. Its depths and shallows, streams and waves. Its darkness and light. I'm open to all of it now.

Pulling Aspen's lips to mine, I initiate the night's revelry with a kiss.

EPILOGUE

ONE YEAR LATER

Foxglove leads the way through a stand of slim white birches surrounded by an elegant citrine wall. A canopy of crimson leaves dance in the mild breeze overhead, the sun shining through the boughs to create the ideal climate. The air that caresses my skin feels like the warmest day of the most perfect autumn, warm enough that a lightweight dress will suffice, but cool enough that I wouldn't be sweating if I chose to wear a cloak or jacket. Foxglove extends his arms. "Here you'll find the autumn garden. There's a pond, several benches, a brook. Then on the opposite side of the palace, there's a lovely desert courtyard with cacti and succulents. I selected each one myself. It's also a great place for sunbathing. Oh, and your pool is there too. Shall I take you to it?"

Aspen and I exchange a glance. "Perhaps show us inside the palace first," Aspen says.

Foxglove adjusts his spectacles. "Very well. How about your bedrooms?"

Hand in hand, my mate and I follow after the ambassador-turned-palace-designer into a set of double doors. There we enter an enormous hall with intricately carved marble walls and a blue tile floor. Heads of servants bow as we pass, while guards in bronze armor stand at attention.

"It seems the palace staff has already settled in," I say.

Foxglove grins. "Yes, most of your households have already arrived. The rest will be coming tonight. Well, except for Lorelei. She'll be staying at Lunar a few more days."

I purse my lips to hide my smile. Even though I only sent Lorelei to exchange a single message with Nyxia, it seems she and the Lunar Queen are getting along far better than they used to. Or perhaps they've grown fond of their fights and have been unable to extricate themselves from their most recent one.

I return my attention to the elegant halls, finding it impossible to take in all the splendor at once. When Aspen and I brought Foxglove the idea of building a new palace on the border between our courts, he immediately went to work. In every wall, tapestry, table, and vase, I see the beauty of Autumn and Fire combined. Leaves mingle with flames in fiery yellows, deep reds, and rich browns. It's even more stunning than I could have imagined.

We make our way up an immense staircase to the sleeping quarters. At the end of the hall, we find our bedroom, which is far larger than anything I've lived in yet. The ceiling is domed and painted like a clear autumn sky, while the walls are carved marble. The floors are deep-orange carnelian. The middle of the room hosts an enormous bed, its posts made from twining roots blooming with red leaves. The windows stand from floor to ceiling across the far wall, filling the room with warm sunlight. I scan the rest of the room, finding a sitting area, a table laden with fruit and wine, and then—

When my eyes land on the tall oak wardrobe, I find Amelie there, resplendent in a gown of lilac chiffon.

"Don't tell me you made me more dresses," I say, crossing the room to join her at my very full wardrobe.

She shrugs, suppressing a grin. "I won't tell you then. But I will tell you, you should see the bathing chamber."

Foxglove claps his hands together. "Yes, the bathing chamber! Your mate was quite specific on the size of the tub you would need."

I eye Aspen, finding the corner of his mouth quirking up. "It had to be big enough for two."

With a blush, I follow Foxglove into the adjoining room. Everything from the floor to the ceiling is pink and orange sunstone, with an enormous recessed rectangle at the center, filled with steaming water. Sprigs of rosemary and marigold heads float over the surface. Just looking at it makes me want to sink beneath its depths.

"Not yet," Foxglove says, as if my thoughts are written on my face. "We have much more to see."

WE CONTINUE THE TOUR, MOVING FROM ROOM TO ROOM, wing to wing, floor to floor. There's a ballroom, a library, several studies, a medical wing, and countless guest rooms. Of course, Foxglove is most excited to show me my parlor, one that is a near-replica of the one he made for me at Bircharbor, filled to the brim with human knickknacks, doilies, and other atrocities. His pride over the room is so palpable, it's infectious, and I find myself not having to fake my smile at all.

Finally, he leads us to the throne room on the main floor of the palace. "Aspen said he wanted me to show you this last," he says as he throws open the doors. The room is nearly as large as our bedroom, with towering ceilings, long windows, two ornate thrones, and...

I nearly bark a laugh at what rests in the center of the room. An obsidian table, twice as large as Nyxia's. I meet Aspen's smirk with a quirked brow.

"So," Foxglove says, wringing his hands. "What do you think? Is it suitable? The palace, I mean."

I go to him and take his hands in mine. "Yes, Foxglove. I love it more than I could ever say. You've done an amazing job."

His cheeks flush pink at my praise.

A knock sounds on one of the open doors, and we turn to find Marie Coleman. She curtsies, then crosses the room to hand me two envelopes. "Another trade proposal to bring to the Alpha Council, and the most recent correspondence from my uncle."

I take the letters from her. "What's the latest from Representative Coleman?" I mutter as I break the seal of the second envelope.

Before I can open it fully, Aspen's hand covers mine. "Work can wait until later," he says in a conspiratorial whisper.

I lift my eyes from the envelopes and find heat in his gaze. It's enough to send my heart flipping in my chest. "I suppose you're right," I say, tucking the letter into the pocket of my dress.

"Are you in need of anything else, Your Majesties?" Marie asks, cheeks flushed as she suddenly finds the floor at her feet very interesting.

"No, thank you, Marie," I say.

She hurries to the door, but Foxglove remains in my periphery, grinning wide at me and my mate.

Marie pauses and clears her throat. "Foxglove," she hisses in a too-loud whisper. "I, uh. I think Fehr wants you to show him your room."

"Oh!" Foxglove jumps, wringing his hands when he gets the hint. Then, *"Oh,"* when he understands what Marie is suggesting.

As soon as the doors close behind them, Aspen's lips find mine. I retreat toward the obsidian table, and he hoists me on top of it. I spread my knees to pull him closer, wasting no time in getting him out of his jacket, his waistcoat. Then he shrugs out of his shirt with haste, losing a button in the process. I run my hands up and down his golden chest, leaning back as he returns his lips to me. One of his hands cradles the back of my neck, while the other moves up my knee, my thigh, climbing beneath the folds of my skirt to the roundness of my hips.

I pull away, my voice breathless when I say, "I have a surprise for you."

His eyes brighten with curiosity. "Do you?"

I put a hand on his chest to gently push him a step back. Then I reach for the ribbon tied behind my neck, one that holds up the bodice of my lace gown. Once the knot is free, I pull the bodice down to reveal thick black satin stiffened by bone stays.

Aspen pulls his head back at the sight of the under-garment. "What the bloody oak and ivy?"

"It's a corset, remember?"

His eyes lock on my breasts, the tops bulging above the painfully tight torture device. As his gaze moves down the length of it, his brow grows more furrowed. "I thought you hated corsets."

I lean back, propped on my forearms, lips pulling into a mock pout. "I do. I hate them so much I can hardly bear it. In fact, I think I might die if I'm not freed from it at once."

He eyes me with concern a moment more before his mouth quirks with devious delight. Stepping forward to return to the space between my legs, he frames my waist with his hands on the tabletop. "I should rescue you then. Although, I must warn you. The corset might not survive my valiant efforts."

I lift my chin, lips parting as my breaths grow heavier. "Do what you must."

Our kisses return with a fierce passion, his tongue caressing mine as his hands grasp the bodice of the undergarment. With one pull, he has me out of it, and his hands rove over my bare skin. I scoot back on the table until I'm at the center of it, and he follows, kissing up the length of my torso. His tongue stops to rest over each mound of my breast, sending heat burning at the apex of my thighs, then he trails his lips over my collarbone, then up my neck—

"Oh, hello, Your Most Beautiful Majesty. And His Most Handsome Majesty."

My head whips toward the fire sprite, and I find

Breeda fluttering just a few feet away without a care in the world for what she might be interrupting.

"What are you doing?" Breeda asks with innocent curiosity. "Are you expecting the other royals to join soon? This is your meeting room, isn't it?"

Aspen laughs into the crook of my neck. "Where in the hell is that bell?"

Stifling my own laughter, I say, "Will you give us some privacy, please? In fact, will you stand guard outside this room and see that no one disturbs us until we leave?"

Breeda spins in a circle and salutes. "It will be done." Then, in a flash, she's gone.

I bring my left hand to Aspen's cheek, running my thumb along the crease outside his mouth, the one that forms only with his biggest smiles. The light from the windows catches the bright orange of my carnelian ring —one gifted to me from Aspen during the human wedding ceremony we had earlier this year. A sunstone band circles the ring finger on his left hand.

My chest feels warm as I'm reminded of the conversation we had just over a year ago, one I thought was pretend. One I hardly dared to hope would ever come true.

And yet here we are.

Of course, there is one thing missing.

"I can't believe after all the work Foxglove put into this palace, it never once occurred to him to make us a bell," I say.

Aspen snorts a laugh. "You're the metalworker. I thought you were going to make one."

"Perhaps I shall." I look into his glittering irises, breathe in the rosemary cinnamon scent of his skin.

He reaches for my free hand, weaves our fingers together. "Evie, have I ever told you how grateful I am that you almost killed me with an iron blade?"

"Excuse me?"

He lights a kiss on my cheek, then my jaw. "The day we met at the wall."

My grin stretches across my face at the memory. "Where would we be now if I hadn't?" The question takes me down several paths, one to a future where nothing changes, where lives are kept but a tense treaty remains. The other brings me to where we are now, past a history of grief, bloodshed, love, and joy. In between lie several other forks and paths leading to unknown fates. All I know is I'm glad I'm here.

Now.

With him.

"Always and forever, Aspen," I whisper to him.

His eyes lock on mine. "Always and forever, Evie."

Our kisses return slow and gentle, his bare skin warm against mine as our hearts hammer between us, beating a rhythm for our love. My favorite song. One I want to hear every day for the rest of my life, however long that will be. It could be endless. It could be an eternity, and I would never tire of its melody. Not when he's here.

As much as I want to linger in the luxury of our simmering fire, an inferno begs to be released. I smile against his lips. "Let's put all other tables to shame once and for all."

And we do.

ABOUT THE AUTHOR

Tessonja Odette is a fantasy author living in Seattle with her family, her pets, and ample amounts of chocolate. When she isn't writing, she's watching cat videos, petting dogs, having dance parties in the kitchen with her daughter, or pursuing her many creative hobbies. Read more about Tessonja at www.tessonjaodette.com

ALSO BY TESSONJA ODETTE

The Lela Trilogy - ya epic fantasy

Shadows of Lela

Veil of Mist

Shades of Prophecy

YA DYSTOPIAN PSYCHOLOGICAL THRILLER

Twisting Minds

CPSIA information can be obtained
at www.ICGtesting.com
Printed in the USA
LVHW030106281021
701775LV00001B/17